NOT SO PERFECT STRANGERS

NOT SO PERFECT STRANGERS

L.S. STRATTON

UNION
SQUARE
& CO.

NEW YORK

UNION SQUARE & CO.
NEW YORK

UNION SQUARE & CO. and the distinctive Union Square & Co. logo
are trademarks of Sterling Publishing Co., Inc.

Union Square & Co., LLC, is a subsidiary of Sterling Publishing Co., Inc.

ISBN 978-1-4549-4743-1 (paperback)
ISBN 978-1-4549-4744-8 (ebook)

For information about custom editions, special sales, and premium
purchases, please contact specialsales@unionsquareandco.com.

Printed in Canada

2 4 6 8 10 9 7 5 3 1

unionsquareandco.com

Cover collage and design: Faceout Studio, Lindy Kasler. Images: Woman:
Susan Fox/Trevillion Images Car: Bernhard Lang/Gettyimages.com
Building roof tops: Jeiel Shamblee/Shutterstock.com

To Andrew and Chloe, my heart and home.

CHAPTER 1

NOW

GUILTY PEOPLE RUN AWAY FROM THE SCENE OF A CRIME, AND THAT IS what Tasha Jenkins was doing as the Gingells' house burned.

In mere seconds, she made it from the front door, down the flight of stairs. She nearly tripped over the last step. One hand gripped the edge of the gate to stop her from tumbling face-first onto the sidewalk, making her fall to one knee instead.

The urge to flee until she reached the other end of the block, until she was far, far away from there, screamed inside her head like the insistent, ear-splitting beep of the fire alarm now going off inside the home behind her, but Tasha couldn't keep running.

It was too late.

She pushed herself back to her feet and looked over her shoulder at the house that she'd been to only once before, and from a distance. The wide-open bay windows. The stately-looking exterior. The imposing oak front door and wrought-iron mailbox. She'd never told Madison how beautiful it was, how she should feel lucky to live there. Now the house was ablaze.

She turned around completely to watch the flames, entranced as the smoke seeped out the cracks in the three windows on the top floor and the fire licked hungrily at the curtains. It would gobble up the furniture next, and likely devour the couple who lived inside.

"Oh, my God!" a man shouted, shaking her out of her stupor. She wondered how much time had passed.

"Look at that!" the man said.

Tasha glanced to her right to find a couple standing a few feet away from her, gazing up at the house, slack-jawed. They were linked arm in arm and looked as if they had been on a late-evening walk. The woman reached down and grabbed their dog, a Jack Russell terrier, and clutched the dog and his leash against her chest.

"Should we call someone, Brian?" she asked the man beside her. "Do you think someone could be inside? Should we get help?"

Help . . .

Calling for help is something that old Tasha would have done. Before all this had happened, before random coincidence had brought Madison Gingell into Tasha's life, Tasha would have called for help without question. But now she held back.

"What should we do?" the woman asked, like she was posing the question to Tasha, not her companion.

With shaking hands, Tasha reached inside her purse and pulled out her cell phone. Her fingers dumbly followed her command, dialing 9-1-1.

"Hello, what is your emergency?" the dispatcher answered.

She forced the words up out of her throat and to her lips. "A house is on fire. 818 Wicker Street. Southeast D.C. Please send help!"

The dispatcher started to ask questions. *Is anyone inside? Are you near the fire? Do you know if anyone is injured?*

Tasha hung up, unable to speak anymore; it had taken all her effort to say that. Now she would just have to sit and wait. So that is what she did, taking a spot on the curb near the corner, clutching her knees and staring off into space. Because guilty people run from the scene of a crime—but sometimes they stay.

Within minutes, she heard the fire engines. By then a crowd had started to gather. Neighbors walked out of their front doors and huddled on the sidewalk in their robes and flannel, pointing at the blazing spectacle.

"Ma'am," one of the firefighters said. "Ma'am, you're going to have to move. We're clearing this block. It's not safe to sit here. There's an active fire."

"I know," she whispered. Tasha didn't look up. She could only see his heavy-duty boots and the yellow hem of his pants as she spoke.

"What, ma'am?"

"I said I know." She finally raised her eyes, meeting his gaze. She cleared her throat, forcing more conviction into her voice. "I started the fire. I—I did it."

CHAPTER 2
BEFORE

MADISON

"Maddie, you . . . look . . . *fabulous*! You have to tell me where you got that dress!" I hear behind me.

I've heard it several times tonight, but I have to look surprised when I turn away from the window where I'd been staring at penthouse views of the Washington, D.C., skyline to look at the woman who'd complimented me. The Tidal Basin and the dome of the Thomas Jefferson Memorial are now replaced with her smiling, wrinkled face.

Her name eludes me, but I don't let on. I can tell from the chunky gold jewelry at her throat and dangling from her ears, and the colorful print of her gown, that she doesn't work at the firm. None of the female lobbyists here at the party would be caught dead in something so garish. They're all wearing simple cocktail dresses and sheaths, like they'd agreed to the uniform in advance.

I try harder to recall her name, but I'm still drawing a blank. Maybe she's one of the other wives. Not one of the other partners' wives. I've made it my job to know all of them so I could spot them across the room with their backs turned. Or maybe she's one of the high-ranking clients. The head of some corporation.

Nevertheless, my face brightens. I give her a conspiratorial wink. "Now, you know I can't reveal trade secrets," I say playfully.

She throws back her head and laughs.

The joke isn't that funny, but I laugh along with her.

She pats my shoulder. "Maddie, you're a hoot! I swear I've always loved your sense of humor. It's a perfect match for Phil! He's so serious sometimes," she says with an exaggerated frown. "Where is Phil, by the way?" She glances around the hotel suite where his firm, Wyatt & Harris, is throwing this get-together, making her gray hair helmet rotate on its axis. "I haven't seen him all night. Where is he hiding, dear?" She chuckles before taking a sip of wine.

I'm starting to wonder where he's gotten off to as well. I haven't seen my husband since he disappeared 20 minutes ago to use the men's room. I assume he was abducted by one of his colleagues on the way back. They're probably talking in one of the many huddles around the penthouse, having conversations about some piece of legislation on the Hill or new executive order or regulation. All manner of things that would make my eyes glaze over.

"He isn't hiding, but now that you mention it, I should go and find him. He said he wanted to get an early start tomorrow and didn't want to stay out too late tonight. We should leave soon," I lie.

The truth is that I've gotten bored. It's bad enough that I have to attend these things. Even though I'm not on the payroll, partners' wives are expected to make an appearance at the firm's parties. But did he have to leave me alone to fend for myself?

"Well, it was wonderful seeing you again, Maddie! Call me when you get a chance. We should set something up. Perhaps lunch?" she says, leaning forward to kiss the air beside my cheek. "My treat!"

"Of course!" I lie again, air-kissing her cheek as well.

I wave goodbye and turn, winding my way through the crowd in search of my husband. I look for men in the maze of rooms who fit my husband's build, who are his height. Finally, I spot him near a baby grand piano in front of one of the floor-to-ceiling windows.

He's standing with three other men, all in tuxedos. A few of them look familiar.

Phil takes a sip of wine and nods at something one of them is saying. I raise my hand to get his attention and start to walk toward them, but stop short when another woman glides across the room from the other direction. She is a tall, lithe, young redhead in an emerald-green dress that sways around her hips and drapes off her pale shoulders. My husband notices her but not me, lowers his wine-glass, and grins. He reaches out to her, lightly grips her elbow, and pulls her toward the group and closer to his side.

My back goes rigid as I watch the familiar gesture.

The young woman tosses her hair over her shoulder and offers her hand for a shake to the others. They greet her, and the five begin to talk. I can't hear them from this distance, but they all laugh at something she says. As they talk, she reaches up and picks at a piece of lint on Phil's shoulder. She lets her hand rest there.

My cheeks and neck flame with heat, like they've been doused with hot water. I feel light-headed.

My outrage and disbelief seem to take on solid form. They fly across space, spanning the distance between me and my husband, and roughly shove at his back. He finally turns to look at me.

"Ah, Maddie! There you are! I was wondering where you'd gotten off to, honey," he says, like I was the one who disappeared. Phil gestures to his side. "Meet Penelope."

Penelope drops her hand and turns. Her green eyes settle on me and she gives me a "cat that ate the canary" smile that makes me tremble. The bitch practically has a feather dangling from the side of her crimson mouth.

"Mrs. Gingell," she gushes, "it's such a pleasure to finally meet you! I've heard so much about you from Phil."

And that's when I know my fears were true all along, what I've been suspecting for months after Phil's numerous late nights at work and the missed phone calls and texts and the mysterious charges on our Barneys account: my husband is no longer mine.

CHAPTER 3

TASHA

A MAN PASSES ME ON THE WAY TO MY ROOM AS I WALK DOWN THE hotel hallway with a towel wrapped around my waist. He's white with dark hair and wearing a checkered shirt and khakis.

"Hiya," he says with a nod.

"Good evenin'!" I say.

He tucks his hotel key into the back pocket of his pants and looks down at my feet, where chlorine water is dripping onto the burgundy and gold rug. He purses his lips and keeps walking.

I'm a little embarrassed by all the dripping I'm doing, by the mess and noise I'm making. I didn't bring any flip-flops with me. Just my tennis shoes, and my feet are soaking wet so I keep making this squishy sound with each step I take. I can't believe I left my flip-flops back home, but there were only so many things I could pack into one suitcase. I took what was important, what I thought we needed, what couldn't be replaced—and a ten-dollar pair of flip-flops wasn't one of those things.

I'm almost near my room anyway. I turn the corner and see the gold sign on the wall. Room 654. I stand in front of it and steal a look over my shoulder before reaching into my swimsuit, digging between my boobs, and tugging out my key card. I wipe it dry on the side of my towel, unlock the door, and step inside.

"Ghalen!" I call out to my son as the door slams shut behind me. "Ghalen, I'm back and you were right, baby. That Jacuzzi was just what your mama needed!"

Yesterday, Ghalen went upstairs to the tenth floor, to the sports center to swim in the pool and splash around. When he came back to our room, he was all smiles.

"You know they got a Jacuzzi up there, Ma?" he said, shaking out water from his dreads and wiping down his face with a towel of his own. "It's so warm, and it has all these jets. My arms and legs feel like jelly. You should try it!"

I figured I should, since tonight would be my last chance. We're leaving the hotel tomorrow, heading to Reagan National, and taking a flight to Atlanta.

I yank off my towel, kick off my wet tennis shoes, and shiver in the air of the room that's as cold as Alaska. I check the thermostat on the wall by the bathroom and see that the boy set it to 65 degrees for some reason. I suck my teeth and raise the temperature to 70. I told him to make himself comfortable in the hotel room, but I didn't mean to freeze us half to death.

We've tried to pretend that our stay at the hotel is like a vacation to keep the mood light, to ignore what and who we're running away from. I let Ghalen buy movies on the pay-per-view channels and eat potato chips and M&Ms out of the hotel fridge. We ordered room service and stayed up late, eating overpriced sundaes and churro sticks.

On the second night, after Ghalen fell asleep, I stood alone on the balcony and looked out at the city that I've lived in for so many years, the twinkling lights in the night sky, and all the cars and people below. I hadn't felt so free in my whole life. For the first time in years, I could hope. I could feel my life finally changing for the better. I went to sleep with a grin on my face.

The grin is back now, as I look around the hotel room. My double bed is made, but Ghalen's is a mess—as usual. The sheets are all rumpled and the pillows are thrown around, but at least he finally put away his clothes instead of leaving them draped all over the furniture like his bedroom back home. Or maybe he finally started packing for tomorrow, like I asked.

"*Ghalen?*" I walk back to the bathroom door. The light is on inside, and even though the door is cracked a little, I knock. He's a teenager, so he's real particular about his privacy. "Ghalen? Baby, you in here?"

He doesn't answer, so I nudge open the door a little more and find that the bathroom is as empty as the rest of the hotel room.

I drop my hands to my hips, wondering where my son has gotten off to. Maybe he went to grab some ice from the machine farther down the hall, or maybe he went downstairs to the Walgreens across the street to get something.

"I told that boy to tell me if he's leaving the hotel," I mutter under my breath as I walk across the room to my purse. It's sitting on the footstool. I open it and begin to look for my cell phone in all the clutter. Maybe Ghalen left me a text message while I was in the Jacuzzi. That's when, in the corner of my eye, I see the notepad sitting on the night table between our beds. I recognize my son's handwriting. I walk toward it and pick it up.

> *I'm sorry, Ma, but I can't go to Georgia with you. I'd miss my girl and all my friends. And I think I'd even miss Dad too. I don't want to start a new school down there. Not when I'm so close to graduation.*

> *Don't worry. I won't tell Dad where you went, but I gotta go back home, Ma. I'll be alright. Don't worry about me.*

> *Luv,*

> *Ghalen*

As I read the note, my hands begin to shake. I start breathing hard, like I'm climbing up a hill. I rush across the room and pull open one of the accordion doors to the room closet. Even though I knew it wouldn't be there, I still cry out when I see our one suitcase is gone.

"Damn it!" I shout, now near tears.

Ghalen really went back. He went back home to his father. He told me not to worry, but how can I not? I can't leave him there all alone to fend for himself. I can't leave him alone with that man.

I close my eyes, feeling all my hope and happy feelings fade. It only takes me a minute or two to think about what to do next. I take a deep breath and grab one of the plastic dry-cleaning bags from the closet shelf that the hotel leaves for guests. I trudge to the dresser drawers, grab my clothes, and start stuffing them into the bag, packing for my drive back home.

CHAPTER 4

MADISON

We step onto the elevator more than 30 minutes later, and Phil is close at my heels. He may be pissed, but I am furious; so if he wants to be coddled tonight, I will not be the one to do it. Let *her* do it instead.

I don't look at him as I turn and the steel doors close behind us, shutting out the tinkling piano keys, laughter, and loud conversations of the party we've just left, and interning us to a deathly silence. Phil presses one of the many buttons on the panel in front of me, and I step back as if I'm giving him room to do so, but the truth is I don't want him to touch me. I don't even want his tuxedo sleeve to skim the silk of my cocktail dress. If it did . . . if he did, I don't know what I'd do. Lurch back in disgust—or maybe start screaming and pounding him with my fists.

I keep my eyes focused on the digital readout and listen to the light chime in the elevator compartment as we descend from the hotel's penthouse. I count down the numbers in my head.

12 . . .
11 . . .
10 . . .
9 . . .

I'm trying my best to ignore him and pretend he isn't here, but I can feel the heat radiating from his body as he looms beside me. The pungent smell of his cologne—cedar, pepper, and white musk—invades my nostrils along with the undertone of an unfamiliar flowery scent that I assume is *hers*.

As we draw closer to the first floor of the hotel, my eyes are magnetically pulled to our reflection in the elevator doors and I look, despite my better judgment. I see how we present ourselves to the world and what we really are. A tall man and a petite woman. A fetching couple, married almost eight years. Childless by choice. Phil is forty-eight years old, in a single-breasted tuxedo with a loosened necktie, thinning brown hair, and a growing paunch that makes the buttons of his suit jacket pull slightly. I am his fair-haired wife of thirty-four, who spends numerous hours and plenty of money on a personal trainer and esthetician to ensure that I look younger than my years and the needle on the scale stays below 110 pounds.

But while Phil, one of the premier lobbyists in D.C., is still considered virile and in his prime, I am already a wilting flower on the stem. I can no longer deny it. My time is drawing near. I am a younger trophy wife who is no longer young and will soon be put on the shelf. In fact, I suspect Phil has already found my replacement. Maybe that's why *she* was there tonight.

"I can't believe you did that," Phil suddenly mutters.

I turn away from our reflection to glare up at him.

"You were rude to her the entire time, Madison. It was completely uncalled for . . . absolutely ridiculous," he says. "You realize that, don't you?"

"I realize that I'm married to a liar . . . a cheater . . . a—"

"I am *not* a liar."

"A cheater, then? Can you finally admit to that?"

"Please stop this, Maddie. Penelope works at our firm. She's just an intern . . . a law student."

"And lowly interns usually get invited to these types of shindigs? Aren't you generous!"

"I'm mentoring her, for Chrissake! I'm helping her with her career!"

I snort and cross my arms over my chest. "Is that what they call it nowadays?"

"Nothing is happening between us. Certainly nothing that warranted your behavior tonight. You were childish. Spiteful. You were trying to embarrass me in front of my colleagues and—"

"And you are humiliating me by canoodling with her!"

"I wasn't canoodling! I was simply introducing her to—"

"I *know* what you were doing," I say tightly, turning around to point up at him. "I know what you have been doing. I am *not* an idiot!"

I know what he was doing because he did the same with me ten years ago when he was married to his first wife, Ashley, and I was temping at Wyatt & Harris as an assistant. Often, when he told her he was working late or taking a client out to dinner, he and I would meet at the Renaissance hotel—a stone's throw away from the firm's offices—in one of the king suites. We'd fuck like bunnies on poppers, and sometimes we would spend the night together. At lunch, he would sneak out early from meetings and we would drink sangria and eat Catalan cuisine while nestled in the back of our favorite restaurant, feeding each other, licking the sweet residue of pork fat and dates off each other's fingers. But unlike Penelope the Intern, I never flaunted our relationship in front of Ashley. I never attended any of the firm's parties and I would have never . . . *never* been caught by his wife with my hand perched on his shoulder, a gesture as possessive and intimate as a kiss.

"Like I said, this is ridiculous." Phil casually adjusts his shirt cuffs. He's wearing the cufflinks I gave him for Christmas five years ago. Twenty-four-karat gold and engraved with his initials, PHG.

"You won't think it's so ridiculous if I tell your colleagues the truth about you."

He narrows his eyes at me. "Don't threaten me, Maddie."

"Don't tempt me, Phil."

"You're going to say something you'll regret, so let's end this conversation now. I'm tired of it and won't entertain it any longer," he says with a finality that is utterly infuriating.

I want to strangle him. I want to murder him. It takes all my willpower not to turn and wrap my hands around his throat.

The elevator gives one last chime, signaling that we are on the first floor. The doors slide open, revealing the busy lobby, and Phil steps forward to stroll out first, but I roughly shove him aside, hurting my arm in the process, and I step in front of him instead.

I stride under a series of twinkling crystal chandeliers and past a throng of people lingering on banquettes and in chairs, talking to each other and their cell phones. Others walk toward the reservation desk, dragging suitcases and wool coats behind them. I can hear the *click-click-click* of my stilettos over the marble tile, and my shoes pinch my toes as I walk. Four-inch heels were probably a bad choice in footwear, but they make me feel tall and powerful, and I need that tonight.

The hotel's gold revolving doors come into view, and I can see our car—a black Lincoln Town Car—idling along the curb. Our part-time driver sees Phil and me through the glass as we approach the exit, so he steps out of the Town Car, jogs around the hood, and begins to open one of the rear doors.

He has worked for Phil for the past four years. He is diligent, discreet, and more than willing to please the boss. Unfortunately, I am no longer of a similar mind.

I push my way through the revolving doors into the night. The air is so cold that my bare shoulders and legs instantly light with goosebumps, and I breathe in audibly at the shock of it. The brisk wind takes my breath away and yanks at my loose bun, making the hair piled atop my head fly around me, striking my face, neck, and back like I'm standing on the deck of a ship during an impending storm. Instead of walking toward the Town Car and the waiting open door, I continue to trace the semicircular path of the hotel's driveway, past a beleaguered bellman whose cart is loaded down with so many suitcases and shopping bags that it looks on the verge of falling onto its side.

"Maddie! Madison, where are you going?" Phil shouts after me.

I don't answer him. I look for any means of escape, but there are no other cars or taxis in sight. I look at the street in front of the hotel. I remember my younger days, when I was a much different girl . . . a *braver* girl, and I hitchhiked my way cross-country, climbing into strangers' cars without hesitation and doing even more along the way. But I am not that girl anymore.

Or am I? I wonder, as I spot a blue Chevrolet sedan pulling out of a garage adjacent to the hotel's driveway. The sedan stops and the driver turns on their blinker. I can't see who is inside, but I know that there are only seconds before the driver merges into traffic and disappears down the street. I run to the car, wincing at the pain in my feet and shivering against the chill.

"Madison, what the hell are you doing?" Phil yells.

I reach the sedan and tug on the passenger-side door handle, but the door is locked. The only thing I've succeeded in doing is startling the driver, making her whip around to face me. She is a black woman who looks to be my age. A cell phone is in her hand, but she fumbles and drops it to the floor.

"Let me in, please," I ask through chattering teeth, knocking frantically on the window. "Let me in! I can pay you money."

"Madison," Phil says as he stalks toward me. His eyebrows are drawn together. His face is red. He is embarrassed again. Perhaps he is furious now, too. "Stop this now! You can't just hop into some random car. What are you doing? This is insane!"

The woman glances back at Phil, then stares at me again.

I bite down on my bottom lip, making tears prick my eyes. I gaze at the woman through the tinted window. "Please help me?" I ask with a sniff.

My eyes are red now. I'm crying—almost.

But she hesitates. She glances at the traffic and shifts the steering wheel as if she's about to merge and drive away, and I wonder if she will leave me standing here. I watch with pleasant surprise as she reaches for the automated locks and I hear the click signifying that she's unlocked the doors.

I yank the handle again and it opens. I hop inside, slam the door behind me, and we drive off just as Phil nears the bumper.

I can no longer hear my husband as we drive away, but his lips are moving rapidly like a silent film star as he shouts and pleads. I can see him running down the curb and almost into the street in a futile attempt to stop me.

CHAPTER 5

TASHA

Don't go back . . .

"Don't go back, girl!" was what my friend, Monique, was saying to me on the phone just as that white lady started banging on my window, yelling for help. "Why in the world would you go back there? Are you *crazy*?"

But I've got to go back. I can't leave Ghalen behind.

My therapist warned me about my baby boy.

"I ain't a baby anymore, Ma," Ghalen would correct me, but he's still a baby to me.

Yes, he is six feet tall now, with wide shoulders and a goatee. Yes, he has a girlfriend and just got his driver's license a month ago. But in my heart, Ghalen will always be that baby in the incubator with the wrinkled skin and tiny arms and legs hooked up to all those wires. Ghalen will always be the baby who brought tears to my eyes when he finally latched onto my breast to feed and the nurses told me that it was a good sign, a strong one that he would pull through after all.

But my therapist warned me that he might not pull through this time. My son was the weak link in my plan, the one thing on my list that I couldn't check off. I just didn't believe her—or I didn't want to believe her, I guess.

I'd written the plan on a notepad that I use for my grocery lists and my lotto numbers. I scratched out the steps and reordered them about 500 times before finally committing it all to memory. I then did what my therapist had told me to do: I held the paper over one of the oven burners and watched the yellow sheet catch fire. I burned it so Kordell would never find it. I didn't want him to know what I was doing.

Step 1. Pack a bag for me and Ghalen and hide it in the attic crawl space. ONE BAG!

Step 2. Keep copies of my and Ghalen's birth certificates, Social Security cards, bank statements, and insurance cards in my purse.

Step 3. Buy a burner phone.

Step 4. Book a hotel with a parking garage so I can keep my car off the street so it's not easy to spot.

Step 5. Tell my job that I'm leaving.

Step 6. Withdraw cash and deposit remaining money on a debit card not connected to bank accounts.

Step 7. LEAVE!

"Your plan looks good," Dr. Green told me when I showed it to her a couple weeks ago, back at her office. She handed the paper back to me. "It looks sound, but . . . does he want to go with you?"

I was too busy smiling down at my escape plan to hear her. I was so proud that I was finally doing it after all this time. It had taken years to work up the courage to leave Kordell.

"Does what now?" I asked her, barely paying attention.

"Does he want to leave with you? Your son, I mean. I don't recall you mentioning discussing this with him."

I looked up from the paper to stare at her. She was sitting in that big leather chair of hers, staring at me over the top of her glasses. Her long braids swayed when she tilted her head.

What a silly ass question to ask, I thought, annoyed.

"Of course he wants to come with me. Why wouldn't he? I'm his mama."

"But have you asked him? He just turned 17. Things like this can get incredibly complicated, Tasha. Legally, he can decide which parent he wants to—"

"He's coming with me," I said.

At that, Dr. Green went quiet. She sat back in her chair.

She ended our session soon after that, five minutes early.

My voice probably sounded harder than I meant it to, but there ain't no way this was even up for debate. If I left, I was taking my baby boy with me. And why wouldn't Ghalen want to come? He'd heard the fights and the name-calling. They only got worse when Kordell lost one of his big construction jobs making custom cabinets at one of those new housing developments out in Laurel, Maryland, because he'd been caught drinking on the job. But instead of learning his lesson and hustling harder, he got bitter and angry and started drinking more.

I used to tell Ghalen to go to his room when the fights got real bad, and I didn't know if Kordell would be happy with just using his words and breaking things but would start using his hands on me, on *us*. Then a month ago, he finally did it. Kordell backhanded me across the face. I can't even remember why. It was over something petty. Something silly. It was the first time he'd ever done it, and Ghalen saw it. Why wouldn't Ghalen want to get as far away from his daddy as possible after he saw what he'd done to me?

So, when I left, Ghalen *did* come with me. I sort of dropped it on him, but he didn't ask any questions. He didn't argue. He just grabbed the suitcase I packed for us, tossed it into the trunk, and climbed into the car with me. While I drove to the hotel where we would stay a few days before heading to the airport, I told him about my big plans for us. How I wanted to move back to Georgia where the rest of my family lives. He would transfer schools. I'd get a new job. We'd live with my Mama. After I begged her, she said we could stay with her for a little while, at least until we got settled and I got on my feet.

But now that I think about it . . . now that I look back on that day, there was a funny look in Ghalen's eyes that should've told me something ain't right. And the way he kept gnawing his bottom lip—like when he has a big basketball game coming up or a test he didn't study for—let me know he was worried, but I just thought it was because he thought we'd get caught. I didn't know he was thinking about all the things he was leaving behind. I never thought he would ever miss Kordell.

That's the hardest part to take . . . that he'd miss the man who made me feel small and weak, who I was trying to protect him from. But he's probably making excuses for his daddy, trying to explain the meanness away and coming up with reasons to forgive. They're the same excuses I've made for so long. They're partly why I stayed. I know Ghalen is grown. It's his decision, but I worry if I'm not there to stand in between them, what Kordell might do to him, especially if he wants to get the truth out of him about where I went. I can't let Ghalen be his punching bag.

I've got to save my baby. I don't want to go back. I'm scared as hell to go back. But I've *got* to go back.

So that's where my mind was when that white lady came knocking on my window, saying, "Please help me?"

She looked so cold and scared. Then I saw that man coming up behind her with a look on his face like he wanted to kill her right then and there. I thought about Kordell. I thought about Ghalen. For a split second, I saw myself standing out there alone with my hair whipping in the wind, begging to be let in, begging for someone . . . *anyone* to help me.

I mean . . . what else could I do? How could I not help?

CHAPTER 6

TASHA

"ARE YOU ALL RIGHT, HONEY?" I ASK HER AS WE PULL OFF INTO traffic. I keep one eye on her and one eye on the road and the Dodge Caravan in front of me that keeps tap-tap-tappin' on its brakes. "Do I need to take you to a police station?"

She stops looking out the back window and turns around in the seat to face me. I can't see her too well in the dark car, just an outline of a face and big, wide eyes. "*What?*"

I reach over and press the button on the dashboard to turn down the radio. The DJ is talking so loud that she probably can't hear me. "I said do I need to take you to a police station?"

She frowns like I've just said the craziest thing in the world. "Why would you do that?"

This time, I'm the one that looks confused, but I remember she's probably in shock. When Kordell hit me, I couldn't remember what day it was or even my own damn name right after it happened.

"Do I need to take you some place to get help?" I ask more slowly this time. "Aren't you running away from him? From that man?"

Finally, something dawns on her. Her frown goes away and she nods. "Y-y-yes! Yes, I was running away from him! He's . . . he's my husband."

I nod with her like we're doing it to the beat of the same song. The DJ's voice disappears, and a commercial comes on with sirens and honking horns. It's starting to get on my nerves, so I reach over again and turn off the radio.

"Did he hurt you, honey?"

She doesn't answer me right away, and I wonder if maybe I shouldn't have asked her that. She's probably ashamed about what happened. Dr. Green said a lot of battered women blame themselves. They think it's their fault and don't want to tell nobody. I've been there. I'm *still* there.

The white lady lowers her eyes and starts to rub her arm, like her husband grabbed her there, like it still hurts. "Yes," she says almost in a whisper.

"It's okay. Just tell me where I need to take you, and I'll do it. Don't worry!"

She starts to give me an answer, but she stops when a little voice pipes up in the car.

"Hello? *Hello?* Tasha?" I can hear Monique say.

"Damn," I mumble, pointing down to the floor as I drive. "Can you hand me that, sweetheart? I didn't hang up and she's gonna just keep shouting until I say somethin'."

The lady leans down, feels around in the dark, and finally finds my cell phone. She hands it to me.

"Monique, I'm sorry, girl," I say, holding the phone up to my ear. "I didn't mean to just leave you hanging like that. Something happened and I dropped my phone."

"What happened now?" she asks.

Monique is one of the few people I told that I was leaving Kordell, but she moved to North Carolina two years ago and I figured he wouldn't go driving down there, beating down her door to find me. He doesn't even know she moved.

"Nothing. Nothing happened to me. I'm okay. I was just . . . I was just helping somebody," I say, not knowing how to explain what happened minutes ago and not in the mood to do it. I hate driving and talking on the phone at the same time, and now I got this frightened lady in my car. It's too much to focus on all at once.

"Helping somebody?" Monique says. "Who you supposed to be helping, Tasha?"

I stop at a stoplight and realize for the first time that I don't even know the lady's name. I haven't told her mine either. I turn in the driver's seat to face her. I can see her better now because the sign and bright lights from a nearby gas station fill my Chevy Malibu.

She's pretty, though I can't tell if it's from her makeup or if she's a natural beauty, as they say. Back at the hotel, for some reason, I didn't notice she was wearing a dress. It's off-the-shoulder and silver with little sequined flowers on the sleeves. A diamond necklace dangles around her throat and more diamonds dangle from her ears. Besides her crazy blond hair that she's now combing back into place with her fingers, she looks rich and classy, like one of those women on those reality shows, the *Real Housewives of Beverly Hills* and whatnot. She looks like she could buy her way out of trouble if she wanted to, but I guess she couldn't do it tonight. Goes to show you that even rich women . . . even rich *white* women have their burdens to bear.

"Monique, let me call you back," I say into the phone.

"*Huh?* Why?" Monique squawks.

I never should've taken her phone call in the first place; but when I saw Ghalen had left, I was scared and panicked and needed somebody to talk to.

"Just let me call you back, girl. I will. I promise. I just can't talk right now," I say, before hanging up.

The light turns green and I start driving. I toss my phone into an empty cup holder and glance at the lady beside me again.

"I'm Tasha . . . Tasha Jenkins," I begin, finally introducing myself.

"Madison Gingell," she says.

Madison. It's a name a woman like her would have. Sophisticated.

"Nice to meet you, Madison. Now, where do you want me to take you?"

She goes quiet again like she isn't sure how to answer.

"You've gotta pick somewhere, honey. I could take you to 28th Street in Southeast with me, but I don't think you'd wanna go there. Where I'm going isn't much better than what you just left."

She squints blue eyes at me. She doesn't know what I mean.

"My husband has a hard time keeping his hands to himself, too," I confess for some reason.

Maybe because I figure she'd understand, being in the same situation and all.

"Men are cockroaches," Madison says out of nowhere. Her voice sounds different now. Sharper. Deeper. I wonder if that's what I sounded like to Dr. Green. Even so, it catches me off guard.

"*Cockroaches?* Well, I don't know about all that! Yes, there's plenty of bad men out there . . ."

My husband being one of them, I think but don't say it out loud.

". . . but there are some good men, too. My son, Ghalen, for one. I'm trying to raise him right . . . to be a good man, you know? That's why I'm going back home. He needs me."

"He needs you?"

"Yeah."

"How old is your son?"

"He just turned seventeen, three months ago," I say proudly.

"Practically a man already."

I laugh. "That's what he keeps tellin' me!"

"And yet you say he needs you," she says, making me frown again. "Interesting."

She turns away from me and looks out the car window.

I open my mouth to say there's nothing interesting about it. I am his mother. It will always be my job to look out for him, and any mama knows that. I'm about to tell her the story of Ghalen's premature birth that nearly killed us both and those long months in the NICU after, but I don't get the chance because she tells me to make a left and that we're only 15 minutes away from where we need to go. She then gives me an address where I can drop her off.

The moment for me to speak up has passed, so I turn on the radio again instead. I've told enough of my business for one night anyway.

It's the late-night hour, so the music is calm now—lots of old R&B and smooth jazz. The DJ has changed, too. This one doesn't shout, but talks like he's trying to make you drift off to sleep. I need that. I've got a lot on my mind right now about Ghalen. About Kordell. The voices in my head are speaking loud enough; they don't need any competition.

When we get near the address she gave me, I look around. I've never been here before, though I thought I'd been just about every-where in D.C. A park is across the street with big trees and a stone monument with a man on a horse. The houses on the block are tall and made of red brick. Most of the windows don't have curtains, so I can see all the people inside, going about their business. In one, a woman is sitting on a sofa, sipping wine with a remote in her hand. In the house next door, a man is jogging up the stairs to the second floor with a dog running behind him.

My neighbors don't just have curtains and blinds on their win-dows. Some even have bars on them, and ADT and "Beware the Dog" signs in their front yards. But I don't see any of that here. I guess when you've got money and live around people with money, you don't need that stuff. You aren't scared of the world and what it will do to you and yours.

Must be nice.

I can't find a parking space, so I stop in the street. Madison unbuckles her seat belt and opens the car door. She hops out.

"You gonna be all right?" I ask, leaning over the armrest.

I'm more worried for her than I am about me, though I don't know why. Maybe it's easier to worry about somebody else. It can distract you from yourself.

She turns and looks up at one of the houses, the one on the end. "I suppose."

"Are you staying with a friend?"

She pauses, then nods. "For tonight, anyway."

That's a smart move. A lot smarter than what I'm about to do.

But I have no choice, I remind myself.

"Well, you . . . you take care of yourself," I say.

She nods again and shuts the door. I turn off my emergency lights and watch her walk a few steps. Her shoulders are bent and her head is down. She looks so small and frail. Like the heavy wind blowing outside could snatch her away at any moment. I beep my horn. She walks back to my car, and I lower my window.

"Here," I say, reaching for my purse. I pull out my wallet and dig around for a couple of seconds. I pull out a business card. "Let me know how it all works out. Okay?"

She reaches through the open window and takes the card. She frowns down at it. "Knit 'N' Things?"

"It's my side business. I sell stuff I knit on Instagram and Etsy, but you can DM me at the address on the card."

She looks confused at first, but then she smiles. "Why, thank you!"

"No problem, honey!"

A car behind me beeps its horn, and I wave to let the driver know I'm moving. "I should get going. You take care of yourself now."

"You too!" she says as I roll up the window.

I can still see her in my mirror as I drive off. She stands on the curb for a long time before finally walking away.

✳ ✳ ✳

It is a long drive across town to my home—the longest I ever remember it being. More than once I fight the urge to turn around, to take a side street and then another until I'm heading back to the hotel. As I drive, I think of the dozens of times in the past nineteen years that I could've turned around and taken a "different road" than the one I'm taking tonight.

Back when I met Kordell in high school, when I came up here to live with my aunt, he was the smooth-talking senior and I was the shy underclassman. He damn near stalked me until I agreed to go out on a date with him.

Back when we had our first fight when I was sixteen, and I watched him throw a Coke bottle at my feet in anger.

Back when he got jealous of Morris, who I met at my first real office job. Morris had been sweet and funny. He had been kind to me. I liked him a lot. He became a good friend, someone I really cared for, and Kordell must have sensed it. Kordell told me I couldn't talk to him anymore and if he ever found out that I had, he'd come down to my job and beat the hell out of him.

All those times . . . all those years, I should've seen the warning signs and I could've packed my bags and left him. I could've used the sense the good Lord gave me and run—but I didn't. I kept making excuses. I kept waiting for him to change. And, truth be told, the one time before this that I did try to leave, I almost paid the price. A big one. Now, I can't leave. I will not desert Ghalen. So I take the road I know and I keep driving.

When I near the house, I see all the lights inside are out, but the porch light is on. I parallel park along the curb and pop the trunk. I climb out and grab the clear plastic bag that has my clothes and the rest of my things. When I close the trunk, I can see Kordell standing on the front porch in a T-shirt and sweats like he's been there the whole time. The screen door sits open. He's waiting for me.

Seeing him up there, I freeze for a few seconds. I swear my feet won't move.

"Hurry up!" Kordell barks at me.

The threat in his voice makes me pry my feet from the cement, and I run up the concrete walkway and then the porch, dragging my bag behind me. I don't look Kordell in the eyes when I get close. Right now, he's an angry bulldog and he will just see me looking at him as a challenge. He's been drinking. I know because I can smell it. I wonder how much and for how long. I step inside, and the screen door slams shut behind me.

"Taking your sweet time," he mutters as I try to step past him, and he shoves me, almost making me stumble. "Like your ass ain't been gone for three goddamn days and you haven't. . . ."

I stop listening after that. I don't have to hear the rest. It's probably better that I don't, anyway. I close my eyes and take a deep breath.

I'm home and back in jail again.

CHAPTER 7

MADISON

PHIL IS STILL FULL OF APOLOGIES AND SO WILLING TO SUPPLICATE
that I suspect he'd bend down and kiss my feet if I asked him to. I
must have really frightened him when I climbed into that car that
night three weeks ago, even though I arrived home before he did.

Good. He deserved to have a little fear put into him.

"I'm not angry anymore. Please don't think that I am. But,
Maddie, anything could have happened to you," Phil said the next
morning, rubbing my shoulders and kissing my crown before taking
the seat beside me at our kitchen island.

In the merciless light streaming through our floor-to-ceiling
windows, I could see that his eyes were bruised and puffy. The
frown lines around his mouth seemed to have multiplied threefold.

He'd stayed awake, tossing and turning most of the night in our
bed. I'd slept like a baby. At breakfast, Phil barely touched his coffee
and toast while I gobbled an entire acai bowl topped with fruit and
coconut flakes. Thanks to not eating anything at the cocktail party
because of all the fat-laden hors d'oeuvres, I was starving.

"You had no idea who was in that car, Maddie. You could have
driven off with a rapist or a murderer!"

I lowered my spoon into my empty bowl and stifled a sigh, now bored and wishing that I could have more to eat, but I was already at my calorie limit for the morning.

Despite my husband's apparent hysteria, I wondered if he was more worried by what might have happened to me that night—or by what I might have done if I'd *really* left him for good. "Hell hath no fury like a woman scorned," as they say, and Phil had to have been losing what little hair he had left at the prospect of just how vengeful his wife could be.

He'd made sure in our prenup that I would get the bare minimum in a divorce, but there are things I've learned about Phil while working at Wyatt & Harris and being married to him these eight years that could not only embarrass him professionally, but also land him in federal prison. And his private life has just as many skeletons.

Phil's trusted me with all those secrets, and I've been loyal to him and will continue to be—as long as he behaves.

"Please don't ever do that again, sweetheart." Phil grimaced and held my shoulders, begging me. "I couldn't take it if something happened to you! Not in that way. I can't . . . I can't go through that again!"

I didn't respond. I didn't need to. My point was made. I played along and just dipped my head, lowered my eyes, and nodded. Phil embraced me. He held me so tightly that I could barely breathe, but I didn't ease away. Instead, I smiled my own "cat that ate the canary" smile as I lay my head on his shoulder, knowing that Penelope the Intern isn't as clever as she thinks she is. Or at least, she isn't as clever as I am.

I'm not done quite yet, bitch, I thought.

Since that morning, Phil and I have been on a second honeymoon. Honestly, our time together reminds me of the early days of our relationship before we were even married, when everything was new and shiny and I was all that he wanted and needed. When I ranked above the firm. Above Ashley. When I was the air that he breathed.

Now Phil brings me flowers every day when he returns home from the office. A bouquet of yellow tulips. A single rose. Three calla lilies in a slender vase. It is our new love language. He even surprised me with tickets to the National Symphony Orchestra last week. We sat in one of the secluded balcony boxes reserved for use by the firm's partners.

"One of the perks of being the boss," Phil boasted as the house lights went down and we took our seats.

As the *Rhapsody on a Theme of Paganini* began, I reached past the armrest and lowered Phil's pants zipper.

"Maddie, what . . . what are you doing?" he asked with an awkward laugh, like he was clearing his throat. He shifted in his chair and took a quick glance around him to see if anyone was watching us.

I didn't respond. I didn't have to. It was obvious what I was doing.

I jerked him off in the darkened theater while the orchestra played, listening to Phil's labored breathing rise and fall along with the violins, cellos, clarinets, and flutes. Like the conductor with his baton several feet below us, I sped up and slowed down the tempo as I saw fit, shoving Phil's hand away whenever he tried to stop me. And I enjoyed it just as much as Phil did. The power I had over him. The risk of being so brazen. It was just as arousing as if Phil had leaned over and slid his hand up my dress and nestled it between my thighs.

He came in my hand, releasing a strangled groan just as the orchestra reached its climax too. I watched him shudder and his body convulse and go limp in the chair beside me. As the audience cheered, I eased back into my seat and clapped, delighted by both performances.

"You're going to be punished for that later," he whispered hotly against my ear as he raised his zipper, making me tingle all over.

That night, Phil took out the handcuffs and the leather belt—something he hadn't done in almost a year. We thoroughly enjoyed ourselves.

There are no more late nights at work. No more faint whiffs of perfume on his clothes. No more calls that he must take in the downstairs office with the door closed. And no more mysterious charges at Barneys.

She is a distant memory.

My husband is mine again.

CHAPTER 8

MADISON

"I WANT TO THANK YOU, LADIES, SO MUCH FOR HELPING OUT TODAY," Reverend Sutton says.

He adjusts his black vest, where a Rainbow flag and a "Black Lives Matter" pin sit prominently near his clerical collar. He then smiles his beatific smile as he gazes around the table at all the women assembled.

There are a little more than a dozen of us. We are of varying ages—the oldest being Elaine Hausley, the wife of Secretary of State Donald Hausley, and the youngest Gianna Zielinski, the teen daughter of Carla Zielinski, the CEO of one of the biggest defense contractors in the nation. All of us are parishioners of St. Thomas Episcopal Church, Washington's most elite house of worship, only rivaled by the Tenth Street Synagogue a mile and a half away.

Our congregation is full of politicians, CEOs, news pundits, lobbyists, and old money. Former presidents have been parishioners, even kneeling on the velvet padded benches in the chapel for prayer and holy guidance prior to taking the Oath of Office. Needless to say, belonging to St. Thomas comes with quite a bit of cachet, so much so that the church should probably have a waitlist or a velvet rope at its double doors—if churches did that sort of thing. But despite the millions of dollars combined among those who sit in the pews for mass every Sunday, the room in which we now find ourselves is underwhelming and claustrophobic.

We are in the basement of the rectory, a building dating back two centuries, and it shows. There are no windows, and it smells of dust, wet newspapers, and mothballs. I can spot more than one water stain on the ceiling. On two large wooden tables in the center of the room sits row upon row of canvas bags waiting to be filled and transported to the local homeless shelter. Beside the bags are the contents: stacks of pita bread, several containers of hummus, apples, bags of dried banana chips, granola bars, toiletries, and bottles of water.

Elaine has already taken charge, pushing her sleeves up her spindly, wrinkled arms, delegating who will make the hummus pitas and arranging the rest of us into an assembly line responsible for depositing each item into the bags.

I'm not a fan of being bossed around, but I don't speak up. I tug on a polite smile along with my latex gloves. I understand my place in the pecking order. Besides, I'm here to do my job . . . my duty as Phil's wife, to play my part in our social circle, though it would seem a lot easier to me to just write a check to the shelter rather than hand out chapstick tubes and sandwiches. But I've been married to Phil long enough to know that wealthy people absolve their guilt of having so much money with the occasional charitable project like this one. The church's communication manager will likely post photos to the blog and Instagram account.

"Really, I can't praise you ladies enough," Reverend Sutton continues, fawning over us.

He is tall and ruddy-cheeked with long, brown, wavy hair that sweeps his shoulders. He looks more like a youth minister at one of the churches back in my hometown than the reverend of an elite congregation. All he needs is the low-slung jeans and plaid shirt.

"You can't imagine how many in our community you're helping by doing this. You're doing good work today!"

"We're happy to help," Elaine assures him, speaking for all of us. "We should have this all completed by this afternoon. Shouldn't we, ladies?"

A few of us murmur in agreement.

"Shouldn't we, ladies?" a voice whispers mockingly beside me.

Hearing it, the rest of us go silent. Elaine's face reddens.

I glance to my left and find Summer Ross rolling her eyes. She smirks, inviting me to join her in her none-too-subtle ridicule of Elaine, but I don't.

I don't have friends. Never have. Never saw the point of them, frankly. But Summer is my only social acquaintance who is the closest to what you would call a "friend." We've known each other for years, bonding over both being second wives married to older men and former small-town girls in a much bigger small town. Summer is bawdy and irreverent and not boring like most of the women I run into. Usually I find her amusing, but there is a prickliness to her humor lately.

Like me, she's having marital issues, though she doesn't know about mine. Over one too many cocktails after an Amnesty International fundraising benefit, Summer drunkenly confessed that she suspected her husband, Tom, was having yet *another* affair—fucking a policy analyst at a think tank. At least this time it wasn't with one of his underlings, which Summer said cost his company a payoff when the young woman threatened a sexual harassment lawsuit because she said she'd felt pressured by Tom to start a sexual relationship.

I wasn't surprised by what Summer divulged to me about her husband that night; Tom's the stereotypical, hyper-masculine scumbag. The one time we'd had a couple's dinner together at their condo, he kept mansplaining everything from politics to lawn maintenance and made several dumb blonde jokes, obviously at my expense. The kicker was when I excused myself to go to the bathroom and found Tom waiting in the hall when I was done.

"Guess we've got a little line going," he said with a drunken chuckle, like his home didn't have two other restrooms.

I gave a weak laugh and tried to walk around him, but he blocked my path. He did it twice more, chuckling again, and then he finally let me pass, but only after rubbing against my ass as he made his way into the bathroom.

When we both got back to the dining table later, it took all my restraint not to grab my salad fork and jab it into his thigh.

I never told Summer what he did that night. What's the point? The guy is a mountain of red flags. She's a hopeless fool for him; she'd only make excuses. I think Summer would be better off without him, but she wants to make their marriage work. Unfortunately for her, while Phil and I have regained our footing, they're still floundering, and Summer's not even bothering to hide it anymore.

Elaine notices Summer's silent exchange with me. Her lips tighten.

Great. Now Elaine's pissed at me. I hope it doesn't get back to Phil. I won't hear the end of it.

"Well, I'll let you all get to work," Reverend Sutton says before backing out of the room.

I've been assigned pita duty and for three hours I systematically slice each pita pocket open before handing them off to Julie, a stay-at-home mom of four who's married to an executive vice president of the Chamber of Commerce. She slathers each pita with hummus and then drops the sandwich into wax paper bags. As we work, she talks about her kids and their plans to take a trip to the family beach house on the Outer Banks this summer.

I find the conversation and Julie dull and tedious, but I nod and pretend to listen.

The rest of the women fill the canvas bags as we work, though Summer disappears two hours in, mumbling about needing to make a phone call, and Gianna gets bored and starts to sulk in a corner, sitting in one of the rectory's ancient chairs while scanning and typing away on her cell phone.

"Hop to, ladies!" Elaine orders with a maniacal cheeriness, dropping bottle after bottle into each bag. "We can't get the job done if we start slacking now." She stares pointedly at Gianna. "I'm sorry if we're interrupting your phone time, young lady, but would you mind disconnecting yourself from that device and *helping*?"

Gianna lowers her cell and curls her lip.

She is short and pudgy, and has the petulant air unique to teen girls who resent the world but can't yet articulate why. I wonder what she did to make her parents subject her to today's punishment.

"I'm allowed to take a break," Gianna murmurs.

"You've been on your 'break' for more than twenty minutes," Elaine counters. Her smile tightens. "We are here to volunteer. Not to surf the Internet."

"The last time I checked, slavery was illegal." Gianna shoves her curly blond hair over her shoulder. "So, like . . . you can't make me do what I don't want to do. You know?" Gianna then returns her attention to her cell-phone screen.

Julie glances at me with big brown eyes. "Wow," she mouths.

I'm a little impressed too by Gianna's nerve. Pecking order be damned.

"We're equating volunteerism with slavery now?" Elaine laughs and looks around the table at the other women to join her in her laughter. A few chime in predictably. "I weep for your generation! Forgive me for asking you to put the needs of others before yourself. I won't bother you again."

"It's not like you're saving the world or anything with this stuff," Gianna says, still scanning her phone. "You guys practically killed the planet and you think you can save it with a stupid sandwich, baby wipes, and Band-Aids." She sniffs. "The wipes aren't even disposable."

"I'll be back in a bit," I whisper to Julie as I tug off my gloves, having my fill for the time being of manual labor and this generational slugfest. I walk out of the room in search of a bathroom to freshen up, and turn down a series of dimly lit corridors. The wallpaper is peeling in some spots. The parquet floors are in need of a good scrubbing. I get that the church wants to give the air of humility, but this is a bit ridiculous. As I pass one of the open doorways, I hear Summer laughing, making me pause.

I step back, then take a step into the room. It's the rectory's pantry closet. A small maze of eight-foot-tall steel shelves takes up most of the space. On each shelf are canned goods and boxes. On one, I spot a pack of 1,000-count communion wafers.

An eerie sense of déjà vu overwhelms me as I look around the closet, making me pause. The walls and steel shelves start to feel like they're squeezing in tighter and tighter, closing in on me. A sense of panic begins to rise and I start to feel dizzy. I grip one of the shelves to steady myself. But I remember where I am.

Washington, D.C. St. Thomas Episcopal Church.

I remember who I am.

Madison Gingell. Wife of Phillip Gingell.

I take long, deep breaths until the sensation goes away. It was a brief moment of weakness. It happens to the best of us. I'm all better now, though; my grimace gradually transforms into a grin.

"So, this is where you disappeared to," I say, forcing my voice to stay light as I round the corner, spotting Summer's silhouette as she leans against one of the shelves. "Many thanks for leaving me in there with . . ."

My words fade when I realize that Summer is not alone. Her arms are looped around a guy's neck. His arms are wrapped around her waist. I recognize him as one of the workers on the grounds of the rectory—a young Latino guy with dark, spiked gelled hair and a raised scar on his brow. He is kissing Summer's neck as she laughs. When they see me, they startle and jump apart. Her cheeks go pink. His mouth falls open like a dead fish.

"What are you doing here?" Summer asks, closing her shirt.

"I could ask you the same thing," I say.

Her companion rushes past me with his head bowed, muttering, "Excuse me, Miss," as he raises the zipper of his dirt-stained cargo pants.

I step aside and watch him flee into the hall. I then turn back around to face Summer.

"Don't look at me like that," she says, shoving her tousled dark hair out of her eyes.

"Like *what?*" I shrug. "I didn't say anything."

"But I know what you were thinking," she begins, buttoning her shirt. "That I'm being stupid . . . reckless . . ."

"No, I'm not."

I'm not judging her. Tom is screwing around. Why shouldn't she? But still, does she even know that guy?

"Why did I do that? Why the hell did I do that?" Summer flaps her arms helplessly.

"So . . . why did you do it?"

Why would she attempt to have sex with a random grounds-keeper in a rectory basement, of all things? Anyone could have caught them. Luckily, it was me, but I could only imagine if it had been one of the other women. If Julie or . . . *Jesus Christ* . . . Elaine had stumbled upon them, everyone in our circle would know within days what Summer had done. She'd be committing social suicide.

"I don't know! Maybe it's because I've always been a sucker for a Spanish accent, ever since I spent that semester in Madrid when I was an undergrad."

I squint. "*A Spanish accent?* You're joking, right?"

"Don't judge me, Maddie," she snaps. "Not all of us have perfect little marriages like you."

I don't comment. Instead, I watch as she buttons the last button and closes her eyes.

"Tom told me a few days ago that he wants a divorce," she mumbles. "It's over. *We're* over."

"I'm sorry to hear that," I lie.

She and Tom weren't even sharing a bed anymore, and they were seeing a counselor, but I doubted it was going to help. A man like him is the master of his own universe, and there was no way his focus could remain on one individual in all that vastness, a tiny speck known as his wife. She can't see that, though.

"It's okay," she says, raking her hair back. "I think I'm finally coming to terms with everything."

I don't know if I would call trying to fuck a church grounds-keeper "coming to terms" with the loss of your marriage, but I don't mention that.

"You're better off without him," I say. It's my halfhearted attempt to comfort her.

"Yeah, right. I'm better off divorced at thirty-six with no real job and an airtight prenup." She gives a cold laugh. "I thought we were getting better, you know? Tom and I even started to have sex again. We were going to take a trip to Paris next year. Then he dropped this bomb on me! I think his new mistress gave him an ultimatum. They must really be getting serious." She slowly shakes her head. "Our marriage is far from perfect but . . . fuck, when I think about all that I've done! What I've put up with from him. How I've bent myself into a pretzel to try to please him . . . to be the girl I thought he wanted me to be! I even got a nose job. New tits!" She points to her chest. "None of it mattered."

I watch as she blinks back tears.

"It might look better on the other side of this."

"Yeah, maybe. Maybe I'll give the same advice if this ever happens to you." She sniffs and wipes her nose with the back of her hand. "Maybe your marriage won't always be so perfect and one day Phil will ambush you and tell you it's over, like Tom did to me. You never know, Maddie. This could just be the calm before the storm. Tick tock, tick tock."

She then walks past me, shoving her shirt back into her jeans. She exits the pantry closet, leaving me standing in there alone.

CHAPTER 9

MADISON

I RETURN TO THE RECTORY'S WORKROOM A FEW MINUTES LATER TO find Summer there and the rest of the women still working.

"Glad to have you back with us!" Elaine exclaims. "My goodness, just think what we could accomplish if everyone was *actually* here to work!"

I itch to hold the serrated blade of the knife in my hand against Elaine's wrinkled neck to finally silence her bitchy sarcasm, but I fight the impulse. Instead, I resume slicing pitas. I steal a glance at Summer, who is dropping banana chips into each bag. Her hazel eyes are still filled with tears threatening to spill over. Her movements are robotic. She is a ghost of her former self.

What's happening to you? Where the hell is your pride? I think. But I already know the answer. That bastard Tom took it away.

When the canvas bags are filled, we file out of the rectory, climbing up the stone steps. We are greeted by a light snowfall that sprinkles the city streets in white confetti. I turn to wave goodbye to Summer, but she's already walking down the sidewalk to her BMW that's parked at the end of the block. She's talking on her cell phone, looking almost frantic. A bit of her phone conversation drifts on the wind.

"Yes, I'm calling again," she says. "Why are you doing this to me? . . . You know I need you more than she does. . . . Please! I don't . . . I don't know what I'm going to do to myself."

Tom is *such* a bastard. I can't stand to listen anymore.

I see the Town Car parked along the curb. Our driver Tony climbs out and opens the rear door for me.

"Hey, Mrs. G!" he calls.

I walk swiftly to the car and climb inside. As Tony shuts the door behind me, the memory of Summer's words refuses to go away. It is the annoying clump of hair clogging the shower drain; no other thoughts can get past it unless I sit and pick the words out one by one.

Phil will ambush you and tell you it's over, like Tom did to me. This could just be the calm before the storm.

Tick tock, tick tock.

I remind myself that Summer is a bitter woman on the verge of a divorce. Her husband no longer loves or desires her and probably hasn't for quite a while. Misery loves company, as they say. But as Tony settles behind the wheel, my phone buzzes in my clutch. I dig it out and see a text from Phil on the screen.

Sorry. Small emergency came up. Looks like it might be a late night. Don't wait up.

No "Luv you" or "Miss you." Not even a "honey" or "sweetheart."

My hand tightens around the phone. My jaw clenches.

Tick tock, tick tock.

"Where would you like to go next, Mrs. G?" Tony calls over his shoulder. "Did you still want to stop by—"

"Home," I answer succinctly before shoving my phone back into my purse. "I want to go home." I then stare out the window as the car drives off, watching as the city transforms into a snow globe and pedestrians hunch their shoulders and duck their heads against the cold.

When I arrive back at the house, I slam the door behind me. I yank off my boots, toss my coat to the hardwood floor, and walk into our kitchen. I open the fridge and take out the chilled bottle of

Sauvignon Blanc I planned to serve with dinner tonight. I uncork the bottle, sit down in one of the stools at our kitchen island, and pour myself a glass.

I wait for my husband to arrive home from work, even though he told me not to. I do not feel like playing the obedient wife tonight, especially when there is no audience to see it. I sit at the kitchen island hour after hour, until my butt goes numb on the wooden stool, until the snow dusting stops and the gray sky gives way to tiered layers of orange, red, and a ruddy purple, like the strata of rock formation in the desert, and then the view outside my kitchen window finally sinks into blackness. I sink into the blackness too, feeling my optimism and assurance from earlier shrivel and sour like the dried cherries I nibble on as I wait for my husband.

Tick tock, tick tock.

At midnight my bottle of wine is empty, but Phil still isn't home and I reluctantly rise from my stool and walk out of our kitchen. I am solidly drunk now and have to cling to the wall for balance as I climb up the next flight of stairs and enter our bedroom.

The space is filled with modern Japanese furniture. Low-profile. Sleek. The pieces seem diminutive in such a cavernous room that is made even larger because it is decorated in varying shades of white. From the wainscoting to the ceiling, from the sheets to the curtains, and the furniture and bleached bamboo floors . . . not a hint of color invades the space, save for the long-stemmed roses that Phil bought for me two days ago that sit on my night table.

When the designer—an eccentric, nebbish FIT grad with a British accent so pronounced it had to be fake—showed us the 3D renderings two years ago, Phil hadn't been impressed.

"It looks like the inside of a mausoleum," he said, frowning down at the laptop screen. "Can't we add a little more . . . I don't know . . . *color?*"

"No, luv!" Devin, the designer said, before sucking from his vape pen and blowing out a plume of raspberry- and lemon-flavored smoke. "It's clean. Unblemished! *Right?* The chaos of the world will be beyond these walls, but this . . . *this* will be your isle of tranquility. *Right?* Your sanctuary!"

But this is not a sanctuary. Phil was right, after all; it is a mausoleum. Because as I undress and prepare for bed, I can think of nothing but death. Severed limbs, gushing arteries, and broken bones. While I brush my teeth and scrub my face, my vision swims red with blood. I want to find my husband and kill him. I want to hunt him down along with Penelope the Intern, because I know he is with her.

Perhaps he's taken her to a hotel, the very same hotel that he used to take me to a decade ago. Maybe he's handcuffing her to the headboard at this very minute, then wrapping his hands around her throat like he would with me. They're fucking like rabbits on the eight-hundred-count cotton sheets that some poorly paid maid will have to strip off the mattress tomorrow morning. And he will come home to me, reeking of Penelope the Intern's perfume, and I will have to pretend like I don't know where he's been. Because if I don't pretend, if I confront him, he will feign innocence and mutter about how I'm imagining things. How I'm being childish again. He will say I'm paranoid and insist that some blowup over legislation his firm had been lobbying for was really what had kept him out all night.

We will fight. Reconcile. Play out the farce over and over again. Phil will make me think it is all in my head until the very day he pulls a Tom Ross and tells me he wants a divorce. He'll no longer care about the blow his reputation will take if I seek revenge for his leaving me because Penelope the Intern will make him feel invincible. And maybe he's right. Maybe whatever harm I could inflict would only be temporary. A few embarrassing headlines about clients that Wyatt & Harris wouldn't want to admit are on its roster and the under-the-table bribes to politicians that Phil has been coordinating for years. He'd be fired, of course, to make an example. Maybe even serve a short stint in prison—no more than a few months—and then he'll have the white-collar-criminal redemption arc and she'll be patiently waiting for him on the other end. All the while, Penelope the Intern will be making a new home for him. She'll move in and redecorate our bedroom with bright colors and lush fabrics, the way he wants so that it no longer looks like a room for the dead.

But I can't let that happen. I will not be swapped out. I have fought too hard. Done too much. I will not become a walking ghost like Summer, stumbling around recklessly. I will kill Phil before I let him do that to me.

I am wide awake but pretending to be asleep when Phil creeps into our bedroom a little after 2 a.m. His tie dangles around his neck. Several buttons of his shirt are open. His suit jacket is draped over his forearm. He pauses at the end of the bed and leans to his right, peering at me through the dim moonlight coming through our bedroom windows. I let out a faint snuffle and shift on my pillow with my eyes still closed. I count as my rib cage goes up and down, up and down. He nods, convinced now that I am lost in slumber.

A few minutes later, now in his boxers, Phil climbs into the bed beside me. The mattress dips under his weight, then rights itself as he adjusts and turns so that his back is facing mine. Twenty minutes later, I can hear his rhythmic snores.

I slowly open my eyes and stare at long-stem roses on my night table. A petal falls onto the ledge.

I want to reach for the vase, bash it against Phil's head and watch the shards splinter against his skull and puncture his eye socket. Maybe some of the glass will lodge into his jugular and send a red spray across the sheets, giving him the color in our bedroom that he'd always wanted. He will roll off the bed, crumple to the floor, and try to crawl away and seek help, but he will choke on his own blood before he even makes it to the door. And I will watch as he gurgles and goes limp.

But it is all fantasy. I do not reach for the vase. I'm not that stupid. Or at least I'm not anymore. I've learned over time not to let my emotions always get the better of me. So I will not kill my husband. Not tonight, anyway.

Tick tock, tick tock.

CHAPTER 10

TASHA

Maddie20295: Hi! I don't know if you remember me, but you gave me a ride last month from the Hyatt hotel. I hopped into your car. It's Madison. Do you remember? You gave me your business card. It was a crazy night, was it not? I'm sure I was acting weird and rushed, and I wanted to formally thank you for being so patient and kind and doing such a sweet gesture.

November 12, 10:26 AM

KnitNThingsTasha2000: Yes, Madison! I sure do remember you! I was wondering how you made out. You already thanked me, hon. But thank you for reaching out to me. I was happy to help.

November 13, 2:58 PM

Maddie20295: Again, I wanted to FORMALLY thank you for what you did for me. LOL Well, more like repay you. Would you like to meet up for lunch? I'll treat!

November 13, 3:42 PM

KnitNThingsTasha2000: How sweet of you! But really you don't have to do that. You don't owe me anything.

November 14, 11:27 AM

Maddie20295: I WANT to do it! Honestly. Let's meet up this week. What works for you?

November 14, 11:56 AM

Maddie20295: Hi, Tasha! I haven't heard back from you. Are you free for lunch this week or next, maybe? Let me know!

November 18, 10:17 AM

I stare at Madison's Instagram message on my cell and I don't know what to type back.

I just got my phone back a little more than a week ago. Kordell had been keeping it locked in his closet all month. He threw away my burner phone and disconnected all the phones in the house. All you can see now is ragged wires dangling from the wall sockets. Kordell could've just yanked the cords out but he cut them to make a statement, I guess. To show me who was in charge. For weeks, I hadn't been able to text friends or call anybody—one of my many punishments for trying to leave him, to run away. Then one day, out of the blue, while I was making breakfast, he shoved my cell at me.

"Act like you've got some sense from now on," he said, handing me the dead phone, making me drop my spatula in surprise.

I looked down and saw that the screen was cracked. It hadn't been before. I ran my thumb over the crack, wondering what he'd done to my phone to make it get there.

"You hear me, Tasha?" he shouted, making me snap my eyes up and look at him. He was pointing his finger down at me. "Act like you've got some sense from now on. Or next time, you won't get it back. Next time, I won't be so nice and your punishment will be worse. You got it?"

I nodded.

While he sat down at the kitchen table and began to dig into his pancakes and eggs, I closed my eyes and held on to that phone like it was the most precious thing in the world. Like it was worth its weight in gold. You don't realize just how important things like phones, car keys, or a wallet are until you don't have them anymore. Until someone takes them away from you.

When I got my phone back, I was so grateful that I wanted to cry. I almost thanked Kordell for giving it back to me, but then I remembered that my phone never should've been taken away in the first place. Stuff like this ain't normal.

My thumb still hovers over the cracked phone screen even now. I swear I don't know what to write to this woman. That's why I didn't respond almost a week ago. It's why I still haven't responded.

I would like to have lunch with Madison. She seemed like a nice lady. It would be good to get out of the house again, but I don't know if I can go. Kordell says I'm still earning back my car keys. He'd have to give me permission to go to lunch with her and either he or Ghalen would have to drive me there.

Those two drive me everywhere now, though the truth is that I don't have too many places that I go to anymore. I quit my job because I thought I was heading for a new life in Georgia, and I'm too embarrassed to see my friends, to even go to church, since it'll have to be under Kordell or Ghalen's escort. I know how they'll all look at me—the ones that suspect what's going on between me and Kordell and the ones that don't. I don't want to have to see their confusion. That look in their eyes that says, "Girl, what are you doing to yourself? How could you stay with that man?" Or for them to feel sorry for me. My life is hard enough without having to explain it to anyone, or worse, explain why I won't change things, why I came back. They'll all think I'm crazy to just let myself be a prisoner. Shoot, some days *I* think I'm crazy too. Like my mind is slipping away. Like I'm losing myself.

I know I don't have to stay here. All I have to do is open that front door, step out, and keep walking. I could go anywhere. To the police. To my therapist. Dr. Green won't be surprised that I'm back with Kordell. She warned me that most women leave their abusers seven times before they finally leave for good, but I'm disappointed in myself for being just another sad statistic. I could even go to the house next door and tell my neighbor—Mrs. Booker, a nice old lady with two Calico cats and a parakeet she calls Belle—what Kordell is doing to me. But then I see Ghalen smiling. He told me he got a B+ on his chemistry test yesterday. He's doing well. He's thriving. He seems happy. When I see all that, I think, "You can wait, Tasha. Just bide your time, girl."

I can hold out until the end of the school year. Until Ghalen finishes high school and heads off to college. He's applied to a few schools, though he has his eye on Bowie State, which isn't too far from here. After that, I'll leave for real this time. Kordell and I are finally done. But then I wonder: Who will I be by then? Will I recognize myself?

"I'm sorry I didn't write back sooner," I begin to type to Madison in my phone, "but you see I can't—"

I stop typing.

. . . *I can't have lunch with you right now*, is what I was going to say, then make up a lie for why I can't see her.

But I don't want to type any of that to Madison, even though that's what I did with everybody else. I went through a month's worth of texts and voicemails that I missed while Kordell had my phone. I came up with stories for friends and folks from church, trying to explain why I just disappeared. I told Joan at my old job that my mama was really sick and I had to quit, pack my bags, and fly down to Atlanta to take care of her. I was in such a rush that I didn't get the chance to say goodbye. I told the church choir director that I'd miss rehearsals and hadn't been to Ebenezer AME in weeks because I'd caught a really bad flu, was still recovering, and my voice was in no condition to sing.

I try my best, but I will admit it's hard to keep up with all the stories and the lies, what I told to who.

"Why aren't you more forthcoming with your friends and coworkers, Tasha?" Dr. Green asked me once. "Why don't you tell them what's happening to you? You told me that you suspect some of them already know anyway that he's abusing you. Why not—"

"I can't," I said, shaking my head.

"But maybe they could offer help or support. They can be your village. Maybe you can lean on them."

Or they'd just pity me and think I was weak and stupid.

I'd told a few people, and all they did was say leave Kordell—like it was that simple. But it ain't. They said it can't be too bad if I stay. I said it *is* bad, but I'm willing to suffer through it for my reasons.

All they did was talk *at* me, but not really listen to me.

Madison would know things aren't that simple, though. I remember how she was banging on the window to be let in my car, how she held her arm that night like her husband had grabbed her there. She might have gone through what I'm going through now. Hell, she might still be knee-deep in it. She won't judge me. Maybe she wants somebody to talk to like I do. Maybe we can lean on each other, like Dr. Green said.

I delete the message and type a new one.

I'm sorry I didn't write you back sooner. Sure, I would love to have lunch with you! Where and when did you wanna meet?

Then I hit SEND before I can change my mind.

CHAPTER 11

TASHA

"Gay, pass me the syrup, boy," Kordell orders between bites of bacon, pointing to the Aunt Jemima bottle in the middle of our kitchen table.

I watch out of the corner of my eye as our son hands him the bottle, then looks again at the little TV on our kitchen counter where clips from a basketball game play.

I'm supposed to meet Madison for lunch today at a cafe on H Street, but Kordell doesn't know that. I hadn't told him, because if I did, I'd have to explain how I know Madison Gingell, how she and I met, and I know right away that he'd say no, that I couldn't go. So, I've got to make up a lie, and that scares the hell out of me. The last time I lied to Kordell I ended up with all the phone cords cut and my car keys taken away. I can only imagine what he'd do if he found out I'd lied to him again. Probably lock me in the bedroom. Probably give me more than just a backhanded slap or a shove.

"Aww, come on! Would you look at that mess?" Kordell shouts mid-pour, jabbing at the TV. He pounds the table, making the forks and spoons rattle. "I swear that man can't make a two-pointer to save his damn life!"

"I've got a job interview today," I say out of nowhere as I open the fridge and take out a carton of eggs.

Kordell goes still. Ghalen does a double-take.

"What job, Ma?" Ghalen asks. "I didn't know you were even looking for one again."

"Me either," Kordell says.

"It's an office job. Downtown. It's for a nonprofit. They're lookin' for somebody who can handle phones at the front desk and do some assistant work for one of the higher-ups."

Kordell drops the syrup bottle back to the table. He wipes his mouth with a paper napkin and frowns. "Why am I just hearin' about this? Since when did you start job huntin'?"

I pause, knowing that I have to get this right. If I stutter or mumble or if my answer sounds made-up, he's going to know I'm lying. I take a deep breath, open the egg carton, and take out one of the eggs. I crack it and drop the yolk into a bowl and toss the shells into the trash. I do it again and again.

"I wasn't looking too seriously, but I saw this one online and just submitted my résumé to see what would happen. I didn't expect them to get back to me at all, but then they just up and reached out to me this morning and asked me if I could do an interview right away. It's at 11:45," I say, stirring the egg yolks with a fork, looking at it so I don't have to look at Kordell and I don't lose my nerve. "They said they're in a rush to find somebody. I know it's last-minute, but we need the money, don't we?"

We've gone from two incomes to one, and I know carrying the load won't be easy for Kordell. The bills will start to pile up in a few months if I don't get another job, if I don't start bringing home a paycheck.

"It all happened so fast. I told them I'd make it just so they'd hold my spot." I look over my shoulder at Kordell. "You want cheese in these eggs, honey?"

Kordell blinks. His frown goes away as he nods. "Yeah, uh . . . cheese . . . put some cheese in there."

I'm so nervous that when I turn back to the fridge, I bump the bottle of stovetop cleaner on the counter. My eyes stay on it for a while as I open the refrigerator door. God help me, but I think about putting it in Kordell's eggs along with the cheese. Just a splash to get him choking. Maybe he'll even choke to death. Then I wouldn't have to do all this. I wouldn't have to make up any more stories. I would just be free.

"Tasha!" Kordell calls out, snapping his fingers at me. "You gonna make those eggs or just stand there daydreamin'?"

"Yes. Yeah, sorry. Just . . . just got distracted," I say before I open the pack of shredded cheddar and sprinkle it into the yolk.

"So how the hell you supposed to get to this interview of yours?" Kordell asks. "That's what I want to know."

"I thought one of y'all could take me. But if you can't, I'll just tell them no. I can't make it. I can email them again if I need to."

"Well, I don't see how we can do it. I've got places to be! I've got to be on-site at 7:30, and I'm there all day," Kordell says. "And you know the boy has school. Can you ask them to reschedule it for the afternoon? Maybe Ghalen can take you then."

"I would, Pop, but I promised Imani that I'd take her home from school today."

Imani is Ghalen's girlfriend. He's head over heels in love with that girl. He buys her gifts and takes care of her. Whenever I see them together, I think, *Well, at least I did somethin' right.*

"No, you go ahead and take Imani home, honey," I say. "I don't think I can reschedule anyway."

"Maybe you can take the Metro," Ghalen suggests before he digs into his cereal again, and I swear to God I couldn't love that boy any more than I do right now. He turns to his Daddy. "There's a bus stop a couple blocks down. She can take the bus to Stadium Armory, right? Then take the Metro uptown."

Kordell goes quiet. He slouches back in his chair, looks away from Ghalen, and eyes me. I try not to fidget, not to look guilty, but it's hard when he's looking at me like that.

"OK," Kordell finally says, shifting in his chair. "OK, you can go. But you get on that bus. You take that train. You do that interview, and come straight back home. You hear me, Tasha? Straight back home!"

"I hear you," I say.

"Nowhere else. If I find out you went anywhere but to that damn interview, I will—"

"I won't go anywhere else. I promise. Just there and back."

He turns back around in his chair. "All right, then," he says, then reaches for the remote to raise the volume on the TV.

I pour the eggs into the pan, watching them as they sizzle, wanting to cry with relief.

✳ ✳ ✳

When I show up at the cafe, I'm out of breath. There was an accident near my house, so the bus had to take a different route than it usually does, and I missed my transfer and had to wait for the next one. When I finally got to the Stadium Armory train station, I saw the trains were delayed for track service. To make it to lunch, I had to damn near jog from the train station for two blocks, and even then I'm still twenty-five minutes late.

I step through the door and look around me.

It's a lot fancier than I thought it would be. I thought it would be a little bistro with small tables and glass cases filled with croissants and bagels. But the cafe has high ceilings and leather chairs and couches. The diners are eating fancy dishes with clam shells and mussels, steak and potatoes. I'm glad Madison is treating today, because there ain't no way I could afford any of this stuff. The seats are all filled with people, *so* many people that I can't find Madison in the room.

"Can I help you?" I hear someone ask. I turn to find a young man in an apron smiling at me. "Would you like me to show you to a table?" He reaches for a menu on a nearby counter.

"Uh, I don't need a table. I'm here to meet somebody," I say, looking around me again. "Her name is—"

"Tasha! Tasha, over here!"

I turn and see Madison smiling and waving at me. She's sitting at one of the tables in the middle of the room. Diners are on both sides of her on the long leather seat, but on the opposite side of the table a chair sits empty, waiting for me.

I wave back. "Hey!" I say as I take off my coat and make my way toward her. "I'm sorry I'm late!"

"Oh, don't worry about it." She rises from her seat and steps forward to give me a hug, like we've been friends for a long time. It surprises me. "It's so good to see you again!"

Madison isn't wearing diamonds today, or a dress. She's wearing a big fluffy sweater—all white—and it looks like a cloud. She has tan leather pants and boots that go up to her knees. Her long blond hair falls over one shoulder. *Sophisticated.* I can't stop using that word when I look at her. But it's the only word I can think of besides pretty, because she *is* pretty. It's not just the makeup she's wearing. I can see her more clearly now in the daylight than I could back in my car that night that we met. And I can see how some of the men at the other tables look at her.

I look down at myself, wondering if I should have dressed up more. Maybe I should've worn more than just a turtleneck and gray slacks. I tug at my top, wishing I could magic it into something nicer.

"I'm so glad you came," Madison says as she sits down. I pull out the chair facing her and sit down too. "I was worried you were going to stand me up."

"No! No, it was the bus and the . . . the Metro. There was . . . well, there were delays."

She nods. "I can imagine. Well, anyway. I'm glad you made it despite the delays." She claps her hands and opens one of the menus at the middle of our table. "Let's order, and then we can talk." She looks up from the menu. "Our time together was so brief, but I feel like I've known you so much longer. I feel like we have sort of a . . . a bond now. Does that sound crazy?"

I slowly shake my head. I feel like we have a bond now too.

"I want to know more about you, Tasha. I want to know more about the woman who saved me."

My cheeks warm at her praise. "I didn't save you. I just—"

"Oh, yes, you did! I don't know what Phil would've done that night if you hadn't stopped your car and let me in."

"Are you OK now, though? He isn't still . . ." I let my words drift off.

"Things are a little better now, but it's always a guessing game on how long it will last."

I nod so hard, my neck hurts. "I know what you mean. Lord, do I know what you mean!"

"How about you?" She lowers her menu. "Are things any better with you and your husband?"

I stop nodding and purse my lips, wondering if I should lie. I am ashamed of what Kordell has done to me, what I've *let* him do to me. But then I remember that she is in a similar place. There is no reason to be ashamed in front of her.

"Not really," I finally admit. I then look around to make sure no one else is listening. The diners at the tables on each side of us are so deep in their own conversations that they're not worried about us.

"I . . . I had to make up a story to come here," I confess, looking down at my menu. "I told Kordell that I was . . . that I was looking for a job. I used to have one at a nonprofit downtown, but I quit. I thought I was running away to Atlanta and planned to find a job down there. Now the only income we have is from Kordell's cabinetry business. He knows I need to get a job. We need the money, so he let me go to this fake interview. Besides that, I haven't been able to go anywhere alone in a month. Not since that night at the hotel. He . . . he won't let me."

I raise my eyes to look at her. She doesn't say anything at first. She just stares at me for the longest time, and I swear it is the weirdest damn thing. It isn't a normal stare. It's like she's looking past my clothes, past my skin, past my muscles and bones, and into my very heart. It makes me lean back in my chair. It makes the hair stand up on my arm. Then suddenly her eyes change. They go bright again as she smiles.

"That was very clever of you," she says as she reaches out and pats my hand, catching me off guard again. "If you went through all that trouble to come here, you should enjoy yourself. Let's eat. Maybe have a glass of wine?" She wiggles her eyebrows, and I can't help but laugh.

"Sure." I force myself to nod. "That sounds good."

And we eat and drink. We talk about things like the weather, the traffic, and the Thanksgiving holiday coming up. Madison tells me more about herself, how she grew up in a small town out West in a religious family, graduated from college, and came East to find a job.

"I bounced around for a bit, working as a waitress in Philadelphia and temping in New York before settling here in Washington," she says.

I tell her that I came from Georgia originally and came up here to live with my aunt for a couple of years, back when my Mama was between jobs and was having a hard time taking care of six kids. But my two years in D.C. turned out to be closer to twenty.

"I've been here ever since," I say before taking a sip of red wine.

We don't talk about our husbands again, or the night that brought us together. I forget about the weirdness from earlier, that peculiar look in her eyes. The food is good and I am nice and full by the time the waiter brings us the check and Madison pays for our meals.

"Thank you again for meeting me for lunch, Tasha," she says after the waiter gives her credit card back to her and she drops it into her wallet. "I know you went through a lot to come here today."

"Thank you for inviting me! I had a good time."

We rise from the table and walk across the restaurant to the door.

"I would offer you a ride home, but I know it might be a bit conspicuous. It might compromise your story," she says as she puts on her coat.

I shove my arms into mine and we step outside the restaurant onto the busy sidewalk. "Yeah, it would be hard to explain it to Kordell if anybody saw your car, but I appreciate the thought."

"So why don't I walk you to the train station instead, then?"

"Sure! That would be nice."

We start to stroll up the block, passing other people and the restaurants and shops along the street. She doesn't say anything and I don't either, so I look up at the shop windows and at the cars that zip down the road.

"Too bad we can't do this again," Madison says out of the blue, making me look at her. "Meet up for lunch, I mean. I know that might be challenging for you."

"I don't think I'll be able to get out of the house for a while. I don't know if Kordell will believe me if I make up another interview for an office assistant job," I say with a laugh before tugging on my gloves. "He'll figure out something's up."

"Not necessarily. Not if you really have a job prospect."

"But who knows when that'll happen."

It took me seven months to find my last job and I already had a job while I was looking. Who knows how long it'll take for me to find a new one.

"I know people, Tasha! Or people who know people, if you know what I mean," she says with a wink. "Plenty of them run nonprofits around town. I'm sure some of them are hiring. I could make a few calls for you, if you'd like."

I pause when we hit a crosswalk. "*Really?* You would do that for me?"

"Of course! I told you that I'm indebted to you! Text me a phone number to reach you and an email address so they can contact you."

"Sure! Sure!" I say, digging into my purse, pulling out my cell phone. "I'll do it right now. What's your number?"

The light changes and she steps into the crosswalk, giving me her cell number as she walks. I stumble after her, typing my info to her. As I press SEND, I'm still in shock that she's doing all this for me:

she bought me lunch and now she's offering to help me get a job. It all sounds too good to be true. I even start to wonder if it *is* too good to be true.

Kordell has done that to me—always making me imagine the worst, no matter what the situation.

"And I'm a big believer that women should help each other, Tasha," she says as we walk. I can see the Gallery Place-Chinatown Metro sign half a block away. "Don't you think?"

"Yeah, I guess . . . I guess women should stick together."

"*Especially* women like us . . . women in our situation. No one else understands what we're going through. They don't get it! They can't! Who else can we turn to besides each other?"

I nod, keeping my focus on her but trying not to bump into people as we walk. Madison doesn't seem to notice them, but they part for her anyway like the Red Sea.

"I want to help you—and not just with finding a job."

I turn to her. "What . . . what do you mean?"

"Your husband isn't going to suddenly change. Neither will mine," she says as we near the station's escalators. "And to expect them to change isn't just crazy. It's stupid. These are learned behaviors, Tasha. And they've been validated. By their pasts. By society. Every time they abuse us and don't get punished for it, it makes them think they can do it again and again and again. It makes them think what they're doing is OK, when it's not. You know it's not! I know it's not. But they don't! And I don't know about you, Tasha, but I'm tired of it. I got tired of being their prey a long time ago."

I can hear the trains now a hundred feet below us. The whoosh and roar as they pull up to the platform. The noise is so loud that Madison has to shout a little to be heard over the sound. I can feel the wind from the tunnels below snake its way up the stairs. It makes Madison's hair fly around her.

"I know what you mean. I get it, but I told you I can't leave Kordell! Not yet, anyway. I *won't* leave my son behind. I won't let him get hurt."

"Has your husband ever hit him?"

I shake my head. "No, but that don't mean he won't start hitting him."

"You're worried about what your husband will do to your son physically. But you haven't considered what he's doing to him mentally. Witnessing abuse can be just as detrimental as experiencing it. It can become a learned behavior for your son, too. You don't want him to become an abuser like his father, do you?"

I flinch at Madison's words like she's just slapped me.

"My son will never do what Kordell does!" I say, now mad and not willing to hide it. "He knows better." I turn to the escalators. "Look, I need to go. If I don't leave now—"

"But how do you know? How do you know he won't, if Kordell is still around?" She takes a step toward me, like she didn't hear me. The trains thunder beneath us, so she really may not have heard me. "You have to admit that you'd be better off without your husband. Life would be easier! Certainly raising your son would be. I know my life would vastly improve if my husband, Phil, would just . . . just disappear."

"Like I said, I can't leave him and Kordell won't let me go. He ain't going anywhere any time soon, either. Not unless he gets drunk again and is dumb enough to drive. Even then, he'd probably survive. He's fit. He could outrun a man half his age."

"Could he outrun a bullet, though?" she asks.

She's looking at me with those weird eyes again. It makes me take a step back, and I bump into the escalator's rubber handrail. I almost fall, but she grabs me to keep me up—and she doesn't let go.

"I told you that I could help you, Tasha. In more ways than one. You could help me, too! We could help *each other*. We just have to think outside the box. If we did, we could get rid of them both."

I squint at her. What is she saying?

But I already know what she's saying, what this woman is asking me to do. I just don't want to believe it.

Looking at her now is like watching a werewolf movie. When you see the person grow hair all over, fangs, and claws in a matter of seconds. You watch as they change into a monster right in front of you. But Madison still looks the same on the outside. She's still a blond, petite little thing. Still the pretty woman who made men's heads turn at the cafe. And she's still smiling at me even though she's just offered to kill my husband if I helped her kill hers. And she did it as casual as you please, like she was offering me a bite of the quiche she had at lunch.

She's joking. Lord, she *has* to be joking. But I can tell from the look on her face that she isn't. This is wrong. *She's* wrong; something is really off with her.

"Look, I can tell you're scared at the idea, but I also notice that you're not saying no outright." Her smile widens. "That means something. You've thought about doing it yourself, haven't you?"

I can't hold her gaze anymore. I drop my eyes and think about that morning when I was making Kordell his eggs, how I thought about poisoning his food. I feel guilty.

"Come on, Tasha. You can admit it to me! I told you, I understand. And in your heart of hearts, you know I'm right. It's the solution we both need. We just have to see it through."

"Yeah, OK, umm . . . I . . . I h–h–have to go," I say, prying her hand from my arm. "I have to get home. Thank you . . . umm . . . thanks again for the lunch. Thank you for everything!"

I then turn and run down the escalator. I don't look back even when I hear her shout, "Tasha! Tasha!" over the sound of the trains.

I wasn't before, but now I am glad that I can't see Madison again.

CHAPTER 12
NOW

818 Wicker Street. Two-alarm house fire. Two victims. One fatality.

THOSE ARE THE WORDS THAT CRACKLED OVER HIS RADIO. THOUGH the dispatcher had given the address, Detective Simmons could easily find his destination on his own. Even at this distance, while the traffic in front of him crawled to a near stop, he could see the rotating blue and red lights from the D.C. Metropolitan Police Department cruisers illuminating the night sky. The closer he got to the scenic Capitol Hill historic district, the more the smell of smoke and burning embers snaked its way into the car's compartment, seeping through his vents.

Finally, the police barrier came into view. Beyond it, three fire trucks sat in the middle of the street with idle engines chugging loudly. Half of the crews were reloading the hoses, and the rest of the firefighters casually walked back to the trucks in their sweat-stained shirts, with soot-covered faces and gear. The only thing that hinted that something was out of the ordinary . . . that this wasn't your run-of-the-mill, accidental house fire . . . was the webs of yellow police tape.

Simmons noticed that the street was one of the newer developments on Capitol Hill, designed to mimic homes nearby that were older by a century or two. The clue of its true age though could be found in its uniformity, its rigidity. This was a neighborhood where people paid good money for bad things not to happen.

All the towering row houses were assembled like identical red castles of privilege arranged in a neat row. But instead of having moats and stone bridges in front to keep out invaders, they had wrought-iron gates and an army of hedges, cherrywood trees, and white oaks. Despite these fortifications, something bad *had* happened here. That was evident from the last house on the block. Its wrought-iron gate yawned open, along with its front door. The top-floor windows were broken and jagged. A portion of the peaked roof was now gone—a skeleton of its former self. The exterior brick that had once been as red as the other houses was now charred black. The stain bled into the house beside it.

Simmons drew to a stop in front of the red, white, and blue barriers closing off one end of the street. He turned off his sedan's engine and climbed out, shutting his car door behind him. He hacked a few times into his fist as the residue of smoke hit his lungs, a full-on wallop that left his eyes burning. He then strolled toward the police barrier where two uniformed cops now stood. Thirty minutes ago, he'd been on his living room sofa back at his apartment, nodding off with a beer in one hand and a remote in the other. Now he was investigating an arson with one fatality and another victim in the hospital.

"Hey," he said to the cops, flashing his badge when they turned to look at him, "Detective Clayton Simmons, MPD. So what we got—"

"Simmons!" a familiar voice called out, making him pause.

He glanced to his right to see Josh Montrose, his partner, striding toward him.

Montrose had played varsity college football back in Ohio, and even fifteen years later he still had the build of a linebacker—broad shoulders, thick middle, and an even thicker neck.

"Hey," Simmons called back, tucking his badge and wallet back into his pocket, meeting the other man halfway.

"I was wondering when you were gonna show up," Montrose drawled between gum pops as the two walked toward the house on the corner.

"Oh, don't act like you've been waitin' forever. I just got the call a half hour ago." He glanced up at the house. "Did Fire clear us to go inside and look around?"

Montrose nodded. "Yeah, they gave the all-clear about ten minutes ago. I was waiting for you before I went in."

"Well, aren't you thoughtful," Simmons murmured. "I gotta confess. I wasn't planning on gettin' a call to this side of town tonight. Nothing but rich folks and bored old ladies around here. Most we get from this neighborhood at this time of night is a 'suspicious guy' in a hoodie that about half the block called the police on."

"Yeah, I know." Montrose walked toward the stone stairs. He climbed under the police tape, motioning for Simmons to follow. "Not too many shootings popping off around here at *any* time of day. That's more of a Ward 8 thing."

Simmons paused, and not just because of Montrose's reference to "popping off." He hated when his partner used Black vernacular. It rolled off his tongue as fluidly as his Spanish, and Montrose could butcher reading a Taco Bell menu. No, Simmons had done a double-take because he'd thought they'd been called to the scene of a homicide by arson.

"Wait. *A shooting?*" he asked, finally stepping under the police tape. The two men slowly climbed the stairs.

"Yeah, the next-door neighbor called it in about ten to fifteen minutes before the fire department got their call. She said she heard shouting and what she thought were gunshots."

A shooting would explain why he and Montrose were here. Simmons had assumed they'd been called in to assist the department's fire investigator.

"Have you talked to the neighbor?" Simmons asked.

Montrose nodded and stepped through the opened front door. "Yeah, she was rattled as all hell and was holding her barking dog the whole time. Barely could get a clear statement out of her, but she said she noticed the shouting next door because it was so rare. Phillip and Madison Gingell . . . the owners, and two victims . . . never say peep usually. They're a pretty quiet, laid-back couple. Charming, the neighbor said. They threw a garden dinner party for the neighborhood last year."

"Humph," Simmons murmured, making Montrose cock an eyebrow.

"What? What's with the grunt?"

"Nothin'. It's just what the neighbor said . . . I've heard it before. It's the first thing people say about serial killers. He seemed nice. Quiet. *Charming.* Doesn't mean ol' Mr. and Mrs. Gingell was just as charming behind closed doors."

"I guess," Montrose said with a shrug. "Well, anyway, the neighbor heard all hell breaking loose at around eleven o'clock. She heard lots of screaming, banging, and pops. She wasn't sure at the time if they were gunshots, but called the police just to be safe. The firefighters came later to put out the fire and dragged out the Gingells. They were expecting two cases of smoke inhalation. Instead, both of them had been shot."

"Shit." Simmons let out a low whistle of exasperation as he stepped aside to let another one of the crime scene technicians pass. He then walked over the house's threshold and looked around the couple's living room.

The temperature inside the living room felt as hot as an oven. He was starting to sweat. Simmons reached up and undid the top button of his shirt to get some relief. The high ceilings and white walls were now gray. Water pooled on the hardwood floors. The room was filled with expensive furniture and artwork. Combined, the items had probably once cost more than what he could ever make in an entire lifetime. Now it was all junk.

"So, what are we looking at? What's the scenario for this one? A murder–suicide? A burglary gone wrong? Do we have a suspect?" Simmons asked, turning back to his partner, "or are we still looking?"

Montrose broke into a grin. "No, we have a suspect. Believe it or not, she's the one who called in the fire."

"Wait a minute. You're telling me she shot two people, set a fire, *then* called 9-1-1?" The skin between his dark brows furrowed. "That . . . that doesn't make any sense."

Montrose heaved up his hefty shoulders and sighed. "Guess not, but do criminals ever make sense? She told the officers when they arrived that she did it."

Simmons gave a reluctant nod and continued through the living room, toward the floating wooden stairs leading to the second floor. They were now slippery with water, so he grabbed the handrail as he walked and made mental notes of the crime scene along the way. Montrose trailed behind him.

"Have you talked to her?" Simmons asked, glancing over his shoulder at the other detective. "The suspect, I mean. Did we get her name? Have we checked her out yet?"

Montrose nodded as they walked. "Tasha Jenkins. Thirty-six years old. A couple of speeding tickets, but no criminal record as far as we know."

The smell of smoke grew stronger as the two men climbed. The heat was worse, too. It was getting oppressive now. Simmons had once read somewhere that house fires could get as hot as 1,100 degrees Fahrenheit. As he drew near the next landing where the bedrooms were, where the Gingells had laid their heads at night *until* tonight, he bet that the temperature in the home had gotten close to 1,100 degrees Fahrenheit up here at some point. It certainly looked like it.

The remains of the top floor had looked jarring from the outside, but it was even worse up close standing here, peering through the lines of police tape covering the open doorway, barring their entry. Most of the drywall was gone, but one remained on the far side of the room. Besides that, all Simmons could see was exposed wooden beams and the insulation inside. Whatever furniture had been in that room, it was now unrecognizable. Just piles of charred wood and heaps of wet stuffing. Moonlight and ambient city light filtered through broken windows and the portion of the top floor ceiling that was now missing.

"Where's the suspect?" Simmons asked. "We need to question her."

"Yeah," Montrose said, "I think she's . . . uh . . . still here. Last I saw her, she was handcuffed in the back of one of the cruisers."

✳ ✳ ✳

Less than five minutes later, Simmons and Montrose strolled through the front door. The fire trucks were gone, but the cop cars remained. The two detectives made their way toward one of the waiting cruisers. In the back sat Tasha Jenkins, staring vacantly at the wire-mesh screen in front of her. Simmons motioned for Montrose to hang back.

"Let me talk to her first, OK?" he said over his shoulder to his partner. "We don't want to crowd her."

"Whatever," Montrose replied. "She already confessed. Case closed as far as I'm concerned, but if you wanna tie up any loose ends, be my guest. I'll talk to a couple more neighbors to see if they heard or saw anything."

Simmons nodded and slowly approached the red, white, and blue cruiser, staring at the suspect in profile.

He presumed under normal circumstances that she was an attractive woman. She definitely had the features for it with her big brown eyes, full lips, button nose, and shoulder-length hair that was pulled back from her face. And under normal circumstances, she might have even been a woman he would have chatted up on one of his days off. Maybe if he had run into her at the grocery store or the gym. Perhaps, he would have asked her for her number. But today, she looked haggard, almost shell-shocked. She looked older than her thirty-six years.

He asked the uniformed officer standing beside the cruiser's back door to open it for him. Tasha barely seemed to notice.

"Have you already read her her Miranda?" he asked the cop standing beside the rear door.

The cop nodded, making Simmons turn back to face her.

"Ms. Jenkins," he said, holding up his badge, "I'm Detective Simmons with the Metropolitan—"

"I did it," she said dispassionately in a whisper that he could barely hear. "I did it. I set the fire."

There it was. The confession that Montrose had spoken of. *Case closed*, Montrose had said. But there was something that still didn't sit right with Simmons. He couldn't explain why.

"Can you tell me *why* you did it?" he asked.

Tasha didn't answer him. She only lowered her eyes to her lap instead.

"Did you have a vendetta against Mrs. Gingell? Mr. Gingell?"

Again, she didn't answer.

"Were you trying to rob their house or somethin'? Or did they catch you breaking in and trying to steal from them, and that's why you shot them?"

Her eyes snapped up from her lap. "What?"

Simmons paused. "Yeah, they were shot . . . which is something you would know if you did this."

He watched as she closed her eyes. Simmons leaned down, bracing his hand on the top of the cruiser, drawing closer to her. She smelled of sweat and talcum powder. He even caught a whiff of vanilla. It was in so many women's perfumes these days.

"Tasha, *did* you do this? Or did someone else?"

She opened her mouth to answer, but only sobs came out.

He took a deep breath and stood upright, tucking his badge back into his pocket, now more than frustrated. Simmons was used to suspects stonewalling him, but the blockade she'd erected felt unlike the others he'd encountered. It added to his sense that something was askew with her story, with this entire scenario.

"Tasha!" he said again, but she didn't answer him. She continued to sob.

He closed the car door, knowing he wasn't going to get anything substantial out of her tonight. Not with the state she was in.

"Thanks. I'm done," he said to the other officer. The cop nodded.

A few seconds later, Simmons watched as the officer climbed into the driver's seat and pulled off to take her in for booking, likely to face a first-degree murder charge.

Simmons saw Montrose standing on the curb, waiting for him with his brows raised.

"Well, did you get your answer? Did she give you a confession?" Montrose asked.

Simmons nodded. "Yeah, she confessed—but she's lying through her teeth."

Now Montrose was the one frowning. "How the hell do you figure that?"

"Because it doesn't make any sense! A 36-year-old woman with no criminal record and no apparent relationship to the Gingells decides to break into their house in the middle of the night, shoot them, and set their house on fire? What's her motive?"

"Just because the motive isn't clear to us now, it doesn't mean she doesn't have one."

"She didn't know they'd been shot. I saw the look on her face when I told her. That was pure shock."

Montrose shrugged. "Maybe she was just pretending. Maybe she's a good actress."

"She said she set the fire, but doesn't smell like smoke. Not at all. I smelled her. You can't pretend that."

Montrose grumbled. "You're not a bloodhound, Simmons."

"And why call in the fire if you set it yourself supposedly to burn the bodies?" Simmons persisted. "She could've just left the scene and fled. We would've been none the wiser, still digging through the ashes. It could've taken us days . . . *weeks* to connect this back to her. Why call the police at all?"

Montrose opened his mouth and closed it, unable to come up with a response.

"None of this is right. You know it and I know it. Something is off. Way off! Tasha Jenkins didn't do this."

"Okay, so if she didn't do it, then why the hell is she confessing to it? Why confess to a crime . . . *a murder* you didn't commit?"

Simmons stood silently for several seconds, slowly shaking his head. "I don't know. I guess that's the question that we need to figure out."

CHAPTER 13

BEFORE

MADISON

I watch Tasha flee down the escalator stairs, running like her feet are on fire, and I'm disappointed as I watch. Not surprised by her reaction, but still . . . disappointed.

I don't lose faith in her, though. Not yet, anyway. Tasha seems to have some cunning. She was willing to lie to her husband to get here today, and she came up with a believable story. A good liar makes for a good co-conspirator. And the motivation is there. I saw the look in her eyes when I said she's probably thought about killing her husband before. I *know* that look. She's just too scared to admit it aloud, but I'm certainly not, especially when I'm with someone like me, who's been through suffering but hasn't let it break them. Instead, it made us hungrier to break free. I can see that in Tasha.

She can't appreciate any of this yet. She isn't a forward thinker like me, but she could be. To some it comes naturally, but for others it's a gradual process. Like learning how to swim, you have to learn how to float first. I threw Tasha into the deep end without warning or preparation, and now she's panicking. She thinks I'm trying to drown her; but the truth is, I'm trying to *help* her—and admittedly, help myself in the process. And why not? We can help each other.

But it's my own fault. I was too eager. I need to back off a little and be more patient. Being charitable requires patience. I've done enough charitable work to know. And if anyone needs my help, it's Tasha.

I'll give her more time. After all, I needed time, too. Years, in fact, before I was ready to finally stop being prey.

✳ ✳ ✳

It's a miracle I have so much patience. It was never shown to me, not even as a kid, especially by my Father. And yes, that's "Father" with a capital "F." Not Dad or Daddy. He never would've tolerated being called that.

Father was a stern man. Solemn and rugged—the kind of man many of these politicians around town aspire to be, but they're just cheap imitations with a pair of Levis and a carefully constructed photo op. Father believed in hard work and doing your duty as a devout Christian lest you burn in the flames of hell for all eternity. I'm not kidding. The crazy son of a bitch really believed this, like God was the assistant manager at Walmart who, from that great break room in the sky, was carefully tabulating the productive and wasted hours we spend during our lifetimes. Father also played the mandolin—the one soft thing about him. It was the only instrument he was allowed to play in his devout Methodist family in Oregon.

Mom always said Father dreamed that God would bless him with a big family of his own—with him, the stalwart, family patriarch, surrounded by a half dozen children and two dozen grandchildren crowded around the Thanksgiving banquet tables or the Christmas tree. Instead, after seven years of trying and eleven miscarriages, they just had me to show for it.

Father blamed Mom at first for thwarting those dreams. By the time I started to walk, I guess he switched the blame to me. I suppose when you combine the myriad aspirations for a half-dozen children into one child, it's nearly impossible for that kid to live up to all that. Even after Mom and Father adopted my twin little brothers, Joseph and William, I remained his continual disappointment. I was the broken, wobbly wheel . . . the crooked stitch that no matter how many times you pulled out the thread and tried to sew it again, would never straighten. I would always be wonky. Bad manufacturing, maybe. But Father still tried to straighten me out.

When I didn't eat all of my dinner, that was a beating.

When I didn't finish all of my homework, that was a beating.

When I didn't properly make my bed, that was a beating.

And it was always followed by reading a passage from the Bible—the sick bastard.

Phil can get pretty aggressive in bed, but even when he works up a good sweat, his lashes are nothing like Father's used to be. Thanks to the old man, I've built up quite the pain tolerance.

Don't get me wrong. Father didn't spare the switch and the belt with my brothers either, but he always saved the "good stuff" for me. When I figured out that I could never really please him, I gave up trying. There were little rebellions here and there. Not pushing my chair up to the table after breakfast. Leaving smears of toothpaste along the rim of the sink. I even got really crazy and borrowed a copy of *Harry Potter and the Sorcerer's Stone* from the local library. I would read it at night under my sheets with a flashlight and hide it under my mattress during the day. Father found it one rainy evening, though. I still don't know how.

"You're being defiant, Madison," he said, brandishing the library book in my face. "You're being childish and defiant! Is that what God would want you to do?"

I shook my head.

"Obey your mother and father!" he yelled, swatting me along the head with the hardback. "There is no confusion there! 'Do not merely listen to the word, and so deceive yourselves. Do what it says.' Book of James, Chapter 1, verse 22."

I continued to stare at my feet, waiting for him to reach for the belt, to hear it swing through the air before it hit my bare arm or leg. But he grabbed my arm instead, making me yelp. He dragged me out of my bedroom and down the hall.

"*Dale?* Dale, what are you doing?" I could hear Mom call behind me.

"Father?" my little brother Joseph asked, his voice shaking as I kicked and screamed.

I grabbed at anything. The hand rail. The newel posts. Even the area rug in our foyer as Father dragged me down the stairs and across our living room to the front door and then our screened-in porch.

I could hear the rain before I could see it pounding beyond the wire mesh. He kicked the screen door open and then dragged me down the porch's wooden stairs and dropped me face-first in our muddy front yard.

"On your knees!" he shouted. "On your knees, girl!"

I pushed myself up to my elbows and blinked the pouring rain out of my eyes. I blew the mud out of my nose and wiped the rest of it away from my face as I attempted to kneel, though my knees hurt. I hurt all over.

"Get up!" He grabbed the back of my T-shirt, yanking me to my feet. "No more defiance! Get up! We all have to deal with the consequences of our actions."

When I fell to the ground again, I made sure I landed on my knees, despite the pain. Out of the corners of my eyes I could see Mom and my two little brothers standing on the front porch. Mom's face was pale and blank. My brother Joseph was hiding behind her legs, sobbing. My brother William just stared with his face and open palms pressed flat against the mesh, showing a mix of shock, horror, and morbid fascination as he watched me.

"Now pray!" Father yelled, shoving my shoulder. "Pray for holy guidance and deliverance! Pray that you will learn to obey your mother and father! Pray for these demons of rebellion to release their hold on you, girl!"

I closed my eyes, clutched my hands together, and started praying like he'd ordered. I asked God for forgiveness for being such a disobedient child out loud, but inside I begged God to make Father stop. To make him leave me alone. I prayed for the clouds to part and a bolt of lightning to strike Father down so that it would all end—the daily terrorizing and the fear. But there was no clap of thunder and no bolt of lightning; just a steady rain. I could feel Father looming over me as I prayed, but after a while his looming presence disappeared. A minute after that, I heard the screen door on the porch slam shut behind him. I turned to see his receding back as he stalked into the house.

I stayed out there for hours, shivering in the cold and the rain, waiting for him to say I could come back inside. I wondered how long my mother and my brothers stood on the porch watching me. I wondered if the neighbors saw me out there and wanted to intervene, but didn't. I kneeled and prayed until I stopped shivering. Until I went numb and finally passed out on the muddy lawn.

When I woke up, my mother was hovering over me. Her long blond hair brushed my nose and cheeks as light as fingertips. Her face looked so pale and angelic that I wasn't sure whether I was alive or dead. Maybe I'd died out there in the cold and the rain. Maybe Father had murdered the whole family, and we were now in heaven away from him.

But then I shifted and realized, woozily, that I wasn't dead; I was in my bed. I'd been stripped of my wet clothes and put in my pajamas. I was lying under a mound of blankets.

"Maddie, you have to stop this," Mom whispered, holding a cold washcloth against my forehead.

I had developed a fever that simultaneously made my skin scorching hot to the touch and had my teeth chattering despite all the blankets piled on top of me.

"Do you understand?" she whispered to me as I floated somewhere between wakefulness and sleep. "You have to stop this, or your father will kill you, honey."

After I recovered, Mom took me to church to see if someone—anyone—could help rid me of my "demons" so Father would stop trying to beat them out of me.

"She's lost, Reverend," my mother said in Reverend Brennan's wood-paneled office as we sat in the chairs that faced his great oak desk. "My child is lost in the wilderness and she needs help getting out of it. Can the church help her? Maybe one of the youth pastors can counsel her."

She'd worn too much perfume that day—a cheap knockoff of White Diamonds she'd bought at the local drug store. The tick of the clock on the Reverend's wall was loud, so loud that it was almost distracting. And the room was too warm. Even though the Reverend had a portable fan on his desk, his office was stiflingly hot. I remember the way the underside of my thighs stuck to the leather of the chair cushion with my sweat. And I remember the heavy weight of Reverend Brennan's eyes upon me as I sat there with my hands clasped in my lap.

God was still an abstract concept for me back then (rather than the fictional concept that he is now), but the closest thing to God in real life and on Earth was Reverend Brennan.

I saw God when the Reverend stood at the elevated pulpit at our church with the six-foot wooden cross hovering behind him. I heard God when the Reverend spoke in his heavy baritone that boomed all the way to the back pews, even without a microphone. And I felt God's presence at that moment when Reverend Brennan looked at my bowed head.

"The church can help, Mrs. Lulan. Of course it can," Reverend Brennan assured. "In fact, I'll take Madison under my wing myself."

At those words, I raised my head. I saw that the Reverend was smiling now. He had a nice smile. Reverend Brennan wasn't a handsome man—he was awkwardly boyish at best, with freckles and wavy brown hair that was parted on the side that was about two inches too long—but he had perfectly sized, white teeth. They were disarming in their perfection.

"My wife and I would be happy to shepherd her. We've helped many wayward youths in our flock."

"Would you, Reverend?" my mother asked, looking more than just a little relieved. "Would you, please?"

"Of course! This is my job, Mrs. Lulan. The task and gift that God has given me. I am a true believer of his word and my duty to proselytize it, especially to the members of our flock that have gone astray." He then reached across the desk and grabbed my mother's hands. "Now will you pray with me? Let's both pray for young Madison's precious soul."

Mom blankly nodded and bowed her head. Reverend Brennan closed his eyes and began the prayer. Mom closed her eyes too, muttering along.

"Amen," he said.

"Amen," Mom echoed.

The next week, Mom brought me to the Brennans' home. I expected to read Bible verses or listen to a private sermon about obeying thy mother and father, but instead Reverend Brennan stayed scarce behind the closed door of his office for most of that warm spring afternoon. Meanwhile, I washed the dishes and did four bags of laundry while Mrs. Brennan homeschooled her children in the front room and watched them play in the backyard. The same thing happened four days later when my mother brought me back. This time, I scrubbed the bathrooms and vacuumed.

"Are you our maid now?" their five-year-old asked me while sucking her thumb.

"It sure seems like it," I mumbled in reply as I carried the bucket of mucky mop water down the stairs.

I wondered how cleaning and washing for the Brennan family was supposed to make me more pious and keep me on the straight and narrow. Even at thirteen, I suspected Mom had been conned into handing over her daughter for free labor.

On the third day, while hanging the clothes on the line in the Brennans' backyard, I heard Reverend Brennan call my name. I turned to find him standing in the shadow of the back porch's doorway.

"Yes, sir?" I'd asked, pushing the sweaty locks of hair out of my eyes.

"Can you come over here and help me, Maddie?" he asked as he jogged down the wooden stairs, beckoning me to follow him across the yard. "Stephanie wants me to get a few things from the tool shed. I'll need some help carrying them in, if you don't mind."

I forced back a grimace and dropped the damp bedsheet I was holding back into the laundry basket. "Uh, sure. Yes, Reverend."

Like I didn't have enough things to do.

I walked through the thicket of overgrown weeds, swatting at gnats that circled my head while following him.

The tool shed looked old, probably older than the house, with its warped wooden boards, flaking white and red paint, and moss and vines dotting the exterior like bad acne. A rusted lock hung on the door and Reverend quickly pried it off and shoved the lock into his jean pocket. He then pushed the door open and stepped inside.

"Over here," he said, waving me forward.

I took one tentative step inside, then another.

It was mostly dark in there, though dim sunlight made its way through the three small windows along the side and back of the shed. Reverend Brennan seemed to know the space well, though. Without hesitation, he went straight to one of the corners where a pile of flowerpots, several bags of topsoil, and a box filled with packets that were probably flower seeds sat.

"Help me, please," he said. "Take these."

I bent down and took the flowerpots he handed me, but paused when he reached up and placed the palm of his hand against my cheek.

I flinched and lurched back, almost dropping the flowerpots.

I'm not sure why I did it. Maybe out of shock of being touched. Maybe because the last man who had touched my face had slapped me. But Reverend Brennan didn't seem offended by my reaction. His smile widened.

"You are beautiful. You know that, Maddie, don't you?" he asked, caressing my cheek again.

I was stunned into silence, now mesmerized by this voice, by his crystal-blue eyes.

"A beautiful child of God." He then kissed my forehead and stood, holding several of the flowerpots. I watched as he walked out, leaving me alone in the shed.

That night, when I closed my eyes, I dreamed of Reverend Brennan. I dreamed of his cool lips on my brow. When my mother brought me back to the Brennans' home two days later, I wanted to be there. I was eager to see him again.

Over the next month or two, I talked to Reverend Brennan about anything and everything, about God, school, and my dreams for the future. I said that I wanted to be a writer and travel the world. He was the first person that I told what was happening at home. I confessed to him about the beatings that Father gave me and my brothers and how we were all terrified of him. Reverend Brennan listened, told me to pray, and said things would eventually get better.

"You just have to have faith, Madison," he assured me.

He was kind and patient, exactly the opposite of my own father. He cared. So, when he kissed me again in the tool shed—this time on the lips—I was confused, but I didn't push him away.

"I love you, Madison," he told me. "I love you as if you were my own."

I was thirteen. I didn't know anything about grooming. I didn't know anything about manipulation. It seemed odd that a man claiming he saw me as a daughter was sticking his tongue in my mouth, but I trusted him. I kissed him back, unsure of how to do it properly, but eager to learn. We met in secret many times after that. Soon, I started to come to the Brennans' house when Mrs. Brennan was away, scrapbooking with friends and when the kids were on playdates. I closed my eyes and grimaced through the pain the first time he took me to bed. I lay stiff and waited until it was over all those times thereafter, waiting until he finished, because I thought I had to. Girls show their love with their obedience, after all.

I wasn't allowed to tell anyone about us. "They won't under-stand, Maddie," Reverend Brennan explained. "Just know you are my heart, Maddie."

He was full of shit, but I felt it. I truly believed that he loved me.

He told me when the time was right, he would approach my par-ents and tell them that he wanted me to live with him and his family from now on. They would adopt me; I would officially become his daughter. And once again I believed him. I actually *believed* him, and I waited for the day that he would rescue me from the hell I called home and the devil I called Father. I was sure it would come.

A different day came instead.

"You son of a bitch!" Matt Dorsey, the father of my classmate Amelia Dorsey, yelled as he raced down the center aisle with a pistol in his hand before he was tackled to the ground. "You son of a bitch! You'll go to hell for what you've done!"

Mr. Dorsey was known at our church for being a quiet man, an unassuming father of three who volunteered at the church bazaar, who helped build the nativity scene the church had erected on the front lawn last Christmas. He looked nothing like that man now as they wrestled away his gun and held him down while the church erupted into screams and chaos.

Mr. Dorsey had beard stubble on his cheeks. His eyes were bloodshot. He looked as if he'd either been drinking, hadn't slept for days, or both.

"You know what you did!" he shouted between sobs as some of the men dragged him out of the sanctuary. "You know what you did, you bastard! He raped my daughter! He raped my baby girl! And you'll go to hell for it!"

The church went silent, save for a few murmurs, as the doors of the sanctuary slammed shut behind him, and I felt the cold bucket of reality as vividly as one of Father's slaps.

CHAPTER 14

TASHA

I'VE GOT A NEW JOB, AND TODAY IS MY FIRST DAY.

I stare in my dresser mirror, running my hands over my hair, then my blouse and skirt, smoothing out all the little wrinkles.

"You look good, girl," I whisper to myself with a smile. And I feel good—for once.

For almost three straight weeks, I applied for everything. But I didn't hear back from any of them; I got nothing but automated emails confirming my application. Then out of the blue one day, I got my very first callback from Myers Trust for an executive assistant position in the CEO's office.

When the HR director called, asking me to come in for an interview, I was so excited. Truth is, I didn't remember applying, but that's no surprise. I swear I sent out about 50 resumes. I need a job, and not just to help pay the bills—I'm desperate to do something besides cook, clean, and stare at four walls.

The day of the interview, I put on a big smile and tried to sound friendly, to seem sure of myself—even if I wasn't.

"Well, you certainly seem like you have the credentials and the experience," the CEO said after flipping through the pages of my résumé. She rose from behind her big desk and gave me a firm hand-shake. "We'll be in touch, Tasha."

I didn't know for sure, but I felt like I aced the interview. I must have, because within two days they offered me the position.

I give myself one final look before turning away from my mirror. I push back my shoulders, ready to start something new, and maybe something good. I walk to the bed and grab my purse.

"Bye, honey!" I call over my shoulder to Kordell as I walk to the bedroom door. "I'll see you when I get home this evening."

"Where do you think you're going?" he garbles from the bath-room with a mouth full of toothpaste.

"I'm headed to work. It's my first day at my new job. Remember?"

"Hold up!" He pokes his head around the bathroom door. He's all big eyes and frothy mouth like some crazy cartoon. "I got a meeting with a big client today. He's building condos out by Green-belt. It's a chance for more work. I told you that last night."

"OK," I say, waiting for him to explain what his big meeting has to do with me.

"I can't just wear a pair of any ol' jeans, Tasha! I need a shirt and khakis. I need my clothes ironed."

I glance down at my watch. It's already 7:15. "Honey, I would do it if I had the time, but I have to catch the bus. I have to take the Metro."

Thanks to you, I can't drive my car so it takes me twice as long to get anywhere, I want to remind him, but I know better. I don't want him to think I'm picking a fight.

I want today to be nice, to start it off on the right foot.

"I can't be late on my first day," I say. "It won't look good."

"Well, what the hell am I supposed to do?" He stomps out of the bathroom in his boxers. "I don't know how to iron!"

"Yes, you do. It's easy!" I walk to one of our bedroom closets. I open the door and take out the ironing board and the iron from the top shelf. I open it up for him by the bed. "Then you plug in the iron and it heats up on its own."

He roughly wipes the toothpaste from his mouth with the back of his hand as I plug the iron into the wall socket. Kordell glares at the ironing board like it's a complicated device and he's just lost the instructions. He picks up the iron, examines it, and shakes his head before setting it back down again. "Damnit, Tasha, why can't you do it?"

"Because I know you can do it yourself. Anyone can! It's pretty simple, honey. Hand me the shirt. I'll iron one of the sleeves to show you. Then I have to go so I won't be late."

He yanks open one of his drawers, takes out a button-down, and slams the drawer shut. He shoves the shirt at me.

"See now. I put it on this setting for cotton," I say as I adjust the dial and lay the shirt sleeve flat on the ironing board. I grab the iron handle and press a button, sending up a cloud of steam. "Then I do a few quick swipes with the iron, and . . . voila! You're done." I set the iron on its side and shift over. "Now you try."

Kordell grimaces. He steps behind the board, picks up the shirt, and slaps it back down. He grabs the iron and starts swiping it back and forth over the shirt sleeve like it's a windshield wiper.

"Honey, do it a little slower," I say, but he ignores me, dragging the iron at the same pace—maybe even a little rougher—like it'll get the job done faster but all he's doing is making more wrinkles. "If you keep doing it like that, you're never gonna—"

"Goddamnit!" he shouts. He reaches out and flips over the ironing board with one quick swipe, like a kid knocking over a sandcastle, making me jump back in surprise, making the hot iron fall to the floor and miss my feet by only inches.

"Stop lecturing me all the damn time! All this talkin' you're doing, you could be ironing my damn clothes yourself! I told you, I don't know how to iron. I'm the man of the house!" he yells, pounding his chest. "This ain't my damn job! It's yours. So, if you're late for work, it's your own damn fault, not mine! You should've ironed my clothes last night, but you didn't. Stop wasting time and do it!"

I stare down at the iron, blinking back tears.

"You hear me?" he shouts, making me flinch. "Iron the damn clothes, Tasha!"

"O-OK," I whisper.

I watch as Kordell stalks back into the bathroom. He turns on the water to finish getting ready.

With shaking hands, I right the ironing board, pick up the iron, and finish his shirt to the sound of running water and him muttering.

✳ ✳ ✳

"Hi, uh, excuse me," I say as I run up to the glass receptionist's desk, now out of breath. A young Hispanic lady smiles up at me. "My name is Tasha Jenkins. I'm here to see Jessica Bellamy for my first-day orientation. I . . . I know I'm late. I'm so sorry! Traffic was a mess."

It's a new job and I'm already lying. I'm already making excuses to cover up what really happened.

The young lady nods. "Yes, Ms. Jenkins. We've been expecting you. You can have a seat right over there." She points to a group of leather chairs circled around a glass coffee table covered in magazines. She then reaches for a phone on her desk. "I'll let Jessica know you're here."

I walk over to one of the chairs and sit down, adjusting the hem of my skirt as I do it.

I look around me. It's a nice office. I noticed that the last time I was here. Lots of nice furniture and more chrome than a tricked-out Escalade. The windows of Myers Trust face the city, so I can see all the buildings faraway and the street ten floors below. Their building is in the part of town where the commercial rent is high. You can tell because the streets are clean and most of the people walking and driving on those streets are white. I stop looking out the window and pick up one of the magazines on the table in front of me, *Town & Country*. I flip through the pages as I wait, trying to get lost in the pictures and the articles, trying to pretend everything is normal, but I can't.

I keep seeing the iron. I keep seeing it sitting on its side on the carpet in our bedroom. It almost landed on my feet. It could've burned me and sent me to the hospital, and Kordell didn't even care. Instead, he screamed at me to iron his clothes. He told me it was all my fault.

I can feel my eyes prick with tears.

"Your husband isn't going to suddenly change. Neither will mine," I can hear Madison Gingell say in my head. "And to expect them to change isn't just crazy. It's stupid."

I've tried not to think about Madison since I left her standing at the top of the stairs at the Metro station a little more than three weeks ago. But I can't forget her or our conversation. Not when I wake up. Not when I close my eyes at night. Not when I cook breakfast and not when I eat dinner. I can't forget what she said, even more so today. I've played it over and over again in my head, wondering if I heard her wrong or if I misunderstood her meaning. She couldn't have been asking what I thought she was asking. Even if she hated her husband. Even if that man's abuse was pushing her to the very edge . . . *nobody* would be crazy enough to just blurt that out in the middle of the street with all those people around, where anyone could hear.

But when you've been pushed too far, when your situation gets so desperate that you feel there's no other option, maybe you just don't care anymore who hears you. You just want the torture to end.

And now I know how it feels to wish your husband dead. I wished it today while looking at that fallen iron. I wouldn't even need Madison to do it. I could do it myself. I could poison his food or smother him in his sleep. Kordell is a heavy sleeper. Always has been. I'd wait until he started snoring and put the pillow over his head. He'd fight me, but if I kneeled on the pillow and sat on his chest, I might be able to hold him down long enough. I'd wait as he twitched and kicked until he went still. I wouldn't have to. . . .

My eyes go wide. I drop the magazine back to the coffee table when I realize what I'm doing. Am I really sitting here planning my husband's murder?

"Oh, my God," I whisper, blinking back the tears that are threatening to spill over.

What in the world has gotten into me?

I shoot to my feet.

"I'm sorry," the receptionist says, staring at me. "Did you need something, Ms. Jenkins?"

"Uh, no. I mean, yes. I mean, can you . . . can you tell me where the ladies' room is, please?"

"Sure," she says, pointing into the distance. "It's down the hall . . . to your left."

"I didn't mean it," I mumble under my breath as I walk to the bathroom. "I didn't mean it."

I pray to God for forgiveness for what I just imagined, for even thinking such a horrible thing. I would never kill my husband. God wouldn't send me on that path. He wouldn't want me to go that way to kill another human being, but I just don't know which way he wants me to go. He can't want me to just suffer silently like this, can he?

I reach the end of the hall. I must be near the bathrooms now, but I can't tell because my head is bowed so no one can see me crying. I can barely see through my tears. I'm not paying attention to anything, so it's no surprise that I bump into somebody stepping out of the men's room.

"Excuse me," I mumble, wiping my eyes, trying to walk around him. "I'm so sorry."

"Tasha, is . . . is that you?" a voice answers with a laugh.

The voice is warm and familiar, like a wool blanket you keep at the end of the bed and wear every night, like a cup of chamomile tea after a long, hard day. I haven't heard it in years; but the instant it hits my ears, I look up. My mouth falls open.

"*Morris?*"

It's Morris Hammond from way back when, the one that Kordell tried to keep me away from but never could. Life did it instead.

Morris's smile widens behind his beard, and, despite all my fears and worries, I feel a little flutter in my chest—just like old times.

"Well, Tasha!" he says. "Long time, no see!"

And suddenly, it all makes sense. I understand where God was leading me.

He's led me here. He's led me back to Morris.

CHAPTER 15

MADISON

"Headed somewhere, sweetheart?"

I turn around at the sound of my husband's voice after looping a cashmere scarf around my neck and adjusting my beret in the foyer mirror. Phil is standing at the top of the stairs on the landing above, with his reading glasses in one hand and a Clive Cussler paperback in the other.

I'm surprised he's using his glasses. For a year and a half after getting them from the optometrist, he had left them in the leather case on our dresser, content to squint and frown down at text rather than to admit that his sight was starting to fail him, that he is getting older.

And they say women are vain.

I force a smile and nod while I button my coat. "Just going for a drive."

"Sorry, Maddie. I didn't know you had plans today. I gave Tony the day off."

"That's perfectly fine! I'm being adventurous and driving myself. I'm meeting a friend. We're taking a field trip."

"*A field trip?*" he says as I turn to the front door. He walks down a few of the stairs and raises his brows. "Are you going with one of the girls from yoga class or a friend from that new art collective you've been visiting? I know how much you like to help the underprivileged."

I pause as I grip the door handle.

The irony isn't lost on me that the lying bastard is questioning me about who I'm meeting and my future whereabouts, when he arrived home in the wee hours again last night, claiming yet another "work emergency." You'd think Phil was a cardiac surgeon with how often he uses that excuse. I bet he and Penelope the Intern have been *very* busy lately.

I pivot on my heels again. An affable smile is back in place. "I'm just meeting Summer." I incline my head and poke out my bottom lip in an exaggerated pout. "She's been down in the dumps lately. I was going to invite her over again, but I figured I'd surprise her instead and cheer her up with a spa day. Maybe a little shopping."

"Ah! Sorry to hear she's feeling down." Phillip jogs down the remaining flight of stairs. "Well, then, you two have a great time, honey. I hope she enjoys the retail therapy. Judging from our credit card bills, I know you certainly do." He laughs, leans down, and kisses my brow with a loud smack.

You patronizing prick.

I want to take off my cashmere scarf, wrap it around his throat, and tighten it until the capillaries in his eyes burst and the eyes themselves bulge out of their sockets, until his tongue lolls like a panting dog's.

"Bye," I reply brightly before putting on my sunglasses and giving him a wave. I then turn back to the door as my smile fades.

Twenty minutes later, my Mercedes passes the D.C. border. I'm on the Beltway, headed to Maryland. Summer does not live in Maryland. She lives in a tony penthouse condo in Northwest on M Street. She probably isn't even home. She could be off fucking the grounds-keeper at St. Thomas Episcopal Church, for all that I know. But like

I told my dear husband, I *am* going on a field trip—a long overdue one, honestly.

I follow the highway signs, driving for two and a half hours. I pass Baltimore, then Cumberland. The terrain changes from densely packed, towering buildings to suburban sprawl and then finally to vast open spaces with only trees and mountains as far as I can see. The slate mountain rock juts into the roadway, towering over me. These mountains aren't carved by time, but by dynamite explosions that were used to excavate the highway in the 1940s, and it shows. It looks like a giant has taken a trowel and dragged it through the center of the mountain.

The old highway roads zig and zag. They narrow from three lanes to two, and finally give way to meandering single-lane roads with double-wides and rundown ramblers on both sides, hidden among the shrubs and trees. I drive past a small town. I see an old Texaco gas station and a deserted general store with a wigwam on the roof and the carved statue of an American Indian holding a tomahawk sitting in the gravel driveway. My Mercedes stands out like a sore thumb among the pickup trucks in the parking lots, among the rusted tractors still covered in patches of the snow that fell a week ago.

I make a right at a black mailbox where the door is missing and a nest of mail and circulars spills out of it like a bridal bouquet. A "DO NOT TRESPASS" sign sits beside it on a wooden post. My Mercedes bumps along a dirt-gravel road, and I finally reach a clearing where a trailer sits. Smashed beer cans are in the front yard, along with an emaciated pit bull whose leash is tied to a tree. The dog barks and growls itself hoarse while lurching on its leash as my Mercedes approaches. When I pull to a stop, the trailer door swings open with a crash. A rail-thin brunette with stringy hair and gaunt cheeks and a crying baby sitting on her hip, steps out and thuds down the wooden stairs in jeans, a stained T-shirt, and bare feet.

"Hey! Hey!" she shouts. "Didn't you read the goddamn sign? Get the hell outta here!"

I turn off the engine and open the car door. I climb out and wince as the heels of my Stuart Weitzmans sink into thick mud.

"Didn't you hear me?" she squawks. "This is private property!"

"Is Billy home?" I ask, tugging off my sunglasses and shutting the car door, not the least bit intimidated by this hillbilly banshee.

"*What?*" she screeches, going up yet another octave, though I didn't know it was even possible. "Who are you? Just who the hell are you, lady?"

"Would you stop screamin', Charlotte? It's giving me a damn headache," Billy says tiredly as he steps out the trailer door. He lumbers down the stairs in work boots and looks at me warily with bloodshot green eyes. "What are you doing here, Maddie?"

"*Maddie?* You know her?" she asks, pointing at me.

Charlotte is still shouting despite Billy's request. The baby is wailing now and the dog is still barking. I can barely stand all the noise, but I've driven this far and I need Billy's help. It would be too challenging to accomplish what I want without him.

"Yeah, I know her," he finally says with resignation, crossing his wiry arms over his chest. "She's my sister."

"*Your sister?*"

"Pleasure to meet you," I say dryly, though assuredly it isn't.

My little brother William is my only surviving relative; Father died of a heart attack over a decade ago, a few years after our brother Joseph committed suicide, and after that, Mom died of breast cancer. I haven't seen Billy in years, not since I gave him that last envelope filled with $15,000 in cash. He claimed he was going to invest it in a car-detailing outfit that he was starting with one of his buddies, a friend he met when he first moved to Maryland. But I was reasonably sure even then that all the money I gave him would either go to partying or into a needle and then his arm.

Billy had always been slim, but now he looks almost skeletal. I can practically see his hip bones over the top of his sagging jeans. His dark hair is greasy and pasted to his scalp. He's now missing a few front teeth. I can't be sure if it was the result of yet another bar fight or the meth.

"Why is this the first time I'm hearing about you having a goddamn sister, Billy?" Charlotte asks. "You never mentioned it before!"

"Go inside," he mutters, tossing a thumb over his shoulder, pointing it in the direction of the trailer.

"No, I'm not goin' inside!" Charlotte argues, adjusting the baby on her knobby hip. "You're gonna damn well tell me who the hell she is, Billy! Is she really your sister or just some—"

"Dammit, go inside, Charlotte!" he booms.

Both Charlotte's and the baby's faces are red now—the infant from crying and Charlotte from anger. But she doesn't argue anymore. Instead, she mumbles to herself as she turns around and stomps back up the stairs and into the trailer, slamming the door shut behind her.

"Shut up!" Billy shouts at the dog, who ignores him. He then rolls his eyes and turns his withering gaze back to me. "Why are you here, Maddie? How the hell did you even find where I live?"

"Well, hello to you too!" I laugh. "You didn't send me a forwarding address, but I have my ways. Honestly, with your arrest record, you aren't too hard to find."

"So you tracked me down." He shrugged. "Why? What do you want?"

"Why do you assume I want something?"

"Because you're not the type to pay a visit for no reason. You wouldn't do it out of the kindness of your heart. I don't even think you have a heart."

"Really? I had enough of a heart to set you up on the East Coast after Mom and Father died. Who's given you a total of a hundred thousand dollars in the eight and a half years?"

"Yeah, and I had to earn that money, didn't I? You didn't just give it to me. I didn't come by it easy!"

"No, you did not." I walk around him and stare up at his trailer. "And considering all you had to do to get it, I'm surprised this is what you did with the money. This is all you have to show for a hundred grand? A run-down trailer in the middle of nowhere?"

He grimaces and lowers his eyes, now embarrassed.

"But, lucky for you, I have an opportunity available for you to make more money. I have a job for you."

He quickly shakes his head. "No."

"Oh, come on! You haven't even heard what it is."

"I don't need to hear it!" He leans toward me, dropping his voice to a whisper. "Whatever shit you're about to ask me to do, I won't do it. I told you that the last time, and I meant it. I won't do it. Not again!"

"But it'll be easier this time. He deserves it, Billy. You'll be doing the world a favor. He's—"

"*He?* Who's the poor bastard this time? The little boytoy that a rich bitch like you keeps on the side? Or is it your husband?"

Even though I came here to ask him to kill Kordell, he must have seen something in my eyes at the mention of Phil that revealed my ultimate intentions, because Billy chuckles and shakes his head in exasperation. I guess he knows me too well. "Goddamn, Maddie. You are a piece of work."

"Just hear me out," I say, holding up my hands. "This isn't what you think. I don't—"

"That's what you said the last fucking time! You said she deserved it. But she didn't, did she? You lied about who she was. What she'd done. The whole time, you just wanted her out of your way. I can't believe a goddamn word you say!" He turns around and walks back to his trailer. "Just get out of here, Maddie! Don't come here again! You hear me? Whatever you want me to do, I'm not interested."

"You know you could use the money," I call after him. "That baby of yours probably needs it too. You aren't exactly living in the lap of luxury out here." I gaze around me. "Does that conscience you've suddenly sprouted allow you to watch your kid starve to death?"

"Go away, Maddie! And don't ever set foot on my doorstep again, you crazy bitch!" he tosses over his shoulder.

"You're acting like what you did was beneath you . . . like it was that much of a stretch! You had a rap sheet as long as my arm, even back then."

He pauses as he opens the trailer door.

"Drug possession," I continue. "Second-degree assault. Robbery. Should I keep going? You couldn't keep a job. *No one* would give you a place to stay. *Everyone* abandoned you. But I took care of you. Me!" I point at my chest. "I helped you! And I would have continued to prop you up, even though you didn't deserve it. Even though you would've continued to use me like every other man in my life while you slowly killed yourself. All that I asked was for one . . . *one* thing in return . . . *one* little favor!"

I watch as he shuts the trailer door. He then slowly turns back around to face me.

"Making me kill someone for you isn't a little favor, Maddie," he begins in a low voice as he walks back down the stairs. "Making me do what I did to that woman that day isn't some little thing."

Jesus Christ. Not this again.

It amazes me that Billy keeps blaming me for how Ashley, Phil's first wife, died.

Yes, I did ask my brother to kill her, but only after she refused to grant Phil a divorce. Only after she started to call me and leave harassing voice messages. Only after she used dummy accounts to post on Twitter and my Instagram page comments like "Good morning, WHORE!" and "She steals husbands!" I had to delete my online profiles to make it stop. My neighbor said she saw a strange woman knocking on doors in the apartment building, asking about me. It was only then that I knew something had to be done.

I'd hoped Ashley would bow out gracefully, that she would have some dignity and just take Phil's offer of a hefty divorce settlement and move to New York or Los Angeles or Boulder, Colorado, for all I cared—but she refused. The poor deranged woman was unpredictable and unstable. She was far from showing the restraint that I've shown with Penelope the Intern.

I didn't want to kill her. She'd left me with no choice.

"I didn't *tell* you to get high that night before you did it," I say. "You did a lot more damage than was necessary. How gruesome it was was your fault, Billy, not mine."

"I got high because I *had* to! I never could've pulled that shit off if I didn't. But I remember everything, Maddie. She begged for her life! She begged me not to kill her! I still dream about it. I still have nightmares."

"Then try yoga," I say flatly. "I heard that helps with night terrors."

"This is funny to you, isn't it? Hearing about how she died is funny to you." He shakes his head. "You know, I've wondered for years why I was so fucked up. I figured out it was from how we grew up, from being around Father, all those beatings day in and day out and all that mental torture he put us through. But I didn't understand why it affected me so much. I mean . . . you and Joe seemed OK. You seemed fine . . . normal. You weren't getting high every day. You weren't breaking into houses to feed your habit. You had your shit together." He gestures toward me. "But then I realized you guys weren't fine either. Joe put a bullet in his head because he couldn't take it. Because the voices in his head got so bad. And you went full-on crazy, Maddie. Even crazier than Father! You're a psycho . . . a certified psycho! You know that?"

I sigh, now bored with this conversation and bored with my brother, his "poor me" routine, and melodramatics. "My cell number's the same. If you change your mind, you know where to reach me."

I then turn, put on my sunglasses, and head back to my car.

"Stay away from me, Maddie!" he shouts at me as I climb inside. "Don't come back here! Don't show up here or try to contact me again, you psychotic bitch!"

A few seconds later, I drive off.

CHAPTER 16

TASHA

"HERE YOU GO," I SAY AS I WALK ACROSS THE OFFICE AND PLACE A file folder on the edge of the desk. I then look at the clock on the wall, watching another minute tick by.

"Thanks so much, Tasha," Evelyn, my new boss, says. She stares at her computer screen. Her nails click away on her keyboard as she types.

I look at the clock again, seeing that it's already five minutes after noon. He's probably already downstairs, standing in front of the glass doors, waiting for me.

"Uh, if you don't need anything else, I was . . . I was going to head to lunch."

She stops typing and looks up at me. She smiles. "Oh, sure! Of course. Are you finally trying that Moroccan place I recommended?"

"Not yet. I'm saving it for a week when I want to treat myself."

Evelyn nods her curly head and laughs. "Well, enjoy your lunch anyway! *Whatever* you choose."

"Thank you! I'll be back in an hour," I say over my shoulder. I then walk out of Evelyn's office and straight to my desk. I open one of the metal drawers and remove my purse. I try not to run down the corridor to the bank of elevators that will take me to the floors below, even though I'm late now. Just as I'm about to press the button, I stop short, turn around, and head to the ladies' room.

In the mirror, I give myself a quick once-over. I finger comb loose strands of hair back into place, dig into my purse, and find a tube of lipstick that I picked up at the drugstore that very morning. It's a matte red. The gold label on the bottom of the tube says it's called "Warm Passionfruit." Rolling it on my lips, I feel womanly. Almost sexy. Something I haven't felt in damn near forever.

I leave the bathroom and head back to the elevators. When I reach the lobby a minute later, I see through the two-story glass that he is waiting for me outside, like I thought he would be. If he's anything, he's always on time. But instead of standing by the door, he's sitting on one of the metal benches, near the courtyard water fountain. He's staring down at a folded newspaper. He's one of the few people I know who still reads them.

When I step through the glass revolving doors and stroll toward him, he looks up. His dark brown face breaks into a smile. His eyes crinkle at the edges. A flash of white teeth appears and I can't help but smile too.

"I'm sorry I made you wait," I say, adjusting my purse on my shoulder.

Morris shakes his head as he slowly rises to his feet with a soft grunt. "No worries. I didn't have to wait long for you. And remember, I've waited a lot longer."

My smile fades. I know what he means, and my heart breaks a little. As we walk away from the building and turn a corner, I reach out for Morris's hand, unsure if he will take it but sure that no one from the office can see us here. He takes my hand within his own, and squeezes it as we walk.

✳ ✳ ✳

I've been working at Myers Trust for more than a month now. I've gotten coffee with a few of my coworkers, even gone window-shopping during our lunch break, where they gave me the lowdown on all the office gossip. Who always steals lunches from the refrigerator. Who's the office tattletale so be careful what you say to them. It was nice to laugh and talk, to have something like friends again. I didn't realize how much I'd missed it—having my own village, as Dr. Green would say. My boss Evelyn is nice, too, not as stuffy as she was the first week I started. When we aren't discussing work or going over her schedule, she talks a lot about gardening and her dogs—three purebred Lhasa Apsos. She has pictures of them all around her office. She calls them her children. One of them even won a dog tournament two years ago. A blue ribbon hangs on the wall in her office in a big wooden picture frame, like she won it herself.

As her executive assistant, I photocopy stuff for Evelyn all the time. I'm always picking up things for her from the printer, too. It takes me to the copier room on our floor, which isn't far from Morris's cubicle in the accounting department.

I tried to avoid him at first. After that first day on the job when I ran into him, it just felt awkward striking up a conversation. I hadn't seen Morris in more than seventeen years; and the last time I had, it'd left a lot of things up in the air. But since starting my new job, I pass him three . . . sometimes, four times a day. We made eye contact as I passed, so to be polite, I waved. He'd always wave back, then return his attention to his computer screen, like he didn't give me a second thought. After the second week, I just couldn't take it anymore. I saw him in the coffee room. He was the only one hanging around in there, waiting for the expensive dispenser machine the company bought to drip out his espresso into his paper cup.

"Do you want to get lunch sometime?" I said out of nowhere, making him whip around to face me. "Lunch with . . . with me, I mean."

Morris didn't answer right away. He just looked at me real funny and slowly nodded. "Uh, yeah. Yeah, I'll go to lunch with you. I brought mine today, but we could go tomorrow if that's OK."

The first time we ate lunch together was at a little Mexican restaurant three blocks from the office. We didn't talk about much. We pretended like we were just coworkers and old friends, like nothing had happened between us way back when. I talked about Ghalen, like I always do, boasting like the proud mother that I am. I didn't talk about Kordell.

Morris said he had a ten-year-old daughter with his ex-wife. I wasn't surprised he'd gotten married. He'd always been a catch. Morris said he'd moved out to Virginia so he could be closer to his daughter; but now he's thinking of moving back into the city, to a place near his mother who had a stroke earlier this year and needs help getting around. I wasn't surprised to hear him say that, either. He'd always been responsible and kind to those he loved.

It wasn't until the third lunch that Morris finally said it. He finally asked me the big question that we'd both been ignoring.

"Why didn't you show up that night, Tasha?" he asked between chews, staring down at his pasta salad.

When he asked, I exhaled like I'd been holding in that breath for forever. Maybe on the inside, I had been.

"I called you. I emailed you," he continued, "but you never responded. You never told me why you didn't come."

"I—I wanted to come. I tried to, but I . . . I had an accident."

"An accident?"

I nodded. "A car accident. I was in the hospital, and then I gave birth to Ghalen. I had to have an emergency C-section. I just had . . . well . . . a lot going on. A lot to . . . to distract me."

He looked up from his salad and met my eyes. "And even after, you still couldn't call me? You couldn't reach out?"

I hesitated.

For that, I didn't have an answer. The truth was, I didn't have a good excuse for not calling or emailing Morris after I came back home from the hospital or after we brought Ghalen home after his three-month stay in the NICU. Kordell didn't know that I hadn't stopped talking to Morris at work, like I'd promised, so he had no idea that our relationship had gone way further and gotten a lot deeper than work friends. The little excuse I did have for never reaching out to Morris would not make sense to anyone but me. Because the only reason why I didn't call him back was because of guilt.

That night almost two decades ago had been the first time I'd ever tried to leave Kordell. I was six and a half months pregnant and ready to start a new life with a man who said he would love and cherish me and the baby he hadn't helped make. But it felt like the hand of God intervened. A van hit me head-on as I was driving through an intersection, heading to Morris's house with my suitcases in the trunk. I survived the crash, but Ghalen barely did. I felt like God was punishing me for being a cheater, for putting my needs first. He was punishing me by taking my baby away from me. He knew I couldn't be a good mother.

While in that NICU, I did two things. I learned how to knit to ease my mind and give my restless hands something to do when I felt like I could do nothing else to help my baby. And I prayed like I always do in my scary moments. My Auntie Yolanda used to say, "Man may fail you, but the Lord never will. Always trust and turn to Him," and that's what I did.

I apologized to God and promised him I would never speak to Morris again. I said I would be a dutiful wife to Kordell and if God gave me another chance, I would be the best mother to our son. And God answered my prayers; Ghalen got better, slowly but surely. Kordell and I watched as the sleep apnea and bradycardia disappeared. After almost two months, the doctors were able to take Ghalen off of oxygen because he could finally breathe on his own. And one day in the NICU nursery, Ghalen latched onto my breast to suckle and I cried and I cried. He didn't have to be fed through an IV anymore. He was still frail, but he had survived. God had shown me mercy, and I wanted to show I was grateful by keeping all those vows I'd made back at the hospital.

At lunch, I told Morris all of this. He didn't interrupt. He let me tell my story from beginning to end as he finished his salad. When I was done, he wiped his mouth with a napkin, tilted his head, and frowned.

"So . . . what's changed?" he asked. "Why reach out to me now? Why invite me to lunch every week? Why invite me back into your life?"

He was asking a lot of questions, but I knew he was basically asking just one. I thought for a bit before I answered him.

"Well, I figured if God brought you back into my life, he'd finally forgiven me. I've paid my penance and my dues with that man. I've paid it *every* day, Morris. Now I might have a chance to be happy."

✳ ✳ ✳

"You're quiet today," Morris says as we stroll along the sidewalk.

We've passed a few of the restaurants and bistros we like, but so far we haven't stopped and gone inside any of them. I don't know what I'm in the mood for today. Maybe I'm not even that hungry. I guess I'm just happy to be here with him.

"I'm just thinking," I say.

"Thinking about what?"

I'm thinking about how, when the day is over, I'll have to go back home to Kordell. He still has my car keys. I can't leave the house without him or Ghalen escorting me, unless it's to go to work. Kordell has only given me back one credit card, and I know he checks the bill. When I talk on the phone, he always stands nearby, listening to my conversations.

I'm thinking about how I've told myself that I will wait until Ghalen graduates to leave Kordell, but now the day seems even further away, not closer since I know I have something . . . *someone* waiting for me on the other side.

I thought I was done paying my penance, but I feel like I still am.

"I'm thinking about us," I say, squeezing his hand. "About the future and things."

"Do you see us there? In the future?"

"I hope so. But I wonder if you're willing to wait for me after all this time."

"You could just leave him, you know." He raises his brows. "You don't have to wait."

I shake my head. "It wouldn't work."

"Why not? You told me what he's done to you. What he's still doing." He stops on the sidewalk and drops my hand. He reaches up and squeezes my shoulders. Even though I'm wearing my wool coat, I can feel the heat of his hands on my skin. It makes me tingle. His dark eyes lock with mine. "*Just leave*, Tasha. If you're worried about where you can go, you can come live with me. You *and* your son. I hope you know that."

"Thank you. Thank you so much." I shake my head again. "But he wouldn't come, and I won't leave him behind, Morris."

"How do you know? How do you know he wouldn't come? The last time you tried to leave, you said you were moving to Atlanta. That's over 600 miles away. Maybe if he knew you all could stay here, he would—"

"He wouldn't. I think Atlanta was just an excuse. Ghalen doesn't want to leave his daddy. He loves him."

Morris drops his hands from my shoulders and sighs. "Well, let's hope Ghalen changes his mind. Or maybe something will happen that will help change it for him."

At those words, I wince. I know Morris doesn't mean what I'm thinking about, but I can't help thinking it anyway, because the only thing that would make Ghalen leave his father is if his father left us first. Kordell would have to disappear from our lives or die.

I think about his death more and more now, especially now that Morris and I have reunited. I think of how easy things would be if Kordell would just die, and I feel so guilty, but I can't help it. Madison Gingell planted the seed, and now it's taken root. The thoughts won't stop.

But for Madison to free me, I'd have to kill her husband too, and I don't have it in me to do that; I can't kill anybody. And even if I could, there's a big problem with Madison's plan.

I've seen murder mysteries. She probably thinks that because we don't have any relationship to each other's husbands, that no one would suspect us; but the truth is, no one would suspect *her*.

No one would think the pretty little blond white lady with nice clothes and home could harm a fly. But the minute the finger was pointed at me . . . the second they saw my black face, they'd think I did it—even if I didn't. I've seen it too many times before. I will not be given the benefit of the doubt before all the evidence is collected. I am not innocent before proven guilty. Women like Madison get off scot-free for murder; women like me do not.

"I'm sorry. I shouldn't have brought this up," Morris says, mistaking the reason I winced for something else. "We don't have to talk about this today. Let's just eat lunch. Enjoy ourselves. OK?"

I nod as he takes my hand again and I look up at the sign of the Vietnamese restaurant we've stopped in front of. I force a smile. "Feel like some pho?"

He nods too. "Sure," he says, before walking around me to hold open the glass door.

I step inside, and he follows.

CHAPTER 17

MADISON

It's not quite 11 a.m., but I've already opened our fridge and taken out a chilled bottle of Sauvignon Blanc. I pour the wine into a glass and take a sip. It's one of the bottles we brought home with us from our trip to the Sonoma Valley last year. The wine is dry . . . crisp, just like I like it. Maybe I'll head back there and buy another bottle after Phil is dead. Maybe I'll get the same private cottage in Napa where we stayed. I adored the views from our patio and the saltwater pool out back.

But first things first. I have to handle my half of the bargain before I can even think about the day that Phil is gone. I finish the rest of my wine in one gulp and set the glass back onto the marble countertop.

Admittedly, I'm not usually a morning drinker, but I need the liquid courage for what I'm about to do today.

My iPad sits beside the wineglass. I ease back onto a stool and pull up Tasha's Instagram page for Knit 'N' Things. It's filled with photos of her knitted pieces—scarves, socks, gloves, and hats—along with a few photos of her and inspirational quotes. "There is no impossible. Only I'M POSSIBLE," one says with about 40 likes underneath it.

"What the hell does that even mean?" I mutter before pouring another glass.

In the photos with Tasha herself, she's always smiling at the camera. But the smiles seem false. None of them reach her eyes. I can see a difference in only one photo where she's posing with a younger man. Considering the resemblance, I believe he's likely her son, Ghalen. They're sitting at a picnic table in front of trays of Maryland blue crabs. They're wearing plastic bibs with the words "Let's Get Crackin'!" printed on them. Ghalen holds one of the wooden mallets to his lips, pretending it is a cigar.

Tasha's fake smile is back in another photo where she is posing with a man much older than Ghalen. He's broad-shouldered with thick muscular arms and so tall that he practically towers over her in the photo. Her arms are wrapped around his waist. Judging from the body language, he has to be her husband.

"Well, hello, Kordell," I whisper dryly before taking another sip.

Kordell proudly holds up a dead-eyed trout, a fresh catch. He has big hands like oven mitts. Hands that he likely uses to grab and hit his wife. Hands that are potentially deadly weapons. I click on the photo and enlarge it so I can better see the T-shirt he's wearing. On it are the words "KJ Custom Cabinets," his cabinetry business that Tasha told me about at our lunch.

I click on the Google screen icon and search for "KJ Custom Cabinets in Washington, D.C." It doesn't take long to find a website and phone number. From my sweater pocket, I pull out the prepaid cell phone I purchased specifically for this occasion. My finger hovers over the buttons on the screen, ready to dial, but I hesitate before I start clicking.

I've given Tasha time to think my proposition over, but she hasn't gotten back to me. I suspect she's still not on board with my plan yet. But the clock is ticking. One of us has to take the initiative, to make the sacrifice. And as I learned in the diversity and inclusion workshop organized by my women's networking group, one of the "Top 10 Steps of Becoming a Good Ally" is to not make it about you and be willing to make sacrifices to help implement change. Tasha obviously needs to offload her husband, just like I do. He's making her absolutely miserable. The poor woman is practically a prisoner in her own home. She isn't willing to take the steps to be rid of him, at least not yet. Maybe it's cultural. I heard that black women are natural nurturers. But Tasha has to know deep down that her life will be better without him. I just have to show her that the plan will work. Then I'll be able to win her over to my side. She'll realize I was right all along.

Yet I wonder if I can do it. After all, I didn't kill Ashley; Billy did. I haven't killed anyone myself in *years*. And even then, it was done on pure impulse. It still feels like I dreamed the entire thing.

✳ ✳ ✳

After Mr. Dorsey's outburst at church, Reverend Brennan refused to see me again. Even when I wrote him letter after letter, sneaking over the Brennans' rickety fence and hiding the letters by the shed behind his house—the place where he'd first caressed my cheek. It had also become the location where we left our secret messages to each other. But each time I would return for his answer, I would see that the envelopes were crusted with dirt and ants. They were left unopened. When I couldn't take it any longer, I called his home, begging for his spiritual counseling. He refused to take my calls as well.

"I'm sorry, Maddie. The reverend is very busy right now, hon," his wife answered over the sound of her screeching children in the background. "But I can pray with you, if you'd like."

"Thank you, Mrs. Brennan, but I have to go," I said between sniffs before hanging up, going to my room, and crying into my pillow.

The rumors about the Reverend started to spread around our town and the church, especially after the Dorseys filed charges against him. One night, someone spray-painted "PEDO PER-VERT" in big red letters on the side of the Brennans' garage. We noticed that the pews weren't as crowded on Sunday and figured out that some of the parishioners were now going to churches in Snohomish or West Lake Stevens. Only the loyalists among the flock like my parents remained.

Watching people turn on the Reverend made me angry. I thought he was a good man and a kind one. Mr. Dorsey's daughter, Amelia, was obviously lying, I told myself at the time. Or maybe he'd tried to counsel her, to become a father figure for her, too, but she got confused. Of course, I didn't realize that I was the one who was confused, who didn't know my ass from my armpit.

The Dorseys would eventually drop the charges. Not because Amelia had lied, I found out years later, but because she would have had to testify in court and the Reverend's sleazy lawyer was ready to present evidence of Amelia getting drunk at a party and giving a blowjob to one of the football players at Richard Johnson High. But even without the charges, the damage had been done. The Reverend announced from the pulpit one Sunday that he and his family would be leaving our town, that they would be moving out of Washington State.

I know most of the church parishioners were secretly relieved. Even if they didn't think Reverend Brennan was guilty, they didn't like the infamy that came with him being the head of our church. But I wasn't relieved. After hearing the news, I burst into tears. There went all my hopes of escaping Father, of living with the Brennans. I sobbed so loudly that Mom had to almost carry me out of the sanctuary and take me to the ladies' room.

"Maddie, you have to pull yourself together," she said, shaking my shoulders as I wailed. "People are going to think you're off your rocker, sweetheart."

I only cried more. She chalked up my outburst to teenage hormones and dramatics. At home, Father slapped me to make the incessant tears stop, but it didn't work. I was inconsolable. The Reverend couldn't leave me. He'd promised me that he would rescue me, that I could become part of his family.

I would die if he left, I told myself.

I wrote one last letter. It said that I had to see him. I threatened to tell my mom about us, about everything that he had promised, if he didn't agree to see me, breaking my vow to keep everything that he had done and said secret.

It was an idle threat—I would never do anything to hurt him—but it worked. That time, I did get a response. It was succinct, almost terse.

Wednesday at 4 p.m. In the church pantry. Come through the back door. I'll give you 15 minutes. That's it.

I took the long way there, a path through the woods so I wouldn't be seen by anyone. But I still arrived at the church on Wednesday at 4 o'clock on the dot in my prettiest dress. In one of the pockets, I hid my Mom's boning knife. I would show the Reverend how serious I was. If he and his wife didn't adopt me like he said they would and take me away with them, I was going to cut my wrists right in front of him.

The back door to the church was unlocked. I walked down a flight of dimly lit stairs to the floor below, listening to my footsteps and watching my shadow stretch on the linoleum-tiled floors. The church basement was a series of corridors filled with rooms. It was where the younger kids gathered for Sunday school and where the church stored its music equipment and other supplies, including our pantry. As I turned the corner, I half expected that he wouldn't be there. That he'd stood me up. But my worries were unnecessary. I saw the Reverend in the open doorway. He was standing in between the shelves, staring down at his watch. He loudly grumbled, then crossed his arms over his chest.

"You came!" I squealed, racing toward him. I attempted to wrap my arms around him, to give him a kiss, but he roughly shoved me away.

"Don't . . . don't do that," he muttered, his face now grim.

I gazed at him, crestfallen. "Don't do what?"

He grumbled again as he stepped around me and closed the pantry closet door. "Maddie, just say what you have to say, please. Steph and I still have a lot of packing to do. I have to get back home."

This isn't what I had envisioned our reunion would be. I hadn't anticipated that he would be so aloof, so cold.

"I . . . I want you to stay. Things are easier when you're here, when I have someone to . . . to talk to," I stammered. "Or if . . . or if you do leave, I want to come with you and your family. I want to live with you guys."

He shook his head. "That's not possible."

"Yes, it is! I can live with you. I can help! Tell Mrs. Brennan that I'll clean the house and babysit whenever she wants. My parents don't have to know that I left with you guys. I can run away! It wouldn't take me long to pack. I could—"

"Maddie, you cannot live with us. There is no way I can have a runaway . . . some thirteen-year-old girl living in my house. My wife would never stand for it, and I'd get thrown in jail."

Some thirteen-year-old girl . . .

He had never called me that before. And the way he said it, with such derision, like a girl wasn't a real person. Like I was an inanimate object, maybe one of the steel shelves in the pantry.

"But you said you loved me," I said weakly as tears flooded my eyes. "You loved me like I was your own. You told me you always would. You said you would help me. That you would—"

"I'm sorry." He furiously shook his head. "I'm . . . I'm sorry."

"I'll kill myself if you leave me!" I yelled. "Take me with you. Please!"

"I'm sorry, Maddie, but I can't. It's out of the question."

He then turned away, like he was about to walk out of the pantry. I reached for the knife in my pocket and pulled it out.

I swore it was to take the blade and place it to my wrist so that I would cut the veins and tendons like I threatened him I would. But something strange happened. My grief turned into rage. Rage that he'd fooled me into trusting and believing in him. Believing that he cared about me. That he would rescue me. In an instant, I finally saw him for who he truly was. I was just some thirteen-year-old girl that he had used and discarded, that he had lied to. Instead of cutting my own wrists, I raised the knife and plunged it in between his shoulders, making him cry out in alarm and pain. He turned, reaching for the growing red stain on the back of his shirt where I'd stabbed him.

"Maddie," he gasped, staring at me in shock. His face was drained of color. "Maddie, what are you—"

And I kept stabbing. Over and over again. He collapsed to the floor. He didn't fight me. After a few minutes, he gave his last gurgle. One final shuddering death rattle. It was only then that I stopped and realized the blade had already broken off inside of him. The plastic hilt was still in my bloody hand. I rose to my feet and stared down at myself. My dress was splattered with blood as well. So were my bare legs. I walked carefully around the body, giving the pool of blood on the floor a wide berth, and rushed out of the closet and up the stairs. I shoved the back door open with my shoulder, careful not to smear it with the Reverend's blood, and took the same path through the woods that I had used when I came.

Luckily, Father was still at work and Mom was away at the library. My brothers were playing at a friend's house nearby. I tore off my dress and stuffed it, my shoes, and the hilt of the knife in a garbage bag. I scrubbed and scrubbed in the shower, removing all traces of the Reverend's blood from my body and hair. By the time Mom's station wagon pulled into our driveway, I was dressed again and sitting at the kitchen table, pantomiming doing my homework. She walked past me, setting her canvas bag on the kitchen counter.

"How was school today?" she asked cheerfully.

"Good," I answered, forcing my voice not to shake.

"Glad to hear it. Almost done with your homework, Maddie? Do you want to help Mom with dinner?" She leaned over my shoulder and frowned before running her palm over my head. "Why is your hair wet?"

I shrugged, still looking down at my science textbook. "I got hot and sweaty during gym class, so I decided to take a shower when I got home."

"Ah," she said slowly, but the frown didn't disappear.

The Reverend's body was discovered that same day by the choir director. Soon, the gory details of the murder of the town reverend who had been accused of molesting a young girl were splashed all over the evening news. The police began their murder investigation, questioning suspects. Mr. Dorsey was high on the list, especially considering that he had publicly threatened the Reverend, but he had a solid alibi. People in town speculated that maybe the culprit was a vigilante who felt Reverend Brennan should be punished for his crimes. And only a few of them wanted the vigilante to get caught.

I waited for the cops to come for me. I had nightmares for weeks of them bursting through our front door and dragging me away in handcuffs while Mom cried and Father looked on. But they never did. They only questioned me once, on our front lawn with Father standing nearby, asking if I had ever seen anyone lurking around the Brennans' home while I babysat. I told them no, not hesitating before I answered because that was the truth. By then, I'd buried my trash bag of bloody items in the woods.

It's twenty years later and the case still remains unsolved in my hometown. No one suspects I did it. But about two months after the murder, while I stood in the kitchen helping Mom prepare breakfast, she asked me out of nowhere, "Maddie, do you have any idea what happened to my boning knife?"

I paused mid-stir of pancake batter and raised my eyes from the bowl to look up at her.

"The one in the butcher block," she elaborated, pointing to the wooden block near our farm sink. "It disappeared weeks ago. I haven't seen it since."

Her blue eyes were unwavering. Her face was stern.

I shook my head. "No," I said, not trusting my voice to utter more than that.

She gradually nodded. "All right."

I started to stir the batter again. She tossed slices of bacon into the pan that was already heating on the stove.

"I never should have taken you to that man," she said over the sound of crackling bacon. "It was like taking a lamb to the slaughter. He was not a man of God. He sinned and God smote him. He got what he deserved, in my opinion. May God have mercy on his soul."

✳ ✳ ✳

I take another sip of wine before I dial, now resolved that if I did it before, I can very well do it again. Kordell deserves to die just as much as that pedophile bastard Brennan had. And now I have maturity and resources on my side. I raise the cell phone to my ear and listen as it rings on the other end. After the third ring, a baritone voice rumbles, "Hello? KJ Custom Cabinetry. Kordell here."

"Hi, Kordell!" I say perkily, leaning my elbows on the cool marble. "My name is Vivian Newsome, and my husband and I are renovating our kitchen at our getaway home in western Maryland. I saw your work online and I was just amazed by your talent. I wondered if you would mind coming there and giving us an estimate for work we'd like done."

Kordell hesitates on the other end. "Well, I don't know about that. I'm kinda booked right now and I don't usually work that far out of the city."

"I understand, but I hope you're willing to make an allowance for us. I've just been at my wit's end trying to secure good contractors." I laugh. "We could make it worth your while. Double your rate, if necessary. And we would pay for your consultation, of course, so your time and mileage wouldn't be wasted. How does $500 sound?"

"Well, I guess I could work it out," he says. "Can I stop by on Saturday? Say around . . . uh . . . two o'clock?"

"That would be perfect!" I gush.

"All right then. Text me the address. OK?"

"I certainly will! See you soon." I then hang up and finish the rest of my wine.

CHAPTER 18

TASHA

"Good job today, Tasha!" Evelyn says as we walk out of the glass-enclosed meeting room.

It's the end of the day and we've had back-to-back meetings since nine a.m.

"I really appreciate your work on those PowerPoints," she says. "I know it was a rush job, but you couldn't tell."

"No problem," I say, holding back a yawn while we walk down the hall back to her office and my cubicle. I'm bone-tired and ready to go home, but I'll pretend I'm not until I'm out the door or at least in the elevator. "It's my job!"

"No, don't downplay yourself or your work." She pauses mid-step, making me stop next to her. "I've had plenty of executive assistants. Some not so great, unfortunately. I know a good assistant when I see one. You're really talented and whip-smart. Have you ever thought about getting additional training? Maybe some college courses. I don't know what your off-hours schedule is like, but it might be beneficial for your career. The company could help supplement the cost."

"Well, I . . . I always thought about getting my associate's degree . . . maybe in business administration."

Evelyn nods. "That's something to consider."

I'd always wanted to go back to school, but Kordell said it was too expensive. If the company was paying, maybe he'd be more willing to let me go to college. But then I think about the late nights I would spend in class, away from home. I think about the weekends I'd have to set aside doing homework and not catering to him. Would he ever stand for it?

Probably not. But Ghalen graduates from high school in June. I plan to leave Kordell soon after. I wouldn't need my husband's approval to take any classes; I'd be able to do what I want.

"Do some research," Evelyn says, "and get back to me. Let me know what courses you'd be interested in taking, with price estimates. We can work on it together and submit a proposal to HR."

"Thank you, Evelyn," I gush. "Thank you so much. I will!"

Fifteen minutes later, my cell phone buzzes as I step into the business-complex courtyard. I shove my hand into my coat pocket and yank it out, juggling my purse on my shoulder and the plastic strap of my umbrella on my wrist as I walk. When I see the message on my phone screen, I suck my teeth because even though I've had a long day, I know my day is about to get a lot longer.

"Oh, Lord," I mumble.

"What? What's wrong?" Morris asks beside me as we walk.

Every evening after work, he walks me to the Metro Center train station before he heads back to the garage to get his car and drive to Vienna, Virginia, where he lives. We don't hug or kiss goodbye just in case someone from the office sees us, but we always whisper, "See you tomorrow," and it feels just as good.

"Metro has delays," I now say. "I swear a day doesn't go by when some train isn't malfunctioning or a track hasn't caught on fire. I better text Kordell now and tell him that I'm going to be late, or he's gonna have a fit."

I pull up his number and start to text him, to tell him what happened.

Metro is a mess today, hon. Will probably be home later than usual. Will keep you updated.

I then send Kordell a link to the Metro alert to let him know I'm not lying before he can question me, which I know he will. He's been questioning me a lot more lately. Why'd it take you so long to come home? Who are you emailing? Who are you calling? I guess if I'm not miserable all the time, he gets suspicious. He can see the little light inside me that's starting to burn bright, now that I have a job, doing well at work, and I feel more independent. He wants to stomp it out.

"I can drive you home," Morris says without even hesitating, making me look up from my phone to stare at him.

"Are you crazy? You can't drive me home, Morris!" We leave the courtyard and make a right, heading toward the train station. "What if somebody sees you? *Sees us?* What if Kordell is home and—"

"I won't drop you off at your house. Not at the door. I'd let you out blocks away, if that makes you feel any better. No one would have to see us."

I begin to shake my head, but I stop as I watch all the people hustling to the escalators twenty feet away, teeming like fish to the tunnels below. I see myself doing the same, then standing on a crowded platform, then squeezing into an even more crowded train car. I'll stand for 30 minutes to an hour with sore feet and strangers rubbing up against me, with my hand gripped around one of the metal bars overhead until my arm goes sore, then numb. And then I'll miss my bus transfer and have to wait until the next one comes. Who knows when I'll finally make it home? Long after the sun goes down, I'd imagine. And when I do get home, Kordell will still expect me to slave over a kitchen stove and put food on the table for him to eat.

I close my eyes. "OK," I say.

Morris smiles. "OK? You'll let me drive you home?"

I nod. "Yes, I'll accept a ride. Thank you. But you have to drop me off at least four blocks away. I'll have to walk the rest of the way there."

"Understood. But in the meantime, we can finally try that Greek takeout place I've been telling you about that opens at five o'clock. It's about six blocks away, and they make the best falafel that—"

"Morris," I moan, "I can't get dinner with you! I have to go home."

He turns to look at me. "But didn't you just tell your husband that the Metro was backed up and you'd be home later than usual? Won't it be strange if you show up home early instead?"

I purse my lips. Morris does have a point.

He places a hand on my shoulder. "Try the falafel. We can be in and out in twenty minutes. You can eat it in the car as I drive." He gives me a wink. "You won't regret it. I promise."

I laugh, always finding it hard to resist this man's charm. "All right, but we buy it and get it to go, but that's it! *Understand*, Mr. Hammond?"

"Understood." He chuckles, grabs my hand, and guides me down the block, in the other direction from the Metro station. I am happy to follow him.

✳ ✳ ✳

I climb the stairs to my home and open the chain-link gate. I close it behind me with a loud squeak and the scrape of metal over concrete before I tiredly follow the path to the front door. The sun is down and the lights shine bright inside my house. Judging from the pickup truck parked out front, Kordell has beat me home. Before I can pull out my keys, the door pops open. Ghalen stands in the doorway. His dark eyes are wide. His face looks stricken, making me frown.

"What's the matter, baby?" I ask him, taking a step closer and reaching for his face. "Did something happen at school today?"

He shakes his head and swallows, making his Adam's apple bob over the collar of his T-shirt. "Dad's been waiting for you."

"Well, all right," I say, waiting for Ghalen to explain more.

Of course, Kordell is waiting for me. I've been sending him text messages all throughout the evening while I was with Morris, typing fake updates, letting him know I was still on my way.

I take another step forward to walk through the door, but Ghalen blocks my path.

"I don't know what you did, but he's mad, Ma," he whispers to me. "*Real* mad."

I bite down hard on my bottom lip, the lips that Morris kissed only minutes ago before we said goodbye. I can still taste him there somewhere under all the cumin, onion, and garlic. We kissed over five blocks away in his darkened car so none of my neighbors could see us. Had Kordell been nearby? Could he have seen us?

"Is that your Mama?" Kordell shouts over the blare of the TV, right on cue. "Is she out there?"

Ghalen looks over his shoulder, but doesn't answer him. His whole body goes tense. I take a deep breath and ease my son aside. "It's OK, baby. No need to worry," I whisper, rubbing his shoulder, hoping to reassure him though I'm just as scared as he is, not knowing what I'm about to walk into. "It'll be fine."

I step past Ghalen, take off my coat, hang it in the hall closet, and make my way to our living room. Kordell is sitting on the sofa, glaring up at the flat-screen TV that's hanging on our wall. He has a beer in one hand and the remote in the other. Three empty beer bottles sit on the coffee table in front of him. When I walk into the room, he turns away from the television. He raises the remote and mutes the volume. His glare is on me now.

"Well, there she is!" Kordell cries. "Your lying ass is finally home, huh?"

"The . . . the Metro was . . . was delayed," I mumble. "I–I told you it was."

He laughs and slowly shakes his head before taking a drink from the bottle. "You weren't on no damn Metro train, Tasha. Don't keep lyin' to me."

I nod. "Y-y-yes, I was. I took the Red line . . . then the . . . the Blue line. Then I took the—"

"Stop lying to me!" he explodes, shooting to his feet and throwing his bottle to the floor. Glass flies everywhere. Beer oozes into the living room rug.

Ghalen rushes to the living room entryway and I hold up my hand and look at him. I shake my head, motioning for him to stay back.

"You think I'm stupid, don't you? You take the same damn path everyday, woman," Kordell says. "The same goddamn route. And today you didn't take it." He grabs his phone that's sitting next to the other beer bottles and holds it up, shoving it at me. "I saw it here! Right here!" He points at the screen. "You didn't get on any train. You went to a restaurant in the city and you stayed there for 23 minutes. To get home, you went through the Third Street Tunnel. What were you doin', Tasha? Who the hell were you with?"

I stare in shock at his phone screen that shows a yellow line tracking my route for the day. I see all my twists and turns like a mouse in a maze. Did he install an app on *my phone?*

"Answer me!" he yells.

But I don't. I can't find any words. My mind is racing with thoughts, and they all pile up on each other, clogging in my throat.

"I was nice to you! I trusted you and let you out of this house. I let you have your phone back. Didn't I? Didn't I, Ghalen?" he shouts to our son. "I let her go to work every day, and this . . . this is what she does to me?"

Ghalen hasn't moved an inch, and I hope it stays that way. I don't want him to get in the middle. I don't want him to get hurt.

"Well, I'm gonna fix her ass!" He kicks aside the coffee table, making me jump back. "You're not leaving this house until *I* say you can." He points at his chest. "You hear me? You're gonna call that office and you're gonna tell them you quit and—"

"No," I say, catching us both off guard.

Kordell narrows his eyes at me. "What the hell did you say?"

"I said . . . I said no." I can't meet his eyes as I say it. I know if I do, I'll lose my nerve, but I can't leave Myers Trust. That would mean no more Morris and no more work friends. No more independence. I'd lose my chance to go back to college. I'd just be stuck home again, staring at four walls. "I'm not . . . I'm not gonna quit. I like my job. I want . . . I want to stay," I say.

"I wasn't asking you what you wanted to do," Kordell says through clenched teeth. "I'm telling you."

"I'm not quitting my job, Kordell, and you can't make me stay in this house." I finally raise my eyes to look at him, and the fury on his face terrifies me, but I keep talking. "This isn't a jail. I'm a grown woman. You can't make me do it."

Our living room goes quiet, so quiet that I can hear the cars driving down the street outside. I can hear the neighbor's screen door open and close with a thwack. One of her cats lets out a yowl. The quiet stretches for I don't know how long until Kordell finally breaks it by leaping for me with arms outstretched, but I'm faster than he is and I jump out of his reach. I run down the hall toward our bedroom and he grabs for me again. He gets the back of my shirt, but Ghalen wraps an arm around his waist and tries with all his might to hold him back. I wrench away and watch helplessly as they both fall to the hallway floor.

"Get off me! Get the hell off me!" Kordell yells, shoving our son away. He rises to his feet first, turns, and grabs Ghalen by the collar of his shirt with his fist raised as if he's about to hit him, and I scream for Kordell to stop. He freezes.

"I've never called the police on you before, but I swear to God, if you lay a hand on that boy, I will do it!" I say, pulling my cell out of my purse. Tears flood my eyes.

He turns to look at me, but he doesn't let go of Ghalen's collar.

"I'll call them right now, and they will take you away in hand-cuffs. I'll tell them how you abused me, how you held me prisoner here and took away my car keys . . . my credit cards." My tears start to spill over and race down my cheeks. "And I will let you rot in jail! You hear me?"

He slowly lowers his fist and lets go of Ghalen, who falls back to the floor again. Kordell stares at me.

"You'd really do that to me, Tasha?" he asks, having the nerve to sound hurt. "You'd do that to your own husband?"

"You stopped being my husband a long time ago."

He stares at me a bit longer before looking down at Ghalen. He then steps over our son and keeps walking down the hall.

"Dad!" Ghalen calls after him as Kordell cuts through the living room. Ghalen pushes himself up to his elbows and knees just as the front door slams shut. "Dad, where you going?" he shouts.

We hear the rumble of Kordell's Ford truck engine next, and Ghalen goes racing for the front door, racing after his father.

"Ma, we can't let him drive! He's been drinking!" he yells as he thunders down the hall, almost tripping over the rug as he enters the living room. "He could kill himself!"

But I don't move. I don't budge one inch, not even to wipe my runny nose or my eyes.

I stay flat against the wall and mutter words I'd never thought I'd say.

"Then let the bastard die," I whisper.

CHAPTER 19

MADISON

"OK, YOU GUYS! NOW I WANT YOU TO PUSH IT! WE'RE ALMOST AT the finish line," the instructor yells over the heavy bass of the dance music pounding its way through the concealed speakers. "You can do this! Ready? One, two . . . one, two, three! Go-o-o-o!"

At her rallying cry, I rise on my stationary bike, gritting my teeth and feeling sweat pour into my eyes. My legs burn as I pedal. So does my throat. But I will not stop. I refuse to.

"Oh, my God! Oh, my God!" Summer moans beside me.

I glance over my shoulder at her in the flashing blue and purple lights. Summer's arms are trembling as she grips the handlebars. Her eyes are closed and her mouth is slack. She looks like she's on the verge of dry heaving, even though she's the one who suggested we take this morning spin class in the first place.

She isn't the only one who sounds like she's in sheer agony. A woman behind me lets out a series of yelps as if she's mid-labor and is pushing out her baby on the hardwood floor. In contrast, two rows in front of us, another woman in a ponytail is whooping at the top of her lungs with her head thrown back. She's whipping her hand towel around and around in the air as she bikes like some deranged party raver pumped full of ecstasy. It isn't a surprise since the atmosphere in the workout room is a weird mix of club vibes and sadomasochistic torture. The blessed few who've crested the mountain of pain are high on endorphins and dopamine. Or maybe she actually took something before class and is just high.

"I want you to hold it! Hold it! Hold it!" the instructor orders. "For ten . . . nine . . . eight . . . seven . . . six . . . five . . . four . . . three . . . two . . . one! You made it!" She lowers herself onto the seat and grins. "Give yourselves a round of applause!"

Several of those around me begin to clap, including the woman in pseudo-labor. Summer emits another groan. Nearly an hour later, we stroll out of the women's locker room and into the gym's center lobby. Instead of feeling tired, I'm now energized and ready to face the day and the task ahead of me.

"That was *insane!* That completely sapped me. Seriously," Summer says as we head toward the doors. Her hair is still damp so it hangs limply around her shoulders. She turns to me, snapping her fingers. "Hey, you know what we should do? You should tell your driver to pick you up later. We can walk to Fruitive at CityCenter. They have these wellness shots that will—"

"I'm sorry, but I can't." I adjust my scarf around my shoulders. "Unfortunately, I have to get going. I have something else I have to do today."

"Oh, no!" she says. Her big hazel eyes go wide. Her voice goes up a little. It comes out like a whine.

Since Tom filed for divorce, she's been emotionally needy, calling me two or three times a week, offering to meet for lunch or dinner or a spa day at the Four Seasons. I finally conceded and agreed to take this spin class with her. I realize not everyone is as resilient as I am. She needs reassurance, something to distract her from what her life has become, and I was willing to humor her for a while, but even I have my limits. Besides, I have a full schedule and I can't afford any delays.

"What do you have to do?" she asks.

I shrug and smile. "Just a few errands," I say, then push the glass door open. As we step outside, I kiss her cheek, which is still warm from the steamy showers. Tony is at the curb, illegally parked and waiting for me. "I'll see you soon."

"Well, O . . . umm . . . OK," Summer replies limply, watching me as I climb into the back of the Town Car and Tony shuts the door behind me.

I give Tony the rest of the day off after he deposits me at our front door. When I get inside, I check the clock on the living room wall. It is 10:48 a.m. I don't have much time.

I drop my gym bag to the floor, but I don't take off my coat. I climb the stairs to our bedroom and head to Phil's walk-in closet. At the back, hidden behind his neckties and suit jackets, is a wall safe. I shove the garments aside and tap in the combination. The metal door pops open with a click. I shove aside the lockbox of important documents and the few velvet cases filled with jewelry and reach for the leather case toward the back. I take it out and open the zipper. A loaded pistol is inside.

Phil bought it about four years ago, surprising me by setting it on the bed one night as I was brushing my teeth. Though he hates guns, a string of robberies nearby in our neighborhood led him to conclude that some form of protection was necessary.

"I'm storing it here, in the top drawer," he said, before tucking it into his dresser and hiding it beneath a nest of black trouser socks. "I hope we don't ever have to use it, but I remember what happened to Ashley. She'd probably still be alive if she'd been able to protect herself from that animal that day. I don't want either of us to be put in the same predicament. To be . . . you know . . . caught off guard."

Like most responsible gun owners, we went to a firing range in Virginia a few times to practice, but that was the only time we ever fired the pistol. After a year or so, the robber Phil feared never manifested, so the gun made its way from Phil's top dresser drawer to the wall safe and was gradually forgotten. I think Phil was happy to be rid of it, to not have to see it every time he got up in the morning and dressed.

I hold the gun now. I don't remember it being so heavy the last time I handled it, but it's been a while. I make sure the safety is on, take the stance the instructor told me to take at the range, and point it at the wall. I then sigh, close the safe, and tuck the pistol into my purse, hoping I still know how to use it when the time comes.

At 10:56 a.m., I step out my front door, locking it behind me. I walk swiftly for five blocks. As I turn the corner, I see a young man with a soul patch standing beside a tan 2018 Jeep Cherokee—the rental car I reserved. He's blowing hot air into his bare hands as he waits for me while shivering in the late-January cold.

"Hello!" I call cheerfully to him.

"You Madison Gingell?" he asks, pushing himself away from the SUV as I approach.

"Yes, I am." I glance at the keys he's holding in his pale, chapped hand. "I'll take those," I say, but he pulls them out of reach.

"I have to see your license first. Then you have to sign this." He lowers his jacket zipper and tugs out a digital tablet.

I slowly exhale, nod, and open my purse, pulling out my wallet. I attempt to hand him my driver's license, but he doesn't reach for it. He's staring at something else. I follow his gaze and see that his eyes have landed on the pistol, which is nestled between a gold compact and my tube of hand cream. I reach down and close the zipper. I clear my throat, making his eyes snap back to my face, making his mouth snap close.

"You said that you needed to see my license," I say firmly, shoving it at him again. "Here it is."

He gradually nods and takes it from me, confirming my name with the one that is on his digital screen. Five minutes later, I'm behind the wheel of the Jeep Cherokee, heading to the Beltway to drive out of the city.

✳ ✳ ✳

Kordell is late. Very late. I rushed here and arrived an hour early for absolutely no reason, and now I'm irritated. I hope he doesn't usually behave this way with potential clients. It shows a lack of professionalism.

I glance at my watch as I lean against the side of the Cherokee where the back tire is now lying in the trunk space and a spare lies on the ground near the rear bumper. I am partially blocking the lane along an isolated back road a few miles outside of Hancock in western Maryland.

There isn't a house for miles around, with the exception of an old barn in the distance that is completely stripped of paint and covered in frost and snow. It leans at an odd angle and a few of the boards are missing. It is the stuff that ghost stories are made of. The road itself also feels ghostly. The howl of the Appalachian Mountain wind is the only thing that keeps me company as I wait. No cars have driven past me since I've been here, but I purposely chose this desolate place.

Not only will it be nearly impossible for me to miss Kordell *whenever* he arrives, since it is the only road en route to the address I gave him, but I also can do what needs to be done without interruption.

Finally, I hear what sounds like a car engine. I push myself away from the SUV and squint into the distance. I can see a blue pickup truck, drawing closer and closer. As it nears and the driver comes into view, I force a smile, stand in the center of the roadway, and wave my arms. Kordell slows to a stop. He hops out of the cab. He isn't smiling in return. His brows are furrowed. His face is marred with a deep frown. Now that he's standing at his full height, I can see that he is as tall and big in person as he seemed in the Instagram photos.

Inwardly, I bemoan that Billy isn't here himself or here to assist me. If this turns into a struggle, I could use my little brother's help. But I hope it doesn't come to that. I'll just have to keep my wits about me, and they have never failed me before. I've been underestimated. I was by Reverend Brennan, Phil, and many other men in my past. But I am not a weak, helpless woman. I have no need to fear, because I am not the prey. Kordell should be afraid of me.

"Good afternoon!" I nearly sing, striding toward him. "Are you Kordell Jenkins?"

He closes his driver's-side door and nods. "Uh, yeah. Are you Mrs. Newsome?"

His eyes are bloodshot. His face isn't cleanly shaven. Dare I say, he looks hungover. That might explain his tardiness.

"I am indeed!" I offer him my gloved hand. "I hope it wasn't hard to get here. I was wondering if you got held up by traffic."

He shakes his head and my hand. "No . . . uh . . . no traffic. I just had a busy morning. My apologies. I would have called, but I left my—"

"Oh, that's fine! Actually, you've come at the perfect time." I gesture to the Jeep Cherokee. "I was heading to the house and got a flat along the way. I tried to change the tire myself, but it's been a struggle." I give a self-deprecating laugh and toss my hair over my shoulder. "I was wondering if you could assist me and I can escort you to the house?"

"Oh, yeah! Umm, no problem." He walks back to his truck. "Let me pull out of the road and see what I can do."

A minute later, he strolls toward the SUV. The Jeep Cherokee sits at a diagonal with the front tires in the right-hand lane. The rear is only two or three feet away from a steep slope that leads to a thicket-filled ditch—what will be, if everything goes according to plan, Kordell's final resting place.

"Again, I got the tire off myself," I say as I trail him. "I even got the car jack to work, which was a miracle in itself, but I'm having a heck of a time getting the spare on."

"You did all that by yourself?" Kordell looks over his shoulder at me, sounding incredulous.

"Is that so surprising?"

He shrugs and doesn't comment further before dropping to his knees on the asphalt near the missing wheel. He then gets to work.

"I wish my husband had come with me today, but he couldn't get away from the city. He had to go in to the office for meetings. He's an investment banker," I say, making small talk as Kordell puts the spare tire on. But he doesn't join me in conversation. He continues to work silently.

"My husband grew up in the country," I begin a few minutes later as I reach inside my purse and grip my hand around the pistol. "We bought the property as a weekend getaway. Something to break up the monotony of city life and remind my husband of home. You know?"

Kordell grunts in reply as he begins to screw on the lug nuts that are sitting in the overturned hubcap. I disengage the pistol's safety.

"We also saw it as an investment property," I drone on as I stand over his shoulder and he screws on the second-to-last nut. "We got it at a cheap price and figured with the upgrades that we'll be able to make double our money back if we try to resale it." I pull out the gun and raise it.

Smooth sailing so far. This looks like it's going to be easier than I thought it would be. If the traffic works with me, I can make it back to the city, kick off my shoes, put on a robe, drink a cup of my fav turmeric and chili loose-leaf tea, and decompress before Phil arrives home.

Kordell grunts again, then reaches for the last lug nut. As he does, I level the gun so the muzzle is pointed at the back of his head. Then everything goes haywire. As he grips the lug nut, he catches my reflection in the hubcap. Our eyes meet for a brief second or two. Just as I'm about to fire, he jumps back like something bit him, knocking into me, making me tumble to the icy cold asphalt. The gun fires into the air.

"Shit! What the hell!" he shouts.

My head hits the asphalt and I blink at the stars that explode in my vision. I hear him scrambling as if he's reaching for the gun. My heart jumps into my throat and I clutch the pistol even firmer in my hand. Though it feels like minutes, it actually only takes me a few seconds to get my bearings. I see that Kordell isn't reaching for the gun. I thought he would fight me. I should have known better. Bullies like him expect submission. They don't know what to do when they get the opposite. Instead of fighting, he's racing for his truck, trying to get away, and I can't let that happen.

"This crazy bitch is trying to kill me!" he yells to no one in particular. The ghosts in the barn, perhaps. "She's tryin' to kill me!"

As he wrenches open the door, I fire. I fire again and again and again, until he crumples to the ground.

CHAPTER 20

TASHA

"You two leavin' now, Ghalen?" I call from my bedroom. I set the book I'm reading on my night table and rise from my bed.

I can hear movement in the living room. I walk into the hall and find my son and his girlfriend standing by the door, putting on their coats—*finally*.

"Yeah, we're headin' out," Ghalen says. His voice is as flat as paper.

He and Imani are supposed to go out tonight. Ghalen's basketball team is headed to the finals for the first time in years, so the school is holding a rally and his coach is throwing a party at his house after to celebrate. I know Ghalen doesn't want to go. He's worried about his daddy. He's been calling him all day, leaving texts and voicemails. That man still hasn't called him back, and it's been eating away at him. I know that not wanting to offend or disappoint his teammates and his coach is the only thing that's getting my son out the door tonight, and I'm grateful. Ghalen needs a distraction from Kordell and his madness. We *both* do.

"Be safe," I say before I give Ghalen a hug and rub his back. "Try to enjoy yourself, OK?"

Ghalen gives a halfhearted nod. He has that same sad, lost look on his face. It hasn't budged at all. I really do hope he can cheer up a little tonight. Our lives will be better without Kordell around. Just wait and see.

I turn to Imani, give her a hug too, and cup her face. "You make sure he doesn't mope around the whole time and try to have some fun yourself. You hear me?"

She giggles. "Yes, Mrs. Jenkins."

"Ghalen, you be careful driving home. Imani, you tell your folks I said hello. All right?" I wave as they walk out the door. "And don't stay out too late! Be home by midnight."

"OK, Ma," Ghalen says, shutting the door behind them.

When I hear the lock click, I reach into the pocket of my wool sweater, take out my cell phone, and type a quick text to Morris. I've been waiting to send it all evening.

They're leaving now. I'm ready whenever you are.

In seconds, I see three blinking dots.

I'm on my way, Morris types back. He's probably been ready all night to hop out the door, just like I have.

I drop the phone back into my pocket and start to walk back to my bedroom to change my clothes, but stop short when I hear a shout. "Just get in the car! Damn!"

It sounds like my son.

I rush to the window facing the street. "What in the world," I mutter as I part the blinds. I watch the kids climb into my car to drive to the rally.

I see Imani in the passenger seat, buckling her seat belt. She's frowning just as much as I am right now as Ghalen slams her door closed. He climbs behind the wheel and slams the driver's door, too. They drive off with tires squealing.

I close the blinds.

Did he really shout at her? Ghalen knows better than to talk to Imani like that, even if he is upset about his daddy. He can't take it out on anyone, especially his girlfriend.

I want to call him, to give him a piece of my mind over the phone, but I know I don't have time for that. Morris is on his way, and I know we only have three to four hours together before Ghalen gets back home. I'll have to talk to my son later about being more respectful to his girlfriend, to not forget himself again; but for now, I have to get ready to go.

It's time for me and Morris to have our own celebration.

✳ ✳ ✳

"I know you don't usually drink," Morris says as he walks out of his kitchen, "but it seems like the occasion calls for it."

I turn around on his sofa to look over my shoulder. I find him grinning and holding a bottle of champagne in one hand and two champagne flutes in the other. He sets the glasses on the coffee table and sits down on the cushion beside me.

"Are you up for it?" he asks.

I can see a twinkle in his dark eyes.

I pretend to think it over for a while, then nod. "I guess I can try just for one night."

He pops the cork and the champagne shoots out like it's coming from a garden hose. It spills on the table and his carpet like in the movies. We both laugh.

It's my first time at his place. Morris offered to take me out to a restaurant so we could celebrate my finally being a free woman, but we eat out so much at work that a dinner at a nice restaurant didn't feel as special as a dinner alone with him that he cooked with his own two hands. And I like it here in his place.

The furniture is simple. There are lots of grays and blues. There are pictures of his daughter, his parents, and his fraternity brothers on his bookshelf and the walls. There's soft music playing in the background. I smell the butter-shrimp casserole cooking in his oven. It's peaceful here. Calm. It's not like my home that has a coffee table missing. It's now sitting in the garage because Kordell broke one of the legs last night when he kicked it over. I'm still finding pieces of glass in the rug from where Kordell threw down his beer bottle. The walls at my house have so many scary and sad memories. I'm glad to be away from it.

I try to imagine living here in this home with Morris some day. Barefoot in his kitchen cooking meals on the stove. Snuggling beside him on this sofa as we watch television after a long day at work.

You never know. Maybe it's possible, now that Kordell is gone.

Morris pours the champagne, and I take a sip. The bubbles make my nose tickle, and I laugh again.

"I'm really proud of you, Tasha," Morris says after taking a drink. His grin disappears. He looks serious now. "I know what you did wasn't easy, but you stood up to him."

"Truth is that I was gonna run away from him that night, hide in the bedroom, and lock the door. I was prepared to stay in there all night if I had to. But he turned on Ghalen—something I was always scared he was gonna do—and . . . and something in me just . . . it just snapped, Morris. I just got tired of running away."

"Well, whatever reason, I'm glad you did it," he says, reaching out to grab my hand.

I stare down at our hands, at the way his fingers fit through mine.

"I know it hasn't been easy for you either," I whisper. "All these years. The distance between us."

"We don't have to talk about that anymore. It wasn't like I sat around waiting. I told you—"

"No, we do need to talk about it." I put down my champagne flute, look up from our hands, and gaze into his eyes. "You didn't sit around, and I'm happy that you didn't. You got married. You had your beautiful daughter. But when we came back into each other's lives, it was just like we were back then. Back before the car accident. Back when I told you I was going to run away with you. It was like time hadn't passed. Very few men would have done all that you've done. Few would be as patient and kind. Thank you for supporting me. Thank you for encouraging me. Thank you for loving me, Morris."

I lean forward and kiss him, trying to show Morris with my lips what I'm struggling to say with my words. He puts down his glass, too, and pulls me close. He kisses me back. His lips are firm and strong. His beard is rough and coarse against my cheek, but I still love the feel of it against my skin. When I pull back from him more than a minute later, we're both breathless.

"Take me to your bedroom," I whisper.

He frowns, surprised by what I'm saying, by what I'm asking.

We've never been intimate before. Not fully, anyway. But I'm ready tonight. I've had seventeen-plus years to get ready, and I don't want to wait any longer.

I cup his face. "Take me there, please," I repeat. "Unless you don't want to."

"No, I want to. I *want* to," he says, all eager. "I just . . . I . . ."

"You just what?" I lower my hands from his face and shift back. "What's wrong?"

He glances over his shoulder at the kitchen. "I gotta take out the casserole. It's gonna burn."

I laugh and give him a quick peck. "OK, don't burn the casserole. Meanwhile, point me to the bedroom and I'll meet you in there."

"Up the stairs. Second room on your right."

Five minutes later, I can hear Morris banging around in the kitchen downstairs as I undress. I hear a loud clatter that sounds like he dropped a dish. Maybe a pan.

"Is everything OK down there?" I call out, frowning.

"Uh, yeah. Yeah, I'm . . . I'm fine! Just . . . uh . . . just cleaning up! I'll be up there in a little bit. No worries," he calls back.

I can hear the nervousness in his voice. Even though I want this, I'm a little nervous too.

I turn and look at my reflection in his bedroom mirror.

I'm in my underwear. I wish I had worn something nicer tonight, something sexier, but I haven't owned anything lacy or sexy in years. I hadn't been in the mood to wear it. Not for Kordell. But I want this moment to be special, and instead I'm wearing the same beige bra and panties that I put on when I go to the grocery store.

I run my hands over my breasts and the softness of my tummy. I stare at my dimpled thighs, not feeling so appealing, trying to find a desirable woman and not a tired mother and wife.

"Damn, you're beautiful," I hear Morris say, like he was reading my mind. Like he knew the perfect moment to utter those words. "You know that?"

I turn away from the mirror to find him standing in the bedroom doorway, leaning against the frame. There's so much love in his eyes—and want. He wants me, despite the beige underwear and butt dimples.

"You make me feel beautiful," I whisper as he walks across the room and wraps me in his arms.

When he lowers his mouth to mine, all my nerves smooth over. I feel as much want and need as Morris does. When he eases me back onto his bed, I pull him toward me and don't want to let go. Morris is as gentle with my body as he's been with my heart. We make love slowly, savoring every minute, every kiss, and every touch. At the end, I lie on top of him and close my eyes, feeling his warm skin pressed against my cheek and his heartbeat under my ear.

"Do you remember the first day we met?" I ask him out of nowhere.

"Of course I do."

"There's no 'of course'!" I laugh. "It happened almost two decades ago."

"Doesn't matter," he says, making his ribcage vibrate beneath me. "I remember anyway. I let you use my key badge to get back through the door on our floor."

"I was so embarrassed. I'd only been on the job a few weeks and I'd already lost mine. I was so happy you walked by. I thought I was going to have to stand out there forever until someone finally came out and opened the door for me."

"I didn't mind. I'd been waiting for the chance to talk to you."

I raise my head to squint at him. "Huh?"

"I'd seen you around the office a few times." Morris gives a sly smile. "The pretty new assistant. I knew your name but hadn't introduced myself yet."

"I didn't know that! Why didn't you just stop by my desk and say hello?"

"I didn't want to come off too strong. But then I saw you waiting by the door that day, looking desperate. It seemed like the perfect opportunity to say hi. I could play the hero and you'd think I was sexy."

I laugh again before giving him a quick kiss and resting my head back on his chest. "And we hit it off right away."

"And then I found out you were married."

"I know. But we still became friends. We couldn't keep away from each other. You were always so easy to talk to. And I liked the way I felt about myself . . . about the world, whenever I was around you. Everything seemed . . . nicer, warmer. It still does, Morris."

His breathing goes deeper and deeper, slower and slower. He's starting to drift off to sleep.

"Being with you is like being in a magic bubble. It's not like the world outside of it disappears, but it just feels like a happier place. Like nothing bad can touch me here. It's why I always find it so hard to leave you."

But I have to leave tonight. Even if I don't want to. Morris knows that, too, which is why I nudge him when I start to hear his snores.

"Morris," I say, nudging him again. "Morris, wake up."

His eyes pop open. He yawns and smacks his lips. "Huh?"

"It's already almost eleven o'clock. I have to go. Ghalen will be home soon."

He grumbles. "Why do I feel like we're teenagers and I'm taking you back home so you can sneak through your bedroom window before your parents find out you're gone?"

"I don't know," I whisper as I leave a trail of butterfly kisses along his bare chest and shoulder. "But I would have been more than happy to sneak out the window for you."

"That's what all the girls say," he mumbles as I slide off him. He throws back the sheets and climbs off the bed. "Give me ten minutes, and I'll be ready to go."

✳ ✳ ✳

When Morris pulls up to the curb, I see the lights are on in the house like I left them, but my car is still gone. Ghalen and Imani must still be at the party. I beat him home, but I'm not eager to hop out of Morris's car and head inside. I want to drag the moment out a little longer.

"I'm sorry we didn't get to eat dinner," I whisper.

"We skipped dinner and went straight to dessert," he says, making me laugh. "Trust me, I didn't mind at all. Besides, I can always eat the leftovers. That casserole will last me all week."

"I enjoyed tonight. And I mean more than just the sex!" I smack his arm as he wiggles his eyebrows and chuckles. "The only thing that would've made it more perfect was to wake up there in bed with you. It would've been nice to spend the night together."

"We will one day." He leans toward me. "One day very soon, I hope."

I hope so, too. Next week, I plan to head to the courthouse to officially file for divorce from Kordell, but I don't tell Morris this. I want to give him a copy of the paperwork. Maybe wrap it in a big, red bow, because it feels like it's just as much a gift for him as it is for me. Something to reward us both for being so patient for so long. So instead of telling him about my plans for divorce, I hold off on the surprise and grab his hand and squeeze it. I raise my other hand to his face, lean over, and give him a kiss. Morris kisses me back, and then kisses my knuckles so tenderly it makes my insides melt.

"You better head in before Ghalen gets here, or you really will have to climb through a window."

I nod and unlock the car door. "Text me when you get home."

He nods back. "I will."

He waits until I climb up the stairs to my front door and I close it behind me. As I turn the lock, I hear his car drive off.

CHAPTER 21

TASHA

That Monday morning, I stand in my kitchen and pour coffee into my mug, replaying this weekend in my mind. Morris's kisses on my skin. Him holding me tight. It keeps coming to me in flashes. Without even thinking about it, I smile and start singing with the music playing on the TV commercial, but I stop myself. I remember that I'm supposed to be sad and worried like my son is right now, not happy and singing.

His daddy still hasn't come back home. I thought he'd come back by now to at least get some change of clothes. A man can only walk around but so long in dirty underwear, but we haven't seen hide nor hair of him. Ghalen keeps calling, but Kordell still hasn't called him back. He hasn't replied to one text either. I look over my shoulder and find Ghalen with his elbows on the table. He isn't looking at the TV on the kitchen counter, but staring down into his cereal bowl. He's slowly stirring the spoon around in his Cheerios, but not taking a single bite. He hasn't really eaten anything since Kordell left. I even made him waffles and eggs yesterday, and it just sat on his plate, getting cold. He can't keep this up.

I walk across the kitchen and rub his arm. "You've gotta eat something before you head out to school, baby. Try a few spoonfuls."

He looks up from the bowl, gnawing his bottom lip. "I don't know why he still hasn't come back. Why hasn't he even called, Ma?"

I pull out one of the other chairs at the kitchen table and sit down. "I don't know, honey."

"How could he just . . . just *leave*? I was talking to the guys at the party, and they said he could've had a car accident. He could be in the hospital right now and we don't even know it. He was drinking that night, Ma."

"Your daddy drinks every night. A few beers ain't gonna hurt him."

The morning news is on, and the woman and man at the news desk are laughing at something on screen. A dog in sunglasses balancing on a surfboard, I think. The sound of laughter doesn't feel right at this moment, like someone breaking into giggles at a funeral. I grab the remote and turn down the volume so that the kitchen is quiet again. I rest my hand on top of Ghalen's. "Look, your daddy was real angry that night and he did stuff he probably isn't . . . well . . . that he isn't proud of."

Like almost punching his own boy in the face, I think, but don't say it.

"Maybe he's just embarrassed, so he's staying away for now," I say instead.

"But why not tell us where he is, though? He could let us know he's OK . . . where he's stayin'. Why hasn't he done that?"

I shrug. "I don't know, baby."

And honestly, I don't care. Kordell could stay gone, as far as I'm concerned. I'd be happy to pack boxes of all his things and ship them to wherever he's disappeared to, but I know that's not the answer my son wants to hear.

The throaty sound of a big car engine fills the kitchen, making us both look up. Ghalen's eyes jump to the kitchen window in search of Kordell. His face looks hopeful and eager. Meanwhile, I suck in a deep breath, bracing myself for the thud of Kordell's footsteps on the front porch, the creak of the front door as it opens, and the crash of the screen door as it shuts behind him. Then he'll shout, "Where are you, Tasha? Get in here!"

But I don't hear any of it. The car engine keeps revving, and the truck drives away. It isn't Kordell. He hasn't returned home. Thank God. Ghalen's face falls, and he stares into his cereal bowl again.

"How about this?" I say, squeezing Ghalen's hand. "How about I call a few of your daddy's friends and ask them if he's staying with them, or if they've heard from him. I'll let them know you're waiting to hear back from him. They'll tell him to finally call you."

Ghalen looks up at me again. He stops gnawing his lip. "Thanks, Ma."

I reach up and brush his dreads out of his eyes, smile, and point at his bowl. "Now eat."

He blows air through his nose, giving me that annoyed look he always gives when he thinks I'm babying him. He then shoves the spoon into his mouth with a slurp of milk. "Happy now?" he asks between chews.

"Yes." I kiss his cheek and raise the volume again on the TV.

✳ ✳ ✳

"So, you still haven't heard from him? Not since Friday night, right?" Morris asks before taking a bite of his taco.

I nod as I sip my soda. "Not one single word."

We are on our lunch break at the Mexican eatery where we had our first lunch together. It isn't crowded today; most of the tables are empty. The waitstaff behind the counter look bored.

"Well, you know how I feel about it," Morris mutters, wiping his mouth with a napkin. "You're much better off without him around. Good riddance to bad rubbish."

"Amen," I whisper, then sigh. "I don't want him back, but I know he won't stay gone forever. We're still married, Morris." At least for now. "The house is in both our names. He left with just the clothes on his back that night. Except for the tools he keeps in his truck, all his stuff is still at home."

"You aren't really going to call his friends, are you? Why should you have to track him down? He's the one who walked out."

"I shouldn't, but I told Ghalen I would. I guess I could call at least one of them. Just to keep my promise."

Morris slouches back in his chair and drops his napkin onto the table. He doesn't say anything.

"What?" I ask. "What's wrong?"

"Nothing. I mean . . ." He looks like he's fighting to find the words, making me wonder what he's about to say. "I mean, I get that you want to be a good mother and all, but . . ."

"But?"

"But don't you think you take it just a little too far sometimes, Tasha?"

"Take what too far?"

"With the self-sacrificing . . . with putting him first? Calling after the man who abuses you, just to keep a promise to your son . . . that doesn't sound crazy to you?"

"Morris," I say, feeling irritated with him for the first time in a long time.

"I'm just saying, you don't—"

"I *know* what you're saying, and I don't want to argue. I'm not gonna argue. You're a father. You'd do anything for your daughter too, wouldn't you? Risk your life if you have to. Take a bullet for her."

"Yes, but—"

"There's no buts. Mothers . . . *parents* who love their children take care of them. They do what they have to do. Calling his friend isn't that big of a deal."

"Tasha, it *is* a big deal when—"

"I don't want to argue about this! I've got enough drama in my life right now. I don't need any more. OK?"

He's reminding me of Dr. Green now, of the way she would needle me whenever I talked about Ghalen.

"You talk often about protecting Ghalen and sacrificing for him, though you never seem to consider that *you* may also need protection and nurturing, Tasha," she said once during one of our sessions. "Why is that?"

"Because I'm the mother and he's the son," I said. "And it's not just that. You're a black woman. All you have to do is turn on the TV and look at the news to see why I'm doing what I'm doing. A black man in America, *especially* a young black man, needs nurturing and protecting."

"Understood. But I see our faces on the news as well. *We're* suffering too, Tasha. And we deserve to be cherished and uplifted. *You* deserve it. You're a human being with needs and wants. Motherhood . . . having a black son . . . doesn't negate that, does it?"

"No. No, it don't, but . . . but . . ."

"But what?" Dr. Green asked.

"If I'm not there for him, who will be? Who's gonna take care of him, if I don't? I can't abandon my baby."

"Abandon," she said, before writing something on her notepad. "It's interesting that you use that word. You use it often. Let's unpack that."

Let's not, I thought back then, but didn't say it. Instead, I just slouched on the couch in her office, hoping the session would be over soon.

"Why do you equate putting your needs first as abandoning Ghalen?"

"I don't know." I crossed my arms over my chest, a lot like my son does when he's tired of listening to me lecture him. "*You* tell *me* why."

"Tasha," she began slowly, "you're being defensive again."

"I ain't being defensive. I want to know! You're the doctor with the fancy degree. Explain to me why I'm equating it with abandoning him."

Dr. Green looked up from her notepad. "Honestly?" She set down her pen on the desk beside her and adjusted her glasses. She clenched her hands in her lap. "I wonder if your worries about abandoning your son have something to do with your relationship with your mother. With her sending you away when you were a young teenager. You being the *only* child she sent away. Did you believe she didn't put you first? Do you believe that maybe . . . *maybe* she abandoned you, and you're still dealing with those feelings and projecting them onto your relationship with your son?"

I couldn't answer her. Her words felt like one of Kordell's slaps that left me dazed for the rest of the day. What she said hurt; it hurt because part of me wondered if it was true.

But I remind myself that Morris isn't Dr. Green. He isn't trying to call me out or lay me bare. This isn't a therapy session. Morris closes his eyes. He thinks I'm shutting him out, but I'm not. I reach across the table and cup his face, making him look at me again, letting him know I want him here with me.

I hate that we're arguing. I want the closeness and calm, which we felt back in his bedroom, to stay in place, not to be ruined like this.

"I don't want drama," I say again. "I especially don't want drama with you. You're my peace, Morris. Please stay that way."

He reaches up and takes my hand. He rests them both on the table. "Well, if you do find Kordell . . . and if you do talk to him, stay firm, Tasha. He couldn't bully you, so he might try to charm you."

"I know," I say with a nod.

Dr. Green warned me about the pattern, the cycle of abuse. How things seem to get worse and worse, then the abuser has this big explosion, then they apologize, try to make up for it, and say things will get better, lulling you into thinking that they mean it this time around. But it always goes bad again. There will always be another explosion.

"Don't back down. OK?" Morris says.

"I've waited too long to finally be free. Don't worry. I won't let him talk his way back in. I'm done with all of it."

When I get back to the office a half hour later, I peek around the corner, through the office doorway, to see if Evelyn is at her desk. She isn't. She hasn't gotten back from lunch yet, so I have some time to make a personal phone call without her hearing me.

I sit down at my cubicle and look through my phone contacts. It doesn't take me long to find Kordell's friend, Jared Humphries, in the list.

Kordell and Jared have been close for years. They started in the construction business together in the same trade-apprenticeship program when they graduated from high school. Kordell would go on to cabinetry and woodworking. Jared would become a plumber. These days, they did just about everything together, from bowling to watching football to getting blackout drunk. We even went on a couples vacation with Jared and his wife, Destiny, to Las Vegas five years ago. If Kordell went to stay with anyone, it would be Jared.

I dial Jared's number and listen to it ring on the other end.

"Hello!" Jared shouts. I can hear the sound of banging hammers and zipping buzzsaws in the background.

"Jared," I say, "hey, it's Tasha."

"*Tasha?* Damn, I thought it was Kordell using your phone. The big dummy left his cell at my place. I figured he'd need to get it back at some point. Tell him he can stop by this evening to pick it up if he needs to. I might have to work late on site, but Destiny should be home to give it to him."

"So he *is* staying with you, then?" I roll my eyes. Mystery solved. "When you see him, can you tell Kordell to call Ghalen back as soon as he can? His son has been calling him for the past few days. He was worried."

Jared doesn't answer me. All I hear is banging and buzzing.

"Jared, did you hear me? Can you tell him to call Ghalen?" I repeat, talking louder.

"Tasha, I haven't seen Kordell since Saturday afternoon when he left the house."

I frown. "What do you mean you haven't seen him?"

"I mean I haven't seen him! I thought y'all had made up and he went back home. He told me that's what he was gonna try to do after he finished looking at that job way out in Maryland for some rich lady."

At that, I go still. A bubble forms in the pit of my stomach. My heart skips a beat. "What . . . what rich lady, Jared?"

"I don't know. She said she had a vacation home out near Cumberland or something or one of them places out there. I don't know the area that well. It sounded like it was in the boonies. She was paying Kordell good money just to look at the job, though, to give her an estimate. He was excited. He told me that there might be work in it for me too, since she said she was looking for contractors. That's where he was driving when he left my house."

I squeeze the phone in my hand. The bubble in my stomach is getting bigger and bigger, crushing into my lungs, taking my breath away. "Did he tell you the rich lady's name?"

"If he did, I can't remember."

"Was it . . . was it Madison? Madison Gingell?"

Jared pauses for what feels like forever. "Naw, that doesn't sound familiar."

"Are you sure?"

"Yeah, that wasn't the name."

The bubble in my stomach shrinks. It doesn't disappear, but it's small enough that I can breathe easy again. It was a real job prospect. It wasn't Madison who called Kordell and lured him out there to kill him. I'm just letting my imagination run away from me. It was all talk. A crazy rant. Madison hadn't meant what she said months ago.

I place a hand to my chest, where my heart is starting to slow to its normal speed.

"Thanks for telling me about Kordell's phone, Jared. That would explain why he hasn't gotten Ghalen's messages. He didn't come home, but maybe he got held up or is staying with another friend."

"Let me know when he checks in!" Jared says. "He's a good guy, Tasha. He wouldn't tell me what happened, but he says he hopes you take him back. Y'all built a family together. Don't throw it away over one little thing. I hope you give him another—"

"Bye, Jared," I say before hanging up, not wanting to hear any more.

For the rest of the day, I wonder where Kordell has gotten off to, and it annoys me. That man doesn't deserve all this space in my head, but he's stuck there anyway and I can't get him out of it. I know he started at Jared and Destiny's house, but where is he now?

Is he with a friend? I think, as I get photocopies for Evelyn from the copier room.

Or does he have a woman on the side, I wonder as I sit on the Metro train during my ride home, *and he's staying with her?*

But why didn't he come back to Jared's to at least get his phone? I think as I stand to give an elderly woman my seat on the bus that will take me to my last stop.

I don't have all the answers, but I have to tell Ghalen the truth, what I know and what I don't. A half answer is better than no answer at all.

About ten minutes later, I open the front door to my house. I see we have a guest tonight; Imani has come over. She's sitting with him on the sofa. He's lying back with his headphones on. One of his workbooks sits open on his chest. He's bobbing a pencil in his hand as he reads. His legs are draped over hers as she scribbles on notecards.

I don't normally like it for those two to be in the house by themselves. Who knows what kind of mess they could get up to without supervision and, as I tell Ghalen, I am too young to be a grandmother, but today I am happy to see Imani here. Maybe she can distract him from worrying about Kordell.

When I step into the room, they both look up. Imani smiles. "Hi, Mrs. Jenkins!" she cries.

"Hi, Imani," I say tiredly as I close the door, take off my coat, and hang it in the closet. I lower my purse to the floor. "So, what have you two been up to? What are you studying?" I begin, just as the phone rings.

"We have a Spanish test tomorrow, so I was making cards to help us quiz each other," she says, holding up the notecards.

"Sounds like a smart idea." I walk across the room to the cord-less phone that sits on one of our end tables. It's still ringing. I pick it up and glance down at the Caller ID. I see the words "WASH-INGTON SHERIFF" on the screen. My thumb freezes for a second before I press the green button.

"Hello?"

"Hello," a man's voice answers, "this is Sergeant Myers from the Washington County Sheriff's Office. Is this Tasha Jenkins?"

"Yes, this is her."

"The spouse of Kordell Isaiah Jenkins?" the sergeant asks.

I close my eyes. "Yes."

"Well, I'm sorry to inform you, ma'am, but we found your husband and his truck not too far from Red Rock Road and—"

"Is he OK?" I ask and Ghalen must hear something in my voice, because he tugs off his headphones.

"Ma, what's wrong?" Ghalen asks.

But I already know what's wrong. I know that Kordell isn't OK. I feel it. It's the same feeling you have when you're riding a rollercoaster and you're going up, up, up, and you know the drop is coming. You're holding the railing to brace yourself when you see the top, because you know that drop is going to be steep. You're going to feel weightless for a couple of seconds, like you could go flying off into space, then you'll be yanked back down to earth so hard that your teeth rattle.

That's what I'm doing as I wait for the sergeant from the Washington County Sheriff's Office to answer. I'm holding on tight. I'm waiting for the drop.

"No, he is not, ma'am," the sergeant finally says. "I'm sorry to inform you, but your husband is deceased."

I then let go of the phone and fall to the floor as my legs buckle beneath me and I come crashing down to earth.

CHAPTER 22

MADISON

"Oh, my God, I needed this! I needed this so badly. You just can't imagine, Maddie. When I tell you I have been so stressed out lately," Summer laments, as she gets her dermalinfusion facial. Her words are garbled a little, thanks to her lip injections.

I recline in a padded leather chair about two feet away from Summer. I'm wearing a white robe and my hair is wrapped in a white towel turban. I'm trying not to wince as the esthetician applies the plasma pen along my brow and eyes. She used the numbing gel, but I can still feel the stings like a dozen bees are doing a country line dance on my face. It's painful, but I must bear it along with Summer's incessant griping. Like her, I need this badly.

Two days ago, Phil leaned in toward our bathroom mirror and stared at my reflection as if I'd grown a second head. "You look tired, honey," he said.

"Tired?" I instantly raised my hand to my face and leaned in closer to see what he was seeing. For the first time, I noticed the purple bruises under my eyes and the crow's-feet that had sprouted at the edges, seemingly overnight.

"Have you been sleeping well, sweetheart?" Phil asked. "I noticed you've been somewhat restless lately."

"No, I haven't been sleeping well," I admitted.

I haven't because the nightmares are back. I first had them when I killed Reverend Brennan. I had dreams for weeks of the door being kicked in by police officers, who then put me in handcuffs. I had dreams of the bag of bloody items being unearthed in the woods, and finding it one morning sitting on our front porch like a misbegotten gift.

The nightmares came back years later, within days of Billy murdering Ashley. When I wasn't tossing and turning in bed, I would lie awake late at night and well into the morning back at my old apartment, wondering if the cops would be able to trace her murder back to my brother, and my unreliable brother would in turn connect the murder back to me. Had Billy been as careful and meticulous as I told him he needed to be? Had he left fingerprints? Would they find samples of his blood under her fingernails? Would they find an imprint of his shoes in the mud? The nightmares only ended when the Metropolitan Police Department announced at a press conference that some drug-addicted vagrant, who lived in a tent only a quarter of a mile from where Ashley's body had been found, would be charged with her murder. Only then did I breathe a sigh of relief.

And now I can't help dreaming about the day I shot Kordell. I certainly don't regret killing him. Just like I don't regret killing Reverend Brennan or Ashley. Sometimes death is unavoidable. But I do regret how that day went, how I wasn't in control of the situation from beginning to end, and how I was left scrambling to cover my tracks.

I had planned to shove his body into the ditch, covering it with dirt and branches, drive his car to another location, take his wallet and ID, and chuck them over the side of the mountain. Not to leave his bloody body dangling halfway out of his truck on the side of the road like a beacon for all the world to see. I had planned to shoot one bullet, not five—one in the air, four in Kordell. After all those gunshots, I was sure someone had to have heard me, even out there, in the hinterlands of Maryland. I could feel the minutes ticking by until another car arrived—perhaps a police cruiser sent to investigate the sound—as I tightened the last lug nut on my spare, lowered the car jack, hopped into the SUV, and drove away. I didn't realize until I neared the D.C. border that I'd left my hubcap sitting in the middle of the road. By then, it was too late to go back and get it.

I have to admit I fucked up that day—*royally*. The question is, did I fuck up enough to lead the cops back to me? That is the question that keeps me up at night. It's what is putting bags under my eyes and etching wrinkles at the corners of my mouth. But like evidence of my crimes, I have to erase them. Today, I will wipe away all traces of my guilt, no matter how torturous it is.

"You have no idea how hard it's been," Summer continues through puckered, bruised lips. "Tom came by yesterday. He told me that he doesn't want me stopping by his new place unannounced anymore."

I grimace through another bee sting. The pain is made much worse, now that I have to listen to Summer gripe about her misogynistic asshole husband.

"I asked Tom if it's because that toddler that he calls a mistress is living there with him now, but he claims she's not." Summer barks out a laugh. "I know he's full of shit! I saw her walking into his apartment building last week. And she was there the day before and the day before that. She was there for hours, Maddie. She *has* to be living there!"

"How do you know she was there for hours? You weren't following her, were you?" I ask.

"No! Well," she hesitates, "I just happened to be shopping nearby. I'd just come from Saks when I saw her."

You were shopping at Saks Fifth Avenue three days in a row, I think, but don't say it.

I grow tired of staring up into the pinched face of the beauty technician as she concentrates, so I close my eyes. When I do, I see the hubcap sitting on the black asphalt. Goddamnit, why didn't I grab it? It would have taken all of twenty seconds to get it and throw it in the back of the Cherokee. Why did I leave it there?

"And even if I *was* following her, what difference does it make?" Summer says, breaking into my thoughts. "She's fucking my husband! Tom's tried to bring up the fact that I've cheated too, but he can't prove it. And besides, I never would have done it if we'd been in a better place. If he loved me like he should've!"

I guess Tom somehow found out about the church groundskeeper. Oh, well.

"I'm just saying that you need to be careful, Summer. You don't want to be accused of harassment or, worse . . . stalking. You don't want the police at your door."

Speaking of police . . . can they trace hubcaps? Do hubcaps come with little ID numbers? I don't think so. I don't remember ever seeing one inside when I handled it. And even if they could track it, it was a hubcap on a rental car. Who knows how many people had driven that car in the course of a week or a month? Any of us could have left that hubcap there.

"That's exactly what Tom said," Summer snips. "That I was acting like a stalker. But I have every right to visit where my husband lives . . . to know what he's doing. What he's up to. Don't I?"

I don't answer her. I'm still obsessing about the hubcap, and I have to stop. It won't change anything. The cops have probably found his body by now and the hubcap anyway. The case will follow its normal process: collecting of evidence, questioning of witnesses, and developing a list of possible suspects. They may charge someone with the crime. They may not. I've done this before. And so far, I've been lucky; I've never been a suspect. Maybe my luck will hold. But honestly, I can't help but resent that I'm going through all this worry and agony when Tasha hasn't lifted one finger. She should bear some of the burden for this.

"It just isn't fair!" Summer is blubbering now, and not just because of her lips. "I've done everything for my marriage . . . for *him,* and now he just . . . just dumps me like some bad prom date, and moves on to someone else! And now he's accusing me of . . . I'm sorry, but why are you laughing? What is so funny?"

The country line-dancing bees along my brow take a break, and my eyes pop open. I look up to find that the esthetician has stopped working on my face and is instead staring over her shoulder at Summer, who is now sitting upright on her leather chair and glaring at the dark-haired woman in the lilac-colored scrubs who was giving her the dermalinfusion facial. The woman is holding up the facial wand and her gloved hands as if Summer has a gun pointed at her.

"Is it something that I said that you find amusing?" Summer asks.

The woman's olive skin flares red. She shakes her head. "N-n-no, ma'am," she stutters. Her voice is heavily accented. It is soft and high, making her sound like a chastised little girl.

"You were laughing, and I want to know what you find so funny."

The woman stares at her blankly while we look on in confusion. Summer's face is flushed now, too. Her eyes are wide and bright with rage and tears.

"Summer," I begin slowly while rising to my elbows and adjusting the front of my robe, "why don't we—"

"No! No, that is it! I have had enough, Maddie." She hops off her chair and stands in her robe and complimentary slippers. "Do you know who I am? Do you know who my husband is? Are you aware that I have been a patron of this spa," she says, pointing her finger at the woman, "for three and a half years? In the course of that time I have spent thousands upon thousands of dollars here. Probably more than you make in a year! And I refuse to be treated this way. To be laughed at by someone like you. I expect professionalism and . . . and *respect*. I want respect!"

"I-I-I'm sorry, ma'am," the woman whispers.

"I don't accept your apology," Summer says as the tears spill over in rivulets. The veins are standing up along her neck and forehead. She is almost shaking. "I do not accept it. I want to speak to your supervisor. No, make that the director. I would like to speak to her right now! I want—"

"Ladies, would you mind giving us a second, please?" I interrupt, plastering on a smile.

It's the same smile I use at cocktail parties and fundraising benefits, or when I arrive at a restaurant and the hostess tells me she can't find my reservation. It is polite. Charming. It diffuses misunderstandings and tense situations, like the one in which we now find ourselves.

The estheticians glance at each other. They then lower their devices, quickly remove their latex gloves, and exit the room.

"I want her fired," Summer rasps as the door closes behind them, furiously wiping at her tears.

"No, you don't," I mutter, trying to ignore the pain in my face. But the pain, compounded with Summer's near hysterics and my own obsessing about my missteps in the course of Kordell's murder, is making me irritable, and the affable façade I'm usually willing to put on feels heavier than usual.

"Yes, I do! I want—"

"What you're feeling right now is impotent rage, Summer. You're furious at your husband for what he's done to you, for fucking the toddler and deserting you and your marriage, and now you're pulling the proverbial Karen and taking out your anger on the Ecuadorian beauty technician."

Summer's mouth opens and closes. She's now at a loss for words. She sniffs and blinks like she's on the verge of crying again, and I don't know if I could take it. Honestly, I might slap her.

"You need to pull yourself together, because you don't want anyone to get fired. You want revenge. You want revenge on Tom. That's who you *really* want to punish. He's the real focus of your rage, isn't he?"

She purses her lips. After a few seconds, she nods. "And his mistress," she whispers fiercely. "I *hate* her."

"Obviously." I incline my head. "Can I make a suggestion, though?"

She shrugs and tightens her robe belt. "I . . . I suppose," she answers tentatively.

"Find a better way to handle this than what you've been doing so far. Showing up at his apartment unannounced. Following his mistress. Now screaming in a spa. What is any of that accomplishing?"

"I was flipping out, wasn't I?" She lowers her eyes, now shame-faced. "My mother said I've been acting crazy. She said I should move on and just accept that—"

"*Why?* Why should you have to move on? Tom used you, then he tossed you aside. You're not crazy. He's a selfish, callous bastard. A philandering cretin."

I remember Tom's imbecile smirk. I remember all of his dumb blond jokes. I remember how he rubbed my ass that night during our couples dinner with his wife sitting in the dining room less than twenty feet away, and how I wanted to punch him in the throat.

"You have a right to your anger, Summer—*and* your vengeance. Don't let anyone deny you that. Including your mother. You just have to . . ."

I pause. I'd had a similar heart-to-heart moment with Tasha, offering my advice and even my help. But her response had been rejection. Complete repulsion, in fact. She literally ran away from me. I was right, of course, but she wasn't ready for the truth back then. I don't want to repeat that mistake with Summer.

"I just have to what, Maddie?" she asks.

I shake my head and she grabs my hand.

"No, tell me. What am I missing?"

I gaze at her, pleasantly surprised.

Summer *wants* my advice and the knowledge I've gained from my experiences. This is what I meant when I spoke to Tasha about women . . . victims like ourselves and how we need to help each other, but she refused to listen. She's been repressed. Indoctrinated by rules that only hold us back. She doesn't realize I'm only trying to free her. But Summer seems willing to hear me out. More than willing. She's as eager as a kid on Christmas morning.

I am not wrong. I should have never doubted myself. I *do* have the answers. And now, after all that I've done, Tasha must finally realize it too.

"You can make him pay. You can teach him a lesson, but you have to come up with a plan. You have to think outside the box," I say to Summer. "So that he doesn't see you coming. So that it isn't so obvious."

"What . . . what do you mean?"

I slowly smile, and I tell her.

CHAPTER 23

TASHA

"Sister Tasha, I am so sorry for your loss," someone behind me says.

I turn to find one of the deaconesses with her arms outstretched wide, waiting to give me a big hug. I walk into them like I'm a zombie, letting her hold me and rock me back and forth, as if I were a baby.

I haven't set foot in this church in months, but I am here today, ready to face them all, because it is the day of my husband's funeral. People have been hugging me and crying on me for the past five hours. I've tried to work up my own tears, but I can't. I'm still in shock.

Kordell is dead. He was shot four times in the back and left alone to bleed out on the side of an empty road in western Maryland, and though I can't prove it, I know in my heart that Madison Gingell did it. She killed him. She made good on her promise to get rid of my husband, and now she's probably expecting me to make good, too, on this deal she's made up in her head.

"How are you doin', sweetheart?" the deaconess asks as she holds me tight, so tight that I can barely breathe. She finally lets me go, staring at me at arm's length and frowning like I'm wearing death and grief on my body instead of a black, knee-length dress and uncomfortable pantyhose. "How are you holding up?"

"I'm . . . I'm all right, I guess," I whisper. I clear my throat. "Well, as good as can be expected."

"Oh, I know, honey. What a silly question for me to ask! The world is full of so many evil, hateful people. And now they've taken away one of God's own soldiers—Brother Kordell."

God's own soldier. . . .

Probably half of the people in our church suspected what Kordell was doing to me, how he abused me. No one ever asked me outright, but the gossip and the whispers had gotten back to me. Before my friend Monique left for the Carolinas, she told me that some of the women in the church had asked her if Kordell ever got high-handed with me. "That man seems to be kind of controlling," one of them said. Now that he's dead, it's like he's become some saint.

I've done it a few times myself. In the past couple of days, I've thought about the sweet times and the fun moments he and I had together. Why I fell in love with him in the first place. I thought about the first time Kordell took me to a roller rink and how we laughed as I stumbled around in my skates. He held me up to keep me from falling. I remembered the first time we made love and I was so nervous, but he made me feel like the most beautiful girl alive. I remembered how he clapped when Ghalen took his first steps and shouted, "That's my baby boy!"

But I also can't forget the time he told me I was a "dumb, worthless bitch" when I forgot to put gas in his truck, letting the gauge drop to "E." I remember when he grabbed my arm in the middle of a clothing store in Tysons Corner when he thought I'd been in there for too long and wasn't moving fast enough; he dragged me out in front of all the other customers and the salesgirls. I can't forget the night that he hit me across the face in front of our son, either.

I remember both sides of Kordell—the good and the bad. And though I can agree that how he died wasn't right, I also know my husband was no saint. I ain't pretending.

"I'm praying for you. For you *and* your son," the deaconess says, looking over my shoulder.

I turn and follow her eyes across the church basement where we're holding the repast after Kordell's burial. My eyes land on Ghalen, who's sitting at one of the banquet tables. The styrofoam plate of fried chicken, biscuits, sweet potatoes, and green beans that the women in the church's steam-filled kitchen have cooked for us sits untouched. Instead of eating, he's holding Imani's hand while his bowed head rests on his aunt's shoulder—Kordell's baby sister, Rita. Rita has one arm wrapped around him. She loves that boy like he was her own. She loves him just as much as she loved her brother, even though she knew just as well as I did that Kordell was far from perfect. Kordell lost his temper a few times with her too, but she made the same excuses for him that I made for so many years.

It was the alcohol.

He wouldn't talk to me that way if he wasn't under so much pressure.

I bet she's still making excuses for him even now.

I've had a hard time working up tears, but Rita hasn't. Neither has Ghalen. I know he's been trying to be all manly and hold them back in front of people, but he can't. He lost his daddy, and he can't help showing it.

"Thank you," I say to the deaconess. "We appreciate your prayers."

She pats my hand, nods, and walks away.

I look around me, wondering who will walk up next to cry or give me their condolences, but I stop short when my eyes land on the metal doors on the other side of the room. One of the doors slowly opens, and Morris walks through. He stops under the glowing EXIT sign, and his dark eyes scan the room before he finds me. They lock with mine, and my breath catches in my throat. He gives me a nod and waves, but I can't move.

I thought I saw him at the gravesite, standing in the crowd, but I figured I must have been mistaken.

Morris wouldn't come here, I told myself as I sat in front of the casket, listening to the minister read his final prayer. Not with my son and all of Kordell's relatives standing around.

Some of the other people from work had come to the funeral to show their support and to be kind, but it's different with Morris. He isn't just a co-worker, and he knows that.

He walks across the room anyway, past all the tables and people, straight toward me, and I bite down on my bottom lip, wondering what the hell he's doing.

"Hey, Tasha," he says, stopping in front of me.

"Hi, Morris."

He gives me a hug and I accept it, but I don't hug him back.

I can't tell if it's real or I'm imagining it, but it feels like a hundred eyes are on us as we stand there. Can they see what has happened between us in the way our bodies lean together like two people who've made love? Do we show how we really feel about each other with how we can no longer look each other in the eyes now that we are so close? Do I still seem like a loyal wife who is sad that her husband is dead, or a guilty cheater?

"Thank you for coming. Kordell would've appreciated it," I say loudly enough for those around us to hear. I gesture to the table of food. "Make yourself a plate and grab a seat, okay?" I then turn away, leaving him standing there alone.

Morris stays at the repast, taking a chair at one of the tables, and I try to pretend like I don't see him, like I can't feel him in the room with me. I talk to people. I peek my head through the kitchen door and ask if they need any help in there, but they shoo me away.

"We're here to take care of you and your family, Sister Jenkins," one of them says. "Don't you touch one pot or pan. You hear me?"

But I can't tell her I need to be in the kitchen. I need something to do with myself, because I can't keep thinking about Kordell and looking at the pain in my son's face. I can't be in the same room with Morris without walking over to him and asking him to hold me, because if he doesn't, I might explode into a million pieces. Standing in this room with all these people, I feel myself slowly going crazy, and pretty soon I am going to be nuttier than Madison Gingell.

"Oh, God! Oh, my Lord!" someone wails out of the blue.

I turn to find my mother-in-law sprawled out on the church basement floor, sobbing. It's the third time she's done that today. Relatives crowd around her, fanning her with their hands like she's fainted from the heat, not because her son is dead. They're trying to get her back into one of the metal fold-up chairs, but not succeeding.

"Why'd you take him? Why'd you take him, Lord?" she screams.

I rush across the room to try to help. My mother-in-law looks up at me, like she notices me for the first time. "Why's he dead, Tasha? Why did this happen?"

"Let's get her to the ladies' room," Kordell's cousin, Janae, whispers. She's a big woman. Nice and sturdy. With her help, we finally manage to get my mother-in-law back to her feet. "We'll help her calm down. Get her a little bit of privacy and get her cleaned up too."

I nod in agreement.

We each take an arm and guide her across the room, like she's a blind woman. Then it's a short walk down the hall to the ladies' room, which is mostly empty. Thank God. Janae turns on the faucet and grabs a couple of paper towels. She wets them and begins to lightly pat my mother-in-law's face while I rub her shoulder, hold her hand, and whisper, "It's gonna be OK, Mama. It's gonna be OK."

"No, it's not. It's not ever gonna be OK again." She stops her tears and stares at our reflection in the mirror. "I just don't get it," she says between sniffs, clinging to my hand.

"Don't get what, Mama?" I ask. Janae stops patting her face with the paper towels.

"I don't get why my baby is dead. Why would someone shoot him out there? He didn't do anything to anybody! And then this happens? Why? *Why him?*"

I don't say anything. I don't know what to say.

"Did something happen that I don't know about, Tasha?" she asks, turning away from the mirror to look at me face-to-face. "Did Kordell get mixed up in something? Or with somebody?"

"Huh?"

"Did he say anything to you?"

Now Janae is staring at me too.

I swallow and look around the bathroom and the stalls, feeling cornered. I'm thinking of the right answer to give as my mother-in-law's grip tightens on my hand, crushing the knuckles and making me wince.

"You look like you know somethin', Tasha," she says, sounding desperate. "If you do, tell me now. I want to know!"

I shake my head. "No, I don't know why it happened, Mama. No one does. Not even the police."

But I can tell from the look in her eyes that she doesn't believe me, that she knows I'm a liar. She knows I'm hiding something.

"Janae, if you've got Mama taken care of, I'm going to go check on Ghalen now. Make sure he's OK."

I don't wait for Janae to respond before I tug my hand out of my mother-in-law's grasp and rush out of the bathroom. When I do, I run straight into Morris. I see he's waiting in the hall, like he's been there the whole time.

"Is everything OK?" he asks, frowning down at me.

"It's fine," I mumble, walking around him and trying to head back to the banquet room.

He follows me. "You don't look like it is."

"You shouldn't be here," I say to him over my shoulder.

"No, I shouldn't have to find out from the folks at work what happened to Kordell . . . about the funeral," he whispers back. "You should've told me, Tasha. I wanted to be here for you. I thought you might need me."

"Well, I don't!"

It comes out meaner than I mean it to. Morris blinks and takes a step back, like I hit him. His eyes go flat. He sucks in his bottom lip and slowly nods. "Understood."

He turns to walk away, heading toward the stairs that will take him upstairs to the ground level and out of the church. I watch him and I know in my heart if he makes it up those stairs, everything will change between us. It will go back to the way it was before. Polite hellos as I pass his cubicle on the way to the copier room. "Good morning" when we see each other in the hall and "good evening" in the elevator before I head to the Metro and he heads to the parking garage. He will disappear from my life again.

I rush after him, not caring if people can see me, can see us. I grab his arm and pull him toward a side exit that leads to the dumpsters. I let the metal doors slam shut behind us.

"I'm sorry," I say. "I didn't mean to talk to you that way. I'm . . . I'm sorry."

He purses his lips. "It's OK," he says slowly. "I know this can't be easy."

"You have no idea," I sigh.

"No, I don't. I don't when you don't talk to me, Tasha. I shouldn't have found out from other people that your husband died. I should've heard it from you."

"Like I said, I'm sorry, but I've been busy with other things, Morris. Taking care of Ghalen, organizing the funeral and—"

"*Really?*" Morris frowns. "Because you called and told other people at work what happened. I got details from the damn receptionist. But you didn't tell me."

I close my eyes, feeling too tired to argue.

"And the last time you did that to me, we didn't talk for more than seventeen years. So you could see why I was a little worried."

"I'm sorry, Morris! I can say I'm sorry a hundred times, but it won't mean anything if you're still mad at me. If you don't believe me."

"I'm not *mad*. I told you, I was worried. And stop apologizing, dammit! Your husband is dead. I don't need you to feel guilty about any stuff between us. That's not why I came here. You've got enough weight on your shoulders. And knowing you, you probably already feel guilty anyway. You feel guilty about what happened to Kordell, don't you? You've somehow made it into being your fault, I bet."

"It *is* my fault," I whisper, and he rolls his eyes.

"Tasha, your husband chose to leave that night and frankly, I'm happy he did. Who knows what he would've done if he'd stayed. What happened to him after that had nothing to do with you."

"That's not true. It has everything to do with me!"

"And how do you figure that?"

"Because I know who killed him, Morris." I exhale. It feels so good to finally say it out loud, to get it off my chest. It's not something I'm just screaming in my head anymore. "She . . . she told me she was going to do it, and I didn't warn Kordell," I rush out. "I didn't say a damn thing, but I was hoping she was all talk. How was I supposed to know she would go through with it? That she was going to shoot him?"

"Wait . . . slow down! Who is *she*? What are you talking about?"

And that's when I tell him everything about Madison and our meeting, about the offer she made back then. When I'm done, Morris stares at me in silence.

"You don't believe me, do you?" I ask.

"It's not that I don't believe you," he begins, and I can tell right away that he's lying. "But are you sure? You're telling me this woman really said she was going to kill your husband?"

"She didn't say it outright, but she . . . she basically said it. She said we should get rid of our husbands. That we could help each other."

"Tasha, you told me that even at your low moments, you thought about killing your husband too. That doesn't mean you were actually planning to do it. People just think out loud sometimes."

"But this was different! With her, it wasn't *just* talk. She meant it. And the day that Kordell disappeared, his friend said he was driving to a potential job. He was going to see about doing cabinetry work for some rich lady's house."

"And he said the rich lady was her?"

"No, he didn't, but doesn't it seem like a hell of a coincidence that he was headed to meet some rich mystery woman the day he was shot?"

Morris squints at me and shakes his head again. "Maybe, but that's still a big leap to accusing her of murder."

"Look, I can't explain it, but I *know* she did it."

"You know? You're certain?"

I'd felt certain of it before, but, under Morris's questioning and the doubtful look on his face, I'm starting to question myself too. Am I just being paranoid? Have I let my imagination run away from me? I shake my head.

"I know it sounds crazy, but she did it and now I have to go to the police and tell them. Even though they'll probably think I sound crazy too. Even if they don't believe me."

"It's not just about you sounding crazy. It's very serious to accuse someone of a felony, especially first-degree murder. One of my frat brothers is a cop, Tasha. He works for the D.C. police department. Murder investigations are a big deal. If you become a suspect in a case like that, it can change your life. It can *ruin* your life. Especially if it gets out. If other people find out about it, like the media."

I go still.

If this woman shot my husband, I don't care if her life is ruined. It would be a just punishment for how she ruined our lives. But if Madison didn't do it . . . if she really is just a woman who was fantasizing about the unthinkable, and my own guilt and shame over wanting my husband dead caused me to make Madison into a big, bad monster in my mind, a monster that she isn't, then . . . well, I'd be doing a lot more harm than good by dragging her into this.

I start to gnaw my bottom lip.

"If you're going to tell the cops about her, just make sure that it's what you *really* wanna do. OK?" Morris says. "Not to mention that you could get charged for making a false statement to the police if they think you lied about her intentionally."

My mouth falls open. I don't know what to say. I'm overwhelmed by the choices, and by how nothing seems right anymore. I don't know what to do. I start to blink back tears, and Morris reaches for me again. He wraps me in his arms and rests his head on top of mine as I weep.

"I wasn't trying to make you cry, honey. I'm sorry," he says. "I didn't mean to scare you. But I don't want you to stumble blindly into this." He loosens his hold on me and tenderly kisses my closed eyelids, my cheeks. "Why don't you just . . . just think about this for a bit? OK? Just sit on it for a week or two. You don't have to make the decision now."

I slowly nod and wipe at my tears. I take a shaky breath. "O–OK. I'll think about it more." I glance at the closed doors. "I should go back in there. People are probably wondering where I've gotten off to."

"Whatever you decide, Tasha, I know it'll be the right decision. Know that I support you either way," he says.

The heavy metal door beside us suddenly swings open, and I look through the doorway. I'm shocked to find my son standing there. I wonder how long he's been waiting. How much he's heard. Ghalen looks from me to Morris.

"Grandma is . . . uh . . . Grandma's complaining about chest pain, so they're gonna drive her to the hospital and get her checked out," Ghalen says, clearing his throat. Though he's talking to me, his eyes stay fixed on Morris, staring him in the face. "They asked me to tell you. Cousin Janae didn't know where you went, so I was looking for you. I thought . . . I thought I heard you out here."

"Oh, I was just talking to my friend Morris," I say with a sniff, hoping my eyes don't look too puffy. I step back inside the church and point over my shoulder. "Morris is one of my friends from work who was nice enough to come to the funeral."

Morris follows me inside and lets the door close behind us. He holds out his hand for a shake. "Good to finally meet you, Ghalen. I've heard so much about you from your mother. I'm sorry about your father . . . for your loss, I mean."

Ghalen looks at Morris's hand and then at me. His face tightens and so does his body, and I'm caught off guard by how much he looks like his daddy at that moment. For a split second, I wonder if

Ghalen is about to shake Morris's hand or punch him in the face. But my son relaxes. His face goes slack. He turns back into himself and does a quick handshake.

"Thank you," he mumbles.

"Morris, thanks again for coming," I say, stepping closer to Ghalen and looping my arm through his. "I'll give some thought to what we talked about. I'll catch up with you at work next week."

"OK, let me know what you decide."

I wave goodbye and walk back with Ghalen to the banquet room.

"Did they already take Mama to the hospital?" I ask, watching the trail of people walking out of the room. "I bet it might just be—"

"What were y'all talking about?" Ghalen interrupts.

"Huh?"

He stops walking and turns to stare at me again. "You and that man. What were y'all talking about, Ma? What did he ask you to decide?"

I smile. "It was nothing, baby. Nothing worth talking about now, anyway."

He stares at me a beat longer and then nods. "All right, Ma."

But he gives me that look. It's the same look that I saw on his grandmother's face. On Morris's. He looks like he doesn't believe me.

CHAPTER 24

MADISON

I'm on my yoga mat, listening to Tibetan chants and doing the downward-facing dog pose when my cell chimes.

I've been doing yoga and meditating a lot more lately as a way to taper off my anxiety and worries. The day at the spa didn't work thanks to Summer and her little breakdown. I figured yoga and meditating would do the trick. They're much better ways of achieving serenity than my other options, like climbing behind the wheel and ramming random pedestrians with my car.

It's not like I need yet another trail for police to follow that could lead to my arrest.

I slowly sit upright, push my ponytail over my shoulder, and glance at my cell phone that sits on the hardwood floor beside my mat. I see that it's our driver, Tony, calling, which is odd. Tony never calls me. If he has any questions or concerns, he knows to address them to Phil. Phil's the boss and writes the checks, after all.

I slowly raise the phone to my ear. "Hi, Tony," I answer before taking a sip from my water bottle.

"Mrs. G, I'm so glad you answered, ma'am!" Tony says breathlessly on the other end of the line.

"Why? What's wrong?" I can barely hear him over the guttural moaning coming through the wall speakers. "Alexa, end Tibetan Monks playlist!"

The music stops and I return my attention to my phone.

"Are you running behind today?" I ask Tony as I dab at my damp brow with a hand towel. "You're going to be late picking me up?"

"No, I . . . Ma'am, the car is totaled. We . . . we had an accident."

I instantly shoot to my feet, dropping my water bottle to the floor and sending cold water splashing everywhere. "*What?*"

"Yeah, it was a hit-and-run. The driver came out of nowhere. I locked eyes with her in the rearview when she hit us from behind. Sent the car into a spin."

"She?"

"Yeah, that bitch . . . excuse my French . . . knocked us into the guardrail and we would've gone sailing into oncoming traffic if it hadn't been for the median. She didn't even stop! She nearly killed us and just kept driving."

My eyes go wide as I listen. My heartbeat kicks into overdrive. I pause and count to ten before saying what I'm about to say next.

I know not to sound too eager. I have to sound genuinely concerned, even frightened.

"Oh, my God, Tony! Are you OK? Is . . . is Phil OK?"

"I'm decent. A little banged up, but I don't know about Mr. Gingell, ma'am. That's why I reached out to you. He got knocked around more than I did since he wasn't buckled up in back. He was passed out in the back seat, the last I heard. We got separated when the EMTs and fire engines showed up. I went in one ambulance and he went in the other one. And now I'm stuck in this damn hospital room. The nurses here don't know anything. Nobody's telling me a damn thing! I thought maybe they'd tell you if you called them. I'd hoped he'd even called you by now, but maybe he can't. He seemed like he was in really bad shape, Mrs. G."

"Let's not leap to conclusions, Tony. Just tell me the name of the hospital and I'll see if they can tell me what happened to Phil," I say, trying to keep from smiling.

He'll hear it in my voice.

"You're right. I shouldn't think the worst. I'm at George Washington University Hospital. I think he's here, too."

"OK, I'll call the hospital as soon as I hang up."

"Mrs. G!" he shouts.

"Yes, Tony."

"When you get an update, please call me back. I'm really worried about him. I feel like this . . . this is my fault. I should've been—"

"Of course, I'll call you, Tony. Talk to you soon." I hang up.

When I do, the smile that I've been holding back erupts on my face.

The hit-and-run driver had to be her. It *had* to be Tasha. She did it. Good God, she did it. After all this waiting. I was starting to lose faith in her, but she pulled through. All it took was for me to hold up my end of our bargain, to show her that I was serious. I knew she had it in her all along. She just needed the right nudge, and now I might finally be rid of Phil.

No more pretending that I don't know where he's been all night when he arrives home late with some half-hearted excuse. I no longer have to resist the urge to slit his throat or stab him repeatedly in the chest as he sits beside me in bed or stands next to me at the double sinks.

I right my water bottle and use my hand towel to clean up the mess. Wouldn't want to ruin the hardwood, especially if I decide to sell the house. I then grab my phone again and search for the number to George Washington University Hospital's emergency room. As I do, I can't help imagining life after Phil. Maybe I'll travel the world like I've always wanted. With Phil's death, I'd inherit enough money to do it. I'd not only go back to the Sonoma Valley, but maybe even travel to places more off the beaten path. Borneo. The Maldives. And I'd eschew my old life. My social circles. No more hobnobbing with Washington's elite. I'd just . . . disappear. Strike out on a new path.

Maybe even a new identity. For the first time in quite a while, I will answer to no one. I'd be free.

But before I start researching itineraries and booking plane tickets, I have to make sure that the car crash was fatal, that Phil will die from this.

It was hard to tell, judging from what Tony said. But Phil's losing consciousness could be the sign of many things, from a seizure to a concussion to a heart attack—all giving me reason to hope. I find the number to the hospital and tap the link on the screen, listening as the phone rings on the other end.

"GW University Hospital Emergency," a woman answers. "How may I assist you?"

"Hello, my name is Madison Gingell. I'm calling about my husband."

✳ ✳ ✳

When I arrive at the hospital, I head straight to the information desk and I'm given Phil's room number. They weren't able to give me any details over the phone about his status besides the fact that he'd been admitted, which means my husband is still alive. How alive, and for how much longer, is the question.

As I walk down the corridor, I adjust my sunglasses. They cover the scars from my plasma pen treatment. I check the room numbers and find my husband's. When I do, I enter the hospital room, but I'm confused. The room is empty, save for a nurse in purple scrubs who is assembling a bag in front of a perfectly made bed. I can see clothes inside and what looks like my husband's wallet.

All his belongings are contained in one large plastic bag. That couldn't mean what I think it means, could it? Is Phil dead?

"Ex-excuse me," I say, taking a tentative step into the room.

The nurse looks up. She's short, with red hair that is aflame with the light coming through the hospital window blinds. "Yes? Can I help you?"

I point at her. "Do those belong to Phillip Gingell?"

The nurse glances down at the bag and nods. "Yes, they do. And who are you?"

"I'm his wife, Madison." I take one step toward her, then another. "Is . . . is my husband dead? Is that why you're packing up his things?"

I start to hope again. I'm nearly across the hospital room now, waiting to grab the bag out of her hands and rush out of the door and to the new life that awaits me.

I'll have to sit through the funeral, of course. Pay homage to my husband in front of his family and colleagues. I won't be able to sell the house right away. It'll take time to sort through his estate. I'll wait a few months, then put it on the market, but all the while, I'll start making plans. What to do next. Where to go.

The nurse opens her mouth to answer me.

"No," a familiar voice interrupts, "they're packing up my things because I'm finally being discharged. And it's about damn time," I hear Phil say behind me, making my face fall and my heart sink.

I turn to find him in a wheelchair, being pushed by a plump male nurse.

"Oh, honey," I gush, "I'm so . . . I'm so glad to see that you're . . . you're . . . OK!"

I sound overwhelmed with emotion, basically choking on my words, because I am. He isn't dead. He isn't even maimed. With the exception of a small gash on his forehead, the bastard just looks cold and uncomfortable in a paper-thin gown and a cheap robe. I can see the blue webs of veins in his pale, hairy legs. His wide shoulders are bowed. He looks older and worn.

Tasha didn't get the job done. She didn't kill him. Fuck.

"Yes, I'm fine," he mutters as I lean down and brush my lips across the stubble of his cheek. "I'm just tired. It's been an all-around shitty morning, and I'm ready to go home. I would have called you, but I dropped my phone in the car." He squints up at me. "How did you even know I was here?"

"Tony called," I say, standing upright and forcing a smile. "He was worried about you. *I* was worried about you, too, sweetheart."

"Well, there was no need to worry," Phil says as the nurse pushes him farther into the room, parking the wheelchair next to his hospital bed. "As you can see, I'm perfectly fine." I watch as my husband grabs the handrails and pushes himself to his feet. "And now I want to put on clothing held together by more than loose strings. Let's see if I can salvage what's left of my day. I have plenty of phone calls to make. I guess I'll have to tell Justine to cancel all my meetings. There's no way I'll make it to the office in this state."

"Of course, sweetheart. Of course!" I begin to back toward the hospital-room door. "You should start getting dressed. I'll be right back."

"*Right back*? Where are you going?" Phil calls to me as I step back into the hall.

"Just going to the ladies' room," I call over my shoulder. "I'll be back in a sec."

I turn and nearly run down the hall, weaving down corridors, almost bumping into people along the way. Eventually, I spot a sign showing the restrooms. I burst through the bathroom door and find a bemused-looking older woman standing at one of the sinks, washing her hands. I ignore her confused stare and walk straight into one of the open stalls, slam the door behind me, and fall back against it. I count to ten over and over again. I start a chant to find serenity and patience, but it's not fucking working.

He's not dead.

I want to punch the walls of the stall.

He's not dead.

I want to kick and yell bloody murder.

I reach for the roll of toilet paper and pull sheet after sheet until I have a wad thicker than my fist. I stuff the wad into my mouth, close my eyes, and scream. I don't care who can hear my muffled shouts. I scream so much that my face goes red and my eyes blur.

When I'm done . . . when I've screamed myself almost hoarse, I take the wet wad of tissue out of my mouth, toss it into the toilet, and slowly open the stall door. I stare at myself in the mirror, taking deep, gulping breaths. I turn on the cold water, splashing my face a few times and wiping it dry with a few paper towels. I put on my sunglasses again and smile at my reflection. By the time I open the door, I'm resembling some semblance of normal.

Phil isn't dead, but he damn well better be soon.

CHAPTER 25

TASHA

"GHALEN," I CALL AS I HOIST THE SMALL BOX AGAINST MY HIP AND walk down the hall to my son's bedroom, "I'm finished loading the car and leaving soon! Ghalen?"

I nudge the door open to find my boy sitting in his favorite chair. It's cracked and weathered. It faces his television. One of his game controllers is in his hands. His headphones are on his ears. I look around me and purse my lips.

His room is a mess—more so than usual, though I didn't think that was even possible. But I don't have the heart to tell him to stop playing his video game and clean up. He's depressed and this is his way of dealing with it, with the loss of his daddy: by escaping to a world full of swords and explosions, race cars and spaceships. Dr. Green told me once that stuff like this is what you call a "coping mechanism." I don't know if it's good or bad, but I guess it's better than him drinking or picking fights.

I tap his shoulder, making him jump in surprise.

"I didn't mean to scare you, baby," I say as he yanks off his headphones and looks up at me. "I was just telling you that I was heading to the flea market. I have to get there in enough time to set up a table." I lean my head toward my box of knitted gloves in my arms. "I'm hoping to sell a decent amount today. Wish me luck!"

"Good luck," Ghalen mumbles. He then swings back around in his chair, stares at the TV again, and starts tapping away on his controller.

"You got anything planned?" I ask, lowering my box to the floor. I walk over to his dresser, trying not to frown at all the junk on there. The empty soda cans, dirty socks, protein-bar wrappers, and leftover fast-food bags and containers. I toss one of the bags into his trash can. It reveals yet another pile of trash. I give up. "Are you meeting up with Imani?"

"Nah, she's going shoppin' with her mom today and gettin' her hair done," he mumbles. "I think we need some time apart anyway. We keep arguing."

"Maybe a little break is a good idea." I remember the night I watched the two kids from my living room window. How he shouted at her. The look on her face. "But how about your friends? They aren't doing anything either? You don't wanna hang out with them?"

"I didn't ask them. Plus, it still doesn't feel right going out and doin' stuff. Living it up when Dad's gone."

"You doing the normal things that teenagers do isn't 'living it up,' baby. We have to go on, even if it's hard to do it. Life can't just . . . just stop."

"It definitely hasn't for you," he mutters under his breath, making me frown.

"What's that's supposed to mean?"

"Nothin,'" he says. I can barely hear him over all the tapping and clicking.

"If you mean I shouldn't go to the flea market today out of respect for your daddy, you should know that I planned to do this long ago," I explain, though I'm not sure if the explanation is more for him or for myself. "He even said it was OK for me to go. He was gonna go with me. The organizers are expecting me to be there. I promised them I would. I even put an announcement on my Knits

'N' Things page so that my followers would come. What if they show up and I'm not—"

"I get it, Ma," he says, cutting me off, no longer looking at me. His eyes follow the path of the alien in the dark tunnel on the screen. "Whatever."

"No! It's not whatever! My knitting is for me what . . . well, what your video games are for you."

I raise my hand to the little white shadow box that sits on his bedroom wall. It has a baby blue cap and a pair of booties inside. It was my first project. The first knits that I ever finished after starting them over and over again. I made them back in the NICU for Ghalen while he was there.

"Those yarn and knitting needles have gotten me through some hard times, sweetheart," I whisper, running my hand over the shadow box's cool glass. "You just don't know."

"I do know," he says.

"Huh?"

When I turn around again, he isn't playing his game anymore, but gazing up at me. He doesn't look angry or irritated.

"I said I know, Ma, and I'm sorry for making it sound like you shouldn't go out today. I didn't mean it. I hope . . . I hope you sell a lot of stuff."

I bend down and kiss his cheek. "Thanks, baby."

He nods and puts back on his headphones. I grab my box and head down the hall and then out the front door, not wanting to leave him, but not wanting to hover either. Finally, I close the front door behind me.

✳ ✳ ✳

"It looks like they've got a pretty decent turnout," Morris says to me over the clamor of voices and footsteps. He hands me a cup of hot chocolate that he got from the eatery on the other side of the pavilion, before taking a drink from his own cup.

"Thanks," I say and adjust the stack of scarves on my table. "I'll take your word for it, but you couldn't tell by how few people have been stopping by the table. All the customers must be at the other end of the market."

Morris offered to come with me today, and I said yes because I knew Ghalen wasn't coming; I didn't have to answer questions or make up excuses for why Morris was here. And I miss being with Morris. Since the funeral, we've only gotten a few snatches of time together. This will be our first weekend since that special night at his apartment that we'll have the whole day to do whatever we want. I've been looking forward to it all week. It'll take my mind off things, and Lord knows I need that right now.

"I only had one woman come by ten minutes ago," I say to Morris as he takes the spot beside me behind the table. He's even wearing a name tag so he looks like he's a Knit 'N' Things employee. "She asked if I had any cashmere knits. When I told her no, she turned up her nose and walked off."

He chuckles. "I looked around and saw your competition. None of the other knitted pieces are as good as yours, in my humble opinion. She's missing out." He then leans down and gives me a kiss.

I almost pull my mouth away, but I stop myself. Instead, I take a quick glance around me to see if anyone saw the kiss, but no one's looking at us. The vendors that are nearby—a woman selling wool berets and a couple selling wicker baskets—are either talking to each other or staring at their cell phones. The customers are looking at the merchandise on the other tables.

"What's wrong?" Morris asks.

"Huh? Nothing's wrong. Why do you think something's wrong?" I paste on a smile, but he's still eying me.

"Really, Tasha? Are you ever going to be comfortable with us in public together?"

"What do you mean? We're in public together all the time."

"You *know* what I mean." Morris drops his voice to a whisper. "How long after he's gone before you stop acting like you're cheating on the man? Frankly, even when he was alive, he didn't deserve all these theatrics just to keep him from finding out."

"Morris," I begin tightly, looking around me again, "let's not do this here."

"I *love* you, Tasha Jenkins, and I'm not gonna apologize for wanting the world to know that."

His words are fierce, but the look in his eyes is tender. It smooths over what little anger I feel at the moment. I reach out and grab his hand. "I love you too."

"And don't forget it," he says with a grin before leaning down to kiss me again.

This time I don't even think about backing away, and I try not to think about who might see us. I try to enjoy just being with him, having someone I truly care for who adores me and wants to be at my side.

"I'm gonna walk around for a bit," he says before squeezing my hand and peeling off his name tag. "I'll pretend to be casually look-ing at tables and see if I can drum up some customers. I'll tell them I met this wonderful woman with impeccable taste who's selling knits for amazing prices. They just have to come to her table."

"Well, aren't you sneaky," I say with an eyebrow wiggle and a laugh.

Morris gives me a wink and then walks off.

I examine my table again and snap my fingers when I realize I've forgotten to put out the fingerless gloves. Last year, they were one of my best sellers. I bend down, push aside the tablecloth, and pull out one of the boxes.

"What lovely scarves! Are you really only charging eighteen dollars for these?"

I freeze mid-motion at the question.

Even in all this noise and all the echoes inside the pavilion, I hear her voice as clearly as if it'd been shouted through a bullhorn. I haven't heard it out loud in months, but it's been ringing inside my head almost every single day. I swear I'll never forget it.

I slowly look up and find her—Madison Gingell—standing on the other side of my table, holding up one of my knitted scarves.

"What do you think about the purple and blue?" She brings it close to her cheek and inclines her head. "Does it flatter me?"

I open my mouth, but I can't speak. As much as I try, nothing comes out.

She wrinkles her nose. "Hmm, maybe not," she says and tosses the scarf back onto the table. She then shifts her attention to the assortment of socks. "I saw on Instagram that you were going to be here at the flea market today. I figured I should stop by and pay you a visit, especially after Phil had that nasty car accident on Thursday. A hit-and-run. It was the strangest thing. The car was completely decimated. Luckily, Phil and our driver survived. He was back at work the very next day—the shameless workaholic that he is," she says with a laugh.

She looks up from the socks that she's flipping through and gazes at me. I stare blankly back at her.

"He survived the crash, Tasha," she repeats again.

"O-OK," I stutter, making her squint at me.

"Considering what happened to your husband, I was surprised mine made out so well, with barely a scratch."

I go still again. My heart starts to pound so fast that I think it might seize up.

"I thought it might be you. I mean, our driver hasn't had an accident in *years*. It seemed so random, but now . . . but now, I'm starting to wonder if it was you." She tosses the socks aside. "Maybe you're still sitting around on your ass, doing nothing."

I gaze around me. Can't they hear her? Don't the other people in the pavilion see our conversation? Why don't they hear what's happening? But once again, Madison floats through life. Untouchable.

"You know, Tasha. This deal of ours only works if we *both* do our part," she goes on. "It also works best if our interactions are limited, and here I am, checking in on you, making sure you stay on task. But it looks like you're already distracted." She stares over her shoulder at the crowds walking through the pavilion. "That tall, handsome gentleman that I saw at your table a few minutes ago . . . did Kordell know about him before he died?"

"You leave him alone," I say in a hoarse whisper through clenched teeth, feeling more angry than scared. "Don't you dare hurt him! Don't you—"

"Tasha, I have no interest in him, and I don't give a fuck what you two are doing together, for that matter. But I am frustrated that you're benefiting from the fruits of my labor. From my good will. You're enjoying your new job as well, aren't you? Evelyn told me you're doing swimmingly over there."

"How . . . how do you know Evelyn?" I ask, now even more shocked.

"My husband and I are one of Myers Trust's largest donors. I recommended you for the executive assistant job. Well, to be honest, I told Evelyn if she couldn't do me a favor and hire you for the job, I wasn't sure if Phil and I could continue to donate to the trust, despite its noble causes. There's certainly plenty of other places around town that could use our money. Evelyn said we had to keep it hush-hush, though," she says before raising a finger to her puckered lips, like she's shushing me. "She had to make it look like the real thing. Wouldn't want to give the impression of nepotism. So they brought you in for an interview, contacted your references, and you got the job."

My mouth falls open. That's why I didn't remember applying for Myers Trust. Because I didn't apply for the job. It'd been Madison working behind the scenes the whole time, just like she did with Kordell . . . just like she's trying to do now.

"I wasn't sure if it was too much hand-holding on my part, but I figured you needed the confidence boost. The mobility. The autonomy. You couldn't very well do what I need you to do if you continued to be stuck prisoner at home. I've invested *a lot* in you, Tasha, because I believed in you. You're free to go about your life and do as you please now, but I'm not. And that's not fair. That's not fair at all." She braces her hands on the table and leans forward, making me take a step back. Her face goes stern. Her lips tighten. "We're supposed to help each other. That was the deal. But so far, I'm the one doing all the helping. It's time for you to stop being selfish. It's time to hold up your end of the bargain. We're in this together, remember? So make sure you do your part—and do it soon."

And like somebody flipped a switch, her blue eyes brighten. Her smile is back. She grabs the purple-and-blue scarf off my table.

"You know what? I think I will take this one after all!" I watch, stunned, as she reaches into her purse and pulls out a twenty-dollar bill. She tosses it in front of me. "Keep the change," she chirps. "Oh, and remember what I said. Let me know if you need me to brainstorm some ideas for you," she says before turning and walking away.

I stand there not speaking, not moving. I'm too scared. Too horrified. I was right. I was right about her all along.

"OK, I don't wanna speak too soon, but I think I managed to drum up some customers," Morris says minutes later, walking back to my table. "They're two women. One's wearing a white hat. The other's wearing an orange sweater. They should be coming over soon." He pauses and frowns down at me. "What's wrong? What'd I miss? You look like you've seen a ghost or somethin'."

"She . . . she was here."

"She *who*?" He touches my shoulder to turn me around. "Damn, Tasha, you're shaking."

"Madison! Madison Gingell. She came o-o-ver here. She t-t-talked to me, Morris."

"She did?" The frown lines in his face deepen. He looks through the crowd. "Where is she now? What did she say?"

"She did it, like I thought. She stood right here in my face and said it. It wasn't my imagination. I'm not making this up. She killed Kordell, and I have to tell the police!"

CHAPTER 26

NOW

Long nights and early mornings. That was his usual work routine. Luckily, Detective Simmons had been blessed with a unique circadian rhythm that he'd further honed over the years, after one too many all-nighters in college and his early days as a patrol cop with a hard-ass superior officer who gave him some of the worst swing shifts in the entire department. Under normal circumstances, Simmons had no problem surviving on a mere four to five hours of sleep, but he suspected he'd need several hits of caffeine to make it through today.

He hadn't left the Gingells' home on Capitol Hill until after 2 a.m., talking to more witnesses, retracing his steps, and going over the details of the crime scene and his brief conversation with Tasha Jenkins over and over again in his head, until his lids mercifully creaked shut like metal shutters at around 3:30 a.m.

Now, as he made his way to his cubicle, he took a sip of his first cup of coffee to get a little buzz, a little energy, but winced at the taste. Simmons had ordered a straight black, but he swore he could detect a hint of caramel, even white chocolate, in his drink. He held up the paper cup and examined the label again. The name in black print was Carol, not Clayton. He must have picked up the wrong one.

"Damn," he muttered before chucking the cup into a nearby bin. "I *am* tired."

This didn't bode well for how productive today was going to be.

The overhead lights in the bullpen burned bright, revealing a nearly empty office that would fill up soon. Littered on the desks surrounding him were coffee mugs, calendars, miniature football helmets, a snow globe, and picture frames. Unlike the other frosted plexiglass cubicles, Simmons's desk and walls were almost bare; they looked as if he'd just been assigned his desk that week instead of four years ago.

Montrose, who sat three desks over, had about a dozen pictures on his desk of his wife and three cherub-faced kids, his Lab, his parents, and even one of his dead grandfather in a Santa hat, raising a beer pint to the camera in a toast. The only pictures Simmons kept were on his cell phone: a few of his Tabby cat, Bruno, a pic of a dent in his car door that he'd sent to his insurance company for damage reimbursement, and a couple pics of a sunset he'd taken while on vacation in the Bahamas three years ago. No pics of a wife or kids. Not even a girlfriend.

Like his desk, Simmons's life was, for the most part, uncluttered. He was solely dedicated to his job. He might even call it a vocation on good days. On his darker days, when the world's problems seemed big enough to swallow him whole, it felt more like a burden. That's when being a black man with a badge felt about as useless as a pen with no ink or a truck with no wheels.

He booted up his laptop, tugged out his desk chair, and sat down. He felt like he'd done all that he could do for now as far as old-fashioned detective work when it came to the Gingells' murder case. Now it was time to do some mundane database and online investigating, which wouldn't make the cut of any episode of *Law & Order*, but had to be done all the same.

"Hey!" he heard Montrose's muffled voice call over his shoulder a half hour later. "You're in here *already*?"

Simmons turned in his chair to find his partner stuffing his face with a bear claw as he shrugged out of his windbreaker.

"Oh, who am I kidding?" Montrose said with a chuckle, licking bits of glazed frosting from the corner of his mouth and his upper lip. "You probably slept here, didn't you?"

"Nope. Can't fit under the desk," Simmons muttered before shifting in his chair and returning his attention to his laptop.

Montrose walked toward him and leaned over his shoulder, peering at the screen. "You look like you're concentrating hard. Whatcha' doin'?"

"I'm looking up Phillip and Madison Gingell. I couldn't shake the feeling all last night that I'd heard the name Gingell before."

"Yeah, his neighbors said he's some rich hotshot," Montrose said between smacks and chews. "A big-time lawyer or somethin'."

"It's not just that. Did you know his other wife Ashley Gingell was killed about nine years ago? She was that woman jogger who was murdered near that C&O trail out in Georgetown."

"Oh, yeah!" Montrose snapped his crust-covered fingers and nodded. "I remember now! We had to do that big sweep in the woods to find her. Shit, that was a lot of man-hours for that one! Didn't she get strangled by some crackhead?"

"Hakeem Fletcher," Simmons said, still staring at his screen. "He was charged and found guilty."

Simmons remembered seeing the news clip on television when the jury read its verdict, how Fletcher had screamed that he didn't do it, how the bailiffs had to restrain him and practically drag him out of the courtroom.

"Humph," Montrose murmured before standing upright and letting out a soft belch. "So why are you so interested in the Gingells? Shouldn't you be looking up Tasha? They were the ones who got shot and had their house set on fire. She's the one who's sitting behind bars after a confession."

"False confession," Simmons corrected.

"Jesus, this again." Montrose stopped chewing. "You don't know that, man."

"No, I *do* know that. I know the evidence doesn't match her story."

"Come on, I saw her that night. She even looked guilty!"

Simmons squinted up at his partner. "Looked guilty how?"

"You know." Montrose shrugged. "She had the . . . the look! You know what I mean."

"No, I don't. Explain to me exactly what you mean."

A heavy lull fell between them that was louder than their voices.

"Hey, uh," Montrose began, shifting uncomfortably in front of him, "if you're trying to insinuate that I'm saying this shit because she's black, that's not what I meant. That's not cool either. I'm not some racist. You know me. I focus on the facts."

"I do too. And I know Tasha Jenkins has no motive."

"No, you don't know if she has a motive!" Montrose licked his fingers and pointed at the laptop screen. "Maybe if you'd dig into her and not the Gingells, you'd find out what it was."

"This is your case too. Why don't *you* find out what it is?"

"Maybe I will . . . *after* I finish my donut. But you've got me all riled up. Almost gave me heartburn," Montrose muttered as he took another bite and strolled to his desk while Simmons shook his head in exasperation.

Montrose's possible prejudices aside, he had a point. Simmons's gut told him that Tasha hadn't committed the crime, but gut instinct still had to be supported with corroborating facts. Especially since Tasha kept insisting she'd done it. Maybe there was something in her background that would explain why she would lie. Maybe she had a spouse or another relative who could give him some insight.

He typed her name into the database and once again found a clean record, as expected. He kept digging and hit on a property record that showed the name Kordell Jenkins. Kordell didn't have a police record, but a check online showed that he was now deceased. A murder victim. And like the Gingells, he'd been shot. The crime had taken place less than a couple of months ago.

Three shootings in Tasha's orbit within a matter of months.

Simmons began to gnaw anxiously on the inside of his cheek.

On cue, Montrose burst into laughter, like he was chuckling at Simmons's latest discovery. Simmons turned with exasperation, only to find his partner staring at a cartoon on his cell phone. He continued reading the article on his laptop screen—his frown deepening as he read. According to the article, Kordell Jenkins's body had been found by a local man and his son who had been hunting for deer nearby.

"The guy was on his knees and kind of slumped over like. We thought maybe he was reaching into his truck or something, or was digging around in there because he lost something under the seat. But then we saw all the blood," Fred Muir had told the *Herald Mail*. "We knew he was dead."

"There are currently no suspects in this case," said Sergeant Myers of the Washington County Sheriff's Office in the same article. "We are asking the public to contact the Sheriff's Office if they have any information."

Simmons leaned back in his chair. Tasha hadn't been a suspect in that particular case, but he had to talk to Sergeant Myers. He needed to know more about what had happened to Kordell. He glanced at the digital clock on his screen. It was 9:47. Hopefully, Myers was in the office and would take his call.

Minutes later, he listened to the bleat of a ringing phone on the other end of the line.

"Sergeant Myers speaking," a voice answered after the third ring.

"Hello, Sergeant Myers, this is Detective Clayton Simmons with the Metropolitan Police Department in Washington, D.C. I'm investigating a murder and attempted murder involving the suspect you may have heard of . . . perhaps even spoken to, and I was wondering if you could help me in regard to my investigation. Her name is Tasha Jenkins, and—"

"Yeah, Kordell Jenkins's wife. I know her. So she's involved in another murder, huh?"

Simmons squinted. "Wait. *Another* murder? She's been involved in one before?"

"Well, not really. We couldn't connect her to Kordell's murder, but . . ." The line went silent.

"But what?"

"Look, uh, detective, I wish I could help you, but this is still an ongoing investigation and I—"

"Sergeant Myers, this is an ongoing murder investigation for us as well, but I called you because I have some missing puzzle pieces that I can't quite figure out. I was hoping you could provide me with some insight. Show me what I'm missing."

Sergeant Myers stayed resolutely silent on the other end. Simmons took a deep breath and thought for a second. He decided to change tactics.

"Maybe our investigation could help yours as well, if they're related," he persisted. "And we won't know if we don't talk, right? Just one cop helping another."

Sergeant Myers loudly grumbled. He sounded like he was going to hang up, but he started talking instead.

"You know that old saying, if a spouse turns up dead the first suspect you look at is the husband or the wife," he began. "Well, we weren't able to connect Tasha to Kordell's murder. She had a solid alibi. She was over a hundred miles away at the time it happened. It all checked out, but somethin' has never quite sat right with me about that woman. I'm not shocked to hear she's involved in another case like this. She didn't seem on the up-and-up. First, she said she knew nothing about the murder. Then she changes her story and starts making these wild claims. Some real kooky stuff."

Simmons leaned forward in his chair, resting his elbows on his desk. "What wild claims?"

"She said she didn't have anything to do with it, but she knew the woman who killed her husband. That the lady had offered to kill Kordell if Tasha killed her husband, too. Like some quid pro quo deal. She was ranting about how the woman cooked up this big plan out of thin air. It was just about the strangest thing I ever heard. But when folks make up wild stuff like that, I generally find it's one of two things: they're either nuttier than a sack of cashews, or they want to distract you from what you really should be looking at. You know? They're sending you on a wild goose chase. They don't want you to focus on them, and frankly, I could understand why Tasha wouldn't want us to focus on her in our investigation."

"Why wouldn't she want you to focus on her?"

Sergeant Myers seemed to hesitate on the other end of the line. Finally, he sighed. "We got wind that Tasha might have been having an affair before her husband was murdered. There also may have been some physical abuse. She and Kordell supposedly had a big fight not too long before the shooting. It may have been over the other guy . . . her sneakin' around. If she knew her husband knew she was doing a little hokey-pokey behind his back . . . if she knew what he might do to her if he found out, it would be convenient to have him drop out of the picture, wouldn't it? It would fix all her problems."

Simmons sat up in his chair. The fact that Tasha may have cheated on her husband might or might not be relevant to his case, but it certainly added more complexity to the image of Tasha Jenkins that Simmons had created in his head.

"Did Tasha happen to say who the woman was? The one she claimed killed her husband, I mean? Did she give you a name?"

"Uh, yeah, it was uh . . . darn, her name is right on the tip of my tongue. Let me check my notes for a sec. Hold on."

Simmons heard a loud clatter, then the rustling of paper. A few seconds later, Sergeant Myers returned.

"Yeah, her name was Madison. Madison Gingell."

At those words, Simmons's stomach dropped. "Jesus," he whispered.

"*What?* The name sounds familiar?"

"Madison Gingell is one of our victims."

"Oh, geez," Sergeant Myers echoed.

Oh, geez indeed, Simmons thought.

"Did you ever speak to Madison? Did she give you any indication why Tasha would accuse her of such a thing?"

"Yeah, I followed up with her, though I doubted anything would come of it. Thoroughly checked her out. The lead went nowhere. But based on what you're saying, I'm wondering now if there was more to the story. Maybe Tasha really was convinced Madison had killed her husband. Maybe she wasn't trying to distract us. She really *is* off her rocker."

Simmons closed his eyes. "Well, thanks for sharing all this with me. Is there anyone else I should talk to . . . that you talked to in the course of your investigation who can tell me more about Tasha? A neighbor? A relative?"

"You might want to reach out to her son, Ghalen. He gave me more background on his mother. He lives with her."

Simmons ended the call soon after, with promises to update Sergeant Myers on his own investigation as soon as he could. Sitting at his desk, going over the information he'd just heard, he was now starting to question his original conclusions about the case. There was a connection between Tasha and one of the victims, and it was a big one: Tasha had accused Madison of killing her husband. And with that went Tasha's lack of motive for the arson and shootings. It annoyed the hell out of him that Montrose had been right—at least in that regard. Tasha definitely had a motive, but was she guilty?

Simmons could feel his confusion growing like his craving for a hit of caffeine. He needed to muddle over this some more as desperately as he needed a cup of coffee.

"I'll be back. I need to take a walk," he announced to no one in particular before rising from his chair and heading out of the bullpen. He grabbed his coat, rode the elevator to the first floor, and walked through the glass doors into the cold March morning sunshine, watching the frost in the air as he breathed. Instead of going to the usual Starbucks on the corner, he decided to take a long stroll to a sister Starbucks seven blocks away.

As he walked, Simmons thought about Tasha. Maybe he'd been wrong. Maybe she had gone "off her rocker" like Sergeant Myers had said, and had shot and set fire to the Gingells. She'd certainly seemed distraught last night when he questioned her. Confused. Almost out of it. He remembered those haunted eyes. The shaky body movements.

After all, he was a cop, not a shrink. Maybe her behavior hadn't been a sign of her innocence, but of a mind now in complete disarray—or one that had been in disarray for quite some time. If she was no longer connected to reality, maybe she wouldn't remember if she had shot Phillip and Madison before she set the fire. News of it would have been a surprise to her.

There is such a thing as memory loss from PTSD, he thought as he waited at the crosswalk for the light to change. Perhaps that had been the culprit.

But still, she hadn't smelled like smoke, he acknowledged, as the light changed and he started walking again. He remembered that distinctly.

"If she started the fire, shouldn't she smell like it?" he whispered later as he stood at the coffee-shop counter.

"I'm sorry, sir?" the perky barista asked with a smile. "Did you say yes to ordering a bagel as well?"

"Oh, umm, no. Sorry," Simmons murmured. "Ignore me. I was . . . I was just thinking out loud."

It was one thing to try to find missing puzzle pieces. It was another thing to try to cram pieces together in order to fit a scene you believed should exist. Detectives could sometimes fall into that trap. He didn't believe Tasha was guilty, therefore he was trying to make the evidence support his theory, dismissing anything to the contrary. She hadn't seemed like the usual suspect. She wasn't one of the hardened criminals he usually ran into during his course of work. Tasha Jenkins had seemed scared and bewildered last night. She was still wearing her work clothes at the crime scene like she had just left the office hours earlier. She'd called in the fire herself like a responsible citizen.

But she'd also admitted that she'd committed the crime. She'd said it more than once.

Is Tasha innocent, or is she guilty? Simmons wondered for the umpteenth time as he drank his coffee and walked back through the police station's glass doors fifteen minutes later. Was she sane, or was she suffering from some psychosis?

If they got this wrong, an innocent woman who could be his sister or his cousin or even his wife—if he had one—could end up rotting in prison for something she didn't do. She could be the one screaming as the bailiffs dragged her out of the courtroom after the guilty verdict. He didn't want to be responsible for another statistic, for an injustice.

When he returned to his desk, he looked up her home number. He got a voicemail and left a message for her son to call him back ASAP.

"You look like someone ran over your dog," Montrose said as Simmons tossed his cell back onto his desk. "What's up?"

"Nothin'. Just gathering more info on the Gingell case."

Montrose leaned back and sat on the edge of Simmons's desk. His lips curved into a cocky grin. "Let me guess . . . the info isn't turning out the way you thought it would."

Simmons didn't answer, making his partner chuckle.

"Told ya' she was guilty, bro." Montrose braced his hands on his knees. "Look, I know you wanna cover all your bases, but sometimes a confession is just a confession. Do you know how many crimes happen in this city every day? Hundreds. Probably thousands! You know how many will probably go unsolved?"

Simmons closed his eyes, shutting out his partner visually since he couldn't very well do it audibly with him sitting there.

"And here we have one wrapped up in a nice package with a neat little bow," Montrose droned on. "One that's already solved, as far as I'm concerned. I don't know about you, but I don't turn away a gift like that. I accept it for what it is."

"You're very wise," Simmons muttered dryly.

"Aren't I?" Montrose laughed. "I should do TED Talks!"

Simmons's cell phone started to ring. He opened his eyes.

"I'll let you get that," Montrose said before pushing himself to his feet and loudly slapping Simmons on the shoulder. "Buck up, bro. Live to fight another day."

Simmons grimaced before pressing the green button to answer. "Detective Simmons with the MPD. Who am I speaking to?"

"Umm, you called me a few minutes ago. I'm Ghalen Jenkins."

Simmons suddenly sat upright in his chair. "Hello, Ghalen. Thanks for calling me back."

"Yeah, uh, is this about my mom? Is she OK? Do you . . . do you know where she is?"

"Gay, who are you talking to?" a female voice shouted in the background.

"The cop that left a message," Ghalen said. His voice was slightly muffled like he was holding his hand over the receiver. "I was calling him back. . . . Sorry," he said to Simmons. "That was my aunt. So, were you calling about Ma?

"Yes, I was." Simmons waited a beat before he continued. "Your mom was arrested last night, Ghalen. She's being charged with murder."

"What?" the young man cried. "How . . . why would . . . Ma would never do that! She would never kill anybody. She wouldn't hurt anyone. Y'all made a mistake! You arrested the wrong person!"

"Well, that's why I wanted to talk to you, Ghalen. If we've made a mistake, I was hoping you could help me figure this out."

"Is this about that bitch? That white lady, Madison? It's about her, isn't it?"

"You know her?"

"Yeah, I know her! She killed my dad! That's why I was gonna—"

"Oh, hell no!" his aunt shouted in the background. "Hand me the phone, Gay. Hand it over!"

The sound muffled again and then was so loud that Simmons had to pull his cell phone away from his ear. He winced.

"This boy just got out of lockup two hours ago, and I'm not about to see him go back!" his aunt shouted. "Why are you asking him all these questions? What's this about Tasha being in jail?"

"Ma'am, who am I speaking to?"

"Like he said, I'm his aunt. Rita Jenkins. He's only 17 years old, and since his daddy is dead and his mama's in jail, I guess I'm his legal guardian for now. So whatever you have to ask or say to him, you can ask or say it in front of me. I'm not gonna have him blurting out something stupid and end up back in jail. Not today, sir!"

Simmons bit back a smile. The woman on the other end of the line reminded him of one of his own aunts. Loud, fearless, and protective.

"I understand your concern. I have no problem speaking to you both. Could I come there and interview you and Ghalen today? Say at around two o'clock?"

His answer must have caught her off guard. For the first time, she went silent. "Make it four o'clock. I want Ghalen's lawyer there when we talk to you, and he won't be available until that time."

He needs a lawyer present? Simmons thought with raised brows.

He was investigating Ghalen's mother, not the boy himself. But Ghalen did have a right to an attorney present, if he wanted one, and his aunt had mentioned that he had just come out of lockup. Simmons wondered what he'd done to get there. Did it have anything to do with his mother?

"Fine by me," he said. "See you at four o'clock, ma'am."

He hung up, wondering whether what Ghalen had to say would finally wrap the mystery of Tasha Jenkins and Madison Gingell into a neat package with a little bow, or make their story even more complicated.

CHAPTER 27

BEFORE

TASHA

POINTLESS. DRIVING ALL THE WAY UP THOSE MOUNTAINS TO HAGERS-town to talk to the police had been a waste of my damn time. I could've saved myself the headache, the gas, and the day I took off from work to go there.

I turn the wheel and make a right at the corner, rubbing at the soreness in my neck as I do it. I'm finally near home, but I don't know what I'm going to do when I get there. Take a warm bath with epsom salts and try to relax, or fall onto my bed and break down into tears.

I don't know what I was thinking. Why would they ever listen to me? I could see the doubt in the sergeant's eyes and hear it in his voice as he spoke.

"So, she offered to kill your husband over lunch?" Sergeant Myers asked me back at the Sheriff's Office.

He looked like one of the cops in those TV shows: short silver hair, plain white shirt, and skin so pale you could see all the purple and blue veins in his face and hands.

"Not over lunch," I explained as I sat in the plastic chair in that plain white room, trying my best to get comfortable but making a poor job of it. "She did it after lunch, as she was walking me to the train station."

"Uh-huh," he said as he scribbled on his notepad. "And what did you say?"

"What do you mean?"

"What did you say when this woman offered to kill your husband for you? Did you tell her no?"

"Yes. I mean . . . umm . . . no."

"Which is it? *Yes* or *no?*"

I swallowed. "I didn't tell her yes."

"So you *did* tell her no?"

I opened my mouth, then closed it.

"It's a simple question, Mrs. Jenkins. What did you say when she offered to kill your husband? What were your exact words?"

I thought back to that day, to that moment standing at the top of the escalators with the sound of the trains thundering beneath us.

"I'm right," Madison had said to me, still smiling. "It's the solution we both need. We just have to see it through!"

"Yeah, OK, umm . . . I . . . I have to go."

Sitting there in that police office, my eyes went wide at the memory. I was as still as a statue in my chair.

"Mrs. Jenkins, do you need me to repeat the question?" Sergeant Myers asked slowly, cocking his eyebrow at me.

No, I didn't need him to repeat it. I'd heard him loud and clear. But now I wasn't sure how to answer. I'd said yes that day. But I hadn't meant it. I would never have said it if I'd meant it. But I couldn't tell him that, so I told him only half the truth.

"I-I-I told her that I . . . uh . . . that I had to go home. I had to go because . . . well . . . because my husband would expect me back soon."

He stopped writing and looked up from his notepad. "So a woman tells you that you should kill your husband and she's willing to do it, and your response is to tell her that you have to go home?"

"I didn't know what to say! I hadn't expected her to bring up somethin' like that out of nowhere. It . . . it caught me off guard."

"Uh-huh," he said, looking at his notepad again. He wrote something down. I couldn't see what.

I told him everything else that had happened. Her check-in at the flea market. All that I remembered. I even gave him a printout of our phone bill that showed all the incoming calls to Kordell's cell phone in the weeks before he died.

"I put names next to the phone numbers I recognized and an asterisk next to the ones that I didn't," I told him. "Kordell's buddy told me he was headed to meet a woman the day he was murdered. He was meeting her for a consultation. I think it was Madison. One of the calls on there has to have been her. It'll show she called him."

Sergeant Myers took the papers and flipped through the stapled stack. "There's more than a hundred numbers here, Mrs. Jenkins."

"I know it's a lot, but my husband did all his business over his cell. Personal calls, too," I explained.

"Do you know what day this woman supposedly called him?"

I shook my head.

"And you're sure she called him? He didn't call her? Would we only be looking at incoming calls?"

"I think so. But . . . but I'm not sure."

"Uh-huh," he grunted, flipping through the stack again. "I'll let you know if anything turns up."

But I knew, from his expression, not to hold my breath.

✳ ✳ ✳

As I parallel park in front of my home, I shake my head again at how the sergeant treated me. I look up. The lights are on inside my house. That used to mean that Kordell was home from work, but it doesn't mean that anymore because my husband is dead, and it looks like his murderer won't be punished. Madison is going to get away with this. She killed my husband and is going to harass me until I kill hers. The police aren't going to help me. No one is going to stop this.

I turn off the engine of my Chevy Malibu and sit, staring out the windshield at the dark city street. I'm starting to feel cornered again. All that freedom I had the day after Kordell walked out was yanked away so fast that I can't remember what it even felt like. I'm not dancing on his puppet strings anymore, but now Madison is breathing down my neck, waiting for me to dance for her. But I won't do it. I can't do it. I refuse.

I open my car door and climb out. A minute or so later, I step inside my home and shut the front door behind me. I fall back against it, drop my purse to the floor, and close my eyes.

"You're late," a deep voice says, breaking the silence.

My eyes flash open. I almost jump out of my skin.

I half expect to see Kordell standing in front of me, still wearing the pancake makeup from his funeral and the suit he was buried in now covered with the soil from his grave plot. But instead, I find Ghalen staring at me. He's standing on the other side of the living room in the entryway leading to our kitchen with his hands shoved into the pockets of his jeans.

"Oh, Ghalen," I say, dropping my hand to my chest, where my heart is still beating fast, "you scared the hell out of your mama! How long have you been standing there?"

"Where were you, Ma? Usually you're home by now."

I take off my coat and hang it in the closet. "I'm sorry, baby. I didn't go to work today, and I didn't know I would be back home so late."

"If you didn't go to work, then where did you go?"

I don't want to tell Ghalen about my drive to the Sheriff's Office. I haven't told him about Madison Gingell, and I don't plan to. He's already grieving the loss of his daddy. I don't know what he'd do if he found out that I know who killed Kordell and told the police about it, only for the police to refuse to listen to me. It might be like hearing the news that his father has died all over again.

"I just ran a few errands." I flap my hands, shooing away his question, and smile. "Did you make yourself dinner? I think there were some leftovers in the fridge. Want me to heat you up somethin'?"

"No, I want you to tell me where you were."

There is a hardness to his voice that catches me off guard. My smile disappears. I narrow my eyes at my boy, but he doesn't flinch. He doesn't blink.

"The last time I checked," I say, crossing my arms over my chest, "I was the mother and you were the son. When did you start asking after me? When did you give me a curfew?"

He lowers his eyes. "I was just worried about you, Ma. Especially after . . . well . . . after what happened to Dad. I didn't know if you were coming home."

"Oh, honey." I reach up and cup his face, seeing all his worry and sadness. I give him a hug and he holds me tight like he did back when he was little and wasn't embarrassed for me to hug him. I rub his back to comfort him. "Your mama is fine. I should have called and told you I was running a little late. I guess time got away from me."

"Were you with him?" he says against my shoulder, and I wonder if I heard him right.

"What, honey?"

He raises his head. His eyes meet mine. "Were you with that dude? That guy you were talking to at the funeral?"

I step out of my son's arms. "You mean Morris? Why . . . why would you ask me that? Why would I be with him?"

Ghalen starts to chew his bottom lip.

"Why would you ask me that, Ghalen?"

He couldn't have seen us together. I had been so careful.

"Everybody saw you walk off with him at the funeral, Ma. They were wondering who he was. I thought . . . I wondered if maybe he was—"

"You wondered if maybe he was what?"

"Nevermind," he says, shaking his head and backing away from me into the kitchen. "Forget I asked."

"Is that the real reason why you thought I wasn't coming home? You thought I was going to run off with a man . . . with Morris, and what? *Leave you?*"

I love Morris, but I would *never* do that. I would never walk out on my baby, not send him away or leave him behind.

"I said, 'Nevermind,' Ma." Ghalen's holding up his hands and shaking his head so hard, his dreads whip his face. "I don't wanna know."

"There's nothing to know! I'm not hiding anything from you!" Not today, anyway. "I was at the Sheriff's Office talking about your father's murder, Ghalen. I was answering more questions. That's where I was *all* day! I wasn't with Morris."

"OK, Ma," he mumbles before walking to the fridge and opening it. He stares at the crowded shelves.

"That's exactly what happened. The police said they want to talk to you too. Just a few questions about your dad. I know it can be scary to talk to the police. If you want me to, I can be there with you while they—"

"No," he says, taking out a plastic container filled with three-day-old spaghetti from the fridge, "you don't have to sit with me. I'm fine talking to them by myself."

"All right. Whatever you want." I watch as he pops his spaghetti into the microwave and turns on the television on our counter. "Look, honey, I'm sorry about everything. Let's start over again. How was school today? Did you do OK on your English test?" I ask, placing my hand on his shoulder. "I know you were worried about it."

"I did fine." He shrugs off my hand and stares at the microwave, no longer looking at me.

I don't have to read minds to know my son doesn't want to talk to me anymore, so I decide to give him some space. I walk out of the kitchen, down the hall, and into my bedroom. I close the bedroom door behind me, but I can still hear the laugh track on the television and the microwave beeping.

I prayed for so long for the day when Kordell would finally be gone and I could spend an evening alone, doing whatever the hell I wanted, not being under his thumb. But I never thought this is how I would get it. I never thought it would turn out this way.

I stare through the doorway at my bathroom, but instead of turning on the water to relax, I sit down on my bed and cry. I cry until it feels like I can't cry anymore. Until the tears run out.

CHAPTER 28

MADISON

"Have you had a chance to look at our menu?" the waiter asks, pausing at my table. I shift my eyes away from the floor-to-ceiling windows to find him gazing at me expectantly. "Are you ready to order?"

"I'm not quite ready yet. Sorry! I'm waiting for my friend, and she's running a little late," I say, with an exaggerated pout.

He smiles and nods. "I understand. I'll give you more time. In the meanwhile, I'll take your glass and get that refilled for you, if that's OK. You had the Louis Michel, right?"

"Yes, I did. Thank you so much."

When the waiter leaves with my glass, I glance at the time on my phone and turn back to the windows in search of Summer among the throng of people walking along the sidewalk and idling by the granite stairs leading to Zaytinya, the Mediterranean restaurant where we've agreed to meet for lunch.

We chose Zaytinya because the multi-level restaurant design and table placement make it easy to talk without worrying that other people will overhear our conversation, and based on our last phone call, Summer has plenty to share. The mezze-style dishes also allow the more calorie-conscious diners like myself to be less conspicuous as we nibble from a "meal" on a plate no larger than a saucer. Nothing worse than hearing "Is *that* all you're eating?" when you already feel like a fat cow for bingeing on three dark chocolate truffles the night before.

But Summer is ruining the dining experience by making me sit here in boredom as I wait for her. And I'm already on my second glass of wine.

"Two-hundred and forty calories and counting," I mutter as the waiter approaches with my glass.

After he places it on the table and I nod in thanks, I notice glossy dark hair bouncing in my periphery. I see Summer rush to the restaurant's glass door and walk to the marble desk where the hostess stands. Summer leans forward, breathless and frazzled, while unwrapping the camel-colored wool shawl from around her shoulders. She says something to the hostess, probably asking if I'm here yet. Of course I am. I raise my hand and wave at her. She notices me and leans back before striding to our table.

"I am *so* sorry, Maddie." She tugs out her chair and sits down. "I didn't mean to be so late. I hope I didn't keep you waiting long."

"That's perfectly fine. I barely noticed," I lie. "So, you look much better than the last time I saw you! I guess you took my advice. How did it go?"

She opens the napkin at her place setting, drapes it onto her lap, and gives an impish grin. "It went perfectly!" she squeals.

The last time we spoke in person was at the day spa when I shared my idea for how she could get back at her asshole husband, Tom. Ethylene glycol in the form of antifreeze. It was perfect. Cheap, easily accessible, and sweet-tasting so it could be masked if you paired it with the right food or drink. Also, it eventually dissolves in the blood system, making it virtually untraceable. Not too much—less than a cupful could be lethal—but just enough to get results.

She'd balked at the idea at first.

"You think . . . you think I should *kill* him?" she whispered in shock.

"Jesus, you're not really going to kill him, Summer! You'll just give him enough so that he *wishes* he were dead. That's the point."

I had considered using a similar method to get rid of Phil, but I thought killing my husband by way of slow poisoning so that I wouldn't draw attention to myself was an unpredictable process that would take too long. I thought enlisting help with his murder from Tasha might go faster. That it would be a more successful route. Joke's on me, though. Working with Tasha has turned out to be infuriatingly slow and far from predictable. So much for being allies.

"I don't know," Summer said back at the spa. "What if I get caught?"

"If you do it right, you won't."

She still looked doubtful.

"Just think about all the pain he's put *you* through. All the suffering. He doesn't regret any of it, I bet. This might give him a chance to reflect a little. To consider his life choices."

Like his choice to feel me up without my permission. I probably wasn't the first woman Tom had done that to—nor the last. He's a putz. A predator. Tom is someone who is well overdue to be taught a lesson.

"I see your point," Summer said, "but I don't know if I can. I mean, even if I don't get caught . . . isn't it still *wrong*?"

I resisted the urge to roll my eyes.

Right and wrong. Why are people so preoccupied with those concepts? This warped sense of goodness and evil. These arbitrary rules. It's so annoying. So pedestrian. Father constantly preached about righteousness—only to leave me with so many welts on my arms and back that I couldn't wear a tank top or short sleeves for most of my childhood. Reverend Brennan stood at the pulpit every Sunday, professing to us about how good deeds brought us closer to God—only to molest underaged girls. But they both knew the truth: right and wrong, good and evil, aren't rigid concepts. They defined them as they saw fit. Like most people do when it serves their purpose. We just pretend that they don't.

"You know what, Summer? Then don't do it," I said, patting her hand. "Don't do anything you aren't comfortable doing. I'm not going to twist your arm. Maybe you should move on and let him move on with his life. Maybe he'll even marry the toddler, but the joke's on her in the end, right? He'll use her like he used you. He'll make her waste *years* on a man who sees women merely as acquisitions that cater to his ego. No better than a sports car or a piece of art. She'll change for him like you did. Put aside her needs. Her dreams. And he'll trade her in, too, when the time comes, and she'll have to fend for herself like you will. She'll have to reconcile with what her life has become. At least you're rid of him, though. Huh? He's not your burden anymore."

Summer looked stricken. She seemed to consider my words. In her hazel eyes, I could practically see her moral compass shifting in real time. "No . . . no, you're right," she whispered. "Tom should suffer a little. He . . . he deserves it."

Now Summer is all smiles as she digs into one of the plates of fattoush the waiter brings to our table, along with the fruity cocktail she ordered. I dig in as well. I'm starving.

"So start from the beginning," I say. "Tell me *everything*."

"Well, I told Tom that I thought it was time for us to stop being immature and finally discuss how we're going to proceed with our divorce. We have the prenup, but there are still some things we need to decide, like what are we going to do with the half dozen embryos of the babies I *thought* we were going to have, but will now stay stuck in a freezer at a fertility clinic in Silver Spring." She pauses to wipe her mouth with her napkin. "I told him we didn't need an arbitrator or a judge to help us decide this stuff. We could just sit down like two civilized adults and talk about it. I suggested that we do it at my place . . . our old condo."

I nod as I stab a piece of cucumber. "Smart move. What did he say?"

"He wasn't open to it at first. He said it would be better to have a discussion like that in 'neutral territory,'" she says, using air quotes, "like an office, so that way I wouldn't get emotional on him."

"Asshole," I murmur between chews.

"Exactly! But I promised that I wouldn't get emotional. No tears. No begging. No arguing. I told him I'm seeing a therapist now. I've been meditating. So he caved. I made us dinner. Pasta primavera. A nice salad. He refused to eat them, but he drank a couple of glasses of wine and had one crostini with olive tapenade while we talked. He left after an hour. We still haven't decided what the hell to do with the embryos," she says before taking a drink from her cocktail.

"So, I assume you added something special to the wine?" I ask, swirling my own wineglass.

She grins. "*And* the tapenade."

"Good job! I guess the question now is, did it work?"

"Well," she says, dropping her voice to a whisper, leaning across the table, "I called him today to ask him when we were going to finish our discussion. He sounded horrible on the phone. He said he's been sick for the past two days. 'It feels like I've come down with a bad flu. I can't keep anything down.'"

I laugh and raise my wineglass to her. "Congrats!"

She toasts my glass and grins. "Thanks! I just have to figure out now how to handle the toddler."

"One at a time," I warn. "You don't want to rush something like this. That's when you make mistakes."

"You're right. You're right." She nods in agreement before taking a bite of the orange slice topping her cocktail. "I'll just focus on Tom for now."

We drink and continue eating our lunch, basking in her win. But I can't help but feel a little jealous. Summer is exacting her revenge on her bastard husband. Tasha's husband is dead. When will I finally get my moment of victory?

I hope Tasha finally gets it after our little chat at the flea market, that she finally falls into line. I have to admit that I'm starting to lose my patience; but from the look on her face, I think I got my point across.

I arrive home a couple of hours later to an empty house. As I remove my coat, I hear the phone ringing. I stroll into the kitchen.

"Call from Washington County Sheriff's Office," the automated voice of our phone system calls out, freezing me in my tracks, making the blood drain from my head.

Why is someone from the Sheriff's Office calling me?

You know why, the voice in my head screams. *It's because of that fucking hubcap! That hubcap that you left on the side of the road like an idiot.*

I guess they finally tracked me down. They know I was driving near the scene that day.

Should I let it go to voicemail? Should I answer?

The phone stops ringing. The decision is made for me. Less than a minute later, I see the red light flashing on the phone unit in the kitchen. With shaking hands, I pick up the receiver and dial to check our voicemail.

"Hello, this message is for Madison Gingell. This is Sergeant Edward Myers at the Washington County Sheriff's Office," the man drawls. "Ma'am, I need you to give me a call back as soon as possible. I'm conducting an investigation into the murder of Kordell Jenkins and I'd like to ask you a few questions. You can reach me at—"

I delete the message before the sergeant can give his phone number. I hang up and fall back onto one of the kitchen stools as the floor seems to shift beneath me, as I become light-headed. I know this isn't the end of it. Deleting his message won't change anything, and I feel the first stab of panic, but I remind myself to take long, deep breaths. In through the nose, out through the mouth. Stay calm. Stay in control.

This is definitely a curveball, but the game isn't over. Not yet. Sergeant Myers will call back eventually, but by then I will be prepared for him. I will know what to do.

CHAPTER 29

TASHA

"I'M SORRY THAT HAPPENED. THEY SHOULD'VE LISTENED TO YOU," Morris says.

While we're on our lunch break and walking to what Morris thinks is the deli where we will eat today, I tell him about my trip to Hagerstown two days ago and just how bad the interview with the sergeant had gone. I didn't tell him about what happened when I got back home.

I didn't mention Ghalen asking about our relationship, and I didn't tell Ghalen the truth. I didn't tell him Ghalen was worried that I was going to leave him, that we were going to run off together. I haven't said anything, because I don't know how Morris will react. He expects that now that Kordell is gone, we will be together. We'll finally be the couple we always wanted to be. I thought the same thing, too, until I saw the look in my son's eyes when I talked about Morris.

"So, what's the plan now?" Morris asks as we make a right at the corner.

"Huh?" I say, a little bit distracted.

The sidewalk is busy with people. A fire truck pushes its way into the intersection, blaring its sirens and horns, making the cars in the street pull over to the side and get out of its way. When it passes, I see the big glass building I was looking for come into view.

"Are you going to try to call them back?" Morris asks as the sound of the sirens fades. "Maybe talk to another police officer?"

"I don't see the point. Not without more evidence, anyway."

"And how are you gonna get that?"

"I gave the sergeant a list of phone numbers. I don't think he'll do anything with it, though, so I've been calling the ones I don't recognize to see if maybe one of them is Madison's. It'll show she did talk to Kordell. That she lured him there that day. But so far, all I've gotten is a lot of telemarketers and a couple of his old customers. Sometimes the phone just rings and rings and nobody picks up."

"Sounds like it could be like looking for a needle in a haystack."

"I know. Believe me, I know."

"You sure you don't wanna reach out to another cop? Maybe local police. Not the ones in Maryland, but in D.C. I can ask my frat brother who to talk to. Because if this woman is as dangerous as you say she is, she should be behind bars, Tasha. What she said to you at the flea market is some scary stuff! Other people could get hurt, like her husband."

Or like you, I think but don't say out loud. Or she could come after Ghalen. To get me to do what she wants, I wouldn't put anything past Madison, which is why I'm doing what I'm doing today. I have to protect them and myself. I have to try every option short of killing that woman with my bare hands.

We are nearing the building I was searching for. I see the plaque on the granite wall leading to the entrance. It shows the four businesses housed inside. "I'll make sure that no one else gets hurt," I say, making Morris squint down at me.

"And how are you gonna do that?"

I stop and point to the sign and to the name, Wyatt & Harris, etched in black. "Her husband works here. I came here to warn him, to tell him what Madison is trying to do. The police won't listen to me. But I know they'd listen to him."

It was easy to find out more about her husband, Phil. The couple seem to be popular around town. I figured she was rich, but Google showed me that not only do Madison and her husband have a lot of money, they've got power too. But those two things tend to go hand in hand, I guess.

I saw a couple of pictures of Madison and her husband in the *Washingtonian* online—one from an opening gala of a new museum in town, another from the White House Press Club dinner a few years ago, and one from one of his lobbying firm's parties. I recognized Phillip Gingell right away. I remembered his face from that night months ago when I saw him back at the Hyatt, except he didn't look like he wanted to wring Madison's neck in the pictures online. He was smiling at the camera. He was smiling on his firm's website too, where I found a phone number, but no email address. I've called him three times at that number and left messages, but he hasn't responded. I didn't fully explain things, because the truth is there isn't a good way to tell a stranger that his wife is trying to kill him and not sound crazy.

"*What?*" Morris looks at the building, then me, and back again. "You're serious? You're really going in there?"

"Yes, I'm serious! I tried calling him, but that didn't work. If I have to see him in person to get him to listen, then I'll do it. I didn't warn Kordell, but I've got to warn her husband. He needs to know what's going on and maybe he'll go to the cops. Maybe they'll finally arrest her."

Morris looks at the glass doors leading to the lobby just as a few people walk out of the building. He takes my arm and pulls me aside, close to a small atrium out front.

"Tasha, you can't just walk in there and tell him his wife is trying to kill him." He looks over my shoulder through the glass into the lobby again. "And there's about four security guards at that front desk. They probably won't let you upstairs to talk to him anyway."

"So, I'll wait for him to come downstairs to the lobby. I know what he looks like." I try to turn away, to take back my arm, but Morris stops me.

"Tasha, I *really* don't think this is a good idea." He looks serious, almost like he's worried for me.

"Why not?"

"Just think about how all this sounds. How you'll look going in there saying these things."

"But it's all true!"

"I know. I know, but hear me out. What if . . . what if they think you're just deranged? *Unstable?* You could get arrested. They could haul you off to St. Elizabeths. Just think about that. OK?"

"I *have* thought about it, and right now this is the best choice I have," I say, tugging my arm out of his grasp.

"Tasha," he calls after me as I stride toward the doors. "Tasha, wait!"

But I don't wait. I keep going so I don't lose my nerve.

Morris doesn't understand how hard it was to talk myself into doing this, to fight all the excuses I came up with last night and this morning for not coming here. I even thought about what could happen to Madison—a murderer—if her abusive husband finds out that she has plans to kill him. But I *have* to do it.

Right now, she and I are in a battle of wills, and she thinks she's going to win. But she forgot that I was with a man for almost twenty years who tried to break me, to make me bend to his will. And even on our last day together, I still rebelled. He couldn't do it. I ain't bending to her either.

I pull the glass door open and fall into a crowd of people who are talking, laughing, and walking to the elevators on the other side of the lobby. I pass the front desk, and no one notices me. Thank God. But when we near the elevators, I see the metal gates where the employees are running their badges. It beeps as each of them steps through. I stop, unsure of what to do next. I can't just stand here.

Either I keep going or turn back. I hesitate some more and then take a few steps forward. I'm through the gates and a few feet away from the elevators now, but a loud alarm sounds. All the security guards look up. A few of the employees stare over their shoulders at me.

I've been caught. I should've known it wouldn't be so easy. I'm not that lucky.

"Excuse me! Excuse me, ma'am!" one of the security guards calls out over the sound of the alarm. He's tall, black, and has gray and white flecks of hair in his beard. He has a bit of a gut, too. He could've been one of Kordell's drinking buddies.

He walks from around the counter and jogs across the lobby toward me. "If you don't work here, you have to sign in and be escorted upstairs by someone in the building."

"Oh, I'm so sorry. I-I didn't know."

"It's not a problem. You can sign in over here," he says, gesturing to the marble desk.

I walk back toward him and the sound of the alarm fades. One of the other guards—a heavyset white man—is already holding out the clipboard with the sign-in sheet and ballpoint pen clipped on top. I take it and write my name, the time, then Phillip's name, and under "Reason for Visit" I write "Interview." I then hand it back to the guard, who eyes what I've written and then looks up at me.

"You're here to see Mr. Gingell?" he asks, sounding surprised.

I nod. "We have an appointment. It's . . . it's scheduled for 12:30."

He shrugs, picks up the desk phone, and types in a number. I assume he's calling upstairs, and I wait, though I already know what whoever answers the phone is going to say, and it's not that I have an appointment with Phillip Gingell and that someone will come down shortly to escort me upstairs.

Morris was right; they're not going to let me up there. I won't get to talk to Phillip and warn him. He'll be murdered just like my husband. And there goes my chance to stop all of this. To protect myself and the people I love. To stop her.

"Hey, uh," the guard says into the phone, "I have a Ms. Jenkins here at the front desk. She says she has an appointment to speak with Mr. Phillip Gingell. Uh-huh . . . uh-huh. . . ." He looks up at me. His eyes have changed. They've gone from surprised to suspicious. "OK . . . Understood, ma'am. I'll tell her that. . . . Yeah, I—"

I don't know what possesses me to do it, but I reach over the counter and grab the phone out of the guard's hand. He's still staring at the empty hand when I start talking.

"Hello," I say to whoever's on the other end, "I really need to talk to Mr. Gingell. Tell him that his life is in danger! I've tried calling him before, but I don't know if he's just deleting my messages. I have to speak with him. I—"

"OK," the black guard says, yanking back the phone and hanging it up, "that's enough." He shoves me away from the counter and points to the glass doors. "You're gonna have to leave."

Everyone in the lobby is looking at me now. The guards. The employees. They stop, point, and whisper. I see the looks on their faces. They're all scared of me, but I'm not the one they should be frightened of. I'm only trying to help.

"I'm sorry. I didn't mean to do that. I'll wait for him outside in the atrium," I explain, backing up. The rest of the guards are no longer sitting behind the desk. They're all walking toward me, like they want to tackle me and wrestle me to the ground. "I'll sit out there. I won't bother anybody."

"No, you're gonna leave *right now*! Leave this property or you will be arrested," the guard closest to me says, grabbing my arm and dragging me so roughly that I almost trip over my own feet.

I've been dragged like this before. It reminds me of my dead husband, and my jitters only get worse. I yank my arm away. "Don't do that! I said I was leaving! You don't have to touch me!"

He's reaching for his hip holster now. A gun isn't there, but I can see a black canister. Maybe it's Mace. I hold up my hands to show him—*all* of them—I mean no harm. I hold up my hands to protect my face and my eyes if he decides to spray me. And then I hear behind me, "Tasha! Tasha!"

It's Morris. He runs across the lobby and grabs my shoulders. He pushes me behind him, standing between me and the security guards.

"My apologies," he says to the guards. "You see, her husband just died. She's still grieving and under a lot of stress. She's not thinking clearly. Please don't arrest her."

The guard in front looks at Morris and then glares over Morris's shoulder at me. He slowly moves his hand away from his holster. The others seem to relax a little, too.

"Then your friend needs to be stressed out somewhere else. Not in here," he says to Morris before jabbing to the doors again. "Get her out of here, or she gets taken out in handcuffs!"

Morris nods and steers me away. "I will. Don't worry."

I don't want to, but I follow him outside. He smiles and waves at the guards behind us before turning to me. When he does, his smile disappears and he lets me go.

"I told you not to do that," Morris says as the glass doors close and we walk away from the building. "I said it was a bad idea, and you didn't listen. You could've been carted off to jail if I hadn't come in there."

"I was just trying to make them listen to me. You know how important that was! I wasn't doing it to—"

"Damnit, Tasha!" He stops walking and turns to me again. "I can't keep rescuing you like this!"

"I never asked you to rescue me!"

"You're right." He nods and closes his eyes. "You are absolutely right. You never asked me to rescue you, and yet I keep stepping forward to do it over and over and over again like some chump. I've been sucked into this damn cycle for the past seventeen years, and it just . . . it just feels ridiculous." He opens his eyes. "You won't even tell your son about us! We sneak around now like we used to sneak around back then, and pretend like we mean nothing to each other. Like I'm just your damn work friend. Nothing's changed. Nothing's ever gonna change. You do what you want to do. You make your decisions without me, and each time, I . . . I feel like a fool."

"What are you talking about?" It feels like he and I are speaking two different languages right now. "What does any of this have to do with what just happened back there?"

"It has *everything* to do with it!" He grabs my shoulders. "I love you, Tasha, but I'm tired of waiting in the wings to sweep in when you need me and then being pushed away when you feel you don't. This isn't working. Frankly, it never worked." He lets go of my shoulders. "And I have to stop lying to myself. This has to stop."

"What has to stop? What do you mean?"

But I know what he means. He shows me by turning and walking away.

And he doesn't stop, even when I call his name.

CHAPTER 30

MADISON

Hair up? Hair down? I've been debating it for the past ten minutes and I still can't decide. How exactly should you wear your hair when you're about to lie to police to cover up a murder?

Sergeant Myers called back, as I predicted, and asked would I mind moseying down to western Maryland to talk with him for a bit.

As if I had a choice.

But I quickly agreed, because now I have a plan of attack.

I frown at my reflection in my bathroom mirror and decide to split the difference with my hair. I pull it back into a low ponytail, letting one stray lock fall forward slightly. It makes me look more vulnerable. Like most men, the cops will respond well to that.

My scars from my beauty treatment have healed thankfully, so I can keep my makeup minimal. A light concealer. Pink blush. A few quick flicks of a mascara wand. A dewy lip. I want to look fresh-faced. Sweet. Innocent. Not like someone who could shoot a man in the back four times.

I turn to my left, then my right, now happy with the results. Less than five minutes later, I lock the front door behind me and walk to my car.

I'm driving myself to the Sheriff's Office today. It would have been less taxing to let Tony drive me, and I could mentally prepare myself for questioning by the sergeant on the way, but pulling up in our newly purchased Lincoln Town car with the driver won't convey the image I'm reaching for. When I arrive there, I want to seem more demure housewife, less rich bitch. And I don't want to have to explain to Phil why Tony and I had to make the trek down there in the first place. I told him I had back-to-back dentist and doctor appointments instead, that I would be gone all afternoon.

As I press the button to unlock the car door to our Mercedes, my cell phone chimes. I check the screen and see that it's Summer. She's texted me four times already today, asking in all caps for me to call her back. I hadn't gotten around to it, thanks to other priorities.

"Hi, Summer," I say as I pull out, "I'm kinda busy right now. Can I call you back?"

I can hear sniffing and whimpering over my car's Bluetooth speakers, making me frown as I make a right onto Benning Road.

"Summer, are you OK?"

"No. No, I'm not," she sobs.

"Why? What happened?"

"Tom's dead! He's dead, Maddie!" she screams hysterically. "And it's . . . it's all my fault!"

She starts wailing, and I loudly exhale. She overdid it. She gave him too much. I should have known Summer would screw up a simple poisoning, and now she's killed Tom. But I don't have the bandwidth to comfort her right now, to work her through her angst and guilt. I can only focus on one dead husband at a time.

"Well, it may not be my fault," she continues, not as loud but still blubbering. "He had a heart attack, but I mean . . . he turned fifty only two months ago, and he was so fit! He ran a marathon last year. He was even training to climb that mountain. You know, the one in Washington State."

"Mount Rainier."

"Yeah, that one, but Tom does have a history of heart disease in the family. His mom told me that when I called her to tell her the news. She said his uncle and his grandfather both had heart attacks in their fifties."

"Well, there you go!" I say before beeping my horn at a car that jumps into my lane. "So then it wasn't your fault."

And honestly, why waste tears over an asshole like Tom Ross? Fuck Tom.

"But what if it was my fault, Maddie?" She drops her voice to a whisper. "What if what we did caused his heart attack?"

"I'm sorry . . . but," I squint at the traffic outside of my windshield, "what *we* did? We who? What do you mean by that?"

"What do you mean by 'what do I mean'? You told me about the antifreeze, Maddie! I put it in his wine and food that night and it made him sick. He was sick for days before he had his heart attack!"

"I also told you that you didn't have to do it. I even encouraged you to go your separate ways and live your lives. *You* put it in his wine and food and made him sick. Not me. I wasn't even there. I didn't supply you with anything. It was your choice, Summer. Not mine."

She goes silent on the other end.

"We all have to deal with the repercussions of our own decision-making." I finally merge onto the Beltway. "Please don't try to blame me for this. It's very hurtful."

"B-b-but you . . . you told me to do it! I never would have come up with something like this on my own. Not if you hadn't suggested it. You said if I gave him the right amount, he would only get sick. He wouldn't die. And now he's dead and they're going to do an autopsy. What if they find it in his system, Maddie? What if it didn't all dissolve? Should I just confess now and tell them everything?"

"You can—and go to jail for murder. Do you really want to do that?"

The speakers go silent again.

"I didn't think so. It's an unfortunate fact of life that people die, Summer. They die every day! None of us are exceptions, including

Tom. So I suggest you be the widow-in-mourning that you are, go to your husband's funeral, and when they read the will, try not to look too happy or excited when you see how much you're getting."

I glance down at my dashboard and see it's already after 1 p.m. At this rate, I'm going to have to break a few speed limits to get to my interview at the Sheriff's Office on time.

"Now I *really* do have to go, Summer. I promise I'll call you back as soon as I—"

"Wait! Wait! But what do I do if they *do* find something in his system? What if they question me? What am I going to say?"

"I don't know. Tell them to talk to the toddler, maybe? Tell them you and Tom started being amicable again and you heard she wasn't responding well. Jealousy is a wonderful motive for murder."

"Hmm, that *is* a good idea."

"Isn't it? So don't worry anymore. I'll talk to you later. Bye, sweetie!" I say before making kissing sounds. I then press the button on my steering wheel to hang up before she can drag out our conversation any further.

✳ ✳ ✳

I speed so much that I arrive at the Sheriff's Office five minutes early. In the parking lot, surrounded by police cruisers, I give myself one last critique in the visor mirror before walking inside. I will myself to get into character, to prepare for this performance. I used to do it all the time, assuming whatever personality was necessary to get what I wanted. I even did it when I first met Phil.

I knew from whispers around Wyatt & Harris, back when I served as a temp assistant there, that the cute vice president who locked eyes with me and gave me the flirtatious smile when he passed me in the hall was married to a high-powered attorney like himself. They'd even gone to Yale Law School together. I made it my job to learn more about Ashley, even visiting his office and examining the many pictures of her that dotted the space. Ashley in her snow gear. Ashley holding up her triathlon medals. Ashley in her mortar-board and robes. She was assertive, opinionated, and accomplished in her own right. They were a D.C. power couple, but I could tell even then that Phil secretly resented her. That he believed that he was better off without her, but he'd never admit it aloud, let alone to himself. He needed to be the lead, not in a duo. He wanted to be the star of the relationship, so that's what I let him be.

In the beginning, I pretended to be shy and meek and intimi-dated by his intelligence and virility. I told him that I hadn't finished college, that I came from a simple family. I played up the fact that I was a small-town girl and feigned being overwhelmed by living in a new, big city. He never had to worry about my stealing his thunder; I would always be his backup singer, the supportive player. It didn't take long for him to fall in love with me, because I was what he needed me to be.

And as I got to know him even better, I could smell the darker side of him that was eager to get out, to have an outlet. He reeked of it, like cheap cologne. I figured Phil wasn't as straitlaced as he seemed. I wouldn't find out until much later about his funneling bribes to politicians to get his clients favors, or how he worked under the table—if the fee was right—for Russian oligarchs who wanted to have their voices heard by the folks on the Hill and at the White House. The first time we had sex, I brought the handcuffs and blind-folds. Instead of balking, Phil bit down on his bottom lip, took off his belt, and looped it around his fist.

I knew I had him in the palm of my hand.

I'll have to do something similar with Sergeant Myers. I'll have to read him, to figure out what he responds to. But I just need him to trust me, not to fall in love with me. That's much easier.

A few minutes later, I walk into the Sheriff's Office—an unas-suming brick building that could be a post office or the Department of Motor Vehicles. It has an equally unassuming front lobby where both the Maryland and American flags are featured prominently. I stroll to the center desk and tell the officer sitting there that I'm here to speak with Sergeant Myers. I then wait, sitting in one of the cheap plastic chairs in the lobby. Within minutes, the sergeant arrives.

"Mrs. Gingell?" he says, walking toward me.

He grimaces behind his bristly silver mustache. He has a lumbering gait like a grizzly bear forced to walk upright.

I rise from my chair, all smiles. "Yes, I am. Sergeant Myers, I presume?"

He nods and shakes my hand. Two quick pumps. "Pleased to meet you. Follow me, ma'am," he says, turning to one of the lobby doors.

My eyes scan over him as I follow. I can tell Sergeant Myers is a no-nonsense kind of guy. This is underscored by his suit and shoes that look like he purchased them from one of the outlet department stores my mom used to haunt when I was a kid. TJ Maxx. Maybe Marshalls.

Flattery and flirting isn't going to work with a guy like him. I have to seem earnest. Honest. Salt of the earth and all that bullshit.

"Have a seat, Mrs. Gingell," he says to me about a minute later, motioning to yet another cheap plastic chair. This time it's in a white room with cinderblock walls and a drop ceiling. A metal table sits at the center. A notepad and pen sit on top of the table. "Can I get you anything? Water? Coffee?"

"No, I'm fine. Thank you." I shrug out of my coat.

"Do you understand why I invited you here today?"

"Yes," I say, taking a seat. "You're investigating a local murder. But I'm confused as to why you brought me in for questioning. The only thing I've ever murdered is my mom's beef stroganoff recipe."

He chuckles.

I've made him laugh. That's a good sign.

"I'm just gonna ask you a few questions, Mrs. Gingell. Answer to the best of your ability, but answer honestly."

"Of course."

He grabs the notepad and begins to write. "Can you tell me where you were on Saturday afternoon on January 18th?"

"I was here in Washington County."

He looks up from his notepad in surprise. "You were here?"

I had already considered how I would answer this question. It's always better to give a little bit of the truth when you're lying, to sprinkle in facts. It makes the lie more believable. Besides, if they did find my hubcap and can trace it back to my vehicle, they'll know I rented the SUV that day. I have to have some explanation for why I was on that road.

"Yes, I was visiting my little brother. Well," I pause, "I was *attempting* to visit him. He lives here. I hadn't seen him in a while, and he doesn't usually return my phone calls. I came out here to make sure that he was OK."

"OK? Why wouldn't he be OK? Were you concerned about his welfare?"

"Billy has a . . . well, he has a bit of a drug problem." I lower my eyes to my lap, looking ashamed. "He's been an addict for quite some time. But he and his girlfriend have a baby now, so I wanted to check on them. See how the baby is doing. I wondered if maybe they needed my help."

The sergeant nods. "If I follow up with your brother, can he verify that you were there that day? Can he say how long you were there?"

"Honestly, Sergeant, I don't know." I shake my head. "I didn't stay long and he wasn't exactly sober. He seemed barely cognizant. I don't know if he realized who I was, let alone that I was there."

I sniff and blink, forcing tears to my eyes. The sergeant stands up and grabs a box of tissues on the other side of the room. He hands them to me.

"Sorry," I whisper, dabbing at my eyes with one of the tissues, "it's a touchy subject for me. I love my little brother so much, but I hate what his addiction has done to him. I barely recognize him anymore."

"We have a big meth problem out here," Sergeant Myers says. "A lot of families are going through what you are going through, Mrs. Gingell. I've seen plenty of it. I'm sorry it's happening to you."

I nod and sniff again. "Thank you," I whisper.

He writes on his notepad again. "Mrs. Gingell, do you know Tasha Jenkins? Have you ever been in contact with her?"

This time when I blink, it's not a performance. His question isn't what I expected.

"I know of *a* Tasha Jenkins, but we aren't close."

"And how do you know her?"

This is starting to veer off script. I don't like that.

I shrug. "She gave me a ride once, and I saw her again a few months ago, but we haven't spoken since."

"Uh-huh," he says.

"Umm," I begin, watching as he continues to scribble on his notepad, "may I ask why you're asking about Tasha?"

Sergeant Myers looks up. He stops writing. "Well, she's the wife of our victim, Kordell Jenkins. His murder is what we're investigating."

"Oh, I didn't know that was her husband!" I try to look shocked and hope I'm not laying it on too thick. "I didn't put it together. Jenkins is such a . . . a common last name. Poor Tasha. She must be devastated!"

"So you and Tasha never discussed her husband?"

"Not that I can recall."

"Not at all?"

I slowly shake my head. "No."

"Mrs. Gingell, I know this might sound like a strange question, but . . ." He takes a deep breath and tilts his head. He's grimacing again. I have no idea why. "Did you and Tasha ever discuss murdering your husbands?"

I am speechless.

Oh, Tasha. What did you do?

I realize now that this interview isn't about a hubcap. Tasha has spoken to the sergeant. She went running to the police and told them about our plan. I can't help but feel betrayed. After all that I've done for her. After the sacrifices and stress I've put myself through. I thought she would finally understand what I was trying to accomplish for us both, but I underestimated how brainwashed and weak she is.

"Mrs. Gingell, would you like me to repeat the question?" he asks.

"No! No, I'm sorry. I was just . . . I'm just so . . . so shocked by it."

I look flustered now, which rings true because I really am.

"I don't understand why she would say this. Why would she do such a thing?" I slowly shake my head in bewilderment. "She seemed so nice. So . . . so . . . I just wanted to thank her for the nice gesture and now she does this? It's insane!"

Sergeant Myers sets down his notepad before leaning forward with his elbows on his knees. He sighs. "Look, uh, Mrs. Gingell, I'm gonna be honest with you. The story sounded pretty crazy to me, too, when it was told to me. And now talking to you, seeing what a kindhearted lady you are, it sounds even crazier. So, I guess you're saying it didn't happen."

"No, of course not!" I cry. "I would never do that!"

He gazes at me a few beats longer, tapping his pen in his hand. It ticks like a metronome in the quiet room. I wonder if too many of my lies have outnumbered my truths and the sergeant no longer believes me, but gradually he nods.

"Thank you for coming down here and answering my questions, Mrs. Gingell. I know it was a long drive from the city. I'm sorry I wasted your time—and mine."

As I drive back, I can feel my rage building. It is a caged animal, ramming itself against the bars, begging to be let out.

That ungrateful bitch.

That coward.

She turned on me.

But some part of me knew she would do it all along, from the moment she ran down the escalator stairs like a scared little rabbit. I did her a favor, and this is how she chose to repay me, by blabbing to police, by having me called in for questioning.

"I swear you can't help these people!" I remember Father shouting at the kitchen table one day over a plate of bacon and eggs.

Some of the workers at the logging company where he was an assistant manager had walked off the job, protesting low pay and bad working conditions, leading to the shutdown of the worksite for almost a month. Every day that Father stayed home, waiting for a call from his site manager to say he could come back to work, the more angry he became, and the more beatings I and my brothers suffered.

"They're lucky to have a job! All of them are uneducated. Some of them can barely speak English. They're always begging for help, when the truth is they don't want to do the work. They just want a handout!"

"Dale, honey, please," Mom whispered as she stood by the fridge, filling glasses of orange juice. "Can we just eat breakfast?"

We were all bracing ourselves for some tirade, but for once it wasn't about us.

"The one who is unwilling to work, shall not eat! That's what the Bible says, doesn't it? In the Book of Thessalonians. So, what makes them think they're any different? And it's happening all over America! The welfare checks," Father continued, ignoring her. "This Affirmative Action nonsense. Just another handout! But let me tell you something," he said before ripping into a slice of bacon, gnashing it between his teeth, "We're the real victims. *We* carry the load! *We* do all the work, and they sit around on their fat bottoms and complain, complain, complain, and tell us about how bad we are. How unfair we are. They want to make us feel guilty when we've done nothing wrong! Thank God I'm a Christian, because some days . . . some days I could pick off all those little whiners and complainers with my 12-gauge."

Joseph's green eyes went wide over the top of his glass of milk. I kept chewing my toast.

"I'd do it one by one," Father said, "and the world would probably be a better place for it."

Mom didn't comment. We didn't either. We all just sat at the table and continued eating our breakfast in silence.

Father was not the most mentally stable man and yes, plenty racist, but he was right about one thing: the world would probably be better off without so many whiners and complainers, and I can think of one whiner in particular who wouldn't be missed.

I underestimated Tasha, but she has also underestimated me, and now I have no choice but to make her pay for that mistake.

I arrive home to what I expect will be an empty house where I can give full vent to my anger, but as I open the door, I see Phil's office door is open. The light is on.

"*Honey?*" I call out.

"In here, my love," my husband answers back.

Fuck. Now I will have to pretend that I'm not angry and put on a shit–eating grin when I really want to start throwing things and screaming so loud that the neighbors will hear.

Enough with Tasha and her backstabbing and unreliability. I should just kill him now. I have enough rage and reason to do it. I should march into the kitchen, grab the butcher knife, and just start stabbing him over and over again. But I know I can't. The whole point is to have an alibi that would distance me from my husband's murder. That's what Tasha was for. None of that can happen if I use a knife from my own kitchen or if I'm covered in his blood, no matter how elaborate a story I contrive for police.

Back to acting it is.

I erase my frown and furrowed brows. A smile replaces them both. I remove the clip from my hair, letting it fall around my shoulders. I turn to the hallway mirror and close my eyes, take a deep breath, and open them again.

"What are you doing home, sweetheart?" I ask him as I drape my coat on the banister and stroll toward his office door. Phil is wearing his robe and a T-shirt as he sits in his rolling chair. He reaches for a box of tissues on his desk, wipes his nose, and looks up at me.

"I was just feeling under the weather and decided to take the afternoon off," he says before coughing into his fist. His face is flushed pink.

"Oh, poor baby!" I stroll into his office.

It is the only room in the house that Phil has decorated on his own—and it shows. It is absolutely hideous. The walls are painted navy blue and the curtains are a tartan plaid. It's all heavy dark wood and leather furniture. A Manchester United flag hangs on the side door leading to our terraced backyard, a memento from Phil's four-year stint in the United Kingdom back in his twenties. A signed football from Tom Brady is enclosed in a glass case, perched on his desk. The bookshelves are filled with espionage thriller paperbacks.

I place my hand on my husband's brow.

"You don't feel warm. Maybe it's just a cold, but don't overdo it. Don't work too hard." I lean down and kiss his crown. "Get some rest."

"I will, as soon as I finish this," he says, gesturing to his laptop screen.

"All right." I rub his back and kiss him again. "I'll make you some lentil soup. That might help."

"Thank you, honey." He reaches up and gives me a quick pat on the rear end. "I'd love that."

I turn back toward the office door to head into our kitchen to make him soup and to consider what I will do with Tasha Jenkins.

CHAPTER 31

TASHA

I've passed Morris's cubicle for the fifth time this morning, trying to catch his eye, but he doesn't look up at me. We haven't spoken since that day I tried to sneak upstairs to speak to Phillip Gingell. He won't answer my phone calls and keeps making excuses not to talk whenever I stop by to see him, claiming that he's busy.

He really is done with me. But I can't let it end this way. Not after all this time. Not after all we've been through. I deserve more than this.

"You aren't headed to lunch?" Evelyn asks when noon rolls around. She strolls out of her office with her handbag on one arm and her coat draped over the other.

I paint on a smile and nod. "I was just about to leave."

I'd been waiting at my desk for a text from Morris that says "Meet you at the elevators" or "Gotta stop to do something. Will meet you in the lobby today," but I don't receive either.

Instead of heading straight to lunch like I normally would, I go back to his cubicle. He's not there. I have to admit it—I'm stalking him now. I take a detour to the office kitchen in search of Morris. I find him standing next to one of the big industrial refrigerators, taking out a plastic container of food, talking to a lady from the department that sits next to accounting.

"Hey," I say to him as she walks out of the kitchen.

It's just him and me now.

"Hi," he says back, glancing at me and then putting the container in the microwave. He presses a few buttons.

"Can we talk, please? You don't seem busy now."

He shoves his hands into his pockets, watching as his meal heats up. "There isn't anything to talk about, Tasha."

"Yes, there is. You know there is. Don't do this. Don't shut me out," I whisper.

"You've *always* shut me out," he says, still staring at the microwave. "I'm just doing what needs to be done to protect myself."

"Protect yourself from what? *From me*?" I ask, just as my cell phone begins to ring in my purse. I suck my teeth and reach inside, annoyed at being interrupted and Morris being so stubborn. When I see Ghalen's school's phone number on the screen, I frown.

"Hello?" I say.

The microwave beeps. Morris opens it, takes out his container of food, and walks out of the kitchen, leaving me standing alone in there.

"Hi, is this Mrs. Tasha Jenkins, Ghalen's mother?" the woman on the other end says.

"Yes, this is she."

"Ma'am, we need you to come down here. Your son has had an altercation."

"What?" My heart is now in my throat. "What happened? Is he OK?"

"He's fine. We just need you to come down here right away, Mrs. Jenkins."

"I'm on my way," I say before rushing out of the room and heading straight to the elevators.

✳ ✳ ✳

When I get to Ghalen's high school, I burst through the metal doors and hightail it straight to the front desk. My heart is beating so fast that I can hear it pounding and the blood whistling in my ears. My hands are shaking. The school wouldn't tell me what happened to my son, and I don't know why. It's only allowed me to imagine the worst, and I'm hoping that whatever I find will be better than what I've imagined in my head.

Before I get there, I see his girlfriend, Imani, in the hall. She's with her father, who I've met a few times before. She's crying like someone just died, and he's rubbing her shoulder as they walk.

Imani's father is usually a friendly man. Kordell used to call him black Santa Claus because of his big belly and how he's always smiling and cracking jokes when you see him; but this time, he isn't smiling.

"What happened?" I ask, drawing near them. "Is Ghalen OK?"

They stop walking. Imani's still crying, but she tries to wipe her tears away. "I'm so sorry, Mrs. Jenkins," she says between sobs and hiccups. "I told them he didn't mean to do it! I didn't want them to—"

"No, he *did* mean to do it," her father says, cutting her off. "That wasn't an accident, baby girl. And they should've called the cops on his ass. I have half a mind to do it myself."

"What are you talking about? Imani, what did he do, honey?"

Her father shifts his eyes from Imani to glare at me. "Just keep your son away from my daughter. You hear me?" he shouts, making my eyes go wide. "That boy touches her again and I'll break his goddamn hands."

"Daddy," she whimpers.

"Daddy, nothin'! If you ask me, he's getting off easy." He then gives me one last glare before they walk away.

I stare after them until they reach the end of the hall and disappear through the double doors. Something sinks in the pit of my stomach. When I reach the front desk and one of the secretaries takes me into the principal's office, the sinking feeling only gets worse. It turns into nausea.

I see Ghalen. He's sitting in one of the leather chairs facing the principal's desk with his head down. Two of the school's security guards are standing behind him, like he's some criminal. Ghalen's wrists are bound in front of him in flex cuffs, making my baby look like one.

"Ghalen," I call to him.

He slowly looks up at me. His eyes look empty.

"Mrs. Jenkins?" the principal says.

I turn to find her standing by a water cooler on the other side of the room. I was so fixated on Ghalen that I didn't even realize she was over there.

She points to the empty chair beside him. "You can have a seat."

I ease past the guards and sit down next to my son.

"Why the hell is he in handcuffs? What in the world happened?" I cry.

"I'm happy to explain, Mrs. Jenkins," she says calmly. Too calm for my liking.

"Somebody better explain! What did you do, Ghalen? Did you really hurt Imani?" I say to him, but he doesn't answer. He turns away from me like he can't look me in the face anymore.

"Ghalen had an altercation with another student," the principal begins, pulling out her chair and sitting down at her desk. "He assaulted her."

"I didn't *assault* her. We were just talking in the lunchroom and we started arguing because she wanted me to—"

"He grabbed her hair, then shoved her out of her chair to the floor. Several students and one of our cafeteria monitors witnessed the attack," the principal says, speaking over him. "The other student suffered a few bruises."

"She got it from the chair, man! Not from me!"

"And when the monitor attempted to intervene, Ghalen shoved him and threatened him. He had to be subdued. For the protection of our staff, he was placed in flex cuffs."

Listening to her talk about my boy is like hearing her talk about another person. Someone I don't know, and I swear to God, I'm horrified.

I'm horrified at what he's done, that he could hurt somebody that I thought he cared about, and instead of being ashamed or even apologizing for it, he's defensive. Indignant. Like he hasn't done anything wrong. Like he had the right to do it. He reminds me so much of his daddy right now that it scares me.

"I've decided to suspend Ghalen for about a week," the principal says. "I understand from one of his teachers that he recently suffered the loss of his father. I tried to keep that in mind before I determined his punishment, considering that he may be under *severe* stress right now. But I can't emphasize enough with you, Mrs. Jenkins, that if something like this happens again, Ghalen will be expelled."

"I understand." I'm nodding and fighting back tears as I rise from my chair. "Thank you. I'll take him home now."

I'm still fighting back tears as I drive to the house with Ghalen in the seat beside me. He's staring out the passenger side window while I keep my eyes locked on the windshield. He's rubbing his wrists, which are now free of plastic cuffs. Neither one of us has said anything since we left the school; and the truth is, I don't know what to say.

I remember again hearing Ghalen shouting at Imani to get in the car the night of the pep rally. Had there been other times he'd shouted at her? Had there been bruises I hadn't seen? Had this been happening right in front of my face this whole time, and my son had been abusing her for months, and I didn't even notice? I didn't help her.

I'm angry. I'm heartbroken. Though I didn't hurt Imani, my son did, and I thought I'd taught him better than that. I thought I was teaching him to respect women, to never raise a hand to one, but I guess I was wrong.

"You don't want him to become an abuser like his father, do you?" I can hear Madison's voice mock inside my head.

That witch knew. That day at the Metro station, she could see it coming, or willed it into being, and it makes me even angrier.

"Don't you ever put your hands on her again, do you hear me?" I say out of nowhere, making Ghalen turn away from the window. "Do you hear me, Ghalen Jenkins?"

"But you don't know the whole story, Ma."

"I don't care what the whole story is!" I scream inside the car, making him flinch. "There is no excuse! There is no excuse for what you did to her! I will not sit by and let you become a man who bullies and hits women. I won't let you become a monster like your father!"

It's out of my mouth before I have a chance to stop myself.

"You thought . . . you thought my dad was a monster?"

I keep driving, refusing to answer him. I should take it back, but I don't want to because it's the truth. Kordell was a monster who terrorized me until the day he died. And he's haunting us even now from the grave.

"Is that why you cheated on Dad with your little friend?" Ghalen says with a mean smile. "Is that why you lied to him that day he left us? You were really with that dude that night, weren't you? You were gonna leave Dad for him."

I shake my head, wondering who is this person sitting next to me, because it ain't my son. Not with the way he's talking to me. He's not that baby in the incubator anymore. The one that I nursed at my breast, who I needed to protect.

I realize now that the reason Ghalen left me alone at that hotel months ago to go back to live with his father wasn't because he was going to miss school and his friends, or because he was making excuses for Kordell abusing me. He came back because he saw himself in his daddy. He didn't think Kordell had done anything wrong. I get it now. Ghalen is a full-grown man capable of bad things. He is a stranger to me.

"Don't shake your head!" he orders. "Stop lyin' to me! Dad saw through it. He saw right through *you*! How you were trying to play him and—"

"*Trying to play him?* That man made me a prisoner in my own house and acted like I should be grateful that he didn't beat me every night." I grip the steering wheel as I drive, squeezing it so hard my knuckles hurt. "And every day I woke up thinking about the moment I could finally get away from him. That I could escape him.

If you really wanna know the truth, I *did* want to run away with Morris, and I even tried to do it once. Packed my bags, put them in the trunk, and drove away. I planned to never see your father again in my entire life. There! I finally told you the truth! You happy now? Does hearing it make it any better?"

He sucks in his bottom lip and bites down hard on it. For the first time, his eyes flood with tears.

"I would've packed my bags and run off again, but the only thing that kept me there with your father in that prison was you. I wanted to protect you. I thought you needed me." I stop at a red light and turn to him. "But I see now I didn't save you, because staying in that house with him was like feeding you poison. It rotted you. It made you turn into him. It made you no better than him!"

I wait for Ghalen to shout back more cruel words, but he doesn't. He doesn't say anything.

When we get back home, he stomps into the house and goes straight to his room, slamming the door behind him. I tiredly walk into the kitchen and crumple into one of the chairs like a broken doll. I drop my head to the kitchen table. In the quiet, now all by myself, my tears finally spill over. My husband's been murdered, I've lost Morris, and now I'm losing Ghalen. It's all slipping through my fingers.

After about an hour, I rise from the table and walk down the hall to my bedroom. I pass Ghalen's door and I pause to stare at it, wondering what my son is doing on the other side. Packing his bags? Punching a pillow, pretending it's me? Or staring at the wall thinking about his daddy? Part of me says to keep walking. I couldn't save Kordell and I couldn't stop Morris from leaving. But I don't want to keep walking and leave Ghalen alone in there. He's my own flesh and blood. He's a part of me. I still want to help him. I still want to try. I can't protect Ghalen. I know that's out of my hands now, but maybe I can help him save himself.

I knock on the door, but he doesn't answer. I try the handle and see that it isn't locked, so I ease the door open. I find Ghalen sitting on his bed, staring out the window. His back is to me. He doesn't turn around when he hears me walk into his room.

"Sometimes, I forget that when I met your daddy," I begin, "we were younger than you are now. When we got married, we were only a few years older. I was nineteen. Your daddy was twenty. We didn't know anything about anything. We were just starting to figure things out. Probably had no business getting married or starting a life together, but I needed your daddy. He came at a time in my life when I was scared and lonely, to be honest."

Ghalen shifts on his bed and turns to look at me. I lean against the door frame and keep talking.

"Your grandmother sent me away to live with Aunt Jessie up here when I was fourteen . . . almost fifteen. I didn't want to go. I didn't want to leave home, all my friends, and everything I knew back in Georgia. But she just couldn't afford to take care of all of us kids anymore. I understood." I pause, think for a minute, and slowly shake my head. "That's not true. I didn't understand. I still don't. She said I could stand on my own. That I was old enough and didn't need her like my brothers and sisters did. 'You're damn near a woman now, Tasha. You can take care of yourself.' But that wasn't true. I wasn't a woman; I was still a child, and I needed her. I needed my Mama, and she just . . . she just gave me away. So here I am in D.C. with nobody. No friends. And your daddy came up to me one day at school, smiling his big smile. He asked me for my name. Offered to show me where my first class was. I was so nervous that day, but he made me feel better."

I walk farther into the room.

"I didn't know at the time what your daddy had going on in his life. That *his* father was using drugs. Stealing money from your grandma's purse. Selling their TV and their clothes when the money ran out. I didn't know that he used to see his father high and out of it, and how his mother tried to pretend like none of it was happening." I sigh. "So, you have two young people—two *hurt, broken* young people—deciding to build a life together."

I chuckle and shake my head.

"And I had the nerve to be surprised when it all turned out the way it did. The mess we made of it."

I sit down on the bed beside Ghalen and place my hand over his. He doesn't pull away.

"I'm not saying that what any of your daddy did was right. I'm not making any excuses for him, because I mean it when I say there was no excuse. But there was a lot that went into who he was. A lot went wrong that he couldn't control. But he didn't try to fix what he *could* control. He didn't try to make it right. And that's what broke my heart. I don't want you to do the same thing, honey. That's all. I want you to be better than your daddy. Better than me. I want so, *so* much for you."

Ghalen drops his head on my shoulder and I close my eyes. We sit there for a while. Me, listening to the quiet of the house. Him, looking out his bedroom window. We stay there until dinner time, until the sun finally sets.

CHAPTER 32

MADISON

As I wait for Tasha to make her appearance, I sit in the court-yard, listening to the trickling of the nearby fountain and observing all the eccentricities that only a major city can offer. A homeless man sits on a metal bench about twenty feet away, meticulously laying out smashed soda cans in a straight line on the bench beside him while muttering to himself. A panhandler who one of the security guards has already tried to escort away twice reads bad poetry aloud about his childhood pet parakeet. A few people have thrown coins into his McDonald's cup to either encourage him or shut him up, I can't tell which. And a woman in a gray business suit smokes a cigarette and paces the circumference of one of the planters while having a heated conversation with someone over the phone.

"You tell that son of a bitch that if he wants his Air Jordans so bad that he can come to the house and get it his goddamn self," she barks into her cell before taking a drag. "What do I look like? A damn delivery service?"

The rest are just workers walking around the business complex, pinging like pinballs from building to building.

I don't miss those days, back when I used to work in offices like the ones towering above me, back when I squeaked out an income to pay for overpriced apartments and my student loans. Back when I had to cater to bosses who didn't have half my intelligence and not even a quarter of my drive.

The modern working world is soul-crushing. Mind-numbing. A place where only cowards and drones can survive. Which is why Tasha seems to be doing well here, I suspect.

She's too much of a coward to seize her own destiny, and too much of a mindless drone to achieve it. But I'll be damned if she ruins my chances, if she continues to get in my way. I'm all for solidarity, but I can't allow her to be my albatross.

I had a similar talk with Ashley. Even after she refused to grant Phil the divorce, even after she posted those tweets that defamed me, I tried to have a heart-to-heart with her. To issue a subtle warning and tell her she was much better off if she moved on. Why fight so hard for a man who doesn't love you anymore? Why suffer? But she literally slammed the door in my face. Three weeks later, she was dead.

A little after noon, Tasha finally appears. Her head is bowed. She's staring into the depths of her purse while walking across the courtyard. She digs around, in search of something. Her phone. A compact, maybe. Either way, she doesn't notice me even when I rise to my feet, even when I begin to follow her out of the courtyard to the sidewalk.

"You should be more aware of your surroundings," I say to her after we turn a corner, passing the entrance to a parking lot. I'm only two feet away. "A woman walking around alone in the city. It's not safe. Anyone could sneak up on you."

At the sound of my voice, she halts mid-stride. She stops delving into her purse and raises her head. She slowly turns around to look at me.

The expression of sheer horror on her face almost makes me laugh. I must really be intimidating.

I like that.

"What . . . what are you doing here?" she asks breathlessly. "Why are you following me?"

"We need to talk."

She shakes her head. "I don't have anything to say to you."

"No, but you seem to have *plenty* to say to Sergeant Myers at the Washington County Sheriff's Office."

"Because you killed my husband. You killed Kordell."

"*Did I?* Or was your husband possibly killed because of a drug deal gone wrong? Or a racist redneck followed him down a deserted road and decided to attack him and shoot him? Or he was having an affair, decided to meet his mistress in secret, and she ambushed him and shot him when he refused to run away with her?" I raise my brows. "Any of those scenarios are possible. A smarter person who is as relieved to have her abusive husband gone as she claimed she would be . . . the *very* same husband she tried to run away from less than six months ago . . . could have told the sergeant any one of those things. But you chose not to."

"Because it's not true," she says in a harsh whisper. "I told them the truth. You killed him."

"And a lot of good that did you, huh? A lot of good that did either one of us. Telling the fucking truth. When are you finally going to figure out that this whole good-girl routine gets you nowhere, Tasha? Just abused and ignored. Meanwhile, someone like me who you've painted to be the bad guy was actually willing to help you. I got you a job. I gave you freedom from a horrible situation. I did more for you than anyone has *ever* done for me. You'd think you'd be grateful. That you would—"

"*Grateful?*" Her face suddenly changes. She doesn't look frightened anymore, but has the gall to look furious. "Grateful? I never asked for this. You turned my life upside down. You took away my son's father. I stood up to Kordell. I told him to get out. He was gone. He had left. I didn't need you to *kill* him!" she screams.

Her voice echoes around the lot, making the guard in the nearby booth look up from his desk and stare at us.

"Keep your voice down," I say through clenched teeth, taking a step toward her.

"Why? You wanted to have it out. Didn't you? That's why you came all the way here! That's why you're stalking me. You wanted to talk. I'm talking. I'm just not gonna say what you want me to say, Madison! I am *not* your puppet."

"You think because you kicked him out once, that makes you brave? You would've let him back. Women like you always do! You're weak. Stupid. You're—"

"And you're a bully! A crazy, mean ol' bully. You're worse than my husband! Deep down he probably knew what a bastard he was, but you've built yourself up to believe that you're some big savior. Like I should bend down and kiss your feet, when the truth is you didn't give a damn about helping me. It was all about you. What you could get out of this. I bet you liked killing him, didn't you?"

I don't answer. I don't have to.

"And now that I won't fall in line . . . now that I'm not gonna march to your beat, all your 'we've gotta stick together' goes out the window, I bet. You're coming after me, too, aren't you?"

"Maybe. Or maybe I'll work my way up to that." I casually shrug. "I've already taken care of Kordell. What's one or two more men along the way?"

She takes another step toward me. Her lips tighten. "You lay one hand on either one of them," she says through clenched teeth, "and you will regret it. Come near me again, and you will regret it."

"Well, look at you! *There's* the fire I was looking for all along," I say with a laugh. "Too bad it's a day late and a dime short, huh?"

"I'm not joking, Madison," she says in an even, grave voice. "Don't push me into a corner. Don't do it. Do you understand me? Because you won't like what I'll do."

"You can save the threats. You don't have it in you."

"You don't know what I have in me." Her gaze doesn't waver, and my grin evaporates. "You were right. I *did* want Kordell gone. And if he hadn't left that night, or if he had come back the next day, God help me . . . I might have killed him myself. He pushed me too far, and I got tired of running. Don't do the same to me, Madison."

Her eyes blaze, but her voice is deathly calm. "What I didn't do to my husband, what I held back . . ." She gives a shrug. "I may have all saved up for you."

Her words surprise me. Not because she said them, but because she might actually mean it. She's warning me to back off. So, there *is* some backbone in her, after all. Good for her.

Too bad I'll have to kill her for what she's done, for fucking up my plans and getting in my way. But I'll punish her first. And I'll make it slow and painful.

I turn to walk away.

"So be it, Tasha. Game on," I call to her over my shoulder.

CHAPTER 33

TASHA

OVER THE PAST WEEK, IN MY MIND I'VE MADE A LIST. IT'S A LOT like the checklist I wrote when I was coming up with my plan to leave Kordell, but I didn't write it down and burn it over the stove this time around. It's a list just for me. It's how I keep from going crazy. It's how I'm going to fix things. I feel like I'm about to head off to war; but before I do, I want to set a few things right.

First, I reached out to Dr. Green. I figured I should finally let go of my shame and disappointment in myself, and let her know what's been going on with me—minus the stuff about Madison. Maybe I'll tell her one day, though.

I told Dr. Green I needed to make an emergency appointment.

"I have to admit, Tasha," she said in her office the next day, "I was surprised to hear from you, since I haven't heard from you in months. And I see you've brought someone with you as well." She smiled and turned to Ghalen, who was fidgeting in the chair beside me.

His eyes were low, and his dreads were drooping into his face. He didn't want to be there, but I told him that we had to, if we were going to move forward as a mother and son.

I reached out, grabbed his hand, and squeezed, making him go still in his chair.

"I know," I said to her. "And I'm sorry for disappearing for so long, but I need your help. *We* need your help." I glanced at Ghalen. "It's a lot that we need to work on as a family. To be in a better place and to be better people. Can you help us, Dr. Green?"

She tilted her head. Her smile got wider. "I can certainly try, Tasha."

The second thing on my list was to check in on Imani. Ghalen said that, according to his friends, she hadn't been back to the school since that day in the lunchroom. She wasn't there when he returned either. I wasn't sure why she hadn't come back. Was she fighting shame that everyone knew the truth of what was going on between them, just like I had for so long with Kordell? Or had her injuries been worse than I thought? Was she depressed?

"We withdrew her from school," her mama told me over the phone.

This was after Imani's daddy had hung up on me as soon as he heard my voice. I left them a message, explaining to them that I was sorry about what had happened and I only wanted to see if Imani was OK. The next day, her mother called me back.

"We don't want your son anywhere near her again," Imani's mother said. "And we're making sure of it. If we find out he's contacted her, we're callin' the police. You tell him that!"

I closed my eyes. "I understand. Believe me, I do. Just tell Imani that I'm thinkin' about her. I'm praying for her. I . . . I went through the same thing with Ghalen's father. He . . . he abused me, too," I confessed, feeling tears prick my eyes. "And Ghalen saw it. He saw it all. Just tell her not to blame herself. I'm not saying that she *is* blaming herself, but if she does . . . if she does, because a lot of victims of abuse do, just . . . just tell her that she didn't do anything wrong. She's a good girl. I know that."

Her mama got quiet on the other end of the line for a long time. She cleared her throat. "I will," she said, and I could hear that she was close to tears, too. "Goodbye, Tasha. Please don't call here anymore."

She hung up, and I respected their wishes; I won't ever call them again.

The third thing I did was to contact the home security company and have them install cameras around our property. I told Ghalen that a neighbor told me there had been break-ins near our block. I didn't tell him who we really needed protection from. And I got a gun. It isn't mine, though. I thought about buying a gun on my own, but getting a permit in D.C. can take months. I figured I don't have that much time, so I asked Kordell's friend, Jared, if I could have one of his guns. He's got plenty of them, being a hunter and all.

"What the hell do you need a gun for, Tasha?" he asked me, sounding worried. "You wouldn't swat a fly!"

"Ever since what happened to Kordell, I haven't felt safe," I told him honestly. "I thought this might help."

He gave it to me with some bullets. He said to use it only if I really needed to, only if I have no other option. I promised him that I would.

I hope I'll never have to use it, but I'm not so sure.

And I felt if I was doing all this to protect me and Ghalen, it was only right to warn Morris to protect himself too. I sent him an email, telling him we needed to meet up.

"What do you want, Tasha?" he asked me at one of the delis we used to go to at lunch together. "Why did you call me here? I told you, I'm done."

I saw in his eyes that his heart was closed off to me now, and maybe that's a good thing. Maybe staying as far away from me as possible will keep him safe.

"I just wanted to tell you to be careful from now on. Madison knows about you. She knows about us. If you're at home or driving to pick up your daughter or walking to your car one day and something doesn't feel right, or if you think you're being followed, get on your cell and call the police. I don't care if it feels silly or stupid, do it, Morris."

He slowly shook his head. "What . . . what are you talking about?"

"I don't want her to hurt you, and she might do it. Kordell drove to his death without knowing what was happening. I won't let the same happen to you. Watch out for her." I then stood from my chair, leaned down, and kissed his cheek. "Take care of yourself," I whispered before grabbing my purse and walking out of the deli.

And tonight, I'm about to check the last thing off my list.

I tug down the front of my suit jacket just before I open the glass door. It was the nicest jacket I could find in my closet. It's navy blue, and I paired it with a matching skirt and a set of simple heels. I figured it'll help me blend in with all the lawyers in the room. I want to fade into the background until it's time for me to do what I came here to do.

I see a reception area where people are huddled around highboy tables, talking to each other and sipping wine. I see a long, wide table along the right wall covered with name tags. A white woman sits behind it with a name tag on her chest too. She's staring down at her clipboard. Behind her is an easel with a posterboard on the front with the words "American Institute for Lobbying & Ethics: Ushering the Profession Into a More Ethical Future." On the board is also the face of tonight's featured speaker, Phillip Gingell.

Morris would say I'm a fool for trying this, for seeking out this man yet again—and he'd probably be right, but I feel like I still have to try. I have to make one last effort to reach out to Phillip.

It's less about protecting him and more about protecting myself and the ones I love. Madison is coming after me . . . after both Morris and Ghalen now. She said it with her own lips, and I believe her. I don't know what I would do if something happened to them. I wasn't making an idle threat that day at the parking lot—I think I might really kill her. I've already started to imagine it, to plan it out without even trying. My dreams of murdering Kordell have switched to dreams of shooting or stabbing Madison. So, to avoid all that—her killing me or mine, or me killing her first—I'm trying again to put it in Phillip's hands.

Maybe Phillip has seen the side of Madison that I have. Maybe he knows what she's capable of. Maybe he'll believe me when I tell him the horrible thing she's done and what she has planned, and he will go to the police to stop her.

I didn't get to talk to him before. To see him in person. Perhaps, if we're face-to-face, he'll see that I'm not crazy. He'll finally hear me out.

And if this doesn't work, if Phillip doesn't listen, then . . . well, I'll do what I have to do.

I look around the room. I don't spot Phillip yet, and none of the other faces look familiar, which is a good thing. No one is here from the time I tried to sneak into Phillip's office building. This time, I'm at a building just over the border in Arlington, Virginia. It looks like a gallery. I can see pictures on the walls and sculptures in the corners.

I walk to the table with the name tags and look through them, though I don't know why. It's not like my name will be there; I'm not one of the guests. But the woman with the clipboard looks up and smiles like I am a guest here. Like I'm supposed to be here.

"Hi, can I help you? Have you signed in?" she asks, pointing at the clipboard.

I turn from the name tags to look at her. "Uh, no. No, I haven't. Not yet."

"Oh, well, can I have your name? I can look it up for you."

I freeze for a second and then say, "Samina. Samina Houston."

It was one of the names I saw on the table.

The woman stares down at her list and puts a checkmark on the page. She rises to her feet and reaches for the tag and hands it to me along with two red cards. "Here are your drink tickets. We're having a brief cocktail hour for now, but the presentation will begin at exactly 7:30. Please enjoy yourself, Ms. Houston."

"Thank you, and I will." I turn away from the table and peel the sticky backing off the name tag and put the tag on my chest, next to my suit lapel.

As I walk across the room, I pray to God that Samina Houston is running late or doesn't show up at all tonight. I hope none of her colleagues are here to point out that I'm not her. I don't want to get escorted out by security guards again.

I still don't see Phillip, so I go to the bar to grab a glass of wine. I don't usually drink, but tonight I might need one. The bartender hands me a glass of Chardonnay and I take a sip.

"Hi, I'm Josh Langley," a man says beside me, catching me off guard. He's a little shorter than me and holding out his hand. I lower my wineglass and give his hand a shake.

I thought mine were clammy from nerves, but he seems to be even sweatier.

"Samina Houston. Pleased to meet you," I say.

He leans forward and squints at my name tag. "Your name sounds very familiar for some reason. Are you with the CGE Group? I think we both worked on the drug bill that went before the Ways and Means Committee last year."

I shake my head and start to look around the reception again, hoping that Langley will take the hint that I don't want to start a conversation. "'Fraid not," I mutter.

"Ah!" He laughs. "My mistake then. Maybe it was another Samina. I'm with Wheeler & Associates, by the way. And you're with . . . ?"

He stares up at me, waiting for me to say who I work for.

"I'm with Wyatt & Harris," I say. It's Phillip's firm and the only one I know.

He nods. "So, I suppose you've come here to support your compatriot. The guest of honor."

Out of the corner of my eye, I finally spot Phillip Gingell standing with a group of men and women on the other side of the room, about twenty feet away. They're all talking, and he's center stage. That's no surprise. He is the "guest of honor," after all.

Phillip looks a lot like his pictures, though he's taller than I expected. He shifts his head when a pretty redheaded young woman taps him on the shoulder. He leans down and she whispers something into his ear. He nods before saying something to the group, then Phillip and the woman walk off.

"Yes, and I should go and say hi to him. Excuse me," I say to Langley. I set down my wineglass on one of the nearby tables and scurry across the room after Phillip.

He and the woman head down a corridor and I rush after them, trying not to lose them.

"They have us set up back here," I hear her say. Her voice echoes down the hall along with the sound of their footsteps. I round the corner just as she pushes open a door at the end of the hall. "I told them that you needed the—"

"Phillip!" I call out just before they stride through the doorway.

They both pause and turn to look at me.

"Phillip Gingell," I say.

His brow crinkles. He looks confused. "Yes? And you are?"

"Samina Houston. Uh, can I . . . can I speak with you?"

The redhead grimaces. "Actually, Mr. Gingell is holding a Q & A session after his speech. So if you would—"

"This isn't for the Q & A. I . . . I need to speak with you now, Mr. Gingell. It's very . . . very delicate."

"Delicate how?" he asks.

"It's . . . it's about the drug bill," I blurt out. "The one that went before the Ways & Means Committee last year. I wanted to get your opinion on part of the bill, and I didn't want to . . . to ask my question in front of everyone. It won't take long."

He looks at the woman and gives her a quick nod. "I'll be there in just a sec, Penelope. We still have time to go over my speech."

The young woman nods and slowly walks inside the room just as Phillip walks back down the hall toward me.

"Sorry. Penelope is subbing for my assistant, who called out sick today. She does a good job but can be a little overzealous about maintaining my schedule." He chuckles. "And I should tell you that I'm only vaguely familiar with that drug bill. We had a few associates work on it last year. I can try to answer your question as best as I can, though. So . . . shoot!" He crosses his arms over his chest. "What did you have to ask me?"

"I . . . I . . ." I begin but can't think of what to say next.

I'm not here to talk about a damn bill. I'm here to tell this man about his crazy wife. About a murder. About how our lives are in danger. And now that I finally have him in front of me, I'm tongue-tied.

Where do I start? I've practiced this over and over again in my head, but the words are piling up in my throat and refuse to come out.

But then I remember that special night with Morris and how happy I was. I never wanted to hurt him, and I couldn't stand for anything to happen to him. I think about Ghalen and how much I love that boy. He made me breakfast this morning—burnt toast and runny eggs. It was the first time he's ever done it for me in his whole life, and he was so proud of himself. Ever since that first family therapy session with Dr. Green, he's been trying to help around the house more, instead of acting like I always need to wait on him and clean up after him. I can see that he's trying to be better. To be nicer. To be a better man. I want to help him do that, but I can't if Madison succeeds. If she wins this battle that's raging between us.

She's certainly been winning so far. The odds are in her favor, and she knows it. She's a cute, rich white woman who manipulated my boss, who manipulated the cops. All she had to do was make a call or bat her damn eyes. They've all been eating out of her hand this whole time.

If I did anything close to what Madison has done, I'd be in jail right now. But they won't put her in prison—at least not on my word alone. I don't have the same power she does. I can't cast the same spells. The only person who has as much power, who has even more, is the one standing in front of me right now: her husband—a rich white man.

I need his help to save me, Ghalen, and Morris. Because if I take this into my own hands and use the gun Jared gave me, I know how this will play out. I know what will happen—and she knows it too.

I am not getting off scot-free. If her life is over, so is mine. Or it may as well be with how long I'll be in prison.

I've been silent for so long that Phillip starts to frown. "This must be a really complicated question," he says.

I let out a hollow laugh. "You have no idea."

He glances over his shoulder at the closed door. "Look, Samina, I would love to help you if I can, but I really have to prepare for my—"

"My name isn't Samina," I begin. "It's Tasha. Tasha Jenkins."

He snaps his eyes away from the door to look at me. "What?" He stares down at my name tag. "Then why are you—"

"And I'm not a lobbyist, Mr. Gingell. I just pretended to be one to get in here today. I'm a woman who knows your wife, Madison. I've been trying to talk to you about what she has planned. She's trying to kill you."

He lurches back from me like I've punched him. The look on his face and in his eyes changes. "You're that woman who left me those messages, aren't you? You came to the firm."

"Yes," I say, taking another step toward him just as he takes another step back. "I've been trying to warn you for the longest time. Madison killed my husband and she wants to kill you too. She wants to kill us both because I wouldn't kill you for her! You have to go to the police! Tell them that—"

"Are you out of your mind? I will do no such thing," Phillip says. I expected him to be alarmed, maybe even scared by what I'm saying, but instead he looks angry. He points a finger down at me. "Leave now, or I will call the police. Don't contact me again."

"No! No, you have to listen! You don't know your wife. She's—"

I stop short when he grabs my arm, catching me by surprise. "Don't presume to tell me about my wife," he says in a harsh whisper. "I know who my wife is, thank you very much. And I will no longer allow you to interfere in our lives. Do not call or email me. Don't come to my office. Stop following me! If you do this again, you will live to regret it. Do you understand me?"

His grip tightens around my arm, making me wince. He looks angry enough to hurt me, and he just might. Madison had said he was abusive, that he'd hurt her before. I can see it in him now. Now I'm the one who's afraid of what he might do.

"Do you understand me?" he repeats slowly. His blue eyes bore into mine.

"Y-y-yes," I stutter. "Yes, I understand."

"Phil?" a voice calls out.

We both look down the hall to find the young woman from earlier gazing at us.

"Is . . . is everything OK?" she asks.

I don't know how long she's been standing there or how much of our conversation she's heard, but now that she's looking, Phillip drops my arm, finally letting me go. The scary look in his eyes disappears. His fake lawyer smile is back.

"Everything's fine, Penelope. I'll be right there." He then leans down and whispers in my ear, "Remember what I said. You've been warned."

I watch as he turns and heads to the room to prepare for his speech and realize when the door closes behind him that I'm shaking.

That hadn't gone at all like I'd planned, even worse than I thought it would. Remembering that look in Phillip's eyes and feeling the soreness in my arm now, I think maybe Madison isn't the only crazy one in that family. I guess you'd have to be a little crazy to be married to that woman. Maybe she really did have a good reason for killing Phillip. Maybe he ain't worth saving. I just couldn't be the one to kill him for her.

I wouldn't help her, and he won't be of any help to me. I can see that for sure now.

It's all in my hands.

CHAPTER 34

MADISON

THE PACK IS GETTING DENSER NOW. IT'S PROBABLY BECAUSE WE'RE nearing the finish line. I can see the inflated archway and colorful columns of balloons in the distance, a little more than a half mile away.

People line the route of the charity 10K race, standing behind plastic barriers. They cheer us on and hold up signs written in all caps, covered with glitter, hearts, and stars, urging us to think of the cancer survivors we're raising money for, begging us to finish.

"Finish Strong!" one sign says.

You're lucky I'm finishing at all, I think, wiping sweat from my eyes.

Some lining the route have pom-poms. One has a bullhorn.

"Go! Go! Go!" he shouts like a drill sergeant, and even though I'm practically gasping for air and my legs are burning, I think I have just enough energy to run to the sidelines and punch him in the throat. But of course, I don't. I have to stay focused.

"Water?" two volunteers shout at us as we draw close to the water station. "Water?"

The guy in front of me, Number 2457, grabs one of the paper cups they hold out to him, guzzles some of the water inside, then tosses it over his shoulder, sending back a stream that the rest of us have to dodge. I wave the cup away that they hold out to me and keep going. My eyes are locked forward. I breathe in through my nose and out through my mouth, counting each stride and ignoring the pain.

I wasn't always a runner. In fact, I could barely do a mile. I much preferred pilates or yoga to cardio.

But all that changed nearly a decade ago with Ashley.

After Phil told her he wanted a divorce and she told him over her dead body, I started running the same trails she did. I rose early in the morning just after dawn, tucked my hair under a baseball cap, slapped on a pair of sunglasses, grabbed a hoodie, and hit the pavement. I waited until she left their house, watching her as she stretched, put in her earbuds, and checked her sports watch. Then she was off, and I followed.

We ran through Georgetown, past the shops and parked cars. We sprinted over the uneven brick sidewalks and through the leaf-strewn paths on the hiking trails in Dumbarton Oaks and Rock Creek Park. The first couple of months, she easily lost me; I just couldn't keep up. But after a while, I was able to keep pace with her, staying close enough to see Ashley but far enough away so that she didn't know she was being followed.

Ashley was predictable; she usually took the same three routes, only changing them slightly on her longer weekend runs. I'd done the routes so often that I was able to map each of them from memory. I gave copies to Billy. It was on one of them that he killed her.

I try to imagine her final run now as I near the finish line. Did she hear it coming? Maybe the rhythmic thump of footsteps behind her, or the snap of twigs underfoot right before it happened. Or was she blissfully unaware, listening to some empowering track by Katy Perry or Maroon 5 or glancing down at her watch to check her heart rate just before Billy grabbed her and dragged her off the trail?

I wonder if Tasha will see it coming when it happens to her. Will she hear a noise that will make her sit up in her bed at night, wondering if it's me? Will she be looking over her shoulder whenever she's alone, searching for me? And unlike with Ashley, I'll be there to see it this time. The fear and then the look of sheer terror when she knows her final moment is about to happen.

The giddiness from anticipation almost makes me forget the pain while I'm running.

"There she is!" someone shouts just as I cross the finish line. "She made it!"

I collapse onto the sidewalk with heart pounding. I'm gasping for air. I drop my head between my knees and I hear the same voice say, "We were wondering where you were. Phil finished eight minutes ago. Guess one of you had to bring up the rear, huh?"

I slowly look up to find Nate, one of the other Wyatt & Harris partners, grinning down at me. He's pushing seventy, has a potbelly that strains against the belt of his khakis, and is sporting a double chin. He probably couldn't have finished that race, let alone run faster than me, but I force my own smile and shrug. "Well, Phil has always been a faster runner than I am. I'm not surprised."

"Don't listen to him, honey. You did a great job," Phil says, stepping forward to lean down and kiss my crown. A towel is thrown around his shoulders. His Yale Law long-sleeve shirt is damp with sweat and pasted to his skin in some spots. He offers me his hand and I take it so he can hoist me to my feet. "I'm proud of you."

"You should be proud of you both! Thank you for representing the firm today. I would've done it myself, but my knees weren't quite up to the challenge," Nate says with another chuckle before slapping Phil on the back.

Yes, your knees were the problem, Nate. Not your fat ass.

Phil waves him off. "It's fine, Nate. Really."

"No, I know you've had a lot on your plate lately. And now with that woman stalking you . . . it's a lot to deal with, but you still came through for us today. We can't thank you enough."

I nearly do a double take. "Wait. Wait, someone's been stalking you, Phil? Who?"

My husband shakes his head. "I don't have a stalker."

"Of course, she's a stalker! What else would you call it?" Nate exclaims. "She's come to the office building and now I hear she's followed you to one of your speaking engagements." Nate looks pointedly at me. "I heard she's even mentioned you a few times."

I look back at Phil. "Why would she mention me?"

"It's nothing," Phil says, shaking his head again.

"It's not nothing!" Nate insists. "See if you can convince your husband to contact the police and take out a restraining order. He won't listen to—"

"I don't need a restraining order. I took care of it," Phil says tightly to Nate. "Please . . . can we just . . . just change the subject?" He grabs my elbow, ushering me away. "Come on, honey. Let's get you some water."

The ride from the race thirty minutes later is carried out mostly in silence. The entire time I wonder about Phil's supposed stalker and why he hadn't mentioned her to me.

Besides a mistress, what else is my dear husband hiding?

I have a sneaking suspicion of who his stalker could be, but I hope I'm wrong. Tasha wouldn't be that reckless, that stupid.

"So what was that thing Nate was talking about?" I ask him after we arrive home. I shut the front door behind us as he strolls toward the lower landing stairs. At my words, he stops. "What's this whole business about you having a stalker?"

Phil slowly turns to look at me. "I already told you, I don't have a stalker. I took care of it." He then starts to walk again, crossing our living room and climbing the second flight of stairs back to the top floor with me close at his heels.

"But why didn't you mention it to me at all, sweetheart? Why didn't you mention that this woman has been following you? Do you know who she is?"

"Not really." He walks into our bedroom.

"Not really? What does that mean? Do you know her or not, Phil?"

He lets out a long sigh that sounds a lot like a grumble. "Before all this happened, I hadn't met her before. She started calling me a little more than a month ago, leaving messages. My secretary said the guards at our front desk had to escort her out for being unruly. She claimed she was there for an appointment with me. But she didn't have one. She made it up."

"Why would she do that? Did she say why she wanted to talk to you?"

He takes another deep breath as he wrenches off his Yale Law T-shirt and drops it to the floor. "It was just nonsense, Maddie. It's not worth talking about."

"It *is* worth talking about. Especially if she mentioned me, like Nate said. What did she say about me?"

He seems to consider his words. "She said . . . she said you want to kill me. That you solicited her to murder me and that you killed her husband."

For fuck's sake. Tasha has been busier than I thought.

"That's insane!" I cry with wide eyes.

My husband nods grimly and sits down on our bed. "I'm aware. She's insane, obviously."

"Oh, honey!" I take the seat beside him and grab his hand. "So, what do you want to do? Did you want to call the police? Were you going to file a restraining order?"

I wait for his answer, but I hope desperately that he says no. I don't need yet another police department questioning Tasha, then probably me. First the Washington County Sheriff's Office. Now the D.C. Metropolitan Police Department. I've already thrown one cop off my trail. I don't need to contend with another.

"I don't think so," he says, to my relief. "I warned her off. I don't think she'll come back."

I gaze at my husband. At his tense shoulders. His flushed face. I can tell he's worried, but he's pretending not to be. My mind is spinning like the lock tumblers in the wall safe.

"You're probably fine, sweetheart. We're probably fine, but maybe, for insurance, in case she ever comes here, we should take the gun out of the wall safe and keep it in our bedroom from now on," I suggest.

Tasha thinks she's given me a setback by running to Phillip, but she's done the opposite. Not only did my husband not believe her, but now with a gun readily available and accessible in our bedroom, I see more possibilities for how I can still get what I want in the end. I can feel a new plan falling into place, a new way for me to finally take care of my husband even without enlisting Tasha's help.

Phil squints at me. "Are you sure that's what you want?"

I nod. "Remember what happened to Ashley. It's good to have it around for peace of mind."

He seems to consider my suggestion. He then rises to his feet again and heads to our walk-in closet. I toss his sweaty shirt into the nearby hamper and stand at the closet doorway, watching as he shoves aside his suit jackets and ties. A minute later, he takes out the leather pouch that contains the gun I used to kill Kordell.

I stare at the gun and try not to grin.

"I won't call the police. I don't want to make a big thing out of this," he says as he opens the pouch and pulls out the pistol; "but if it makes you feel better, I'll keep the gun in our bedroom again. We can keep it close to us in case . . . well, in case anything happens. Anything unexpected. So at least you'll be protected if things get out of hand."

I watch as my husband walks out of the closet, around our bed, and opens his night-table drawer. He places the gun inside, then closes the drawer.

"Thank you, honey." I step forward and give him a kiss on the cheek. I run my fingers through his hair and rake my nails down the back of his neck, leaving four red lines on the pale skin. "Well, I guess that's enough excitement for one morning. I'm going to take a shower. Want to join me?"

"No, you go ahead. Maybe I'll join you later. I need to, uh . . . I need to do something downstairs first."

"OK," I call to him as he walks out of our bedroom.

Thirty minutes later, I'm freshly showered and dressed and Phil is nowhere to be found.

"Honey, I'm making lunch!" I call out to Phil, but he isn't in the kitchen or our living room or the backyard. He doesn't respond at all. I turn and see that his office door is closed. I can faintly hear his muffled voice on the other side. I tiptoe across the hardwood and stand in front of it, glaring at this obstinate slab between us. Instead of knocking, I press my ear flat against the door.

"I know . . . I *know*," he says. "I love you. You know I love you, but something like this just takes time! We will be together, though. Just be patient, honey."

I pull my ear away from the door, having had my fill of eaves-dropping on my husband's conversation with Penelope the Intern.

So, Phil has decided that he's no longer content with philandering and now wants a divorce. I'm not at all surprised. I suspected it would happen eventually. My replacement would start to get restless and ready to step into her new role. Even more of a reason to accelerate the plan I have percolating in my head.

I turn away from his office door and remind myself of the gun that's now in his night-table drawer, waiting for the right moment to be of use. And that moment will come soon. I decide to fine-tune some of the details a bit more as I make lunch, but I think it's already about time to proceed to step one.

CHAPTER 35

TASHA

"TASHA, MAY I HAVE A WORD WITH YOU?" I HEAR, JUST AS I HANG up my coat on my cubicle hook and drop my purse into the steel drawer beneath my desk.

I look up to find Evelyn standing in her doorway. Her face looks different. She isn't smiling like she usually is when I first see her in the morning. She looks like she ate something bitter.

I nod. "Sure, Evelyn."

She turns around and walks back into her office and I take a long, deep breath.

I know what this is about. I figure it out before I even shut my drawer and make the walk from my cubicle to her office. Madison got to her, and now she has to fire me. I'm surprised it's taken this long.

When I step inside, Evelyn points to one of the leather chairs facing her desk.

"Please shut the door behind you. You can have a seat."

I do as she asks while she sits down at her desk. She starts shifting things around. Her coffee cup. Her pens. A stack of Post-it notes. I kind of feel bad for her. I can tell she doesn't want to do this. She doesn't want to fire me, but she's going to. Madison wants to punish me, and what better way than to take away the gift she thinks she gave me, to take away my livelihood? Evelyn isn't going to risk angering her.

What Madison says, goes.

"I received a call yesterday and heard some disturbing information, Tasha." She clasps her hands in front of her on her desk. "Very, *very* disturbing. It's my understanding that you've been stalking and harassing one of our major donors. Phillip Gingell. Is that correct?"

"I wasn't stalking him. I was trying to talk to him. To help him."

"And that required you to show up at his place of work unannounced and follow him to an event in Arlington?" Evelyn asks, cocking an eyebrow. "To call him repeatedly?"

"Madison wants to kill her husband."

Evelyn blinks. Her mouth falls open. "W-what?"

"She wanted me to do it for her, and I told her no. Now she's punishing me. She wants to kill me, too."

She stares at me for a long time. "Tasha, I don't . . . I don't understand any of this! What are you saying? Have you had some kind of mental breakdown? I know you've been through a lot, especially with your husband's death, but—"

"Murder. He was murdered."

"But you can't accuse Madison of something like this. It's . . . it's just insane. Unfathomable!"

"I'm not crazy," I say through clenched teeth. "I've worked for you. You've seen what I'm like every day. You know who I am, and I wouldn't lie to you. I'm telling you the truth!"

She doesn't say anything, making me shake my head.

"But you don't believe me, right? *No one* will believe me. And now you don't either. I'm tired of trying to explain myself. It's like I'm a broken record, stuck in a loop."

She closes her eyes and purses her lips. "Tasha, what you're saying . . . this type of behavior is not only alarming, but it's . . . I have no choice but to terminate you. I'm sorry, but I'm letting you go. A security guard will be at your desk shortly to help escort you from the premises."

I nod and rise from my chair. "I'll pack my desk now," I whisper before walking across the room.

"Tasha," she calls after me, making me stop at her door. She's standing at her desk. She's slowly shaking her head. "Please get help. I hate to see you like this."

Just like with Phillip Gingell, I tried to tell her the truth. I tried. But it's more breath wasted. I step out of the office and shut her door behind me.

The security guard arrives about ten minutes after I've started packing. He looks to be only a few years older than Ghalen, and he's nervous, like he isn't sure what to do if I start yelling, crying, or fall down in the middle of the floor. But he doesn't have to worry. I have no plans to do any of those things. I've accepted what's happening.

Because I've been on the job for less than six months, there isn't too much to pack except for some pictures of Ghalen, my wall calendar, and a neck pillow I brought from home. Most of the rest belongs to Myers Trust.

"I'm ready," I whisper to the guard, lifting the cardboard box into my arms. It's lighter than I thought it would be.

As I walk down the hall to the elevators with the security guard at my side, I hear the sound of footsteps thumping behind me. I turn to look and see Morris running in our direction.

"What are you doing?" Morris asks. Then he looks up at the guard. "What's happening? Why are you taking her out of here? They didn't really fire you, did they?"

The guard is starting to look nervous again. He hadn't planned for this one.

"Everything is OK. It's fine, Morris," I say.

"No, it's not fine! Why are they firing you? Is it that thing with Madison? Did she get you fired?"

"I told you, it's okay. I'm not fighting it."

"But . . ." He looks between me and the guard. "But you can't just let them do this! Make them listen! Go back and talk to Evelyn. Explain to her how—"

"I did. It didn't make a difference. Now don't make a scene. You know you need this job. Besides, you said you had a bad habit of trying to rescue me." I give a little smile. "Don't start up again now. All right?"

He goes quiet.

The guard and I continue to walk to the elevators, but I stop when Morris grabs my arm. I look up at him.

"Did you ever get evidence connecting her to Kordell? Did you find her phone in that list of numbers?"

I shake my head. "I went through all of them. If one of them was hers, she didn't answer."

"Then get a recording of her admitting to what she did . . . what she has planned. Do it and I swear to you, I'll give it to my frat brother in the MPD," Morris says. This time, he gives me a little smile. "Some bad habits die hard."

"Ma'am," the security guard says, nodding to the now open elevator doors. "It's time to go."

"Get a recording, Tasha!" Morris calls to me as he watches us board. He's still standing there, still looking at me even as the doors close.

CHAPTER 36

MADISON

I CLIMB THE STAIRS TO OUR BEDROOM AND READ THE EMAIL FROM Evelyn Lancaster on my phone screen. It's full of profuse apologies. Lots of kowtowing. I expected as much. Considering that Phillip and I gave them more than $95,000 last year and the same the year before that, she should be offering to babysit our child. Lucky for her, we don't have one.

"The situation has been taken care of," the email says. "Tasha Jenkins is no longer an employee of Myers Trust. I'm sorry for the pain and suffering she has inflicted upon you and your husband. Let me know if there is anything else I can do."

I lower my phone, smile, and take another sip of wine.

I'm glad I decided to pivot to a new plan. It's only been a week, and I've already accomplished step one. I give it an imaginary checkmark. Maybe even a smiley face. Now that Tasha has been fired, she has to be devastated. I'll give her a week or so to fret about what's going to happen next.

It was hard to decide what to tackle next: her son or the boyfriend. It's the flip of a coin between the two, honestly. It's obvious she's very attached to both.

I finally settled on the boyfriend, since he's easier to get to. I found out through Evelyn that he also works at Myers Trust. Morris Hammond of Honeysuckle Court in Vienna, Virginia. It seems that he and Tasha have been engaged in a not-so-secret office romance. I could follow him in their office-complex courtyard. Hopefully, he's as unaware of his surroundings as Tasha. Or I could wait for him at his townhome. It seemed like a nice neighborhood. Quaint. Not too many people around at night to see a man get shot in the back of the head as he walks out of his garage.

Then I'll handle Ghalen. I'm still perfecting that part of the plan. But I think it has the most potential, with the downside of more unpredictability. He's a teenager, after all. They can get emotional. Hotheaded. But that can also work in my favor. I need to get him here, in this house, to do what I've planned. But how?

I set my wineglass on the night table just as I hear the front door slam shut. "Phil?" I call out with a frown. I walk out of our bedroom and back down the stairs. "Honey, is that you?"

"Of course it's me," Phil says with a loud sigh as he takes off his coat and tosses it onto one of the stools. He cocks an eyebrow. "Were you expecting someone else?"

"My lover," I say with a saucy smile, dropping my hand to my hip. "He's running a little late."

"Well, tell him to reschedule." Phil opens one of the doors of our refrigerator and stares inside. "Your husband is home."

"I thought you would be home late again." He'd been working so many late nights lately that he didn't even bother to text his excuses anymore. "I wasn't expecting you until well after midnight."

"Well, not tonight." He starts shoving items around on the refrigerator shelves, giving me no more explanation.

Poor Phil. I guess Penelope the Intern was busy tonight.

"Would you like me to make you dinner? Or I can order something."

"No, I'm fine, sweetheart. Don't worry about me," he says from the depths of our freezer. All I can see is his torso and rear end.

"OK, then!" I sing after turning around to head back upstairs. "I won't," I mutter under my breath, adjusting the trinkets on our hallway console as I walk by.

When I enter our bedroom again, the house phone rings.

"Can you get that, sweetheart?" Phil yells upstairs.

I roll my eyes and reach for the cordless on one of the night tables. When I see who's calling, I'm stunned.

"Call from Kordell Jenkins," the automated voice for the Caller ID says over the speaker.

But it isn't Kordell Jenkins. Kordell is six feet under, thanks to four bullets from Phil's pistol. So the only person it could be is his darling wife.

"Oh, this is too perfect," I whisper.

I glance over my shoulder at the doorway, looking and listening for any signs of Phil climbing the stairs and coming into our bedroom. I then walk into our master bath, shut the door behind me, and turn on the faucet to drown out the sound of my voice—a tactic Phil should use when talking to Penelope, but doesn't.

I sit on the edge of our bathtub, press the green button on the phone to answer, and raise the receiver to my ear, now smiling.

"Hello, Tasha. Isn't this a nice surprise?"

CHAPTER 37

TASHA

I'VE HAD ALL THIS NERVOUS ENERGY SINCE I LEFT THE OFFICE TODAY, since Evelyn fired me. I spent all of it on thinking about this moment.

Morris said to get recorded evidence that he can give his cop friend, something that will prove once and for all that Madison killed my husband and wants me to kill hers. All day, I've been practicing in my head what to say to her, how to get her to confess. I know I have to be careful. Madison ain't a stupid woman. If I don't do this right, she'll figure out that I'm trying to trap her. But she also thinks she's smarter than me, that she has me on the ropes. She's the type that likes to see people squirm. She'll want to gloat. I'm just giving her the chance to do it.

Ghalen is down the hall in his bedroom, playing video games, and my bedroom door is closed and locked. My cell phone is sitting next to the cordless, already recording. Madison's voice comes over the cordless speaker. I can hear water running in the background.

"Hello, Tasha. Isn't this a nice surprise?" she says like we're the oldest of friends. "I didn't know you knew my home number but then again, you found Phil's work extension. You're an industrious woman when you want to be, aren't you?"

"You got me fired today," I say.

She laughs on the other end. "You got yourself fired."

"Yeah, I guess I deserved it, huh? How dare I not do exactly what you tell me to do. I told Evelyn about you, too, you know? How you killed Kordell and keep harping on me to kill your husband, too, to repay you."

"Oh, really?" She laughs. "And I bet that got quite the reaction."

"She thinks I'm crazy. She doesn't know that *you're* the crazy one. You're dangerous."

"Tasha, I'm not crazy. I'm *determined*—which turned out to be a good thing for you, right?"

"My husband being murdered wasn't a good thing."

"Oh, please! It was the best fucking thing that ever happened to you, but you're too stubborn to admit that. You want to play the good Christian wife and mother, the bereaved widow who would never, *ever* say or do a naughty thing," she simpers, "when you know you really aren't. You're a woman who fucked around on her husband, Tasha. You're a woman who wanted her husband dead. But don't worry. You still get to play the angel and the victim, but this time for real."

I close my eyes. "You're gonna kill me, aren't you?"

"Now, why would you say that?"

"Because you keep saying it. Just not outright. I got in your way. I didn't do what you wanted, so you're gonna kill me."

She stays silent a long time. "Eventually," she finally says. "Yeah."

"When is that? Tomorrow? *Next week?* Will I get a chance to say goodbye to my friends? My boy?"

"Oh, good God!" she says, and starts to laugh again.

"Ma, who are you talking to?" I hear Ghalen shout over the phone, making my eyes flash open, making me freeze.

When did he pick up the line? How long has he been listening?

"Well, who is this?" Madison exclaims. The laughter is still in her voice. "Ghalen, is that you? Don't tell me we have a group chat now, Tasha!"

"Ma, what is she saying? Why is she talking about Dad?" he asks, sounding near tears. I shoot up from the bed and rush to my bedroom door.

"Oh, don't act so heartbroken! You and I both know that man deserved to die," Madison answers before I can. "I did you two a favor, but your mother refused to show her appreciation. Now I'll have to kill her, too, for being so rude."

"You stay away from us!" he yells. "Don't you touch my mama!"

"Ghalen, stop talking!" I scream as I unlock my door. "Hang up! Hang up now!"

"Aww, 'don't you touch my mama!' Don't you sound so big and brave?" I hear Madison say over the phone's speaker as I rush down the hall. I look in his bedroom. He's no longer there. "Much braver than your father," Madison continues. "He doesn't mind beating up women, but he ran like a scared rabbit when one of us fought back. Will you do the same, Ghalen?"

I reach our living room, where Ghalen is clutching our other cordless.

"Don't you talk about my father, bitch!" he shouts.

"Ghalen, get off the phone!"

I can't hear Madison anymore in here. I can't hear what she's saying but Ghalen suddenly explodes, "Fuck you, bitch! Fuck you! I'm comin' for you! I'm comin' for you first!" Then a few seconds later, he throws the phone against the wall. It bursts into pieces.

I jump back.

"She hung up on me! She hung up!" he yells, still pacing. "And you knew! You knew this whole time that bitch killed Dad. You knew who did it and you never told me! You never told the police!"

I hold up my hands and slowly walk toward him. "I did tell the police, baby. But they didn't listen to me. No one would listen to me." I reach out to wrap my arms around him. I didn't want him to hear any of this. I didn't want him to ever cross paths with her. I never meant for this to happen. "I'm so sorry, honey. I didn't tell you about this to protect you. I tried to fix it. I tried to take care of it on my own. And I will do it. I have a plan. Just . . . just calm down. All right? And listen to me."

"Don't tell me to calm down!" He shoves me away. "Don't tell me to calm down, Ma! Who is she? Why would she kill Dad? What the hell is going on?"

And that's when I know I no longer have a choice. I have to tell him everything. I can't protect him anymore. I never could. It's a hard lesson that I keep learning over and over again.

So, I tell him the story about Madison, how we met, and the offer she gave me. I tell him about what Jared told me about the last day Kordell was seen alive, where Kordell was headed and the mysterious woman he was going to meet. I tell him about how Madison showed up at the flea market and my job and the threats she made. I even tell him about how I tried twice to reach out to Phillip Gingell for help but it was pointless. When I finish my story, he isn't pacing anymore or breathing as hard, but that furious look in his eyes hasn't changed.

"That bitch was making fun of what she did to Dad. You heard her. She doesn't regret it at all. And she said she's coming for you next!"

"I was recording her, honey. I wanted her to say it. I wanted her to threaten me. I need more evidence to take to the cops."

"But you went to the cops, Ma! You went to her husband. We gotta take care of this ourselves! She even told me where she lives. She told me to come and get her if I was so big and bad. She was practically daring me to do it!"

I raise my hands to his face and slowly shake my head. "No, baby. You can't. *We* can't. It's a trap. Can't you see that?"

"No, it's not, Ma! She deserves what's comin' to her. What difference does it make if you always do the right thing when it means letting people hurt you? When it means standing by and letting people get hurt? You keep waiting for somebody to help, but they're not gonna help us, Ma! We need to go down there and—"

"Ghalen," I begin, holding his cheeks and gazing into his eyes, "listen to me. Listen to me! That woman has already done everything to ruin my life. I'm not going to let her do the same to you, because that is what will happen if you do this. It will put you in jail for a very long time. For the rest of your life. It will take away your future. Do you understand me?"

Finally, he stills. The veins in his forehead begin to fade.

"We'll be okay. I'll be okay, honey." I drop my hands from his face and wrap my arms around him. "I will take the recording to the police. Not the ones in Washington County like last time. This time, I'll try the ones in D.C. I'll do it tomorrow. I swear to you!"

I watch as tears slide down his cheeks.

"I've got this. Let me handle it. Please, just . . . just go back to your room and . . . and watch some TV. Or call one of your friends. Take your mind off all this. Try to calm down. We'll work on it in the morning. I'll go to the police in the morning. Will you at least wait until the morning?"

I watch as he slowly nods and staggers down the hall to his bedroom. When he shuts the door behind him, I look at the busted cordless phone. I decide to clean it up later. Instead, I walk back down the hall to my bedroom. I grab my cell phone and listen to the recording, wincing at the pain and anger in my son's voice.

"818 Wicker Street," Madison taunted. "You know where to find me, kid."

You know where to find me.

I swear that woman is the devil, but I'm relieved to finally have something that shows Madison for who she is. I clutch the phone against my chest and say a prayer.

"This has to work, God. Please, God, this has to work!" I whisper.

I set the phone back on my night table and lower my head. I'm exhausted. By Madison. By my son. By all that has happened. A wave of fatigue sweeps over me out of nowhere.

I just want a few moments. Some quiet time when I don't have to think about Madison or murder or what she's done and is still doing to me and my family. I just want some peace before I have to face it all again in the morning.

I lie on the bed and stare at the ceiling. I stare at it so long that I fall asleep. Maybe because I'm just so damn tired. Maybe because all the sleepless nights tossing and turning have finally caught up with me. I don't know how long I doze.

The sound of a door slamming shut is what makes my eyes pop open. I push myself up to my elbows with a yawn.

"Ghalen?" I call out, but he doesn't answer me. I rise from my bed and stagger down the darkened hall to my son's bedroom. When I push open the door, I see my son isn't in bed. I turn on the lights to make sure and I'm right; he isn't there.

"Ghalen?" I say now in a shaky voice. "Where are you?"

That's when I hear the car engine and the squeal of tire wheels. I race to the front door and throw it open in just enough time to see him driving off in my Chevy Malibu.

"Ghalen, stop!" I scream, running out the front door to our chain-link fence, but the car is already gone by the time I get there. Its rear lights disappear around the corner.

I know where he's going: 818 Wicker Street.

I rush back to the house to get my phone and call a Lyft, hoping I can get there before he does.

CHAPTER 38

NOW

DETECTIVE SIMMONS WRENCHED OPEN THE GATE BEFORE CLIMBING the concrete stairs leading to the Jenkins's home, with Montrose close at his heels.

Where Tasha and Ghalen Jenkins lived was a modest rowhouse, similar to his childhood home in Baltimore. He bet the neighbors were similar, too. Simple middle-class black folks going to 9-to-5 jobs, hoping to make just enough money to pay their bills, put enough gas in their cars, and go to a vacation in Ocean City or Disney World once a year.

"I don't know why we're even here," Montrose muttered behind him.

Simmons glanced over his shoulder at his partner. At that moment, the 32-year-old detective looked a lot like a sullen child forced to take piano lessons.

"We're here investigating an arson and murder," Simmons whispered to him.

"One that we already have a confession for."

"You have something else to do today? Is this not under the purview of our job?"

Montrose gave an exaggerated shrug. "I just prefer to put my energy toward cases that aren't already solved, but I guess that's just me."

"Look," Simmons began with a loud sigh, "I didn't tell you this, but earlier this afternoon I got Tasha Jenkins's cell phone out of the evidence locker. I listened to her old voice mails and went through her text messages."

"Why didn't you tell me?"

"Because you're so damn sure she did it! I'm not saying you're wrong. I just want to make sure. To cover all our bases. Anyway, nothing in the voice mails and texts raised red flags, but I noticed she made a recording the night of the murder. I listened to it."

"And?" Montrose asked, shrugging again. "What was in the recording?"

"There was an . . . an exchange, shall we say, between Tasha and Madison Gingell."

Montrose nodded and chuckled. He sucked his teeth. "That's why you didn't want to tell me. Because it's even more proof that she's guilty as hell! See, I told you. I told you she was—"

"Tasha's son, Ghalen, was on the recording too. The two exchanged words, Montrose. Tasha believed Madison had killed her husband, and frankly, from that recording, I'm starting to wonder if it's true."

It had been startling to hear the exchange. It had raised the hair on the back of Simmons's neck.

"That woman came at Tasha. And she came at the son—she came hard. She mocked him. Basically, called his father a coward. She threatened Tasha in the recording and told the boy to come to her if he wanted to do something about it. She egged him on."

Montrose frowned. "So what? What are you saying? That *he* shot the Gingells? *He* set the fire?"

"No, I'm saying that before we jump to any more conclusions, we need to consider every possibility. We need to talk to him. This little excursion isn't a waste of time. We need at the very least to clarify things. All right?"

Montrose grudgingly nodded. "All right."

Now with his partner onboard, Simmons turned back around and banged on the screen door. Within seconds, a petite, plump black woman appeared in the doorway. She scanned Simmons up and down through the wire mesh.

"Hello, ma'am, I'm Detective Simmons," he said, holding up his badge. He then gestured over his shoulder. "This is my partner, Detective Montrose. I'm here to speak with Ghalen Jenkins."

She didn't immediately answer. Her discerning dark eyes shifted from him to Montrose.

Simmons cleared his throat and tucked his wallet back into his coat pocket. "Are you Ms. Rita Jenkins? I believe we spoke on the phone. You said it was all right to come today at 4 o'clock. Is it still a good time for Ghalen?"

She pursed her lips. "Let's understand somethin'. Ghalen might have agreed to talk to you, but if I see that it looks like this conversation is starting to go left, your little interview is over."

Simmons could hear his partner start to grumble behind him, to form a snarky response, but he held up his hand, motioning him to hold his tongue.

"Yes, ma'am. We understand," Simmons said, broadening his smile.

She hesitated for a few beats longer before she slowly opened the screen door. "You can come in."

Simmons stepped past her over the threshold. Montrose followed. Simmons could feel mutual reluctance radiating from both Ghalen's aunt and his partner, like body heat.

He turned a corner to find a small living room where a tall boy with chin-length dreadlocks sat on a suede sofa and a man who looked to be eighty or older with stooped shoulders sat in the recliner beside the sofa. The boy was in jeans. The man was in a gray suit that practically billowed on his skinny frame.

Now that Simmons, Montrose, and Ghalen's aunt, Rita, were in the room too, the space felt even smaller. Almost ready to bust.

"This is Ghalen," Rita said, gesturing to the boy, who gave a limp wave, "and this is his lawyer, Deacon Roberts."

"Moses Chauncey Roberts, *Esquire*," the old man boomed followed by an abrasive cough as he grabbed the recliner's armrests. "And you two are detectives, then?" He tried to push himself to his feet. After a couple of failed attempts, Simmons rushed forward with his hand extended.

"Yes, sir, I'm Detective Simmons with the MPD," Simmons said, shaking Roberts's gnarled, wrinkled hand.

"Detective Montrose," his partner grunted behind him.

"Well, I've advised my client that he can address any questions you have regarding his mother, but that is it," Roberts said firmly before turning to the young man. "Right, Ghalen?"

"Right," Ghalen answered softly.

Simmons nodded and watched as Rita sat down beside Ghalen on the sofa. The living room fell silent as they waited for Simmons and Montrose to proceed. Simmons noticed that no one had offered him or his partner a seat; but to be honest, there really weren't any other places to sit in the crowded room, short of perching on one of the end tables. Even the coffee table was missing. He didn't want to stand up, though, to tower over them. Their body languages already projected suspicion and an unwillingness that bordered on outright hostility. But Ghalen had called him back. He obviously had wanted to talk to Simmons—at least, *before* he was encouraged to stay tight-lipped by his lawyer and his aunt.

Simmons wanted to endear himself to Ghalen. He wouldn't tell him that he'd heard the recording, that he'd heard the boy's tirade and his threats to Madison Gingell. Not yet. He wanted him to feel comfortable, and the only way he could do that is by coming to him on his level—figuratively and literally. He glanced over his shoulder at the nearby dining room.

"Do you mind if we grab a few chairs and sit down?" he asked.

Rita shrugged. "Go ahead."

He took two of the dining room table's oak chairs, handing one to Montrose. He then set his chair next to the sofa, near Ghalen.

"Thanks for agreeing to talk to us," he said to the young man. "I know you're worried about your mom and just want to help."

"She didn't do it," Ghalen said. "She didn't kill anybody!"

"How do you know that?" Simmons asked.

"Because . . ." Ghalen seemed to hesitate. He looked at his aunt, then Roberts. "Well, because I just know. I know her. My mom's not a killer. Even though Madison killed my dad, Ma kept saying we shouldn't take revenge. We shouldn't take it in our own hands."

"Why would she say that?" Simmons asked. "Did your mother mention taking this into her own hands?"

"N–no!" Ghalen stuttered, for the first time sounding nervous. "She just said it would be better to let y'all handle it. She talked to the cops. She tried to get y'all to help her, but no one did. She wouldn't have even been there if it wasn't for me!" he argued.

"Gay!" Rita barked, grabbing his arm as if to stop him.

"But it's true, Aunt Rita! I'm not lyin'!"

"What do you mean by that?" Simmons asked. "What do you mean that she wouldn't have been there if it wasn't for you?"

Ghalen slowly tugged his arm out of his aunt's grasp. "She was there because . . . because she was . . . following me."

"Wait a minute!" Montrose said, leaning forward. "You're telling us you were there?"

"Deacon Roberts, please say somethin'!" Rita begged.

The old man held up his hands. "Now, now, Ghalen. Hold up! You don't have to answer that question."

"But I want to answer!" the young man insisted, now looking desperate.

Rita shot to her feet. "That's it! Y'all are done." She pointed to the front door. "You can get out *now*!"

"Why won't you let him answer?" Montrose shouted. "Why won't you just be quiet and let him speak for himself?"

Simmons watched as the room descended into chaos . . . as Rita dropped her hands to her hips and told Montrose not to talk to her like she was "a damn child" . . . as Roberts attempted to shout himself and broke down into a coughing fit instead.

"Shit," Simmons whispered. He couldn't take it anymore. He raised his fingers to his lips and did an ear-piercing whistle, making them all fall silent with the exception of Roberts, who continued to cough.

"Can we get him some water, please?" Simmons asked.

"Oh, sure," Rita said before rushing out of the living room and through a doorway. Simmons presumed she'd disappeared to the kitchen. Less than a minute later, she returned with a water-filled glass and handed it to the old man, who loudly sipped.

"Ghalen isn't under investigation. We didn't come here to arrest him," Simmons began, now that the room was quiet again. "I just want to make that clear, Ms. Jenkins. He says he has information that could exonerate his mother, who *is* currently accused of murder. So, if Ghalen could supply us with that information, I would appreciate it." He then turned to the young man. "Do you still want to talk to us, Ghalen?"

Ghalen gradually nodded.

"What did you want to say?" Simmons asked.

"I was going to say that when my mom was asleep, I snuck out of the house to go to the Gingells."

"Why?" Simmons asked.

"Madison had called the house. Or Ma had called her. I wasn't sure. I was playing my video games. I had . . . I had on my headphones. Then I took them off and paused my game to go to the bathroom. That's when I heard their conversation. I heard it through my mom's bedroom door. She had the speakerphone on."

Simmons surmised that Ghalen was referring to the recorded conversation he'd listened to earlier.

"Madison was trying to scare her, and my mom sounded scared. So I . . . I picked up the other phone. I was just telling her to leave

Ma alone, and then she started talking shit . . . I mean *stuff*," he said before glancing sheepishly at his aunt, "about my dad. Talking about how he . . . he beat on women."

As he spoke, Rita looked away, staring at the neighboring wall like she didn't want to hear the rest.

"I thought Madison was going to come for my mom now, too," Ghalen continued. "I was just trying to protect her! So I . . . so I decided to go to her first."

Simmons closed his eyes, unsure if he wanted to ask his next question. If the young man answered it the way Simmons thought he would, it would exonerate Tasha. It would show that Simmons had been right about her all along, and would change the course of their investigation. But it would also mean that he could no longer assure Ghalen that they were merely here to speak with him as a witness. If Ghalen confessed to the murder, Simmons and Montrose would be obligated to arrest him.

Simmons slowly opened his eyes and took a deep breath. "Ghalen, did you shoot the Gingells? Did you set their house on fire last night?"

Ghalen quickly shook his head. "No. No, I didn't do it!"

Simmons exhaled with relief.

"And we're supposed to take your word for that?" Montrose asked, sounding incredulous.

"You don't have to," Ghalen snapped. "I was in jail last night. I never made it there. You can look it up yourself. I got pulled over for speeding on my way across town. The cop asked me why I was driving so fast. I was pissed already and started to talk smack. He told me to step out of the car. I told him no because I already gave him my driver's license. I wasn't drunk. I didn't do anything wrong. It turned into a big thing. He arrested me on some bullshit charge. Failure to obey a police officer. I was in holding until about 3 a.m., until Aunt Rita came and got me out."

"What time did you leave the house before the cops pulled you over?" Montrose asked.

Ghalen scratched his head. "I don't know. Around 10:30."

That would put him within the timeframe of when the neighbor heard the gunshots, only thirty minutes before the phone calls were made to 9-1-1, Simmons realized. He thought for a moment.

"Does your mom know you got pulled over by the police, Ghalen? Does she know you didn't make it to the Gingells' house last night?" he asked.

"I don't know. Maybe not."

Fifteen minutes later, the two detectives walked out of the Jenkins's home and down the concrete stairs to the unmarked cruiser parked along the curb at the end of the block.

"Well, Tasha is off the hook now," Montrose said as they heard the deadbolt click behind him. "That should make you happy."

"This is a change." Simmons looked at his partner in surprise. "You were convinced her confession was legit an hour ago."

"Well, yeah, but that was before you told me about the recording. Before we talked to her son." Montrose yanked open the gate, paused, and glanced over his shoulder at the closed door before looking at Simmons again. "Obviously, he did it," he whispered. "You were right. Her confession was fake. She's just covering for him."

Simmons shook his head as he strode through the gate. "I don't think that's it. I think Ghalen is telling the truth, that he never made it there."

"What?" Montrose threw back his head and groaned. He then jogged to catch up with his partner on the sidewalk. "For the love of God, *why* do you keep making this more complicated than it needs to be? Can no black suspects be guilty now? Is that where we're going with this?"

"I'm not even going to dignify that with an answer."

"We have a recording of him threatening Madison Gingell. The kid admits that he left in the middle of the night around the time that the Gingells were shot, when the house was set on fire. Even if the cops pulled him over, he could have left the crime scene, ditched the gun out the window, and sped away. Maybe *that's* why he got pulled over. He was fleeing the scene."

"*Or* he didn't do it. Everything happened exactly like he said it did, but Tasha didn't know he hadn't made it to the Gingells' house and confessed to a crime neither she nor he committed."

"Oh, come on! Then who did it?"

Simmons shook his head again. "I don't know. I just think there's more here that we aren't seeing."

"*Why?* What the hell more is there to see?"

"On the recording, it isn't just Ghalen threatening Madison. She's threatening him too, and basically admitted to a crime."

"*What?*" Montrose cried.

"She didn't say it outright, but she just about admitted to killing Kordell Jenkins. Whether it was just taunting or she was serious, who knows."

"Which gives Ghalen even more motive to come to the Gingells' house with his gun blazing, shoot them both, and set the house on fire."

"But it also indicates that Madison is a woman who is a lot more complex than we think, and just as capable of instigating carnage as Ghalen is," Simmons countered.

"Jesus Christ," his partner muttered before giving a caustic laugh and dropping his head into his hand. "You are hell-bent on complicating this shit, aren't you?"

Simmons understood why Montrose was frustrated with his equivocating. He was getting frustrated himself. But it was hard to explain a feeling. You couldn't articulate instinct. He still wasn't sure why he thought Tasha wasn't guilty nor her son, but he didn't think they committed the crime. He was just waiting for all the information and evidence he needed to support his feelings. He had collected a few pieces, like priceless trinkets he could carry around in his pocket, but he still needed a few more.

Montrose's cell phone began to chime, giving them both a reprieve. Simmons watched as the other man glanced at the screen, then raised the phone to his ear.

"Yeah?" he said into the phone as they started walking again. "Yeah. . . . Oh, *really?* Hmm . . . OK. OK! . . . Yeah, we're on our way!"

"Who was that?" Simmons asked as Montrose hung up.

"Medstar Hospital," Montrose said, shoving his phone into his coat pocket. "Looks like we're finally going to find out if you're right or wrong, Simmons. Our victim's awake and ready to talk."

CHAPTER 39
BEFORE

MADISON

THE HOUSE IS ACHINGLY SILENT, WITH THE EXCEPTION OF PHIL'S snores, and I'm getting tired of waiting. Finally, I hear what can only be footsteps on the stairs, then the faint creak of hardwood in the hall leading to our bedroom, and I am surprised.

Not by the sound. I just didn't expect him to get into the house so smoothly. Ghalen is cleverer than I thought.

I know it's him. Men are predictable, if anything, and Ghalen is—despite Tasha's vehement protests—a man. I knew when I poked the bear, when I challenged him to come and get me like the big bad boy he said he was, he'd come here tonight. The order is different from my initial plan. Ghalen will go down before Morris Hammond, but . . . fuck it. Sometimes you have to work within your circumstances. The end result will be the same anyway.

Not a single crash of a broken window or the thud of a door kicked open. Nothing to wake up my slumbering husband, which means that I'll have to wake him up myself. In order for this to work, Phil can't be asleep. The pistol in his night table has to be in his hand. He has to be ready.

The show is about to begin.

I can see Ghalen as well as hear him now. The barely discernible outline of a tall, looming figure in the darkness, nearing our doorway. I reach over and shake my husband's shoulder.

"Phil," I whisper. "Phil, someone's in the house."

But my husband doesn't stir. His eyes stay closed.

"Phil!" I shout, shoving him harder. "Phil, wake up! Someone's here." I yank frantically at the sleeve of his T-shirt, and his eyes finally pop open. "Get the gun!"

At those words, Ghalen charges out of the hall into our bedroom. Now that he's left the pitch black of the hallway and has entered the gossamer light filtering through our window curtains, he takes on solid form. Like a faraway figure quickly coming into focus as it nears, details emerge at rapid speed. A black hoodie. The gun in his gloved hand. A ski mask. But something is off. He's not as tall as I thought Ghalen would be, and he's a lot skinnier. Through the holes of the ski mask, I lock gazes with green irises that catch the moonlight.

This intruder isn't Ghalen.

"What are you waiting for?" Phil yells.

I turn to him in shock. He's sitting up now, glaring at the intruder. Who is he talking to? What the hell is going on?

"Shoot!" he orders.

It all clicks then. This isn't the young man I brought here to kill my husband. Phil has brought someone here to kill me.

I leap from the bed just as the intruder raises his gun and fires the first shot. Instead of hitting me, the bullet goes through our headboard. I scramble to the nearby master bath and lock the door behind me.

"Goddamnit!" Phil shouts as I turn on the bathroom lights and look frantically around me for a means of escape. But there are no windows, and the sunroof over our bathtub is twelve feet high. Even standing on our marble counters, it is too high for me to reach. There is only one exit, and it is behind the door that I just came through where my killers are waiting for me on the other side.

I'm pinned in, with nothing to defend myself. There is no boning knife for me to wield. No gun for me to fire. I am the cowering girl again, waiting for my punishment to be meted out.

"Help me!" I scream, pounding my fists against the bathroom wall, hoping our neighbor will hear. "Help me, please!"

"Do you hear that? You were supposed to kill her," Phil says on the other side of the door. "Now she's going to wake up the whole goddamn neighborhood!"

"I told you I'm not good with guns!" a voice whispers back, making me halt. Making the blood turn into ice in my veins.

I know that voice. I know that voice.

"I don't care! Do your job. Get her out of that fucking bathroom and finish this," Phil says.

The darkness in my husband was deeper and vaster than I thought. I hear it in his voice now. The coldness. The brutality. He's going to kill me.

"Fine. You want me to get her out of there. I'll get her out of there!"

They're battering the bathroom door now. It rattles on its hinges, and I can hear the wood splintering with each kick and ram of their shoulders, making me scream all over again. I make a frenzied search around the bathroom for something to defend myself. A soap dish. Scented candles. Bottles of expensive body wash. Toenail clippers. The objects seem so ridiculous now. The search is utterly pointless.

I back into the corner, hiding between the toilet and the counter. Covering my head. Bringing my knees to my chest. The door flies open. This time, the ski mask is gone and I see the face of my killer, confirming what I suspected. But finding out that I'm right brings me no joy.

"Come on out of there, Maddie," my brother Billy says. He reaches for me, grabbing my leg and yanking me from my hiding space.

I kick and I yell so much that my throat burns. My eyesight is blurry from my tears. I grab for anything. The counter. The door frame. The floor rug. But it doesn't stop. *He* doesn't stop.

My brother sits on top of me, crushing my shoulders under his knees, pressing all of his weight on top of my chest. He clamps his hand over my mouth and I bite down on the flesh of his palm, making him squeal and then slap me across the face so hard that my jaw rattles, that my vision goes bright. I taste blood in my mouth, a mix of mine and Billy's.

He clamps his hand over my mouth and nose this time, and I start to asphyxiate. I weakly tug at his hands. I open my eyes, and the world is spinning.

I don't see Billy anymore, but Father. His face is stern. His blue eyes are now pinpricks. His lips are curled into a thin white line as he slowly suffocates me.

I know on some level it's not really him. It can't be. Father is long gone. Phantasms aren't real. But my brain is dying. It no longer knows the difference.

"Don't kill her *that* way," Phil says impatiently, standing over Father's shoulder. "That's not part of the plan."

"Yeah, well, shit happens! Plans change."

"Not this part!"

Phil yanks him back. The suffocating hand flies from my face. I can breathe again.

I gasp, starving for air, ravenously sucking it in through gulps, but my feast is short-lived. Another hand roughly turns my face upward. It is softer, less callused, but the grip is even rougher than before. The hand is my husband's.

Phil is on top of me now. He's been rough with me before, but not like this. There is no thrill in how he's taking control. No pleasure. Just sheer terror. He places the muzzle of his pistol into my gaping mouth. It clicks against my teeth. I start to gag as he shoves it toward the back of my throat. I'm struggling again, fighting my ending with what little energy I have left.

"Damnit, stay . . . still!" he grumbles, like he's trying to adjust my clothes, not attempting to kill me.

He pulls the trigger and—

CHAPTER 40

NOW

"What room is it?" Detective Simmons asked as they stepped out of the hospital elevator.

"Uh, let me check." Montrose glanced down at his cell phone screen, quickly scrolling through a few texts. "Looks like it's 2452."

Simmons wasn't a fan of hospitals. He'd always hated the smell of the antiseptic cleaners that permeated the air and the distinct, irritating squeak of your shoes over the linoleum tiles. And he hated the malaise that clung to the walls, that coated the patients in their rooms. It made him think of death, and not the quick, gruesome kind that he'd encountered in his years as a beat cop and a detective, but the achingly slow, painful kind. The one that came from disease and old age. But despite his growing discomfort, he had to be here at Medstar Washington Hospital Center because he and Montrose were going to talk to Phillip Gingell and finally find out what happened last night. The night that Phillip was shot, his wife was murdered, and their house was set ablaze.

They turned a corner, then another, and Simmons spotted "2452" on a plaque on the wall. The door sat open, but the curtain around the one hospital bed in the room was partially drawn. He could see two men there. One in the hospital bed, the other casually reclining in the leather chair beside it. Simmons knocked on the metal doorframe. "MPD," he called out. "Can we come in?"

"Yes, officers," the man in the bed said. "Be my guest."

As Simmons drew closer, he saw that the patient's face was bruised and scratches were on his left cheek. He was partially covered in bandages on his right side, both his shoulder and his entire arm. The patient smiled weakly.

"I'm Phillip Gingell," he began, "and I presume you are the detectives I'm supposed to speak with today."

Simmons nodded. "Yes, sir. We wanted to hear about what happened last night. As much as you can remember."

"I'm more than happy to tell you, gentlemen. I'd like to keep my legal counsel in the room, though," he said, inclining his head toward the sweater-clad man sitting beside him.

"Kenneth Jensen with Robertson & MacGruder," his companion said, adjusting his glasses. "Pleased to meet you."

Christ. Everybody has a lawyer, Simmons thought glibly.

"We don't have a problem with that," Montrose answered for them. "Can you tell us what happened, Mr. Gingell?"

"Yes, well, I just want to preface this by saying that Madison and I had been having marital problems for quite some time." Phillip lowered his eyes and cleared his throat. "She felt I worked too many hours. That I was never home anymore. We'd tried to make it work, but we'd reached an impasse. We were about to go to bed that night, but I just . . . I just couldn't take it anymore. The pain between us. The silence. The anger. I told her that I wanted a divorce, that I thought I should move out and . . . and things quickly escalated from there."

"Escalated?" Simmons took a step toward the hospital bed. "How did it escalate, Mr. Gingell?"

"She started screaming and threatening me. Threatening herself. I'd . . . I'd never seen her like that before," Phillip said with a grimace. "I tried to talk her down. To even shout her down, but she wouldn't listen. I keep a gun in our bedroom. In my night-table drawer, for defense purposes. Madison knew where it was. Before I knew it, she was digging inside the drawer. She grabbed the gun before I could stop her." He paused to clear his throat. "When I realized what she was about to do, to try to shoot me or herself, I tried to stop her then, to wrestle it away. It fired a few times. One of the bullets hit me in the shoulder," he said, gesturing to his right shoulder. "I guess I fainted from the blood loss. I didn't wake up until the firefighters carried me out of the house. That's when I saw. . . ." He blinked back tears, sniffed, and wiped at his nose with his bandage-free hand. "That's when I saw that Madison had killed herself. I saw my wife was dead."

"Did your wife set the fire, too?" Montrose asked.

Phillip nodded. "I suppose so. When I was shot and fainted, I guess she assumed the wound was a lot worse than it was. She thought I was dying, or at least that I would be dead soon. She didn't try to revive me or call for help. She was just going to let me die. But it wasn't enough to kill me and kill herself. I guess she wanted us to burn together as well."

"Shit," Simmons whispered.

"So, officers," Phillip's lawyer said, "as you can see, this was a very unfortunate incident. My client is lucky to be alive."

"Had your wife threatened you before? Had she tried to kill you before last night?" Simmons asked, remembering the phone conversation that Tasha had taped where Madison had admitted as much.

"No. Never! But she had been very . . . upset lately," Phillip continued. "Moody. Like I said, we had been arguing more. Maybe she was depressed and wasn't in her right mind anymore. She usually keeps to herself. She doesn't have very many close friends. She wasn't happy, but I didn't know things had gotten that bad. My asking for the divorce may have pushed her over the edge. I would have gotten her help, if I'd known. None of this had to happen."

It seemed there were a lot of things Phillip Gingell didn't know about his wife.

Simmons had heard the woman on the recording. She'd seemed calculating and cold. Phillip claimed his wife was behaving out of character, but Simmons doubted it. Maybe she hadn't taken the gun out because of depression or hysterics, but had planned to shoot Phillip all along. She was a woman who very much wanted her husband dead, based on the recorded phone conversation. Simmons guessed if she couldn't get Tasha to do it for her, she'd decided in a moment of desperation to do it herself.

And with that, Simmons finally felt the unease that had plagued him since he walked into the Gingells' home last night loosen its hold on him.

It *was* an attempted murder-suicide—one of the original scenarios that Simmons had suggested when he'd arrived at the crime scene. Simmons finally had his solution to the puzzle, and all the pieces supported his instinct that neither Tasha nor Ghalen were guilty.

Ghalen hadn't made it to the Gingells' house that night like he said.

Tasha had taken responsibility for the fire because she thought Ghalen had done it.

It made Simmons speculate how bad things could have turned out for the mother and son if fate hadn't interceded. What if Ghalen hadn't been stopped by the police that night? Would he have killed Madison before she killed herself? What if Phillip hadn't survived the shooting and fire, if he hadn't been able to explain what really happened? Would Tasha have been found guilty of a crime she didn't commit?

What had happened that night at the Gingells' had been a tragedy, but it sounded like the tragedy could have been ten times worse if things had been just a little different.

"Well," Montrose said as he gave Simmons a knowing look as if he was bracing for his partner's impending gloating, "we appreciate your talking to us, Mr. Gingell. We'll likely have to follow up with you, though, after our crime scene techs finish their analysis. Of course, we have to make sure it all corroborates what you're now saying."

"That isn't a problem, detectives," Phillip said, nodding. "I understand."

"We'll be in touch," Simmons said before turning to head out of the hospital room. When he did, he almost ran smack-dab into a woman holding a styrofoam cup of coffee.

"Whoa!" Simmons said. "I'm sorry, ma'am!"

"No, my apologies!" She laughed softly. "I didn't know Phillip had . . . uh . . . guests."

She blushed slightly, bringing a pink flush to her ivory cheeks. Even in her cashmere turtleneck and jeans, he could see that she was curvy. She had long dark hair and big hazel eyes. She was one of those rare beauties you only see in movies or on magazine covers.

"They're the detectives, Summer," Phillip called to her. "They were questioning me about what happened last night." He smiled at the detectives. "Summer is a friend of the family. She came to the hospital when she heard what happened."

Summer gazed up at Simmons and Montrose. "Did I come at a bad time? I can come back again later if you want to continue to—"

"No, ma'am, we're done," Montrose said before stepping around her into the hall.

Simmons nodded goodbye before following his partner. As he rounded the doorway, he paused and glanced over his shoulder, watching as Summer walked across the room.

"This is the best coffee I could find," she said, walking toward the hospital bed. "I figured you wouldn't be able to hold it yourself, so I brought you a straw."

"That was thoughtful of you. Thank you," Phillip said as she drew near. When she leaned over and raised the straw to his mouth to drink, he reached down and lightly cupped her rear, making Simmons do a double-take.

"*What?*" Montrose asked as they walked down the hall back to the elevator a few seconds later. "I'd thought you'd be grinning ear to ear right now, considering everything. You were right all along. Yay for you," he said dryly. "What's with the face?"

"Nothin'," Simmons said, pressing the DOWN button when they reached the elevators, erasing the image of Phillip's hand caressing the woman's jean-clad bottom from his mind. "It's nothin'. If you don't mind writing this up, I'll head to the Correction Treatment Facility now. It's time to get Tasha Jenkins out of jail."

CHAPTER 41

SIMMONS SAT ON THE OTHER SIDE OF THE METAL TABLE, WAITING patiently for Tasha to enter the room, downing his fifth cup of coffee of the day. One of the corrections officers had popped in a little earlier to update him, to tell him they had located the inmate and were bringing her down. Simmons had already initiated the paperwork for her release, but he wanted a final conversation before Tasha went back into the free world.

It was a little after 8 o'clock and Simmons was exhausted. He was basically functioning on caffeine, adrenaline, and three and a half hours of sleep. Now he was approaching the finish line.

One last stretch, he told himself. One final push, and he could go home and crash.

He'd already made good on his promise to Sergeant Myers and updated him on their investigation. He told the other officer about the recording on Tasha's cell phone and about the things that Madison Gingell had said. Myers was as shocked as he'd been.

"She really said all that?" Myers asked. "She admitted it?"

"Pretty much, and she shot Phillip Gingell last night, too. I don't think Tasha Jenkins was lying about what happened with Kordell.

You might want to take a second look at Madison as a suspect for your investigation."

"Maybe we do," Myers agreed.

Simmons now lowered his coffee cup and sat upright as the door suddenly opened. Tasha stood in the doorway in her orange inmate uniform, with her wrists bound in cuffs in front of her. A female corrections officer stood behind her as Tasha shuffled into the room. Tasha looked at him, but there was no sign of recognition on her face. She'd gone from aging decades overnight, to now seeming like a walking ghost.

"You can have a seat, Tasha," Simmons said, gesturing to the chair on the other side of the table.

She slowly sat down.

He then nodded to the corrections officer to let her know she could leave. She silently followed his request, closing the door behind her.

Simmons stared at Tasha's bowed head, at her sunken shoulders. He could clearly see this woman had been broken by everything that had happened, and not just last night. It sounded like even her saga with Madison Gingell—real or imaginary—had taken its toll. He barely knew Tasha, but he knew enough about her and her circumstances that he felt like he did. It was painful to see her this way. He hoped all he had to tell her today would finally give her some relief.

"So," Simmons began, leaning his elbows on the tabletop, "I know that you lied to me last night. I know for a fact now that you had nothing to do with what happened to the Gingells."

"I didn't lie to you," she said, staring down at the table, not meeting his eyes. "I did it."

"No, you didn't."

"Yes, I did."

He sighed impatiently. "So why did you call 9-1-1? Why'd you call for help? It doesn't make much sense."

"I didn't want the fire to spread and for more people to get hurt," she whispered. "I didn't want that on my conscience."

"And yet your conscience went silent when you shot Madison and Phillip."

She didn't reply.

He slouched back in his chair. "What did you do with the gun?"

"I threw it away."

"'Away' where, Tasha?"

She shrugged. "It's all a blur. I . . . I can't remember."

He slowly shook his head in exasperation. "I'll give you one thing. You're sticking to the story no matter what. You've got a ready answer for everything, even if none of it makes sense."

She didn't respond.

"You must really love your son if you're willing to take the fall for him like this, for something you didn't do. I admire that. I don't know if I could do it. But I'm telling you that you don't have to anymore."

"I'm not taking the fall," she said as tears began to fill her eyes, then spill over. "I told you, I *did it!*"

"Tasha, Ghalen didn't make it to the Gingells' house last night. The police stopped him en route. He didn't shoot them and he didn't start that fire."

Her eyes flew up to meet his. Her mouth fell open. "What? How . . . how do you—"

"How do I know he didn't? Because Phillip Gingell told us Madison did. She shot her husband, she set the bedroom on fire, then she shot herself. They had an argument. Phillip was going to leave her and . . . well, she lost it. Phillip told us everything. Ghalen's not guilty—and neither are you."

He watched as a series of emotions flashed across her face: surprise, confusion, the slow coalescence of comprehension, and, finally, relief. The relief expressed itself with loud sobs, with even more tears. She doubled over and lowered her head to the table as she cried into her bound hands. Simmons reached into his pocket and pulled out a stack of tissues. He set it next to her. When the sobs finally subsided, she raised her head and looked at him with bloodshot eyes.

"This was hell. Pure hell," she croaked.

"I can only imagine," he whispered.

"I wish I'd never let that woman into my life. I wish I'd never given her that ride that day." She reached for the pack of tissues, yanked out a handful, and blew her nose. "Kordell would still be alive. I thought Ghalen was on his way to jail, too. I felt like I was being punished for not making good decisions. For all the mistakes I've . . . I've made."

Simmons thought for a few seconds. "Guilt is a funny thing, Tasha. I find that the people who should feel it—don't. And the people who do feel it the most, probably shouldn't."

She opened her mouth and then closed it. She nodded.

"You're getting released today. Your charges have been dropped. I hope that whatever burden you've been carrying around, you can finally let it go, because you didn't do anything wrong. You hear me? There's nothing to feel guilty about anymore." He looked over his shoulder at the door behind her. "We're done!" he shouted.

Within seconds, the door opened. The female corrections officer came inside.

He watched as Tasha stood from her chair and began to walk toward the waiting officer. She gave one last look at him over her shoulder before exiting the room.

CHAPTER 42

Five months later . . .

PHILLIP GINGELL STEPPED OUT OF THE SHOWER, WIPED AT THE condensation on the bathroom mirror, and winced at the image staring back at him.

The bandages were long gone. He'd regained almost all of the mobility in his shoulder. Most of the burned skin along his right arm, shoulder, and torso was now as pink as a newborn's and even more sensitive to the touch. But the doctors said it would all heal in one to two more months, and, when it did, it would be just as good as new. Unfortunately, the rest would remain scar tissue, reddish elephantine hide that would be harder to ignore.

He ran his hands over one of those scars, letting his fingers read the webbed ropes of flesh as if it were braille. He usually covered the scars with his shirts or made up an elaborate story about escaping a burning car after an accident whenever someone at the pool or in the gym sauna asked what had happened to him.

At least the fire hadn't made it to his head; he'd gotten to keep what little hair he had left.

Phillip leaned against the marble counter before grabbing his toothbrush.

Considering everything, he supposed that he'd made out well in the end. The fire, the smoke, and the firefighters trampling throughout his house had done a good enough job of covering the evidence of what had really happened that night. And one mostly superficial gunshot wound and a few second- and third-degree burns were a small price to pay to get rid of his conniving cunt of a wife, to finally be with the woman he adored.

When Madison's brother, Billy—a brother he hadn't even known existed—had called him out of the blue, offering to give him bombshell information about his wife in exchange for $2,000, he hadn't known what to think initially. Mildly intrigued, Phillip had agreed to a meeting at a rest stop in Boonsboro. It was there that Billy had told him the story of Madison's murder plot.

"I think she wants to off you, buddy," Billy had said between smacks and chews of his burger. They had stood in the parking lot, next to their cars, as they talked. "I told her I wasn't interested."

"Why would she come to you to do it?"

"She knows I've got a record. That I've been involved in that . . . umm . . . that sort of thing before."

Phillip had eyed him, not liking his cagey answer. "*Involved? Involved how?*"

"Don't worry about it! Worry about your wife." Billy paused to suck soda through his straw. "Watch your back, because Maddie's persistent and cold-blooded. Just because I said no, doesn't mean that's the end of it. Not for a bitch like her."

First he'd thought it was a hoax. An outright lie. He could see from the tracks and bruises on Billy's arm, from his gaunt cheeks and bulging eyes, that he was obviously a drug addict. The story of Billy's familial relationship to Maddie turned out to be true, thanks to a background check that Phil conducted that showed he was Maddie's brother and did have quite the criminal record. But maybe the rest of his story was made up, an elaborate scheme to get money out of Phillip to feed his habit. There was no way that Madison would want to *kill* Phillip. Sure, she suspected he was having an affair, though she had wrongly guessed with whom. And yes, she was angered by it. She had even threatened to tell all his secrets if he left her, but in no way was she angry enough to have him murdered. It would seem much more likely that he would kill her first.

Phillip had learned the benefits of having a troublesome wife disappear when Ashley, his first wife, was murdered. Before that fateful day on the C&O running trail nearly a decade ago, Ashley had been threatening to take Phil to the cleaners if he decided to go through with their divorce. She was going to bring up his tawdry affair with Madison and how he practically owed Ashley his law career. She'd carried him through law school, even cheated for him so he could pass written exams. He'd used her family connections to help get a position at his first firm.

"Leave me and I will wring you dry, until there is nothing left," she'd promised him.

Though he would never admit it aloud, Ashley's murder had been a fortunate coincidence. Of course he'd played the grieving widower. He'd cried at the funeral. To this day, he still talked about what a wonderful woman Ashley had been. But on the inside, he'd wanted to shout for joy and was relieved she was gone. He'd wanted to send her murderer, Hakeem Fletcher, a fruit basket and a bottle of wine in thanks.

So when history started to repeat itself, and Madison was the one making threats about what she would do to him if he left her, he'd started to consider how convenient it would be to have yet another wife murdered, but he had no idea how he would even go about doing it.

Then Billy showed up and that black woman, Tasha, had started to call him, to leave messages also talking about Madison's murder plot against him. Instead of being alarmed by the confirmation of what Billy had said, Phillip saw it as an opportunity. Circumstances were once again playing in his favor.

And he had yet another motivation to expedite Madison's murder: Summer Ross. He had fallen hard for Summer and, frankly, had been taken with the irreverent brunette since the day Madison had brought her to their home after yoga class for brunch three and a half years ago, but Phillip had never acted on it. It wasn't until he heard mutterings from Madison about Summer's marriage problems that he saw his opening. They'd been meeting in secret for months—except for that brief time that he tried to reconcile with Madison to pacify her when he couldn't see an easy way out of their marriage. Knowing that his wife wanted to kill him meant he was no longer obligated to keep up their farce of a marriage. This was a chance for a clean break, for a new chapter. He could finally show Summer just how serious he was, that this was more than just a casual fling and he was willing to display the lengths he was willing to go to finally have her.

Phillip didn't have Hakeem Fletcher to help him this time around, but now he had Billy. So, he reached out to his brother-in-law and offered him a similar deal as Madison's, asking how much it would cost to employ his expertise and get rid of her. The two men then began to hatch their plan. There had been a few shaky moments and missed opportunities. One evening three weeks before, Billy was supposed to carry out the fake robbery and murder, and had gotten stuck in infamous D.C. traffic that backed up the Beltway for miles. On another occasion, Phil's driver, Tony, had surprised them by showing up in the middle of the night to return Maddie's purse, which she'd forgotten in the back of the Lincoln Town Car earlier that day. Tony had arrived only fifteen minutes before Billy was slated to show up in his ski mask with gun in hand. Not wanting Tony anywhere near the crime scene when the murder was supposed to happen, Phillip and Billy had been forced to call it off that day too.

Even Tasha had started to get in the way. She'd become a nuisance. A real pain in his ass. Her persistence in telling Phillip the truth about his wife and doing it so publicly was starting to bring attention to him and to his tumultuous marriage, which was exactly the opposite of what he wanted. Phillip didn't want police to think he'd have any reason to want his wife dead. He was sure his plan had completely fallen apart when Madison discovered he'd talked to Tasha, but thankfully his wife still believed he trusted her and hadn't listened to Tasha's "delusions." The murder plot could proceed as planned, and he and Billy succeeded in the end. Now Phillip was on his way to see Billy one last time, to give him the last bit of money that would end their arrangement.

Phillip emerged from the bathroom soon after, to find Summer still slumbering in bed, her limbs twisted in the sheets. He smiled and leaned down, pushing aside her dark hair and placing a light kiss on her bare shoulder. Summer stirred and turned to her side to look up at him.

"What time is it?" She stretched and yawned. Her eyes were still puffy with sleep. "Why are you up so early on a Saturday?"

"I have that important meeting today," he said as he opened one of her dresser drawers and began to dress.

He was staying at her condo, now that the house on Wicker Street was uninhabitable thanks to the fire. They planned to sell both properties and buy a new house soon. Maybe even build one. With the money from Madison's insurance policy and Tom's estate that he'd left Summer in his will, they had more than enough to spend.

"Remember I told you I'm giving him the money today?"

She stilled. Her face went from drowsy to alert. "Oh."

He stepped into his chinos and pulled them up to his hips. As he buttoned his fly, Summer shifted upright and climbed out of bed, revealing her nakedness. She strolled across the room, before standing behind him and wrapping her arms around his waist.

Phillip closed his eyes, momentarily lost in bliss. He loved the feel of her body against his.

The scars were definitely worth it. To have all of this and no longer have to hide it. He was sure of it now.

"And this is the last meeting with him?" Summer asked, resting her chin on his shoulder, then nibbling his ear. "Then it's all over, right?"

"It's all over," he repeated, turning around to kiss her. Long and hard. When he pulled his mouth away, she asked "Do you regret it? Do you regret killing her?"

"Absolutely not!" He searched her face. *"Do you?"*

Summer had known about his plan from the beginning. At first, he had been wary of telling her about it, unsure that her conscience would get the better of her and she would warn his wife about their scheme, but he'd been right to trust her.

Summer now seemed to contemplate his question before slowly shaking her head. "Not really. Tom's gone. Madison's gone. People die every day. Besides, as Madison would say, 'We all have to deal with the repercussions of our decisions.' She had to deal with hers."

She gave him a wry smile before turning away and humming as she strolled into the bathroom. She closed the door behind her. He heard the blast of the shower.

Phillip then resumed dressing.

✳ ✳ ✳

It was a little after 10 a.m., but the rest stop was already teeming with people. Truck drivers were grabbing breakfast, attracted by the oversized golden arches perched on a sign forty feet above the roadway, visible from miles away. Tourists noisily disembarked from buses that would take them to other cities and states for their summer vacations. They now scurried to the rest stop mini-mart in search of bathrooms, bottled water, toiletries, and snacks. And among the crowd was a lone man at the far end of the lot, sitting in his Mercedes with the AC cranked up high to combat the August heat.

Phillip tapped his fingers against the steering wheel as he waited. Billy was only a few minutes late, but each second that ticked by made him more restless, more anxious. He just wanted to get this over with.

He finally saw the battered Ford pickup coming toward him, its rusted bumper and missing emblem. It pulled into the space next to the Mercedes. The engine chugged so loudly that it seemed to make the windows of the Mercedes vibrate. He watched as Billy opened the door and hopped out. Phillip turned off his engine and climbed out too, taking out the cup of coffee and the McDonald's bag containing a hash brown and $80,000.

Every time Phillip saw the young man, he was always put off by how ghastly he looked. The scars. His sickly pale skin. His scarecrow-like frame. Billy looked like a criminal. Like a killer. But ultimately, Phillip reminded himself, Billy hadn't been the one to pull the trigger and fire the deadly shot. Phillip had killed Madison, and now, thanks to the fire, he had his own scars as well.

"You got it?" Billy asked before taking a quick look around them. "We're good?"

Phillip nodded and handed him the coffee and the bag.

Billy grabbed greedily for them both and grinned, revealing his missing teeth. As he took a sip of cold coffee, he cracked the bag open, checking the money inside.

"You're going to count it in the open?" Phillip asked, aghast. Why bother with all the subterfuge if he was going to do something so blatant?

"Nah, I'll assume it's all here and I know where to find you if it isn't." Billy chuckled. "Good doin' busy with you," he said before turning to hop back into his truck.

"By the way," Phillip called to him, stopping Billy in his tracks, "I decided to give you all your money though technically everything didn't go according to plan. In fact, it went *wildly* off course."

"Hey, I told you in the beginning guns weren't my forte, bud. You're the one who was hell-bent on that whole burglary-gone-wrong scenario. And I didn't know she was gonna lock herself in the goddamn bathroom. Besides, we got her out, didn't we?"

"That's not what I meant. I get that you had to cover things up," he continued, drawing closer to him, "but knocking me out and setting that fire was incredibly risky."

Billy squinted up at him. "What the hell are you talking about?"

"You know what I mean. I won't belabor the issue, because every-thing turned out fine, but word to the wise: if you're going to diverge *that* greatly from the original plan, make your partner aware of it. Not to mention the fact that if the fire had gotten any bigger, or the fire-fighters hadn't gotten there in enough time, I could've died."

"I didn't set that fire," Billy said, screwing up his face. "I thought *you* did!"

Phillip stared at him in amazement. *"What?"*

"I ran out the back door and left you to call the police and tell them she shot you, then shot herself, like you said you would. I thought you came up with that fire shit on your own."

The two men gazed at each other in silence, listening to road way noise, to the steady roar of the semitrucks entering and leaving the parking lot. The unspoken question between them floated in the fog-filled air above, like a thought bubble. The question of what had really happened that night.

CHAPTER 43

"How much more do you have to go?" Tasha asked as her son loaded yet another box onto the U-Haul truck.

"Eh, a few more," Ghalen said before turning away and wiping his hands on the front of his jeans. "Then we have to break down my bed to get it ready for the Salvation Army to pick it up."

They watched as his friend, Mason, loaded yet another box with a label written in magic marker on the side. It said "Jenkins, Room 435." She'd told him the labels were a good idea just in case his box got mixed up with any of the other students who were moving into their dorm rooms at Bowie State University this weekend.

Tasha couldn't believe she was finally at this moment. The goal-posts had seemed so far away for so long. During her last year with Kordell, she'd practically checked off the days on her calendar.

Just one more, she'd told herself, whispering it like a mantra in her head.

And then, before she knew it, the day had arrived. Her son was now headed off to his freshman year of college. Her "baby" was moving on—and so was she.

Ghalen turned and looked longingly at their house, at the gray siding, white shutters, wilted lawn, and chain-link fence. "Are you finished packing too?"

She glanced at her car, which was now brimming with her own boxes and suitcases. "Yeah, I think so."

Tasha had put the house on the market a few months ago. Last week, she'd accepted a full-ask offer. The house was now mostly empty save for a few items tucked away in the attic. What Ghalen didn't take with him and she couldn't fit in her car, she had either sold or donated. Tasha would leave the last of the scrubbing and vacuuming to her son and told him to give his keys to the realtor when he was done. Now she was off.

"I don't see why you can't stay a couple of days longer, Ma," he said, almost pouting. "At least wait until I'm at school and settled in."

"Boy, stop being all dramatic! You'll be fine," she assured him with a laugh. "You've got a mattress and there's still some food in the fridge. You don't need me watching over you."

Tasha felt like she had already done her duty as his mother. She'd kept her vow and been willing to make the ultimate sacrifice for him. That fateful night at the Gingells' home had tested her to her core. In some ways, she still wasn't sure if she had passed the test or failed.

She hadn't planned to go inside the house that night of the fire. She'd hoped that she could catch Ghalen before he'd even arrived, but then she heard the noise coming from the back of their property.

She'd been surprised to discover that she had been to the house before, the first night that she and Madison had met. Tasha hadn't remembered the name of the street from months earlier, because she'd been following Madison's directions, making rights and lefts in the dark. But as the Lyft driver pulled off after depositing her on the curb, she could see that Madison's home—818 Wicker Street—was the house on the corner that Madison had claimed was her friend's home. The safe house she'd fled to when she was supposed to be running away from her husband.

Now Tasha knew it wasn't a safe house. It had been Madison's home all along.

She'd thought she heard Ghalen in the backyard. She'd thought he might be trying to sneak inside the home or had already done so. She'd gone toward the sound, intending to stop him.

A side door had been left open just a smidge, so she walked in and shut the door behind her. It led to a small office. She'd left the office and heard noises upstairs, lots of thumping and moving around.

She'd wanted to whisper her son's name, to tell him to come back, but she'd been too frightened to speak. Maybe what she was hearing wasn't him. Maybe it was the Gingells instead, so she climbed a few more stairs to get a better view of the top floor.

That's when she saw the chaos in the bedroom, the aftermath of whatever melee had taken place in there. She saw Madison's dead body on the floor in a pool of blood. Her empty eyes stared up at the bedroom ceiling. Her hand clutched a gun. Meanwhile, Phillip was muttering to himself as he paced in front of Madison's body. One hand held his bleeding shoulder. The other held his cell phone.

Where had Ghalen gotten a gun? Had he found the one that she'd gotten from Jared and hidden under her pillow? Tasha didn't know, but it was obvious to her that he had killed Madison, like he'd threatened he would. But he must have missed the mark with Phillip, or hadn't intended to kill him and had accidentally shot him instead. Phillip had survived, and he was going to call the police. He was going to tell them what had happened, what Ghalen had done.

She'd vowed before to do what she had to do. *I will protect me and mine,* she thought as she silently watched Madison's husband pace around the room.

Tasha didn't have much time to think. Even less time to act. She noticed a black metal cube . . . an object d'art, sitting on a hallway console. When she picked it up, it felt heavy in her hands. Heavy enough. As Phillip started to dial, she rushed toward the door. He was too engrossed in what he was doing to hear or notice her. His back was facing her, too. He didn't see her coming before she hit him with all her might on the back of the head and he collapsed to the floor.

It wasn't hard to set the fire. Madison had several candles in her bathroom, all with a French label printed on the packaging. All a sickeningly sweet vanilla scent. To this day, she would never forget that smell. It would be forever imprinted on her memory. Sometimes Tasha swore she still smelled it on her clothes, in the air. And she would always think of Madison's vacant eyes and her blood-filled mouth whenever she got a whiff of it.

Tasha frantically placed the vanilla-scented candles around the bedroom before kicking them all over one by one in quick succession and tossing the last onto the bedsheets. She was out of the room and down the stairs by the time the fire started to pick up steam.

As she closed the Gingells' front door behind her, ran down the stairs, and watched the flames from a distance, she'd been amazed at how fast the fire had grown. But ultimately, it hadn't been fast enough. Or she hadn't let it grow fast enough to burn the bodies and any evidence of the shootings that she was sure the police would be able to trace back to Ghalen.

She'd called 9-1-1 too soon.

She'd told Detective Simmons the truth: even though she was willing to get rid of the Gingells to protect herself and her son once and for all, she hadn't been able to stomach the idea of the fire spreading, of it burning down the *entire* neighborhood.

What had happened these past few months had changed Tasha. It had made her nimbler, more conniving, and more ruthless. Madison would be proud. But, ultimately, she guessed it hadn't changed her enough to watch *everything* and *everyone* burn to get what she wanted. That's where she and Madison diverged. She didn't have the stomach for that.

Tasha would never repeat the story. She would never tell Ghalen the truth of what had happened that night, what she had done for them. She would take that secret with her to her grave. Besides, what was the point of telling the truth, anyway? It never served her any purpose. Not with Sergeant Myers. Not with Evelyn. Not with Phillip, or even with that kind-hearted Detective Simmons. People didn't really want to hear the truth. She'd learned that hard lesson— one she was reluctant to admit that Madison had been right about.

Tasha now watched as her son continued to gaze at their house. "It's gonna be weird, not having a home to come to anymore," he said, sounding forlorn.

"It's just a house, Ghalen. Just a building."

Even though Ghalen was nostalgic about their old home, she was happy to leave behind many of the memories housed within it.

"And it's not like we're going to be homeless." She grinned and placed a hand on his shoulder. "You have your dorm, and you can always visit your mama. I'll always give you a couch to sleep on at my place," she joked.

"I don't even know where that place is! You still haven't told me where you're movin'."

She shrugged. "I haven't decided yet. First I thought I was going to stay in the area. Then I thought I'd drive around a bit for a few weeks. See other parts of the country, stay at a couple hotels. See what I like."

"See what you like?" He shook his head in disbelief. "That doesn't even sound like you."

"I know!" she said with another laugh.

She knew that she would eventually settle in some place. It might even be right back where she'd started, somewhere in D.C., but she would only settle when *she* wanted to. Only when she was ready.

Ghalen cocked an eyebrow. "You sure you don't have some secret plans to move in with that Morris dude?"

Her smile disappeared. "Ghalen Jenkins," she began ominously.

"I mean . . . it's OK if you do! Dad is gone now. And . . . and you have a right to be happy just like everybody else, Ma."

"Thank you, honey, but no. I'm not moving in with Morris."

But he wasn't completely out of her life, either. She had spoken to him a few weeks ago. He'd called her out of the blue, after news of her arrest and release had spread, to see how she was doing.

"Fine," she'd said. "I'm doing fine, Morris."

"I'm glad to hear it. I was worried about you." He'd gone silent on the phone line a long time after that. "I miss you."

"I miss you too," she'd replied without hesitation.

"Can I see you, Tasha?"

It had been on the tip of her tongue to say yes, but instead she said, "I'm going on a trip. I don't think it will be a long one, but it's one I feel I need to take. That I need to do for myself. I'd like to see you after, though. If you still want to meet up and—"

"I will," he answered right away.

"You don't have to wait for me, Morris." In fact, she understood if he didn't.

"I waited for you before. It's not a big deal to wait a little longer," he'd said.

They'd hung up soon after.

"Well, I better get going," she said, opening her arms to Ghalen. "I want to see if I can make it to North Carolina by this afternoon."

"Why North Carolina?"

"Why not North Carolina?"

Ghalen laughed before hugging his mother. "I love you, Ma."

"Love you too," she said before giving him one final squeeze. "I'll call you from the road and check in with you. Make sure you aren't doing anything crazy in those people's house before they even have a chance to move in."

"I won't," he said, as she opened the driver's-side door and climbed inside. She gave one final wave before starting the engine.

Tasha glanced in the rearview mirror as she pulled away. She watched her son's image get smaller and smaller and then finally disappear as she rounded the corner and drove off.

ACKNOWLEDGMENTS

It's funny. By the time a novel actually makes it to the shelf (or e-reader), so many hands have touched the work, either through inspiration, critique, promotion, etc., despite the author's name being the only one on the cover. I'd like to thank the many folks that "touched" this work of fiction in their own respective ways.

Thanks to my family, for their love and support. Writing this would not have been possible without the coveted time at home I was able to spare and the patience my family showed whenever I had to seclude myself. I know there are weekend family outings that I missed and occasional dinners that I skipped in order to write and edit. Thank you for not guilting me too much when I disappeared. Thank you for cheering me on and making me feel so special.

Thanks to my agent, Barbara Poelle. We've been working together for almost a decade now. You've seen my career highs and some tough lows, and motivated and believed in me the entire time. You treat all your clients like they're your priority, which I know isn't an easy task. Thanks for your dedication and loyalty.

Thanks to my editor, Laura Schreiber. You've made me feel like a literary superstar and my book hasn't even hit the shelves yet! I thought I'd pushed myself with this work, but you showed me there were even more ways to see each character and make the novel better. I've learned a lot from working with you and hope to learn even more.

Thanks to my publicity team at BookSparks. I'm excited to have you guys in my corner.

Thanks to my past editors, English teachers, college professors, and those authors that I shamelessly binge. You've inspired me and my love of the written word. You made me want to become a writer.

ABOUT THE AUTHOR

L.S. STRATTON is a NAACP Image Award–nominated author and former crime newspaper reporter who has written more than a dozen books under different pen names in just about every genre from thrillers to romance to historical fiction. She currently lives in Maryland with her husband, their daughter, and their tuxedo cat.